THE NOAH DOCUMENT

BY

GARY P. GOODNOUGH

Additional copies of this book may be ordered at the website:
www.garygoodnough.com

ISBN: 978-0-9903931-0-8

First printing · 2014

This novel is a work of fiction. All characters, names, incidents, events, places, dialog, plots, and opinions are either invented or used fictitiously.

Published by Gary P. Goodnough

Printed in the United States by Morris Publishing®
3212 East Highway 30
Kearney, NE 68847
1-800-650-7888

Acknowledgements

People make a difference. Many thanks to Anne for providing relentless input and editing. Thanks to my daughter for several book reviews and suggestions. Thanks to my wife for tolerating my "obsession" to complete this work. Thanks to New Vine Media for their production assistance, book cover and website design.

www.newvinemedia.org.

Dedication

I dedicate this book to my mother and father and thank them for the strong Christian morals they instilled in my life.

Chapter 1

Panic set in and my adrenalin level spiked when I spotted the tiny specks of gold on the underside of the leaf. I heard myself gasp for air. I stared at the specks of gold for what seemed like minutes, though I knew it was only a few seconds. Then I remembered the quote from the instructor at my first training session as an inspector. "During greenhouse and nursery inspections you will observe numerous plants and plant species similar to our rare laboratory specimens, but the odds of seeing one of these rare beauties while actually inspecting is about one in two million."

Then my training regimen kicked in. The feeling of panic disappeared as I regained control and focused on the procedures I was required to follow. I lowered the plant I had lifted and turned slightly sideways to peer at the underside of the leaves. As if nothing significant had happened, I nonchalantly lifted my head and turned to see who else was in the immediate vicinity. There was only one other person in the University of Washington Rare Plant Greenhouse. He was standing sideways near the greenhouse front entrance about seventy-five feet from me. He held a clipboard and was jotting notes or sketching. His subject was a large potted plant in front of him. I looked back down at the plant in my hand. There was no doubt about it; the potted plant was aloe vera gold; Latin name, Aloe Barbadensis Aurum. The leaves looked exactly like the aloe vera plant leaves that nine out of ten homes in the United States have sitting on their windowsill shelves and refer to as burn plants. The only difference in these plants I'd just discovered was the speck of gold under each leaf near the base of the plant. That gold speck makes the plant super rare and highly volatile. There were four aloe vera gold plants on the rack surrounded by other diverse plant specimens.

I gently set the plant back on the rack and, without hesitation, reached into my pants pocket to pull out my cell phone. I turned and started walking the fifteen feet back to the main greenhouse aisle.

During the past twelve years, I had inspected over eight thousand greenhouses worldwide. My inspections had uncovered numerous types of mold, plants dead or dying from who knew what, and enough aphids to give anyone nightmares. However, my key role as a greenhouse inspector was to be on the lookout for ninety-six plant species that should never be seen outside a handful of specific environmentally controlled laboratories. Of the eleven other inspectors with experience ranging from two to twenty-three years, only one of them had ever seen one of these ninety-six species outside of our training sessions. This was my second find. Although we are paid well and take our jobs seriously, it is tedious work to look for specific, almost extinct plants that have volatile characteristics.

Our training sessions as inspectors are another situation altogether. Twice each year we are flown to an unidentified laboratory location at night. It is the same location each time, yet the flight time ranges from three and one half to almost six hours. We know the flight plans are staggered so we will have no idea of the exact location of the laboratory. At the training sessions we are required to identify each of the ninety-six plant species that are, as we call them, 'out of circulation'. After two full days of training every six months, we return home and our scheduled greenhouse inspections continue. Of course, as top world-class botanists, we can easily identify all of the common plants we see. Marigolds, geraniums and pansies are like identifying jellybeans in a candy jar. Sometimes the South American orchids and tropical rain forest plants are a little tricky, but we have them pretty well sorted out in our minds and seldom have to look at our plant ID reference guides on our laptops.

When I reached the center aisle, I again scoped out the greenhouse. Nothing had changed. It was probably a grad student working near the entrance. If he only knew the capabilities and inherent dangers of the super rare aloe vera gold plant or that such a plant was housed in this greenhouse, he would have been doing cartwheels. It had been two years since the last inspection at the University of Washington greenhouses on the west coast. My pointer finger quickly pecked out the emergency number I had memorized so many years ago. Twelve years on the job, and this was the second time I had used this number. The phone rang only once before there was a voice at the other end.

"Name, please."

"Hector Rodriquez."

"Code number."

"XR51. Aloe vera gold. Aloe Barbadensis Aurum."

"Confirmed."

There was a click as the line went dead. The call lasted less than ten seconds, and I was anxious to finish my inspection. After searching the remaining sixteen side aisles of plant racks, I ascertained there were no other rare classified plants in the facility. I left the greenhouse and entered the main office area in the adjacent building. After filling out an official inspection report, I reviewed it with the plant sciences department head. There was no mention of the four aloe vera gold plants on the report.

I had no idea what my immediate supervisor's next course of action would be. In the training sessions, we were told the course of action taken when one of the ninety-six rare plants was found depended on the plant species, location, and overall situation. A classified plant recovery operation is a security issue. Our sole job is to spot targeted plants, call the designated emergency telephone number to report our find, and then remove ourselves from the area without raising any suspicions. Our instructions are to be extremely careful and alert if we find one of these classified rare plant species, because our lives are in significant danger from that point on. When we asked what the danger would be, we were told some plants had compounds with potential explosive, life extinguishing capabilities. We were also told that people in possession of any of these rare plants would most likely be from a dangerous criminal element.

My inspection at the University of Washington was complete. I wasted no time leaving the campus.

Chapter 2

Just two hours later a woman wearing a uniform labeled Washington Campus Security entered the plant sciences building with a ten foot stepladder and small utility cart with wheels. Her campus security uniform was on loan to keep her true assignment undercover. Acting alone, she stopped opposite the hallway door leading into the rare plant greenhouse and set up remote wireless surveillance camera number one. The first camera was placed close to the hallway ceiling and focused on the main entry door to the greenhouse. A second camera was placed just inside the greenhouse door on a truss about twelve feet in the air and focused on the main greenhouse aisle looking towards the back emergency exit door. Camera number three was placed at the exact opposite end of the greenhouse over the rear emergency exit door and focused on the main aisle looking towards the main entry door. Camera number four was placed outside, over the rear emergency exit door. It was focused down a sidewalk that led to a campus parking lot. Finally, camera five was placed in the aluminum greenhouse trusses in aisle eleven and focused on the four aloe vera gold plants. Only by breaking or removing greenhouse glass, could anybody enter or exit the greenhouse without being detected.

The view from each camera was monitored twenty-four hours a day on screens in a secure location at Thornburg Genetics, Inc. Day after day nothing unusual happened. Instructors entered the greenhouse, sometimes alone, sometimes with students. Students entered the greenhouse and spent time working on projects with their plants. Plants were carried in and out of the greenhouse regularly. Plants were watered and fed. Night monitoring of the cameras was the most tedious. Nothing transmitted from the cameras but a dimly lit greenhouse with no movement. The unexpected happened on Christmas morning, December 25th at 8:00 AM, six weeks after the camera system had been installed. Camera one picked up a medium height male with a medium build entering the rare plant greenhouse. A composite of camera transmissions showed a frumpy looking bald man with hair that stuck out and covered both ears. His large black frame eyeglasses were out of style, and his disheveled looking clothes did not seem to fit right. With a rubber gloved hand, he held a wooden box by a single handle on the top. In no apparent hurry, he walked down the main aisle, took an immediate right onto aisle eleven, and walked directly to the aloe vera gold plants. He looked up and gave a slight smile at the camera. With flawless precision, he opened the small hinged front door of the wooden box and picked up the plants one at a time, placing them inside. He shut the box door and latched it, then quickly proceeded to the back main aisle emergency exit door. With a gentle push the door opened, setting off a loud alarm. Exterior camera number four showed him walking down the thirty feet of sidewalk toward the rear parking lot. He took an immediate left at the end of the sidewalk and disappeared behind a row of evergreens out of camera range.

Thornburg Genetics had notified campus security as soon as the man placed the first plant in the transport box. According to the video security tape, it took campus security only three minutes and ten seconds to arrive at the greenhouse. There was no sign of the frumpy looking man. Security staff hadn't passed any vehicles on the only road leading to the greenhouse rear parking lot. There were no witnesses in the area since campus was shut down for the holidays with limited security and maintenance staff on duty.

The man had disappeared with four extremely rare and lethal plants. The only immediate evidence left behind was found discarded on the lawn just out of camera sight near the parking lot sidewalk. There, campus security discovered black eyeglasses and a skin-tight rubber mask designed to cover everything from the neck up, which the intruder had apparently pulled off. The mask portrayed the same face and balding head as the man who removed the aloe vera gold plants. The security videos were reviewed numerous times by Thornburg Genetics security experts at an undisclosed location in hopes of picking up some clue to the person's identity. The entire greenhouse and parking area was cordoned off by campus security in an attempt to preserve any additional evidence. The results were pitiful thanks to the Seattle Christmas rainfall. From the videos and a potential footprint of the intruder, it was determined the frumpy little man wore size ten shoes. The clothes could not be identified as any particular name brand and were probably purchased at some yard sale or second hand store. The intruder weighed about one hundred fifty pounds and was approximately five feet six inches tall. Individual employee personnel interviews were conducted. Every person who had legitimate access to the plant sciences building and the numerous campus greenhouses over Christmas break had an alibi for their whereabouts on Christmas morning.

It had been almost one year since that incident and the Thornburg Genetics security task force was no closer to finding the greenhouse perpetrator. A short brown hair found in the mask was analyzed for DNA. There were no hits when the results were run through the national criminal computer system database. Somewhere on planet earth, there were at least four rare volatile plants not under the control of Thornburg Genetics. Whoever had them in their possession might, or might not, know of their volatile capabilities. Too many questions remained unanswered. Where did the aloe vera gold plants originate?

Where were they now? Did the thief possess some of the other ninety-six rare 'out of circulation' plant species as well? The Thornburg Genetics security staff and management continued to earnestly seek the plants and person involved.

Chapter 3

"At most you have forty-five days to live. I wish the news were better, but the chemo and radiation therapies just aren't working. I would suggest you get all of your affairs in order if you haven't done so already."

"Thank you, Brett. I was afraid this was coming, but I really didn't want to face it. When death is staring you in the eyes, it sure is tough to stare back."

Brett and Vince had been friends for years, but they had grown closer after eight months of cancer treatment. As a retired Thornburg Genetics researcher, Vince's philosophy was to relay facts accurately and not to sugar coat bad news. That was the best and most effective way to tackle the issues of life. Forty-five days max left on planet earth. Vince had one major item left to take care of before death. At sixty-eight years of age he felt slightly cheated that death could knock so soon, but he had lived his life to the fullest with few regrets. His wife, Midge, would be well cared for with adequate savings and a decent life insurance policy. Her health was fine, and Vince knew she would miss him very much. They had such a great life together. Midge was a true soul mate. They decided to keep their home intact until after Vincent's death. After his death, the plan was for Midge to sell the house and move to Virginia Beach to be near their son, David, and his wife, Valerie, along with their two grandchildren. Vince and Midge also had a daughter, April. April was a bit of a floater who made every day an adventure. She joined the Peace Corps after college and went off to save the world. Her first stop was Ecuador where she agreed to spend twenty-seven months. She loved the terrain and people of Ecuador and made the decision to stay longer. If she was in touch with Vince and Midge by telephone twice a year, they were lucky. They did receive a letter or card on birthdays and holidays. April was one strong-willed child when it came to being disciplined. Even as a young child she was always determined that things had to be done her way. Spankings and time outs were frequent. At the same time, she was a girl who had a huge heart of gold and loved being around people. She would do anything to help anybody. During high school she would help a neighbor fix a flat tire or run an errand rather than do her homework. It was a constant struggle to keep her focused on school. On occasion Vince remarked to Midge that April must have inherited the trait of stubbornness from her mother's side. They would both chuckle over the situation.

"I want to see you again in two weeks or sooner if anything changes," said Brett.

"You have my word on that."

Vincent thanked God his rare form of lung cancer had caused very little pain until the last couple of weeks. Now there was pain in his lungs frequently, though it wasn't more than he could bear. Dr. Brett had prescribed painkillers, which Vince had only used sporadically up to this point.

"It must be hard to work with suffering people every day isn't it, Brett?"

"Some days it's harder than others. I have to stay focused on providing help and comfort to patients the best way I can. With today's specialized medicines, there are many more cancer survivors every year. I suppose I've grown a little calloused towards patients' suffering over the years though."

"Well thanks for all you've done, Brett. There's no way I can ever repay you for being such a close friend."

"There is nothing to repay. I'm glad our friendship has lasted so many years."

A stiff wind blew the big, puffy snowflakes around Vince's head as he exited the medical center. The Philadelphia, PA winter seemed even colder and gloomier than it had an hour ago. The thermometer on the bank across the street was lit with bold numbers that registered twenty degrees. The cold air bit Vince's cheeks and seemed to chisel its way through his clothing. He knew this feeling wasn't completely due to the weather, but was also related to the diagnosis of his upcoming death. What a weird and helpless feeling. He knew what his future held, and there wasn't a thing he could do to change it.

It was time. Vince had struggled for several years and debated for the last two how he should proceed. In the past he would write two or three pages and then shred them. Two days later he would start writing again, then pop the sheets of paper into the shredder. His wife knew he was agonizing over something, but she never brought the topic up. Vince wanted to discuss his dilemma, but every time he broached the matter he felt like a brick wall was solidly placed between them. Vince's mind would veto any discussion of this topic with Midge. The veto was unexplainable to most people, but through his biological research Vince knew exactly why there was only one family member in his life he could share certain confidential information with. Now the writing project had to be completed. Vince was tired of the wrestling games in his mind and wanted them to stop. The information he would reveal would solve that problem, but he knew the consequences would alter his entire family's way of life. There could be no more procrastination. He would start writing full force right after lunch.

Chapter 4

Michael picked up his office phone and quickly punched in the numbers. "Good afternoon, Midge. How are things going?"

Probating wills was one of Michael's least favorite things to do, but it was one of his law firm's commitments to the community. This one was the toughest probate ever. Vince, one of his best friends for over twenty years, had now passed away. Dr. Brett's prediction of death was correct. Just thirty-four days and Vince was gone. The calling hours and funeral had been held four days ago. Vince was a highly regarded man in the community, and hundreds of people arrived at calling hours to share their sympathy with the family. The pastor that resided over the funeral made mention of Vince's commitment to Christ and explained that those who believed in and committed their life to Christ would see Vince again in heaven. That sure wouldn't make up for the weekly fishing trips and every other week summer golf outings. Vince was a good sport when it came to golf. He was a horrendous player and lost every time he and Michael played together. Michael's wife, Susan, would miss spending time with Midge also, but they both knew it would be better if Midge moved closer to her son and grandchildren in Virginia Beach as planned. There was just this lingering empty feeling inside from the loss of Vince.

"I'm still trying to believe this all happened," said Midge. "April is on Delta flight 6524, which is scheduled to land at 3:35 PM. I'll call you as soon as I talk with her. I know you want to get the will finished, and we want to get everything settled."

"Thanks, Midge. If I can do anything, just let me know."

"Thanks, Michael. You and Susan have been very gracious. Tell her I said hello and thanks again for the wonderful apple pie you brought over. Talk to you soon."

"Goodbye, Midge."

Michael had seen April fifteen or twenty times in the years he had known Vince. Vince always had good things to say about her, but he was concerned about her safety. The way Vince described it; she had seen more back streets and hill country and been in more dangerous places than anybody he knew, including several of his friends who had served in the armed forces. April sure had a knack for staying out of harm's way. Some of the tales Vincent told him were earth shaking. The tale he remembered most was when a truck she was driving with supplies for a village was commandeered by, as she quoted, pirates. She was captured, but somehow managed to escape unharmed. It seems that most of these events were relayed through her brother, David. Vince said that David and April were very close. April was arriving in town very soon. Even the Peace Corps couldn't locate her until two days after they had buried Vince. At least she had been home and spent a few days with her family at Christmas.

Chapter 5

It was 3:45 PM when David said to Midge, "There she is." They both waved and caught April's attention. She fought her way through the loitering plane passengers, ran up to her mother and gave her a big hug as tears started rolling down her cheeks.

"Hi, Mom."

"Oh April, we've missed you so much."

"I know, Mom. I'm so sorry I wasn't here to see dad before he passed away. Did you know it was coming? I love you so much!"

"We knew he was going to pass away, but only for about a month. You know your father. He didn't want to interfere in your life, so he wouldn't let me contact you."

April backed away and put her hands on her mother's shoulders. She looked at her mother through her tear-filled eyes and said, "You look really great, Mom."

"Thanks, honey. I probably look better than I feel right now. I really miss Vince."

"I know, Mom."

April turned to her brother. "How are you handling everything, big brother?"

"I'm doing fine. It's just not a fun situation. Where were you, lost some place in a river basin or peering down from the highest peak in the Andes?"

"You know perfectly well I was in Ecuador helping some villagers with crop management. I just may have been out of the village for a couple of days and a little hard to reach. You know me David, just trying to help the less fortunate survive another day."

"Must be the sun is shining bright in Ecuador. Your face sure is tan. You look a little underfed though."

"Come on, David. I'm in great shape. I feel better than I ever have."

"I'm only kidding, Sis. So do I get a hug?" April smiled and gave David a bear hug and a kiss on the cheek. David said, "Wow, feel those muscles." All three of them laughed.

Suddenly the crowd at the airport came to life; the noise from people talking, the smell of sweat from weary travelers, a microphone blaring a new flight change, and people hustling back and forth with all sorts of odd-shaped baggage.

"Shall we head back to the house?" asked Midge.

"Sure thing," said April. "Maybe we could stop at Carnicelli's Bakery and get a fresh cannoli on the way. It's my treat of course."

"I think we can arrange that," said Midge.

"Maybe we can fatten you up a little," said David.

"Very funny."

Chapter 6

"Good morning, folks. How are things going, Midge?"

"I'm doing fine Michael. I loved Vince more than I can ever tell you, and it's just going to take time to get over his death."

"David; is everything all right with you?"

"I'm handling everything okay, Mr. Anderson."

After a slight pause Michael said, "It's great to see you again, April. We only get to see you around here once in a while. How are you handling all of this?"

"I have to say I'm sorry I wasn't here for the funeral or even here for dad before he passed away. I'm feeling a little angry that nobody notified me he had a terminal illness."

"Your dad knew you would feel that way. He specifically told me to tell you that you were leading your life with meaning and purpose and there were to be no regrets. That is why he didn't contact you before he passed away. You know how passionate he was about his research work. You two are almost a mirror image of each other when it comes to work ethics. Your visit at Christmas time was special and Vince wanted those memories to linger, not memories of cancer."

"Well, I still feel guilty."

"Please don't. This is the way your father chose closure of his life. If any of you need anything at all or just want to talk, feel free to call or stop by to see me. Vince and I went back quite a number of years as friends. I figure it's about twenty-five years. You have a great family here, Midge."

"I sure do. They are very supportive and sympathetic. Thanks for the compliment, Michael."

"Okay. Let's proceed. We are here today to probate the last will and testament of Vincent. I am going to turn on this tape recorder and then my secretary will print a copy of these proceedings for the record. Is there anything you would like to say before we start? This is a simple matter and will only take a few minutes."

Michael looked at Midge, then directed his gaze toward David and finally to April. "Let's get started then." Michael turned on the tape recorder.

"For the record, this is the last will and testament of Vincent James. Today is Friday, March 12. It is 9:00 AM. In attendance at this probate are three family members, all of whom are named in the last will and testament of Vincent James. My name is Michael Anderson, Esquire. For the record, will you please state your first and last name and your relationship to Vincent James."

Michael pointed to Midge.

"My name is Midge James, Vincent's wife."

Midge looked at David, sitting directly to her left.

"My name is David James. I am Vincent James' son."

"My name is April James. Vincent James was my father."

"Thank you. I will now read the last will and testament of Vincent James."

Michael paused. He knew this was the point where all families started to fall apart, and he wanted to make sure he stayed strong for them. "These are Vincent's words: 'As you know, I can thank God I was allowed time to make sure all of my affairs were in order before my death. To my wonderful wife, Midge, I will always love you'."

Midge started to cry as David and April both teared up.

"As we discussed and planned, you will receive the entire estate with two exceptions. David James will receive a cash sum of twenty five thousand dollars. April James will also receive a cash sum of twenty five thousand dollars. I know that both David and April will use these finances wisely. I know the three of you have placed your trust in God's salvation. I will miss you, and I am ready to meet you in heaven on the day God has appointed. Please don't lament over me, because heaven is a far better place than earth." Michael paused. "That is the end of the final will and testament of Vincent James."

At this point all three family members were crying bountifully. They were each grabbing handfuls of tissues from the box on the conference table. Michael reached out and pushed the off button on the tape recorder. He then handed David and April a separate envelope each containing a check for twenty five thousand dollars. Michael didn't say anything more as he fought to hold back tears as well. After a couple of minutes the intense crying settled down to sniffling and a few tears.

"Thank you, Michael," said Midge.

"You are entirely welcome. I know this is a tough time. Feel free to stay here as long as you like. I do need to discuss one other issue with April, in private." Michael stood up. "April, will you please follow me? This will only take a few minutes."

April picked up her handmade, woven, wool sack from Ecuador and followed Michael through a side door, which led directly to a large desk made of cherry. There was row after row of legal books lined up neatly in bookcases along the walls, and stacks of overstuffed file folders on the floor as far as the eye could see. The nameplate sitting on the desk said, Michael Anderson.

April's eyes were red and swollen. Michael hated to see people suffering at a will probate. He motioned to a large dark red leather chair directly in front of his desk, and April sat down. Michael then sat down behind his desk and reached into the top right hand drawer.

"Here is a packet that I was directed by your father to hand deliver. It was not to be mentioned in the will. His limited directions were specific. First, you are to share the enclosed information with absolutely nobody unless they are considered worthy, and second, use the information only as deemed necessary."

Michael slid the manila envelope across the desk to April. The envelope was about one quarter of an inch thick and was completely covered and crisscrossed with brown packing tape. Printed on the front in bold marker were three words: APRIL JAMES ONLY. This was underlined twice.

Michael watched April's eyes, as they remained glued to the envelope. April looked up at Michael. "Do you have any idea what's in here and what those directions mean?"

"None whatsoever, but I have to tell you that the suspense has been painful. I hope I am one of the, quote, 'worthy ones.' He also said to tell you that you would know who was worthy."

"Wow. This is a shocker. Should I open it now? You really don't know what's in here?"

"I have no idea what the contents of the envelope are. Things have been hectic this morning. Why don't you take it home with you and open it when you have some quiet time. After you check out the contents, feel free to call if you have any questions. Here is my business card."

April took the card and slid it into her sweater pocket. Then she stuffed the manila envelope into the sack she was carrying. It settled down between a bottle of water and her change purse.

"Thank you, Mr. Anderson," April said as she stood up.

"You are entirely welcome, April, and feel free to call me Michael." With the packet delivered, Michael escorted April back to the conference room.

"What did you find out?" asked David.

"Dad had a couple of personal messages that Mr. Anderson shared with me."

"Oh. Okay. Are the messages anything you would like to talk about?"

"No. Not really."

"I hate to interrupt, but I think we should go now," said Midge. "I'm sure Michael has lots of work to attend to."

"I could use some fresh air too," said April.

"Thank you for coming this morning, and I hope to see you all soon," said Michael.

Midge, David and April stepped out into the frigid weather. A shiver went up April's spine. She didn't know if it was from the cold weather or the anticipation of opening the packet her father had left her.

Chapter 7

When they arrived back home, April wanted to go upstairs and survey her bedroom. Every time she came home one of her favorite things to do was look at certain photos of her family and friends and reminisce. Many of the photos were framed collections scattered throughout the room on walls and bookcases. Her favorites were two collages she'd made into large wall posters. She had been too tired to check them out the night before. Then she wanted to open the packet her father had left her. Her plans changed abruptly when Korey and Kevin, David's two boys, greeted them at the door.

"Will you play with us, April?" they chimed. How could she say no? Korey was six years old and Kevin was four. They were both cute, blue-eyed, blond-haired and well-mannered kids, but they were still all boy.

"Let's go outside and sled and then throw snowballs," said Korey.

"Yah," said Kevin.

"Let's stay inside and play trucks," said April.

"OKAY," they both chimed at once. They were both smiling, and their eyes were glowing with excitement as they ran upstairs to get their beloved trucks.

David's wife, Valerie, appeared in the living room. "I was in the kitchen and couldn't help but overhear the playtime request by the boys. After all you've been through, don't you need some time to rest or some alone time? They'll play with you forever if you give them the chance."

"Oh, I don't mind. We can play with their trucks for a while."

"Why don't we have an early lunch," said Midge. "There's so much food in the refrigerator. People have been dropping it off for days now."

"I'll help you, Mom," said Valerie. "Just holler when you've had enough play time with the boys."

Truck playing with Korey and Kevin was a rigorous activity. The couch and overstuffed recliner made great mountains for the trucks to scale. There were only a couple of accidents where the trucks slid off their designated course. Kevin told April that she had to drive more carefully. April couldn't help but laugh out loud.

"Where did you hear that?"

"That's what mommy and daddy tell each other."

"I see. Well, I guess I will have to be more careful then."

After half an hour of playing trucks, everybody sat down at the dining room table for lunch. A large pan of lasagna, a huge tossed salad and a basket of sliced Italian bread were spread out. The aroma was inviting. Kevin and Korey each had a hotdog, carrot sticks and a few chips on their plate.

When lunch was over, Midge wanted to look through some family photo albums with David and April. April was going nuts waiting for a chance to see what the envelope from her father contained. It was 2:30 in the afternoon before April finally bowed out of the family get together and walked upstairs to her bedroom. She hadn't realized how exhausted she was and decided to take a short nap before opening the envelope, knowing she wouldn't be able to comprehend what she read anyhow.

It felt good to be in her old bedroom again. Her mother had demanded the room remain unchanged, even though April had moved out seven years ago when she went to college. The yellow and white striped comforter made the double bed look like a puffy marshmallow. April retrieved the envelope from her bag, pulled back the comforter and dived underneath. She tucked the envelope under the spare pillow on her bed and drifted off to sleep.

Chapter 8

April felt refreshed when she woke up. The clock on the bedside table said 3:40 PM. She remembered dreaming about a deep gully with thousands of people on each side jumping back and forth over the gully. April wondered if the dream's meaning had any significance in relation to the day's events. She decided it was not important enough to try and remember more. The house was very quiet, and April smelled a spicy odor in the air. She knew it had to be her mother's famous blueberry pie. It was April's favorite.

April picked up the corner of the spare pillow and peered underneath at the packet she had stashed before her nap. She retrieved it, sat up in bed, and examined both sides. The outside of the packet gave no more clues to its contents. The multiple strips of packing tape crisscrossing the envelope seemed strange, because April knew her father was meticulous when it came to making everything he did neat and symmetrical. She slid her hand in the left front pocket of her jeans and extracted the small pocketknife her father had given her years before. She could still hear her dad's words, "It's a Swiss Army Victorinox. Never buy a cheap knife if you want it to survive the test of time." She opened the small blade and slowly slit the very top of the packet, then removed the contents. There was a business-size envelope inside with the words, Open First. It was on top of a stapled booklet about 20 pages long. On the front cover in bold print were the words, THE NOAH DOCUMENT.

Numerous questions and thoughts flashed through April's mind because of the peculiar heading. She opened the business envelope first and started reading the letter from her father.

"My dearest April, I pray all is well. It was great to see you at Christmas time, and I miss you dearly. While I knew I would be departing from this earth soon, I didn't want to distract you from your work. You are as passionate about working with people as I was in my research work."

April started crying as she read her father's last communication to her.

"Our time on this earth is but a brief moment. It flashes before our eyes and then it's gone. I know I will see you in heaven someday, but for now, stay passionate and in touch with God in all you do. Enclosed is 'The Noah Document.' My research at Thornburg Genetics has fascinated me since the beginning of my career. As I told Michael, you will know what to do with this document and who is worthy to share its contents. You will not be able to discuss the contents with those who are not worthy. Guard it with your life! I will always love you. Goodbye for now." April wondered what worthy meant. She read the communication again, put her pillow up to her face, and bawled. Why hadn't she spent more time with her family? She had always been so concerned about everybody else in the world, and now her father wasn't here. It was too late to spend more time with him. After a few moments she calmed down. Then she picked up The Noah Document and flipped the cover open.

Chapter 9

"When I graduated from college, I was immediately hired and started conducting research at a drug company called National Chemical, Inc. I am sharing this information with you because the medical discoveries I have seen and been involved in are earth shattering. Yet, very little of this medical progress has been made available to the general public. I will use myself as an example. After nine years of research, I was promoted to a position in a sister company called Thornburg Genetics, Inc. About one year after becoming involved in research at Thornburg Genetics, I was diagnosed with colon cancer. The oncologist set up an appointment for surgery and wanted me to start chemo and radiation treatments immediately. I was grief stricken and shared my agony with two of my friends who were researchers in a different department. They asked if they could review the diagnosis. No one knew about the cancer except the outside physicians, my two friends at Thornburg Genetics, a Thornburg research physician, and me. We weren't married yet, so even Midge doesn't know this. I probably should have told her, but I chose not to because of the following. Within 24 hours of the diagnosis, a Thornburg research physician gave me a seven-day supply of pills to take for the cancer; one pill per day for seven days. They called the pill The Blue Mule. I took the pills as prescribed and kept working. Not once did I feel ill, and the only side effect was frequent urination, since drinking large amounts of water with the pills was required. Ten days after my diagnosis, I went back to the outside specialists for more screening before my operation. A few days later my oncologist reported there was no evidence of colon cancer. I was not in remission. I was cured! I was also in complete shock. The oncologist could not understand how their diagnosis had failed, and I could not tell them about The Blue Mule. The oncologist and specialists apologized numerous times for their incorrect diagnosis. At that time the survival rate for colon cancer was poor. Sure you might be able to drag yourself through special treatments and last a few months, but usually you were terminal. I asked my co-workers what the pills were and why they weren't on the open market to treat other cancer patients. The only answer I could ever get was that certain medical knowledge had to be withheld from the general population due to national and global security in an attempt to maintain world peace."

"I eventually worked with plant sterols and genetics associated with The Blue Mule, which our company labeled Constellation Blue. I know the product results from my research could easily be used to prolong life or heal millions of cancer patients. There is a side issue with the Constellation Blue drug that is not medical in nature and certainly should not hold up distribution to cancer patients. Several experimental medications never make it to the open market even after a U.S. Food and Drug Administration approval, but Constellation Blue was never sent to the FDA. I did not delve too deeply into the confusing mechanics of the Thornburg Genetics operation, but there seems to be an almost unlimited amount of funding for research from a combination of the United States government, foreign governments, pharmaceutical companies and who knows whom else. In addition to diverse funding sources, the upper level of the organization is covered in a shroud of secrecy. It has numerous subsidiaries working on sophisticated medical research projects, but does not report to any of the financial backers due to global military security. The Thornburg Genetics company head is only referred to as The Keeper. I will give you more information on that later."

"What piqued my interest in Thornburg Genetics were the genetic and biotech projects. I enjoyed genetic and biotech research because the work gave hope to others. The thrill of seeing people's lives extended by two, five, or even ten years due to our research work was extremely fulfilling. However, this whole situation is dwarfed by the magnitude of what you are about to read."

"On my fifteenth anniversary date as a researcher, I was flown to an undisclosed location to attend a conference. Three gentlemen and three ladies were summoned to a small conference room in the basement of the building. A middle-aged man walked into the room and introduced himself. He said he was called The Keeper, and this meeting was due to our exemplary performance with Thornburg Genetics, which had resulted in a promotion opportunity for each of us to a higher level in the company. This new level would allow us to access special documents that would improve and expedite our research immensely. We were told the special documents were classified, and any information we received could be shared only with other employees at security clearance level seven. Fewer than 500 people in the world had access to these documents. The promotion was optional and did not have to be accepted. It sounded great up to this point. Then we found out why the offer was optional. We were told that although every effort had been made to produce accurate clearance screenings for employee safety, somehow knowledge of this high security level had fallen into the wrong hands in recent years. It could not be determined exactly why or how at this point in time, but Thornburg Genetics security investigators indicated some types of radiation or chemotherapies might alter an individual's genetic makeup, allowing that employee to leak classified information. An almost unbelievable, yet important reason why the six of us were chosen was because of our genealogy as much as our research capabilities. Some type of genealogical background information showed that the six of us had a common ancestor. This had been determined by different written tests we took and individual blood work. DNA screening was in its infancy then and rather archaic. We were given no specifics due to security reasons. Based on our character assessments, some type of genetic code, and our genealogy, we were determined to be eligible for this promotion. The genetic screening determined we each had some specific gene makeup that blocked certain brain cells and prevented us from sharing critical information concerning specific classified documents with most other researchers. In today's high tech world, we would call it a firewall. We would be able to remember classified information but would be physically unable to tell others what research we were involved in. The only exception to this was individuals with the same genetic makeup as us."

"The offer was optional because we would be replacing four other employees that had disappeared about six months previously and were presumed dead. There was a possibility we could be captured and tortured by unethical, power-hungry people in an effort to extract the knowledge gained through our research. The thought of this gave me a scary, gut wrenching feeling."

"The Keeper said we had fifteen minutes to make our decision. There was no pressure to accept the promotion, and we would remain with the company even if we decided not to participate. We were told the opportunity might, or might not, surface again in the future, and acceptance meant no turning back. The Keeper then left the room. Here we were, six Thornburg researchers left to decide our future. There was a pitcher with ice water on the table. A dozen large clear tumblers sat next to it. I poured myself a glass of water, took a sip, and asked if anyone else would like some. The others said, yes please, or nodded their head up and down, speechless."

"Let's face it. Most people have the opportunity to discuss a major life decision with their spouse or extended family and are given a reasonable amount of time to make a decision. We didn't ask, but we knew we would not be afforded that opportunity. We would not have expected it anyway due to the high security classification. The six of us never discussed finances, raises, job security, perks, or any similar issues. We only tried to guess what the unknown future would hold for our families and us. Exactly fifteen minutes later The Keeper walked back into the room."

"I understand each of you has had to make this decision in a short time with very limited information. There is no other effective way to handle this. Let me just say: anyone who has accepted this promotion in the past has not regretted it. I will now ask each of you for your decision."

"The Keeper told us to answer yes if we accepted, or pass if we declined the promotion. He asked the question only once."

"Do you accept the promotion?"

"I had never met The Keeper before, and I assumed the other five hadn't either. However, he knew each of us by our first name. I was the third one to have my name called. I can remember the sound of The Keeper's voice to this day."

"Vincent?"

"And my response: Yes."

"All six of us said yes. What choice did we have? Imagine a researcher turning down the opportunity of a lifetime, and April, it was in fact the opportunity of a lifetime! Are you ready for this? Hold on to your seat."

"The Keeper thanked us and then said, please follow me."

"We walked through several unmarked hallways and stopped at an elevator door. We took the elevator down two floors. When we exited the elevator, there was a massive steel door about thirty feet in front of us. We followed The Keeper through highly sophisticated security equipment straight to the door. When the door finally slid all of the way open, we stepped into a small room where an average-sized young man with a big smile on his face greeted us."

"Welcome to the library."

Chapter 10

"The six of us just looked back and forth at each other. What had been intense, unbearable excitement was now an intense let down. It felt like we had just traveled from the top of the roller coaster to the bottom in two seconds. I knew we were each thinking the same thing. Not library research, no way!"

"My name is Charlie Mantz. I am the coordinator of this library facility. Why do I detect such glum faces? Believe me, you want to be here. You are about to enter the library of libraries. You will see that your research work has only just begun. To put your minds at ease, you will not be involved in literary research. As soon as you leave here, it is back to the test tubes and petri dishes. Here is a pair of lint-free cotton gloves with special rubber grips on the fingers and palms. Please put the gloves on your hands now. You are welcome to touch, hold, or just view the library selections. Since the selections are all categorized, I ask you to place each item back in the location from which you obtained it."

"We each put on a pair of the gloves as directed. The Keeper also put on a pair. Charlie flipped on a light switch as he walked through a beautifully adorned wooden doorway. We were apprehensive, but followed. April, my body literally shook at the sight. What lay before us was row after row of ancient tablets. There were tablets of bronze and silver, marble, baked clay, and sandstone. They ranged in size from two inches square to eight inches square and were anywhere from a sixteenth inch to a full inch thick."

"Welcome to The Noah Library," exclaimed Charlie. "If Charlie's smile had been any bigger, he wouldn't have been able to contain his teeth."

"Let me give you a background of The Noah Library while you look around. First, why do we call this The Noah Library? In this glass showcase you will see one tablet made of solid gold. It was the only gold tablet discovered within this library. This tablet's purpose, as translated from Hebrew, gives honor to Yahweh for allowing life to remain on earth after the great flood and for allowing Noah the honor of passing knowledge on to future generations. There are 3221 tablets in this room. What you see here are actual tablets either made by Noah himself, scribes as dictated by Noah, or Japheth's lineage. Japheth was Noah's son. So far, we have learned that 420 of these tablets describe life on earth before the flood, 690 tablets describe life on earth after the flood, and 10 tablets describe finding the cave after the flood where the tablets were stored. Those ten tablets are extremely interesting. Finally, there are 2100 tablets made of silver. These are the tablets of special interest to our research program. They each contain a plant description with an artwork engraving that shows each plant in finite detail. Most of the plant tablets list a medicinal use for the plant. For example, willow leaves and bark contain salicylic acid, which is a chemical precursor to aspirin. The extraction is used to help relieve pain and fever. A large number of the plants described are believed to be extinct, but many are still in existence today. There are 100 tablets dealing with animal species now extinct due to the flood."

"Hands with cotton gloves were flying in every direction. The six of us picked up and looked at tablet after tablet. The detail of the plant artwork was unbelievable. Of course, we couldn't read the inscriptions as they were written in Hebrew or some other archaic language. I wish you could see this collection."

Suddenly, there was a knock on April's bedroom door. April jumped in shock. She had been so engrossed in her reading she hadn't heard her mother walk upstairs.

Chapter 11

"It's Mom."

April stashed the packet back under her pillow. "Come in, Mom."

"I brought you a slice of fresh baked blueberry pie and some coffee, honey. Is everything okay? It looks like you have been crying."

"I thought that was the smell of blueberry pie drifting up the stairs. Everything is fine, Mom. I was just doing a little reminiscing."

"I'm sorry to bother you. I wanted to bring you up a little snack."

"It's no bother. I will never consider my mother or blueberry pie a bother. I can taste it already. Are you able to cope with this whole situation, Mom?"

"I do so miss your father, but I expect things will get easier with time. I miss his touch, our conversations, and our meals together and that look he used to give me when I asked a question that already had some simple answer."

"Yeah, I remember that look. Like the time I was a junior in high school, and I asked him if I could buy a prom dress. There was that look and then the response, 'well, what else would you wear to a prom?'" Of course, the real question then came up. "Dad, would you buy me the dress?"

"That was the look." Midge smiled. "Well, I'm going to head back downstairs. Enjoy your snack."

"I'll be down in a little while, Mom. Thanks a million for the pie and coffee."

As soon as Midge left, April got up and locked the door. Then she took a sip of the coffee. "Ooh, this coffee is good." Then she dived into the piece of blueberry pie. It only took a couple of minutes to devour. "Nothing like homemade," she said to herself.

April retrieved The Noah Document from underneath her pillow. She had to read more about her father's experiences.

"God instructed Noah to create the 2100 silver plant tablets before the flood that would destroy the whole world. The information on these tablets would give some relief, in the form of medicines, to Noah, his family, and their descendants after the flood. The tablets were placed in a cave somewhere in Mesopotamia. The cave was sealed prior to the flood. After the flood, Noah chose one of his sons, Japheth, as overseer of the tablets. Because the earth was basically ripped to shreds during the flood with debris everywhere, it took Noah and Japheth just shy of two years to find the cave again. Even though the cave had been sealed, the immense pressure from the floodwaters broke through the seal and flooded the cave. We believe all of the tablets survived the flood, but the cave was full of mud and debris. The tablets were carefully mined out, cleaned and stored. Noah recorded that the tablets were replaced in the cave after it was fully cleaned and consecrated. A limited number of Japheth's descendants have maintained the cave and contents throughout history up to this very day."

Then Charlie said, "Guess what my friends. You are six of those direct descendants."

"I went for it hook, line and sinker, April. I asked Charlie, 'Are you telling us we are direct descendants of Noah?' I recognized my mistake immediately. Of course this was a dumb question, and Charlie roared with laughter."

"I always get somebody with the descendant line comment," said Charlie.

"I know", I said, "If Noah and his family were the only flood survivors, we are all descendants of Noah."

"Bingo," said Charlie.

"One by one, numerous questions were asked. Where did all of the tablets come from? How old are they? Why are they made out of different materials? Who interpreted them? Are they all interpreted? Where have they been for all of these years? They must have been housed in other locations weren't they? How did they get here? Who funds all of this? Are there more tablets someplace else?"

"We asked questions for two hours, and Charlie was able to answer almost every question. Now comes the tricky part April. I know your life revolves around helping people and trying to improve impoverished communities. With this background information, I believe you could make some of the biotech research I was involved in available to help improve medical conditions and quality of life around the world. With this information comes a huge responsibility. I was never able to share my research or my experience at The Noah Library with your mother. She was gracious enough never to ask or prod about my work, because she knew I would tell her if I could. As I mentioned earlier, there is some type of sophisticated genetic mental block that does not allow those who know about The Noah Library and the corresponding research to tell those who don't know. Though it has not been determined exactly why, we are within reach of proving there is a genetic code that has been passed through certain branches of the line of Japheth. This code does not allow our brain to disclose locations or information about The Noah Library and its contents. Through different research levels in the company and different written tests we have to take, there is a 99.9% chance that all of those selected for involvement in the Noah research projects will carry their secrets to the grave and will not be able to divulge this information to anyone else not worthy. Of course your question is how can I tell you this information? The answer is I would not be able to write it down or pass this information on to you if you were not an acceptable candidate to receive it. You, April, have apparently inherited this special gene through the Japheth line. We refer to it as The Noah Gene."

"I must give you a severe warning, April. There are influential people and governments that will use any covert action necessary to obtain classified research information from Thornburg Genetics. There is a .01 percent chance that high security level researchers were not screened properly. They may be working behind the scenes or out on the streets trying to mastermind some devious plot to obtain highly classified medical research. Bits and pieces of our research results that have never been released by the company have shown up in different areas of the world. We don't know how or why. We know torture doesn't work. The Noah Gene shuts down the memory system when dealing with select information."

"It is common knowledge that a percentage of the population comes down with diverse types of cancer. We believe the use of certain chemotherapy and radiation treatments alter the makeup of The Noah Gene. This potentially opens a pathway that might allow information to be extracted. A high-level security employee suffered severely from cancer and received chemo and radiation treatments about 4 years ago. Nobody knew she had the cancer until she was very sick. She was cured after receiving the Thornburg seven-day 'Blue Mule' pills. She suddenly disappeared along with her family. We believe her research was forcibly extracted from her and is now in the hands of malicious individuals or government officials who want to commit acts of evil. You now see why this information is valuable, and we cannot afford a leak. It all comes down to the eternal struggle of good versus evil. Only you can decide whether you want to pursue this matter further."

"When you were young, you professed to know God and Jesus Christ as your Savior. For several years now, you appear to have drifted away from that belief. How is your spiritual life now? May God be with you in all your decisions."

April read the document through a second time and had just started her third reading when she heard her mother call that supper was ready. She responded, "I'll be right down, Mom."

April took The Noah Document and slid it into her sack lying on the floor at the foot of the bed. "It should be safe in here for now," she said to herself. She slid the sack under her pillow and went to supper.

Chapter 12

That Monday, April borrowed her mother's car and drove to High-bridge Street. She walked into the Bank of America branch office and secured The Noah Document in a safety deposit box. Just up the street was a Dunkin' Donuts shop. April pulled up to the drive-through window. A young girl smiled at her through the window.

"May I help you?"

"One large hazelnut with just a little cream and sugar please."

April knew where she had to go now. It had been years since her last visit. As she drove through the streets of Philadelphia, the words of The Noah Document crept back into her memory. She could hear her father's voice, the way he used to talk to her, each inflection, and each laugh, and she asked herself again why she hadn't spent more time with her family.

Her destination loomed before her. Had it really been three years since her last visit? The light falling snow encased the entire building and grounds with a look of purity. The cross at the peak was outlined by the light blue sky, which was highlighted by gray and white clouds. Why had she drifted away from God and her faith? She knew part of the reason was disbelief in a God that would allow people to be so cruel to each other. Another was what she considered to be hypocrites in the Christian church. People were so severe in their judgments. If something didn't fit precisely with their way of thinking, it was automatically wrong. They put on their best appearance and acted like saints on Sunday, but any other behavior you could imagine was acceptable the rest of the week. Of course there were many exceptions.

Mr. and Mrs. Brown were two examples. They would do almost anything for anybody and expected nothing in return. They liked April and supported her decisions. She could count on them to send a letter to her in Ecuador once every other month. They never said a bad thing about anybody. Their lifestyle matched their true commitment to God. Commitment; now that was a word to think about. Lots of excuses were used to avoid commitment. That was probably the deep down truth of her separation from faith in God. She needed a reason to commit.

April opened the car door and took a short walk to the garden behind the church. It was white and serene under the fresh coating of snow. The small fir trees looked like sentinels wearing white armor and guarding the property, but April remembered how bright the colored flowerbeds were in summer. Her favorite was the bed with the crimson-colored rosebush tucked away near the back of the garden. A cardinal flitted by and landed in a small bush a few feet away. It took a quick peek at April as if to say, where did you come from? You are in my territory. Then it flitted around the corner of the church to some other unknown destination. April brushed the snow off the end of a bench and sat down.

"Great," April said as she laughed. "I thought I was filling my life with purpose in the mountains of Ecuador. Now my dad wants me to use The Noah Document to reach out and touch even more people. I have no idea what particular research dad was working on. I know he purposely left out that information because he knew I wouldn't rest until my curiosity was satisfied." April lost track of time as her thoughts kept reflecting on her father's written words. A harsh shiver brought her back to the real world.

The sun breaking through the clouds reflected off the beautiful stained glass windows of the church sanctuary. April was cold from sitting outside for so long, yet she felt more content within than she had in months. She glanced back toward the snow covered garden after getting back in her car to leave the church parking lot. Hers were the only set of tracks in the fresh snow. The icy outline of each boot print glistened from the reflection of the sun. She took her last sip of lukewarm coffee, set the empty cup in the holder, and drove back home.

Chapter 13

"Hello, April. My name is Jason Otis. I am glad to meet you."

"Hello, Jason. It's nice to meet you too."

"My sympathy to you about your dad's passing away. I didn't know him well, but I did talk with him a couple of times. I understand he was a great researcher."

"Thank you. My family and I miss him a lot."

"Please let me know if there is anything we can do for you or your family."

"Thank you. I appreciate your concern, but we are working through the grieving stage and slowly moving on with our lives."

"Well, April, the reason I am meeting with you today is to discuss your letter and resume expressing your interest in a position with Thornburg Genetics. As approved by you, we have completed an extensive background check and everything appears in order. Why are you interested in a job with Thornburg Genetics?"

"As I wrote in my letter, I have a passion for helping people. It is very satisfying to see a glimmer of hope on the face of a person that had none. I love to see children smiling at the thought of an improved life or finding out that a dream is within reach. It's amazing to see how family ties can strengthen when a family member is on the road to physical recovery from an illness. Examples like these are what make my life worth living."

"I have to say that you are enthusiastic. What do you personally have to offer our company or how do you see yourself fitting in?"

"I can't be a researcher like my father was. Biology and chemistry were not my specialty. I picture myself as a company spokesperson, promoting the Thornburg Genetics line of pharmaceuticals by using positive consumer feedback and increased product knowledge."

"We already have a marketing department. You don't believe the current marketing program is already accomplishing this?"

"From my research on the company, it appears that Thornburg's pharmaceuticals are marketed mainly to physicians who then recommend and prescribe the medicines to patients. I believe more extensive marketing can make Thornburg products a household name like Tylenol, Motrin, Bayer aspirin, etc."

"But our medicines have much more limited uses, such as treatments for cancer, arthritis, Alzheimer's and so on."

"Yes, however, everybody knows somebody with a serious medical problem. I don't believe most people could pick out a Thornburg name-brand pharmaceutical."

"I see," said Jason.

After more than an hour of interviewing with Jason, April left the office with a new job. It was 11:30 AM, and she was to report back to the interview room at 12:45 PM for a written test. Her father had mentioned that testing was a way of pinpointing employee promotions at Thornburg Genetics. They were starting phase one of determining whether or not she might have the special Noah Gene from the line of Japheth. She wondered how many people in Thornburg Genetics knew about the Noah Gene theory.

April walked out of the Thornburg Genetics building glass front doors and up the street until she spotted a sandwich shop and stopped in for lunch. April decided to eat a light lunch as she wanted to have her full senses and not feel tired when she took the upcoming test. A young man prepared the fresh salad she ordered. April had no idea she would be in this situation even one month ago. She thought about Ecuador and the people and projects she would be leaving behind. Before she ate, she called her mother and let her know she had a new job and would not be home for lunch. Her mom was very excited and asked her if this was definitely the right decision. They agreed to talk more about it later that evening.

At 12:55, Jason walked into the interview room with the test in hand. "How was your lunch break, April?"

"It was fine, but an hour is a little more than I am used to."

"Don't worry about that. Lunch breaks around here are usually pretty flexible. Most people take about half an hour. Now, let me tell you a little bit about this test. There are one hundred and fifty questions. There is no pass or fail and some of the questions may sound a little strange. This test is designed to determine communication skills, situation ethics and problem solving. You have two and a half hours to complete the test. Inside the front cover is our standard, fill in the bubble answer sheet. Use only a number two pencil or black pen. They are in the container in front of you. Are there any questions before you start?"

"None that I can think of thank you."

"Help yourself to the ice water if you would like. There is a restroom through that door if you need one. You may start the test at any time."

Jason left the room and April immediately opened the test booklet and removed the answer sheet. Her name, the date and the last four digits of her social security number were filled in on the heading. She took a quick look at the first few questions. They looked impossible to decipher. Short of being an astrophysicist brain child, who could answer them? Maybe the first few questions were to make a new employee nervous or something. She read the first question out loud.

1) Saponins from Gupsophila paniculata have been shown to significantly augment the cytotoxicity of immunotoxins leading to improvement in the research of:

a) Epilepsy

b) Macular degeneration

c) Lymphoma

d) Osteoporosis

"Are you kidding me?" She went to the next question.

2) Ayurveda is a:

a) Psychological term

b) Plant name

c) Town in ancient Mesopotamia

d) Form of alternative medicine

"This is going to be a long test."

Things looked brighter after the first ten questions as most of the remaining questions were to be answered by either, or.

58) At a family birthday party would you rather discuss your recent new restaurant find or a coworker's slip up at work?

121) Would you rather play fetch with a dog or teach a dog a new trick?

April was glad when the test was over. She was sure the test was based solely on psychological issues and wondered who could create a test like that.

Chapter 14

April was celebrating her one year anniversary at Thornburg Genetics. It was Wednesday, and she had just returned from a one week vacation in Virginia Beach where she had visited her mother, brother and sister-in-law and spent some time playing with Korey and Kevin. Her nephews were growing up so fast. Most of the playtime now revolved around soccer and baseball. The bright yellow Tonka Toy trucks seemed to be a secondhand thought.

Jason was glad April had returned. There was a large bouquet of roses on her apartment table. The small card attached to the vase said, "I miss you and love you, Jason." Jason was such a great guy. April couldn't remember getting along so well with any other guy. He was good looking, had a great sense of humor, though a little dry, and they hardly ever had an argument. His kisses made her feel special. It felt like a match made in heaven. They spent many evenings together. They would catch a movie, go bowling or maybe just grab a bite to eat. Sometimes they would go to his house, and he would make a fantastic supper and spoil April. Other nights they would go to April's apartment, and she would try to outdo him. Though they had talked about sex, April made it clear that sex came after marriage in her life. Jason accepted April's wishes and did not pressure her. He was such a gentleman. His manners reminded April a lot of her father. She called him and thanked him for the flowers.

April had told her mother about him and promised they would meet in the near future. When she discussed him with her two closest girl fiends, they told her not to let him get away, because he sounded like a keeper. She hoped an engagement ring would be coming in the near future. Did she really want to settle down? How could she pass on such an offer? However, she knew in her heart that she had to find out more about The Noah Document before she could make any kind of firm commitment.

Sales for Thornburg Genetics had been rising consistently for the last seven months. April's improved media campaigns and product exposure were giving Thornburg Genetics more and more name brand recognition. The 'Body-New Pharmaceutical' products, renamed by April, were becoming a familiar household name. Now not only physicians, but also individuals, were familiar with names such as Milky Way White, a white pill with blue specks used to decrease inflammation of joints in many people afflicted with arthritis; and Orange Comet, an orange, oval-shaped pill with a comet monogram stamped on it, used to reduce memory loss in the early stages of Alzheimer patients. April was surprised when the company approved the new names, but they were paying off in a big way.

Many of April's colleagues welcomed her back and asked for details of her vacation. She filled each of them in briefly on her activities and showed them her updated family photos on her laptop. The photos of Kevin and Korey received the most attention. As everyone around her settled into work mode, April stared at her inbox. The stack of paperwork was a foot high. "Do I really want to do this for the rest of my life?" she asked herself. "This is only one week's worth of paper." She had refused to check her emails while on vacation and knew they would be backed up as well.

April decided to check her voice mail before she started sifting through the paperwork. Among the messages on her voice mail was a message from Jason to call him as soon as possible. After writing down sixteen more messages she dialed Jason's number.

Jason saw April's phone number flash up on his caller ID.

"Hello, you have reached the one and only Jason Otis."

"And this is the one and only April James. How are you this fine day?"

"I'm great. It's good to hear your voice, April. How was your vacation?"

"You know how it was. I just talked to you yesterday."

"I'm just trying to sound good for the office politics."

"Well, I'll have to remember that one. What are you, too embarrassed to let people know we are dating?"

"I should say not, Miss James."

"So, you left a message on my voice mail. What's up?"

"It appears that you have one full year of service with Thornburg Genetics and rumor has it that you may be doing a reasonably decent job."

"Very funny."

"Someone up the chain of command said they were considering a promotion for some lucky and unsuspecting employee. Of course, they asked me for my professional opinion. You know, because I'm one of the key players they always ask me important questions like that."

"Oh, I know you are on that important who's who list."

"Well, after a lot of thought, my first suggestion was a Miss April James. Can you believe they went for it?"

"Come on, Jason, now you're flirting with danger. Tell all."

"I will. You have a meeting at 10:00 AM to discuss a company promotion. That's only about half an hour from now. Congratulations

April."

"Why did you wait so long to tell me?"

"I just found out about it this morning."

"What kind of promotion?"

"Sorry April, I can't tell you anything more. You know, company policy and all."

"Come on, Jason, you know more than that."

"Sorry. See you in room 101 at 10:00 AM sharp."

"Jason, you are just a pain sometimes. I don't know whether to hug you or smack you."

"A hug would be preferable. See you soon."

Jason could be exasperating, but he was a lot of fun. April went to the ladies room to make sure she looked her best. The next twenty minutes just dragged. April couldn't concentrate on anything. She attempted to sort part of the mail piled up on her desk. After reading the first piece of mail three times and still not knowing what it said, she put it back down and took a walk. She was in her own little world at this point and started talking to herself.

"A promotion, I wonder what they are thinking. Will it be in marketing or some other area? Do they want me to supervise more employees? Are they going to ask me to move to some God forsaken place like Siberia? Do I want a promotion?"

April couldn't stand the suspense any longer and headed for room 101. Originally there was no room 101 in the facility; it was simply called the conference room. Several years before, some jokester dubbed it room 101 and it stuck. Entering room 101 was equated to the nervous, painful feeling you had when you started college and were enrolled in a freshman level course. There were hundreds of new faces in every classroom, and they were all staring at you. You were lucky if you could even find a designated classroom on campus without a map, and you asked yourself exactly what you were doing there. Voilà, room 101 at Thornburg Genetics where all job interviews, promotions, firings, and layoffs, you name it, happened. It had even earned its own brass plaque, which was fastened at eye level on the solid oak entry door. The standard saying was, 'beware of room 101'.

April turned the doorknob and walked in. There was Jason looking at the seascape painting on the wall.

"Hello, April. Aren't you a little early? Have the room 101 gremlins been after you since our telephone conversation?"

"The suspense has been killing me, Jason. I can't concentrate on anything."

"That's natural and expected, April. Do you know how many times I see this as head of the human resources department? I spend more time in room 101 than anybody else at Thornburg. Take a second and look at this painting. Every time I enter this room I'm drawn to it like a magnet. The beautiful golden sunrise and the mist in the harbor are so warm and inviting. The boats are getting ready to set out to sea. But look at the very upper right hand corner. A dark cloud is just starting to work its way into the scene. The painting gives a feeling of calmness in the harbor, yet an unsure feeling of what lies in front of you. Just that one small cloud changes the complexion of the whole painting. I kind of like the unsettled feeling it gives."

"It's a great painting, but I just can't concentrate on it right now Jason."

Jason chuckled a little. "I know. Why don't you take a seat in our favorite room 101 special assignment chair?"

This was called 'the chair of fate'. Every company has one. It's the chair where an employee sits to learn his or her fate, good or bad. This was the same chair April sat in just one year ago and accepted a job offer with Thornburg Genetics. One year seemed to vanish so quickly.

Chapter 15

Jason and April were barely seated when the door behind Jason opened and in walked a tall slim woman with a folder in her hands. She wore a navy blue pinstripe suit. A solid white blouse offset her olive-colored skin. Her dark brown hair was tied in a tight bun on the back of her head. Her facial demeanor gave the impression that she was all business. Behind her was a tall gentleman outfitted in a solid charcoal-colored suit, white shirt, and a paisley print tie. Both of them had an air of importance and a no-nonsense appearance. April had seen both of them before but had never been formally introduced. She felt a little intimidated and out of place. Both Jason and April stood up as they walked in.

"Hello, Jason," said the woman with a pleasant tone of voice. "Would you do the honors?"

"It's my pleasure. This is April James, Director of Public Relations in Marketing. April, this is Tanya Jefferson, Vice President of Marketing, and this is Mark Ellison, Vice President of Sales."

Both Tanya and Mark greeted April with a friendly hello and strong handshake.

"I must apologize," said Tanya. "You have worked here for a full year, and I haven't met you until now. I do my best to meet all employees that work in my area of responsibility, but in your case it seems like every time I tried to introduce myself, you were in a meeting or out of the office. I must do a better job of contacting new employees."

"I don't know what to say. I don't think an apology is necessary. I'm glad to meet you now, and I'm sure your schedule makes it difficult to be everything to everybody."

"Thank you for being so understanding. Of course I keep in touch with your supervisors, and they tell me about your excellent work ethic. It is always good to hear positive comments. So, I understand you just returned from vacation. Could you give us some highlights?"

"My vacation was great," said April. "I had a chance to spend time with my family again. My nephews Kevin and Korey are 5 and 7 years old, and they are constantly on the move. They are the highlight of my visits, but don't tell the rest of the family. I also had time to take a couple of nice long hikes."

"Where do you hike?" asked Mark.

"One day I walked as far as I could on Virginia Beach. It was probably seven or eight miles. Another day I drove across Chesapeake Bridge and walked up Rt. 13 through the Hamptons. I stopped and checked out a couple of small county parks as well. It's not as much fun as hiking in the Adirondacks or on the Appalachian Trail nor is it as rugged as the terrain in Ecuador, but I had a good time. The fresh air and exercise are very relaxing."

"Do you go by yourself?" asked Tanya.

"Sometimes I go by myself. Sometimes I go with friends. It just depends on the day. Sometimes I want to share the experience and sometimes I want to be alone."

"Aren't you afraid of being robbed or molested when you are by yourself? It seems as though every day in the news a jogger or hiker is attacked by somebody."

"Well, I love the outdoors and can't worry that there might be a problem every time I want to take a hike. I depend on God to keep me safe and not allow any harm. I also carry a handgun and pepper spray, just in case."

"Really," said Tanya with a surprised tone in her voice. "Do you know how to use them?"

"I target practice with the handgun at least once a week. A girl can never be too safe you know."

Jason chuckled and smiled. He had been with April half a dozen times when she practiced shooting. She would shoot at least one hundred rounds from several different stances. Her shooting was right on the money. Woe to anyone who thought she was an easy mark for a robbery or hideous crime.

April glanced at Jason as if to say, 'Be quiet.'

"That sounds like something your father would have said," Mark retorted.

"Well, April, the reason we are here today is to discuss a promotion," said Tanya. "Mark and I work closely together in marketing and sales for Thornburg Genetics. Evidence of your hard work and excellent ideas have resulted in increased sales of several pharmaceuticals due to a more personal approach to name brand recognition. In less than one year, the 'Body-New Pharmaceutical' name brand is the talk of the industry. I have to say that I was skeptical about a drug named Milky Way White and the other new names, but the general public has embraced them. Renaming the brands was your idea, and we want to thank you personally for all of your efforts."

"Yes," said Mark. "Your creativity is of great value."

"Thank you very much," said April.

"You are welcome," both Tanya and Mark responded.

"I would like to ask a question," said April.

40

"Sure, anytime you have a question, feel free to ask," said Tanya.

"I realize this is a big company, and I have heard your names mentioned. I have seen you in this facility a couple of times, but I really don't know anything about either of you other than what I have read off our website and the limited information my supervisors have shared with me. Would you mind sharing more background information about yourselves?"

"I like it when people are inquisitive," said Tanya. "I am Vice President of Marketing for both North and South America. And because I know you are dying to ask but won't, I have a slight Portuguese accent because my mother was from Brazil. My father is American. I am fluent in Portuguese, Spanish and, of course, English. Thornburg Genetics has been my employer for 21 years now. I try to meet with as many employees of the company as I can, but my free time is indeed limited. I deal mostly with personnel in upper level management."

Tanya looked at Mark.

"I am the Vice President of Worldwide Sales, April. I worked for another pharmaceutical company for five years and have been with Thornburg now for eighteen years. My job involves extensive travel throughout the world dealing with sales goals and communication, and I'm always monitoring new market trends. I also deal with high level managers in the company."

"Thank you for the background information. I appreciate it," said April.

"Do you have any other questions before we get back to the business at hand?" asked Tanya.

"Not at the moment."

"Okay. April, the reason we have called this meeting today is to discuss a job promotion. We like what we see in you, and we do our best to promote from within Thornburg Genetics. Your quarterly evaluations have been superb, considering you have only been on the job for one year. We know that you must have completed a lot of work, not only on company time but also on your own time, to achieve the level of performance we see. We love employees that go above and beyond the call of duty."

"We are also familiar with your high level of ethics and personal values," said Mark. "Since you are surrounded by excellent employees, we knew you would question the reason why you should be promoted after one year of service when other quality employees with far more time have not been offered a promotion. For that reason, we created a special new position to limit personnel conflicts. The position is called the North and South America Public Relations Specialist."

Tanya continued, "Your main job objective will be the advancement of Thornburg pharmaceutical name-brand recognition. In this position, traveling will be required as your territory will cover both North and South America. You will also be responsible for training other employees in the effective promotion of the Thornburg line of pharmaceuticals. This will include creating and updating a written training manual in both English and Spanish. I hope you have kept up on your Spanish from your time spent in Ecuador. Naturally, there will be a considerable raise in pay and certain perks go along with this opportunity. Jason has all of the facts in a packet, which he will be sharing with you after we leave. The reason I am here today is because you will report directly to me in your new position. I will be available at any time, day or night, and for any reason whatsoever. Of course, we expect continued success to retain this position. Do you have any questions at this point?"

April was awestruck. She had no idea anything of this magnitude would be offered to her. There was a moment of silence. April regained her composure and said, "This is a little overwhelming. I am a confident person by nature, but I have only been with Thornburg Genetics for one year. The offer of a promotion comes as a bit of a shock."

Mark answered, "We believe you can handle this assignment, and we also believe you can continue to advance within Thornburg Genetics. We would like you to begin thinking about employees you would potentially want to hire as your staff. You have worked with several individuals over the past year, and you know their qualifications and work ethics. We are thinking about a staff of four to begin with, one clerical staff and three sales/marketing employees."

"Will I still be able to live here or will I be expected to move to a different location?"

"With this promotion, you will be able to live almost anywhere you want as long as there is internet access and cell phone capability."

"Wow, I'm overwhelmed."

"We thought you might be," said Tanya. "Jason has a packet of material for your review and signature. It is fairly extensive and will probably take about an hour to review. It is eleven o'clock now. Why don't you review the packet and write down any questions you have. We will meet back here at noon to see if you have any additional questions, and once you have accepted we will welcome you aboard in your new position. Mark and I are really excited about creating this position for you. Now, I'm sure you are aware with every company promotion there is a corresponding test. It is similar in structure to the test you took at the time of your initial employment. That will be administered this afternoon. Again, there is no right or wrong answer to the questions."

Mark turned to Jason. "Will you arrange a small luncheon for the four of us at 12:30?"

"I certainly will, Mr. Ellison."

"Thank you, Jason."

At this, both Tanya and Mark stood up. Jason and April followed suit. April shook their extended hands.

"Congratulations," they both said in turn.

"We will see you at noon," said Tanya.

At that, they both turned and left through the side door, leaving Jason alone in the room with April.

"Congratulations, April."

"I don't know what to say. I had no idea a promotion of this magnitude was even possible after working here for one year. And you didn't even let me know it was coming. I hope I looked attractive with my jaw dragging on the floor for the last half hour."

"You looked fine, April, and you know I can't say anything about promotions. I do have to say though; I have only seen a couple of promotions like this in my seven years here in the personnel office. Wait until you look through this packet. It is an exceptional opportunity." Jason set a file folder on the conference table. "I'll be back a little before noon. See you then." Jason turned and exited through the side door of room 101.

April stood up and poured a glass of ice water from the pitcher on the table. Then she walked over to the painting Jason had been admiring when she arrived for the meeting. It was a beautiful painting. The golden sunrise, mist in the harbor, fishing boats ready to trek out to sea. What did Jason say? It gives the feeling of calm, yet uneasiness. She wondered what the artist was reflecting on when he created this piece.

April smiled and giggled to herself. She wondered how her father would have reacted to the proposal. As she looked through the packet her mouth dropped open. She was offered a company car with unlimited mileage, the opportunity to live anywhere in North or South America, full medical and dental benefits, vacation as needed and a salary of $138,000. She would be required to maintain a 15% annual increase in sales in her department and would receive stock option benefits for sales increases over the 15% target. "Unbelievable," she said out loud. The rest of the packet delved into budget restraints, marketing requirements and company policies.

At 11:55 sharp, Jason walked in the side door.

"Well, April, quite a package isn't it? They want your expertise and creativeness and are willing to pay for it."

"I never imagined such a thing was possible."

"Did you sign on the dotted line?"

"Not yet, Jason."

"Is there a problem?"

"There's no problem at all. It's an exceptional opportunity. I just want to talk with Tanya and Mark a little more."

"Sure thing. They'll be here any minute."

It was only a couple of minutes later when Tanya and Mark entered room 101. Tanya held out her hand and motioned for April to be seated. They were sure April was on board, judging by her big smile.

"How do you like the package?" asked Mark.

"Outstanding is the word that comes to mind. I do have one question though."

"Shoot," said Mark.

"It appears that I will be setting up my own program to accomplish all of this. Is that correct?"

"That is correct, April. That is why we are allowing you to hand select staff for the project. You will be reporting to both Tanya and I, but Tanya will be your immediate supervisor. I believe you saw the approved budget in your package. We will work closely with you at first until things start falling in line and then give you more leeway to work with less supervision. Don't worry about all of the logistics. Take one step at a time, keep up your work ethic, and we will make sure your promotion is a success. This is a very important project to us. Are there any other questions?"

"That's the only one I can think of right now. Everything else in the packet is self-explanatory."

"Have you signed the agreement and non-disclosure statements?" asked Tanya.

"Not yet. I am very excited and this is a great opportunity, but I would like to think about it. This has all happened so fast and I wasn't expecting a promotion. I just want a little time to breathe. I am sure you understand."

"To be honest with you, we thought you would sign the contract right away," said Tanya. "We don't offer promotions like this very often."

"I understand that," said April.

April glanced at Jason. He was just sitting there with a blank stare on his face.

Mark broke the short moment of awkward silence. "April, we want you on our team. Is there a problem with the package? Has another company made an offer for your services? Is there some other problem we can help with? We want everything to feel right and we pride ourselves in having content, hardworking employees."

"There are no problems," April assured them with a smile. "I just want a little time to consider the added pressure and responsibility."

"Do you know how much time you need?" asked Tanya.

"I would like to consider the offer overnight."

"Is that okay with you Mark?"

"Well, here's my situation. I have to be on a plane by 9:00 AM tomorrow. I don't want to push this, but would 7:00 AM be too early to meet? We really aren't trying to pressure you April. We just have busy schedules."

"7:00 AM will be fine."

The 12:30 luncheon in room 101 was awkward. April was sure the original intent of the luncheon was to celebrate her promotion and discuss future marketing plans. Instead the time was used for small talk about great vacation spots, new drug results and family fun events. At 1:00 PM, April was given the promised test to complete in anticipation of her acceptance of the promotion. Jason, Tanya and Mark left the room.

Once outside room 101, Tanya and Mark cornered Jason. "What is going on? Why didn't April sign the contract?" asked Mark.

"I have no idea. There was no indication of any problem. Maybe she does need some time to consider her decision."

"Come on, Jason, nobody needs time to think about an opportunity like this one. We want her on our team. Let us know what we have to do to make it happen and if there is a problem, let us know immediately. Do your best."

"I'll make sure everything works out."

"We'll see you here at 7:00 AM, Jason."

"Sure thing."

There were more crazy questions on the second test. April recognized some of the questions as the same ones asked on her initial hiring test. These had to be some type of psychological test questions. There were 175 questions and April blazed through them in one hour and twenty minutes. They were mostly multiple choice and required little thought. As on the first test, most of the questions were would you rather do A or B. She reached for the telephone on the desk and called Jason's number.

"Fought your way through another tough test did you, April?"

"I might even have passed this one," she chuckled. "I need to be rescued from this room. I've been in here all day."

"I'll be right down to collect your test and rescue you. See you in a minute."

"Okay, I'm impatiently waiting."

April stood up and walked over to the painting again. Calm, yet uneasiness she thought.

Within minutes, Jason walked into the room. "Hi, April, it's been kind of a long day hasn't it."

"This has been way too much sitting time. At least when I'm in my office I can get up and move around."

"Would you like to get together after work for a little while? I think a nice dinner to celebrate your promotion is in order. How about Calandra's? Their entrées are the best!"

"That is such a sweet offer, Jason, but I really need to be alone tonight to think this promotion opportunity through. I need to make sure this is the right direction for my life. It's a huge decision."

"Is it really the promotion or is there some other problem? Is something going on with your family? I will be glad to talk with you about anything. This is such a great opportunity, and I don't want you to miss it, April."

"There is absolutely nothing wrong. This promotion is the opportunity of a lifetime," April said with a big smile. "I just don't like to make snap decisions when it deals with my entire future. I want to consider what's ahead of me and pray about the situation. There is a ton of responsibility that goes along with this scenario. There are employees to consider, a budget to follow and lofty sales goals. The work expected from this promotion isn't going to be a walk in the park. You know I like a challenge, but you also know how much of a perfectionist I am. This promotion is nothing to take lightly, but everybody wants an immediate decision."

"You're right, it is a big decision. It is a little bit after 2:30. Why don't you take the rest of the day off? I know you won't be able to concentrate on your desk work."

"I know this is my first day back from vacation, but I think I will leave a little early."

"Call me if you would like to talk about anything, and remember the offer to go out is good all evening." Jason gave April a kiss on the cheek. They had both agreed that even though they were seeing each other, there would be no office romance, but she did appreciate his affection.

"Thanks, Jason. I'll give you a call if I need anything."

"You are welcome to take home the promotion package for review, but it should not be shown to anyone else. Is that workable?"

"Sure Jason, I understand the whole corporate privacy issue."

"Well, I'll see you bright and early, 7:00 AM to be exact."

"I'll be here."

April left room 101 feeling drained of energy. She stopped at her desk quickly to see if there was anything urgent. There was nothing that couldn't wait until later. She stopped to chitchat with a couple of her coworkers. They talked about April's vacation and current events in the office. In half an hour she was out the door and headed for her apartment.

Chapter 16

When April walked into her apartment, the sun was shining into the living room through the sliding glass door. She took a moment to stand in the rays and absorb the warmth before taking the promotion proposal out of her tote bag and laying it on the cushion of her couch. The back of April's neck hurt so she decided a short jog would relieve some of the pressure. After drinking a large glass of water, she slipped on her favorite dark lavender jogging suit, trotted down her apartment building stairs, and slowly started up the sidewalk. Three blocks from her apartment she stopped by a small stream that meandered next to the sidewalk. A great blue heron lifted off, annoyed at the intrusion. April thought about the promotion and the additional work it would require. Then her thoughts drifted to Jason. He was such a good looking guy with his wavy, light brown hair and brown eyes. He was always handsome looking in his required suit and tie at work. Why hadn't some other girl picked up on him before now? He always said he was waiting for just the right young lady. April completed a forty-five minute jog still trying to sort out what mattered most in her life. She had worked up a sweat and her neck ache had disappeared.

When she arrived back at her apartment, she filled her teapot with water and turned on the stove. After selecting a bag of green tea from the white ceramic canister on her counter, she chose her favorite over-sized, porcelain mug and laid the tea bag in the bottom. She raced to her bathroom to see if she could get a shower in before the tea pot whistled.

As she continued to mull over the promotion, her father's words came back to her. You will know what to do with this document and who is worthy to know its contents. Many thoughts about The Noah Document raced through her mind. There was the underground vault, hundreds of tablets, and Charlie the librarian. Did she really have the Noah Gene? Suddenly the whistle of the teapot brought her back to the present. The water in the mug quickly turned dark green as the boiling water covered the tea bag. April took her cup of tea, put on a heavy sweater and walked to the sliding glass door. As she slid it open and walked out on her deck, she felt the cool March air contrasting with the warm rays of the sun. She closed the door behind her, sat down on the black metal bistro chair, and laid the proposal on the matching table. She took a moment to gaze at the pond from her third floor deck. Two ducks flew off the pond and circled over her head, barely missing her apartment roof. The remnants of small waves left behind crept toward the banks of the pond. April picked up her mug and blew on the surface of the hot tea, then took a sip. She picked up the proposal and read it through twice. Then April prayed a brief prayer.

"God, I ask for wisdom in this decision, and I thank you for the offer of a promotion. I ask for your guidance in this matter, and I ask that your will be accomplished, in Jesus' name, amen."

April felt at ease as she picked up her cell phone and called the family attorney. She had devised a plan to see how much of The Noah Document she could verify, and she needed Michael's help.

"Hello, you have reached the office of Michael Anderson, Esquire. May I help you?"

"Hello, this is April James. May I please speak with Mr. Anderson?"

"I'm sorry, but Mr. Anderson is with a client right now. May I take a message?"

"Yes, would you please tell him that I need some legal advice concerning a job promotion? I have to make a decision by 7:00 AM tomorrow morning, and I need to speak with him as soon as possible."

"Let me get your telephone number, April, and I will give Mr. Anderson your message. I expect him to be available shortly. If for some reason he cannot get back to you, I will call you back and let you know."

April wrote a few notes to herself as she again reviewed the promotion proposal. It was about twenty minutes before the telephone rang. April checked the incoming number on the screen and quickly picked it up.

"Hello, this is April James."

"Hello, April, this is Michael. How are you?"

"I'm fine, Mr. Anderson. How are you and the family?"

"We are all doing great, and we are busy as always. So, I hear you are up for a big job promotion. How can I help you?"

"Well, here is the situation. I have just been offered a significant company promotion including a pay raise and benefits. My intent is to accept the promotion, but I need to create an addendum with two items. The addendum has to be ironclad legal, with no loopholes."

"Tell me what you have in mind."

April explained the requirements for addendum number one. According to Michael this could easily be written to produce a legally binding contract. The second addendum was much more difficult to explain. April had to use some hypothetical situations because there were certain elements in the addendum, which were related to The Noah Document. She knew that even with legal confidentiality there were just certain facts she could not share with Michael due to The Noah Gene.

"You want this tonight? That's not much time, April."

"I know its short notice, but I just found out about the promotion today. They wanted an answer almost immediately, but I did convince them to give me until 7:00 AM."

"Aren't they a little pushy?"

"I don't know why it's such a rush job. I guess it's because they are all busy executives, and they want to move on to their next project. Besides, the offer is a great one, and they expected me to jump on it like there was no tomorrow."

"Okay April, I better get to work on it right now, and I will call you back later."

"Thank you so much, Mr. Anderson."

April called her mother and told her all about the promotion. Then she called her brother. Both congratulated her and asked her to let them know how things went. They both said they would pray for her and her decision. She reviewed the entire packet again and still couldn't believe this opportunity was hers. She reminisced about her time in Ecuador with the Peace Corps. It had been just over a year since she left there. What a radical difference in employment. April finally picked up the black pen that had been sitting on the bistro table and signed and dated the promotion agreement and nondisclosure statements. She picked up her paperwork and went back inside. It was just after 8:00 PM when Michael called back.

"Hello, April. I have the information you requested. The two addenda are brief, but legally binding. I will email them to you. I just want to make sure I have the correct email address."

After their telephone call, April retrieved her laptop. She opened her email account and found the email Michael had just sent. She opened the attachment and read the addenda through twice. The first addendum was perfect. Because April could not share certain privileged information with Michael, she had to rearrange and complete the second addendum using what Michael had sent her as an outline. When she finished, she thought the second addendum looked good, but wished she could have sent a copy to Michael for approval. She printed two copies of the addenda and set them next to the signed contract. Now the pressure was off. April went to her bedroom, set her alarm clock and crawled into bed.

Chapter 17

It was 6:45 AM when April walked into her office. She turned on the copy machine as she walked by. After removing her coat, she retrieved the job promotion papers from her tote bag. The addenda were on top of the pile, and she made an additional copy of each paper on the copy machine. She signed each original addendum and sealed them in the envelope she had preaddressed to Tanya the night before. Only a handful of people were in the office at this hour. April glided past them unnoticed as she set course for room 101. Jason was already seated and was just raising a cup of coffee to his mouth when April entered. He set the cup down on the polished cherry conference table and stood up. The smell of coffee radiated through the room.

"Good morning, April," Jason said and then smiled gingerly, "It's good to see your cheery face this morning."

"It's great to be here," April said, as she smiled back.

"Would you like a cup of coffee?"

"It smells good. I would love a cup."

Jason went to the small cherry side table adjacent to the conference table and poured a cup of coffee for April.

"Cream as usual?"

"Yes and maybe just a little sugar today."

"Sure thing, ma'am, here you go."

"Thanks, Jason."

"Tanya and Mark should be here any minute. Do you need anything before they arrive?"

"I believe I'm all set."

"So, did you get everything sorted out, April? I had hoped you would call me last night. You seem so secretive for some reason."

"I did a lot of praying and thinking last night. I thought about calling you, because I knew you were concerned, but I just had to figure things out in my own way. There's nothing to worry about, Jason."

"Well, let's take a seat, shall we?"

"Yes," said April. "Mmmm, this coffee is good. Did you make it?"

"It's one of my secret blends. I ground it just this morning for someone special, such as you. It's called coffee d'April. That's French of course and means coffee just for April."

They both laughed. April was glad to hear Jason talking with his normal self-esteem again. "I shall require coffee d'April often from this day forward."

Jason and April were both sipping their coffee when Tanya and Mark entered room 101. They both looked calm and collected even though April knew there was tension carried over from the day before. Jason immediately asked them if they would like a cup of coffee.

"I would love a cup with just a little sugar, please," said Tanya.

"I would like a cup too, Jason. Straight black for me, please," said Mark.

"Good morning, April," they both said in turn.

Jason poured and distributed the two cups of coffee.

"Shall we get right down to business?" asked Tanya.

"Yes," said April.

Mark nodded his head up and down in agreement.

"We assume you have reviewed the job promotion proposal," Tanya said, looking at April. "Do you have any additional questions or can we congratulate you as our new Public Relations Specialist?"

April could sense an air of uncertainty in both Tanya's and Mark's actions and facial expressions. "I have come to a decision. All of the job promotion documents have been signed, and I am ready to start my new assignment. It is a magnificent offer, and I thank you for this opportunity."

April could see a look of relief come over Tanya and Mark's face. "However, I have two contract addenda, which I would also like to include."

A new look of tension appeared on both Tanya and Mark's face. April saw Jason's jaw drop as he stared at April.

"I have to say this is a little unusual, but what do you have in mind?" asked Tanya.

April took the sealed envelope with the addenda and handed it to Tanya. The room was silent as Tanya opened the addenda and read them. April had never seen anyone turn so pale so fast. Tanya completed reading the addenda and folded them back up. Then she turned her head toward Jason.

"Will you please leave the room, Jason? We will call you when we are ready to move forward."

Jason glanced at April with a look of, what did you just do? He silently rose from his chair and left room 101.

Tanya turned and stared at April. She handed the addenda to Mark. April watched his face as he also read the addenda. She could see the look of shock on his face. Mark looked up at April.

"I think it is safe to say you have caught us entirely off guard, Miss April James. I am sure addendum number one can be arranged. Creating a charity fund to help provide medical assistance to impoverished countries and people groups is of major interest to Thornburg Genetics. I will have to get approval from my superiors to put you in charge of such a fund, and I am sure a board of directors will also be required. Your requested addendum number two will have to be discussed at some length. Do you have any idea what level of security is required in order for us to accomplish this request?"

"I really have no idea," said April, "but I think you are about to inform me, aren't you?"

"Oh yes indeed! Where did you get this information?"

April knew she had to concentrate and think quickly. She was treading on dangerous ground, and if she didn't answer certain questions correctly she could be in big trouble.

"I would really rather not say."

"Have you shared this information with anyone else? That means anyone at all in any shape or form?" There was silence in the room. Mark and Tanya both stared at April with stern, tense eyes.

"I have told no one about this."

"Did you discover this information here at work?" asked Tanya.

"Again, I would rather not say."

The room was silent. April knew that Tanya and Mark were not sure what to do or say.

"Will you excuse us, April?" asked Tanya.

"Of course."

Tanya and Mark left the room and walked down the hallway to a small side room known as the control center. Mark closed the door behind him.

April stood up, took a deep breath and let out a sigh of relief. She knew the second addendum was not going to be an easy request, and she had certainly caught them off guard. They didn't know what to do. She smiled a big smile. Now it was time to wait. April poured herself another cup of coffee and a glass of ice water.

Chapter 18

Mark immediately picked up the telephone in the control center and dialed an outside long distance number.

"Hello. This is Mark Ellison and Tanya Jefferson. We are in control room number 1 at the Philadelphia, Pennsylvania Thornburg Genetics location. My security clearance number is E188247. Is this room and telephone line secure?"

"Give me just a minute, sir. Please turn on the scrambler device." There was a pause. "The room and telephone line is now secure."

"Thank you. The room is clear, Tanya."

"What are your thoughts, Mark?"

"I don't know what to think. April shouldn't even know about this as a security level one employee. Only level six and seven employees know this information. I have only one theory. Vincent James, her father, must have been involved in this. He died over a year ago now. He must have shared some inside information with April. If all of our Noah Gene theories have been correct, he shouldn't have been able to tell her anything about classified Thornburg Genetics information."

"Is it possible that she stumbled onto something here in the work place? Maybe some research work or paperwork was misrouted or something. She is extremely sharp, and she could have put two and two together given the right circumstances."

"What were the numbers on the test she took yesterday?"

"She was in the 92 percentile on the test yesterday and in the 98 percentile on the initial hire test."

"Those are high scores. That at least puts her at a security level two and probably three."

"Do you think she'll make a security level seven? She may have the Noah Gene."

"The potential is there, but it is just too early to tell. This is a major security issue. We must know how she found out. I hate to do this to you, Tanya, but I have to catch that 9:00 AM flight. Can you handle this without me?"

"What choice do I have?"

"None, I have to run. Good luck and I'll talk to you later."

"Thanks a lot, Mark. I can't believe this whole scenario is going to go smoothly."

Mark left the room and Tanya remained in the brown leather chair thinking about the next move. How did April find out? Like Mark said, it must have been her father. There wasn't any other reasonable explanation. Maybe this whole situation could turn one hundred percent positive. April has the potential to be a security level six or seven employee. On the other hand, this situation could be a complete mess. This could mean a major information security breach within Thornburg Genetics.

After several minutes of brainstorming, Tanya's gut feeling was that everything would work out for the better. April's security test scores were high. According to April, she had told nobody else about this information. Her father had passed away over a year ago. That meant that if Vincent had revealed this information to April, she had remained quiet for over a year. In fact, if nobody else at a lower security level or in the general public knew, the situation should work out okay. Tanya picked up the secure telephone and dialed the direct number. Only one hundred and fifty people in the entire world had access to this telephone number. It was changed every time a level seven security associate retired, died, or left Thornburg Genetics.

"Hello, this is Tanya."

"Hi, Tanya. How are you this morning?"

"I'm fine. It's a beautiful day in downtown Philadelphia."

"You sound a little on edge, Tanya. Do we have a problem?"

"Mark and I are in the process of promoting an employee. Her name is April James. She is a security level one employee and has been with Thornburg Genetics for one year."

"April is Vince's daughter, our Body-New Pharmaceutical marketing girl."

"You have a great memory."

"Does this have something to do with the promotion?"

"Here is the situation. We have offered her a very attractive level two promotional package, which she has accepted. However, she insists on two addenda. The first addendum deals with setting up a charity fund to establish a medical distribution system in third world countries. April would like to be the overseer of that fund. We feel this fund would continue to put Thornburg Genetics in the eyes of the general public and would enhance our marketing efforts while performing a great human service. As you know, our sales have increased greatly in the last few months due to many of April's marketing and promotional ideas. You mentioned the Body-New name brand pharmaceuticals. April created that idea herself. We need to discuss the charity further, but I'm sure April's involvement will be acceptable. The second addendum she requested is a little out of the ordinary. Are you ready?" Tanya paused as she tried to maintain her composure. "April has requested a face-to-face meeting with The Keeper."

There was a moment of silence from this unexpected request. "Really? How did April James find out about The Keeper?"

"At this point in time she prefers not to say. Mark and I just discussed the possibilities. We believe that in some way The Keeper may have been portrayed through her father, Vince."

"Vince was a great guy and a truly dedicated employee. I am a little surprised he would tell anyone about our operations. Based on our research, he could not tell anyone about The Keeper if our genetics theory is correct. Of course, April may have The Noah Gene, which gives her security level seven potential. What are the other possibilities?"

"A possible misplaced research document or mislabeled piece of correspondence, but that seems unlikely."

"Vince died over a year ago. Why would this situation take so long to surface? Is there any indication of a security breach? We know we have a problem somewhere in the organization."

"I'm not sensing a security breach, but April isn't saying a word. We did ask her if she told anyone else about this and the answer was no."

"What were her test scores?"

"She scored a 98 on the level one security test and a 92 on the level two test."

"Those are high scores and definitely welcome. Let's meet with April next week after working hours. I will notify you of the arrangements. Of course she can't know the exact date or time. Make sure Mark is in attendance, and we'll have dinner together before we meet with April. Is that workable?"

"My schedule is open. I will check with Mark."

"Great. Now, I have two things that need to be done, Tanya. First, I want you to put a tail on April twenty-four, seven until I meet with her. Second, let her know that the first order of business will be to discuss how she found out about me. In fact, why don't we give her a level three test before then as well? I have an idea this may work to our advantage."

"Consider it done, Lexis."

"Thanks for everything, Tanya. This is very interesting. I needed something a little different to start my day. I'll see you next week."

"Goodbye, Lexis."

Tanya left control room number one and walked back to room 101. April was standing up with a cup of coffee in her hand. She was peering at the seascape painting on the wall. April turned as Tanya walked in. Tanya could sense that April was excited and anxious. April eyed Tanya and could detect a sense of composure unlike her whole appearance only half an hour ago.

"Will you please follow me, April?"

Tanya led April back down the hallway to control room number one. She let April enter first and then closed the door after walking in.

"Have a seat, April. This is a secure room and no one else can hear our conversation as long as the door remains closed. Just so you know, Mark had to catch a plane and is on his way to the airport."

Tanya studied April's face. "I have conversed with The Keeper. She has agreed to meet with you."

"So, The Keeper is a woman."

"That is correct."

"What exactly does she do?"

"I'm really not authorized to say any more on that subject at this point. However, I do have a few things you must understand. First, only a limited number of people know about The Keeper. This is a top-level secure position in a security conscious company. You said that no one else knows about this matter. It must remain that way. I cannot emphasize how important this is. Do you understand?"

"I understand."

"Good. Nothing more should be said outside of this room. Even this room is checked for security clearance before use. Now, just so you know, The Keeper said that the first order of business at the meeting will be to discuss how you found out about The Keeper title. You have no idea how big a concern there is over a possible security breach at Thornburg Genetics because of your request. Are there any other questions, April?"

"I don't have any other questions at this point."

"Do you fully understand the severity of the position we are in? We are putting a lot of faith in a one-year employee being discreet with a high-level security issue. At this point we can only hope you are telling the truth."

"As God is my witness, I can assure you I am."

"There is one final concern I need to share with you. Your life is now in danger due to the knowledge you possess."

"Why is my life in danger?"

"Again, I wish I could tell you, but until you meet with The Keeper,

57

I'm authorized to say very little."

April was thinking everything through very carefully. She wondered exactly what she was in the middle of. Were there illegal operations going on? What danger could there be to her life?

"So when will I meet The Keeper?"

"I cannot give you an exact date, time or location, again for security reasons. At some point in time it will just happen. I do have some good news for you though."

"Okay, go ahead."

"We would like you to take another written test for us."

"I'm sure there is no sense in saying this, but I just took a test yesterday."

"You were right; there was no sense in saying that."

"That's what I thought. What about the new position?"

"We are on a temporary hold with the new position." Tanya rose to her feet, which signaled that the meeting was over. April was ushered back to room 101.

"I will call Jason. He'll be right down with another test for you. I'll be in touch."

April's mind started to ramble. What am I doing? What am I involved in that could be so life threatening? I don't know if I can sit still long enough to take another one of these dumb tests.

It was ten minutes before Jason slipped into the room. "Hi, April."

"Hello again, Jason."

"I have to say that this is a very peculiar situation. In the seven years I've held this position, you are the first person to take test three within one day of taking test number two. Can I ask what was in the letter you handed them?"

"How many of these tests are there, Jason? What kind of tests are they? Half of the questions make no sense at all. They have to be some type of psychological test aren't they?"

"I really can't tell you any information about them, April."

"That seems to be the story of my day. I can't really tell you anything about my letter either."

"You don't understand, April. The reason I'm not telling you anything is because I don't know the exact purpose of the tests or how many there are. I have had to take three tests, and they have been the same tests as yours. If there are more tests, I am not aware of them."

"I still can't tell you anything about the letter, Jason."

"I can tell you this, April. I never saw Tanya's face make such a drastic, dramatic change in a matter of seconds. Never! When she read your letter, she turned so white I thought she was going to pass out. I don't know what the content of the letter was, but is there anything I can do? Are you in some kind of trouble?"

"Thanks for your concern, Jason. You are very sweet, but I just can't tell you anything right now."

"I thought our friendship had grown so close these last few weeks, but now in a flash it feels like we are living separate lives or something."

"Look, I'm free after work. Would you like to take me someplace nice for dinner? Looking at the inside of room 101 is really getting to me."

"You know I can't wait."

"Great. Now let me take this test and get it over with. Will you pick me up about five thirty?"

"Sure thing, I'll see you when you're done with the test."

Jason left room 101 and made a beeline for the front door of Thornburg Genetics. He stepped out of the double glass doors and walked into the small company garden that ran a full city block along the entire front of the Thornburg Genetics building. He knew the security camera over the front door was recording his every move. After making believe he was admiring a few of the plantings, he walked out of the garden and down the street to the west. He walked a full block before he took his cell phone out of his shirt pocket.

Chapter 19

"Hey, it's me."

"Are you on a secure phone?"

"Of course I am. I think we may have a breakthrough. Remember I told you about this girl named April that is involved in marketing, and her father used to work here at Thornburg?"

"Yeah, I remember, Jason. Every time I talk to you, you're taking her out on another date."

"That's the one. Well, listen to this story. April is in the process of receiving a promotion. I was in the conference room today finalizing some paperwork with her. Mark Ellison and Tanya Jefferson are interviewing her, and they want April to accept this promotion real bad. You should see the unbelievable contract they offered her. They are creating a special position for her, including a significant pay increase, flights paid for by Thornburg, an apartment allowance of one thousand dollars per month, a company car with a gas card, and she gets to hand select her own employees. She's only worked here one year! This contract even makes my mouth water."

"I don't think that takes much, little brother. So far I'm not impressed."

"Will you let me finish! So here I am waiting for Miss April to sign this delicious, perk laden contract, and she says she would like to include a couple of addenda. She then hands a sealed envelope to Tanya. Tanya opens the envelope and starts reading. You should have seen the look on her face. Her jaw dropped, she turned white, and didn't even blink her eyelashes for thirty seconds. I thought she was going into shock. The very next order of business was to bounce yours truly from the conference room. Now, the story gets better. Five minutes after I was bounced, I watched Mark and Tanya hustle to the command center. About an hour later, I'm back in my office cranking out the work I need to get done when I get a call from Tanya saying I need to give our Miss April test number three. She just took test number two yesterday. That never, ever happens. Never! I don't know what it is, big brother, but she has something huge on Thornburg."

"This sounds like the most interesting tidbit of info I've heard in quite some time. So, what next? You know what we're after. I assume you are treating our Miss April like a queen."

"Are you kidding me? We're almost married. I'm the most refined gentleman on two feet."

"You're still seeing Sheila too, aren't you?"

"Of course I still see her. She's only in town once in a while so I adjust my schedule accordingly. She's madly in love with me."

"Sheila is one gorgeous blond bombshell. She's way too unpredictable, though. Maybe a better word is unstable."

"You just don't know how to handle women, big brother. You have to let them know they are the best things on this earth. The smartest move you ever made was introducing me to Sheila. Sheila will do anything for me. So will April before you know it."

"You always were mighty smooth when it came to the ladies, and you're such a good actor, Jason. Keep me posted on any detail no matter how insignificant it might seem and don't blow it with April. It's time for an academy award-winning performance."

Chapter 20

It was four days later when April received the telephone call. It had been a tiring workday with two long, but effective, marketing meetings; and April had managed to clear a large stack of paperwork from the top of her desk. Jason suggested dinner out, and April accepted. They both had a light meal at Pepper's Deli, which consisted of a sandwich and iced tea. The standard potato chips and dill pickle sliver were welcome side dishes. Over dinner, they discussed Thornburg Genetics, their jobs, family and where they would like to go on vacation. They enjoyed each other's company for almost two hours. Then April told Jason she was exhausted and needed to go back to her apartment if she was going to survive long enough to get to work the next day. Jason pulled up in front of her apartment building. April waited for him to circle the car and open her door for her. He was so debonair. She thanked him for the evening as they embraced and kissed for a moment. Then she walked up the sidewalk past the well-manicured shrubs and into the brick building's double glass doors. She turned and gave Jason a smile and a wave with her fingertips. He smiled back and waved, then blew April a kiss.

April walked into the hallway and took the steps to her third story apartment. She unlocked her door and slipped in. After bolting the door behind her, she went to the bathroom and took a steamy shower. The hot water pelting her body made her sleepy. After drying off, she wrapped her terrycloth white robe around herself and headed for the kitchen stove. A hot cup of tea would end the day nicely she thought to herself. As she sat in her overstuffed chair, she thought about Jason and how close they had become. She knew she loved him and was sure he knew it, even though she had never told him. Time after time she thought about why she couldn't say, 'I love you'. There was never a good answer. She was glad Jason was gentle and didn't pressure her in the whole dating scenario. She hadn't seen that before in other men she had dated. He was a true gentleman. It seemed like it was almost a lost virtue. Of course his handsome face and humorous disposition topped off the package nicely. April took a sip of her orange-flavored tea. The aroma and taste blended with her drowsiness. Besides, they communicated well together, and he wasn't one of those control freaks. Some of her girlfriends had dated some real wackos. Their boyfriends demanded that they know about every activity, every available minute be spent with each other, and they scrutinize all cell phone calls and emails. Those relationships were short lived. She never wanted to be in the middle of one of those horror stories. Suddenly she was jostled from her warm little dream world as her cell phone rang. She answered the call on the second ring.

"Hello, April, this is Tanya."

"Hi, Tanya."

"A dark green Ford Expedition will pull up in front of your apartment building in ten minutes. Please stay inside the front door and watch for it. When it pulls up, just walk out the door nonchalantly and enter the front passenger door. Talk to no one between now and then. Dress a little better than casual, but don't overdress. It's time." There was a click at the other end of the line and April hung up her phone.

Then the adrenalin kicked in. April wanted to jump up and down, but she knew there wasn't time. She had to make herself presentable. What should she wear to meet The Keeper? April rushed to her bedroom closet. A black skirt and colorful flowery blouse should work. It was businesslike, yet casual. She stuffed herself into her clothes while looking in the mirror. "What do I do with this mess," she said to herself as she ran her fingers through her hair, still damp from the shower.

April was standing inside the apartment building looking through the double glass front door when a vehicle pulled up and stopped. It looked like an Expedition under the streetlights. As directed, she walked in a normal pace towards the front passenger side door right next to the curb. The dark green color became more visible as she approached the vehicle. She opened the door, but no interior light came on and the street light did little to reveal the identity of the driver.

"Hello, April."

Mark was driving the vehicle. She could only see his outline in the dark, but she recognized his voice.

"Hello, Mr. Ellison. How are you this evening?"

She slid onto the dark gray leather seat and closed the door. Mark waited for one car to go by then pulled away from the curb.

"I'm fine, April. Let's see now. I haven't seen you in what, a whole four days? Are you continuing to make Thornburg millions?"

"I'm doing my best."

"I'm glad to hear that. I assume you know why I'm here this evening."

April thought for a moment. She assumed it was to meet The Keeper, but now other ideas were starting to jump up in her mind. Nobody else knew where she was going, and she wasn't exactly sure what she was in the middle of. Maybe this was some scandalous or illegal operation, and this would be her last ride ever. She suddenly panicked. Then she caught herself and started to think rationally again. It was too late to change anything now, no matter what happened. She glanced at the electronic door lock. It was locked. Pressure started to escalate as April's thoughts turned more horrific. She thought for a moment and then responded.

"I hope this is a trip to see The Keeper."

"That is correct."

April breathed a sigh of relief, which she thought must have sounded like a small hurricane.

"I have to say that you caught us off guard on Thursday. We have a lot to discuss as I'm sure you know."

"What exactly does The Keeper do?"

"Why don't you hold your questions until our meeting?"

After about ten minutes of driving, Mark pulled the Expedition into the motel parking lot of the Days Inn on Thompson Road. Another set of headlights reflected off the side mirror as another vehicle pulled in behind them.

"Is somebody following us?" asked April.

"Yes, that's one of ours, no need to worry. Do you know where you are?"

"Yes, I've been down this street several times. I have a question. I understand this whole matter is a security issue but isn't this going a little overboard? I feel like I'm in the middle of a James Bond movie or something."

Mark laughed, "A James Bond movie huh. Just give it a little time. You'll understand." They pulled up in front of room 117 and parked. There were about two dozen cars in the parking lot. Mark exited and walked around the front of the vehicle to the passenger side. When he arrived at April's door, he opened it. "Just follow me."

April slid out of the vehicle and fell into line behind Mark. They walked down the outside corridor past several doors and then cut through a breezeway. It came out on the opposite side of the motel. They then ascended the steps and stopped on the second floor at room 240. Mark gave two light taps on the door. In a matter of seconds, the door swung open. As they walked in, a tall, solidly built man walked out and closed the door behind him. Tanya rose out of a high-backed green velvet chair and stepped forward.

"Hello, April, it's good to see you again."

"Hello, Tanya, how are you this evening?"

"I have to admit, I'm a little tired. It's been a long week and it's only Monday. You look a little tired yourself. I wish we could have arranged this meeting during the daylight hours, but our security department set this up. We have little say when security is involved. In a few minutes you will meet The Keeper. Again, I must tell you everything that happens tonight is classified, top-secret, company information. Here is a form for you to sign stating that."

April read the form, which consisted of a one-sided sheet of paper. It was straightforward, so April signed and dated the bottom. Tanya took it, signed the bottom, and slid it into a file folder. Then she pushed it into the top of her black leather briefcase sitting on the floor.

"There is one more order of business, which may be a little demeaning. I hope you understand the importance of the security protocol we are required to go through. Before you can see The Keeper you must be frisked."

"A frisk? Are you serious, Tanya? I deal with sensitive information every day. Why do I need to be frisked?"

Mark responded, "I'm sorry, April. Our security staff demands it. They have dibs on every move in this situation. We will be glad to leave the room. You will have to agree to a pat frisk. Security staff wants to make sure you aren't wired or armed. I forgot to ask if you had your handgun with you."

"Of course I do. It's in my pocketbook."

"We will have to ask you to turn it over to security staff until the meeting has been completed. Please leave it in your pocketbook until I notify security staff."

"I hope you know it's not easy for me to part with my handgun, but in the name of security, here goes."

Mark nodded at Tanya. Tanya picked up the telephone and dialed a number.

"We're ready," she said, then she turned to April. "It will be just a couple of minutes now."

April peered around the motel room. It was just a plain motel room. There were two queen-size beds, as well as a television, desk and table with what appeared to be Tanya's paperwork on top. There were two low-class, framed, colored prints, one hanging over each bed. They looked like Monet's water lily paintings. The bedspreads did not even have a wrinkle in them. It was obvious they had not been slept in.

Then there was a single knock on the door. Mark looked through the peep hole, unlocked and opened the door. In walked the toughest, most muscular, yet most beautiful woman April had ever seen. What did they do, steal her from some shot-put team she thought to herself. She turned out to be quite pleasant.

"Hello, April, my name is Emerald. Most people call me Em. I will be escorting you to the meeting this evening. First, I have to give you a pat frisk. It will only take a minute and is quite painless. Don't worry about your pride. It's only a passing thought. Mr. Mark, would you please look the other direction for a minute?"

"I'm just going to wait outside Em, but you do need to know April has a handgun in her pocketbook."

"You're packing heat are you, honey? I don't blame you. A girl can't be too safe nowadays. Okay, just hold your hands out to your side like this and face the other direction. I'm going to run this metal detector over your clothing, then give you a quick pat down. Here we go."

The whole process only took a minute as Em had guaranteed. April had been through the pat frisk scenario once years ago, but she wasn't about to let them know that. It was a memory she did not like to recall.

"There you go, honey. That was painless enough wasn't it? Now let me see that piece. When you take it out of your pocketbook hold onto the grip and make sure the barrel is pointing at the ground at all times. That's right. Let me just get hold of the butt end. That's perfect."

Emerald opened the cylinder, extracted the rounds and slid them into her pants pocket. Then she looked to make sure the gun was empty, snapped the cylinder shut and looked it over. "A Smith & Wesson .357 wheel gun and hollow point ammunition. You are loaded for bear honey. I'd hate to meet you in a dark alley. Do you know how to use this?"

"Of course I do. I've practiced with it for years. I wasn't sure if I wanted to give it up tonight, but when I saw you come through the door like a linebacker I knew that idea was hopeless."

"Like a linebacker you say? This girl's got game and humor. You know, I like you. Don't you worry girl, I'll take good care of your piece for you. Are you ready to go, Miss Tanya?"

"I'm ready."

Emerald opened the door and stepped outside. "We're ready to go, Mr. Ellison."

"You lead the way, Em. We're right behind you." They proceeded down the steps and across the dimly lit parking lot to the motel next door. There was no conversation as they walked. April couldn't remember the name of this motel even though she had driven by it only a few days ago. The outside appeared a little more luxurious than the Days Inn. They followed Emerald directly to a side exit door. When April saw the words Hampton Inn etched on the glass door, she felt a little more relaxed. A doorman pushed open the locked security door from the inside, and they all entered The Hampton. Emerald never slowed down. She was constantly shifting her view, first looking to the right and then left as they walked. They took an immediate right down the maroon and beige carpeted hallway. All of the motel room doors exited to the inside hallways. They had walked past eight doors when Emerald halted at room 125. When Tanya, April and Mark caught up, Emerald knocked on the door. The door was opened from the inside by a tall, athletic looking young man. His red curly hair accentuated the big grin on his face.

"Good evening, Mark. Good evening, Tanya. And this must be Miss April James. 'Tis a great evening, is it not, Miss James?"

April was speechless. For some reason she was captivated by this fellow. His Irish accent and wavy red hair gave him the air of mischief. He saw her gaping at him.

"Are you seeing a ghost, ma'am, or am I that funny looking to you?" he said in a joking tone of voice.

"Oh no, I mean yes, uh no. I'm sorry for staring. I'm just a little tired, and I think the shock of this whole event is just hitting me."

"Well when it hits, I sure hope you are still standing. You wouldn't look very good spread out on the hotel room floor."

"Very funny."

"Shall we?" said Tanya.

"Oh yes. Follow me."

Tanya just shook her head. The red-haired stranger led them through a side door into a small conference room. He then closed the door and stood next to it. The room was brightly lit with a large oval conference table. Standing at one end of the conference table was a woman who looked to be in her late forties. She had a beautiful, warm smile that made her whole face glow. Tanya walked up to her and April followed.

"Hi, Lexis. Meet April James."

"April, this is Lexis."

"Lexis reached out and took both of April's hands in hers. I'm glad to meet you, April. Let me look at you for a moment. You are so beautiful. You definitely have your father's eyes and nose. I hope that's a compliment?"

"It is thank you. I loved my dad very much."

"I am also called The Keeper."

April didn't know what to say. She had expected a woman who was hard featured and all business and had convinced herself The Keeper would be harsh and straightforward. Lexis wore a black dress that showed off her lady-like figure, yet complemented a woman with a position of authority. Her blond hair flowed over her shoulders. April felt like she had dressed too casual in comparison. Lexis continued to hold her hands and look at her. April glanced over toward the door. The red-headed man gave her a big smile. He didn't miss a thing. Lexis also spotted the exchange.

"I'm glad I have this opportunity to meet you April, though I must say that the circumstances are quite unusual. I have coffee, tea and a selection of cookies and fruit for us to enjoy." Lexis let go of April's hands and motioned to the table.

"April. Why don't you go first before we get down to business? Keegan, help yourself."

"Thank you, ma'am, coffee and cookies sound great."

"You did meet Keegan, didn't you, April?"

"We sort of met briefly."

"No formal introduction was made, ma'am."

"I'm so sorry. Keegan, this is April James."

Keegan darted over and shook hands with April. "I'm pleased to meet you, Miss James. My name is Keegan McGrath."

"I'm pleased to meet you as well, Mr. McGrath."

"Keegan is my top security advisor. He goes with me frequently when I travel. He has quite the colorful Irish personality, don't you think? But don't let him fool you. He can turn it on and off like water running out of a faucet."

"It is indeed colorful," said April.

"I'll accept that as a compliment and thank you both," beamed Keegan.

"Now we need to get to work," chuckled The Keeper.

April, Tanya, Lexis and finally Mark each selected a small plate of refreshments and a beverage from the side table before taking a seat at the conference table. Keegan waited until last. He stacked three cookies on a plate, poured a cup of coffee and sat in a chair next to the side door through which they had just entered.

Chapter 21

April looked at Lexis, Tanya, and Mark. She knew she was on the hot seat. They were enjoying their refreshments in silence when Lexis started. April detected an immediate change in her demeanor.

"April, I'm sure you are aware that your name and request has been the buzz since Thursday. Our first order of business this evening is to discuss how you found out about The Keeper. For reasons related to Thornburg Genetics security, we will not proceed any further until this matter has been explained to our satisfaction."

April had rehearsed an answer to this question several times. She had hoped they wouldn't pry too far, but she sensed they would. She knew there was little use in trying to hold back any information. "First, I would like to know what happens if I don't reveal my source. I really have no idea what I'm in the middle of. From what I've seen so far tonight, you may decide that my life ends tonight if I tell all."

All three looked at April. She could see the look of shock on their faces. She heard Keegan laughing out loud and glanced in his direction. His smile reached from ear to ear.

"You think we would have you killed?" asked Lexis. "We aren't talking about that type of security situation here, and God forbid we would ever have to. Our goal is to find high-end quality employees for Thornburg Genetics. We believe you are such an employee. That is why you were offered a high-quality job promotion."

"Our situation is we have a breach of security somewhere in the organization. At all times, we are working aggressively to eliminate this breach. In this instance, we are trying to work with you, April, not alienate you. You requested to see The Keeper. Only a limited number of people know about my title. For security reasons, we need to know how you learned this information and, also, that you don't have some hidden agenda. Let me say this, I believe with my whole heart that cooperation with us will bring you excitement and fulfillment beyond measure. I can guarantee that you will never want to work elsewhere. We have what you are looking for right here at Thornburg Genetics."

"How do you know what I'm looking for?" April said before she could stop herself.

"You are looking for adventure. You are looking for success by making a difference in the lives of others and for freedom to set your own course. That's the job we have offered you. If you choose not to divulge certain secret information, I really don't know what we will do at this point. We have no alternative course of action, because we want you on our team. We certainly aren't going to have you killed. I don't know where you even dreamt up an idea like that. We need you to work with us, April."

There was silence as April considered the points The Keeper had just made. For the most part the points were what April had expected, but she had needed to hear it out loud. She had pretty much determined that she could trust them. Besides, what choice did she have? They were right. The money they were offering her wasn't the most important part of her life. It was the opportunity to help as many people globally as she could. Available medical treatment would help thousands and thousands of people. April decided to reveal the information they wanted.

"When my father passed away, he left me a document. The document was in a sealed envelope given to me in private by the family lawyer. The only one that knows I have this document is my lawyer, and he has no idea of the contents. In a separate letter enclosed with the document, my father said I would know whom I could or could not share the information with. I have no idea why he shared this information with me and not with my brother, mother or somebody else. Apparently, it has something to do with The Noah Gene. Even now I have no problems sharing this information with all of you, but I know you are the first ones I do feel comfortable sharing it with. I couldn't even share the information with my lawyer."

"So you have known this information for over a year now?" asked Tanya.

"That is correct."

"Where is this document now?" asked Mark.

April glanced at Keegan. He held his cup of coffee and smiled at April. He was listening intently.

"It is in a secure location."

"I think we need to know more about that," said Mark.

"What other information did your father disclose in this document?" asked Lexis.

April hesitated for a moment. "He said there existed what was referred to as The Noah Library, and he briefly described it."

"And what do you think about The Noah Library?" asked Lexis.

"It sounds like one of the Seven Wonders of the World, and I would love to see it."

"How many pages was this document and did you make copies of it?" asked Tanya.

"It was twenty-two pages long, and I made no copies."

"What other information was in the document?" asked Tanya.

"Most of the document revolved around The Noah Library and some medical ideology. Dad tried to portray how marvelous The Noah Library experience had been for him. It sounded spectacular. I compare it to watching a National Geographic special on TV. The scenery is beautiful, but you know it's never as nice watching the show as it is being there in person. He also described some cancer curing medicines that were not on the open market."

At this point there was silence.

"How far up the ladder does this organization go?" asked April.

"What do you mean?" asked Lexis.

"I keep taking tests. How many security levels are there at Thornburg Genetics?"

"There are seven security levels in total, though few people are actually told what level they are on. It's not a straight upward progression and many of the employees will plateau at level one or two," said Lexis. Again there was silence for what seemed like minutes. All eyes were staring at April.

Then Lexis spoke, "I think our immediate concern is to obtain this document as soon as possible. We must review it to consider the entire contents. The Public Relations Specialist job offer is still open if you accept. We need to make some decisions about your security clearance level."

"I'm not sure if I want to hand over the document. The document contains the last words my father gave me before he died." Again there was silence. The tension in the room increased a little more with every discussion.

"What if we keep this document under lock and key, but give you access any time you would like to review it as long as you remain employed at Thornburg Genetics?" asked Mark.

"That is a great idea, Mark. Would that be workable April?" asked Lexis.

"I think that would be all right, but I would like a few minutes by myself to think things through."

"I believe we could all use a few minutes to clear our minds and strategize," said Lexis.

April stood up and walked toward the side door.

"Keegan, will you please escort Miss James for a breath of fresh air?"

"It will be my pleasure to escort Miss James to the ends of the earth," Keegan said as he made a slight bow, opened the door and hand gestured April to walk through. "Any place special, Miss James?"

"I just need a little fresh air."

"I will escort you outdoors and then give you some space. If you need anything at all just let me know. I'll be at your side in a flash."

"Are you always this jovial, Mr. McGrath?"

"Please call me Keegan, and the answer to your question is yes. We live but once. I enjoy life, and I choose to live it in a fun-loving way. Now let's get you your breath of fresh air."

April gave Keegan a little smile, and Keegan instantly smiled back. He really was quite handsome with that big smile and the well-trimmed red hair that led to his square, manly jaw. April turned and retraced their incoming steps back to the hotel parking lot. As she walked she thought about the implications of the Noah Document. She knew there were only two options. Either she took the deal she was offered or refused it. If she refused it, then what were her options? She could go back to working and fighting for underprivileged people, having no money, little backing, and following orders from her job supervisors. April also knew that one way or another, Lexis was going to obtain the Noah Document. They were afraid of its written content.

"Keegan?"

"Yes, Miss James?" Keegan said as he walked up to her.

"Do you love your job?"

"I wouldn't trade it for the world."

"Do you ever feel like life isn't fair? Do you ever feel that under-privileged people the whole world over need help and don't get it? That the little person just kind of gets crunched up and spit out with nothing to look forward to?"

Keegan hesitated before he spoke. "Miss James, I have only partial knowledge of what you are involved in here. I know it's very important, because you are meeting with The Keeper, but I can tell you this. God gave us all a specific lot in life. My lot in life is to provide security for Thornburg Genetics. I do the best I can at my job. Someday I will be too old to do this particular task. When that time comes, I believe my next lot in life will be at my very fingertips. Whatever decision you are trying to make, I believe God has given you a lot in life as well. Do you believe in God, Miss James?"

"I do, Keegan."

"Then you probably already know the answers to your questions.

If you have been blessed with the gift of helping others, then give it your best. One person can't take care of the whole world. It has to be done in bits and pieces. I have seen many of the world's underprivileged people. Most of them seem happier with few earthly possessions compared to people like us who have many possessions."

"There is a lot of truth to that. Thanks, Keegan."

"Anything to save a damsel in distress, me lady."

"So you got your accent back did you?"

"Oh, that, ma'am, just trying to keep me Irish background intact," Keegan said with a smile.

April turned and started walking again. She thought about her job, the new job offer and how she could best help underprivileged people with their needs. Then she thought about her father and the Noah Document. Again those words her father had written came to mind. You will know what to do with this document and who you will or will not be able to discuss it with.

Chapter 22

Lexis stood up and checked to make sure Keegan and April had left the immediate area and then she walked back to the conference table. Mark and Tanya were both standing up. Mark poured a glass of ice water and offered it to Tanya before pouring himself a glass of water.

"Would you like a glass of water, Lexis?"

"I would love one. I think I'll have a cup of coffee too. I'm glad we don't have these evening meetings very often. It's exhausting. April James is one smart young lady. Her brain is working full speed every minute. What do the two of you think about this whole situation?"

"I'm sure she will come on board," said Mark. "She has way too much to gain with this promotion."

"I agree with that assessment," said Tanya.

"There are some ideas we need to think about here," said Lexis. "First, I want you to know that I had some significant background work done on both April and her father, Vincent. April was heavily involved in all those save the earth and people movements in college. She received very little pay while helping the mountain people in Ecuador. Just because she is now in the corporate world doesn't mean she has forgotten her past experiences. Helping people is still a priority in her life and thus her request for a formal charity. Second, Vincent was working in genetic research. He was piloting 'The Noah Gene Project'. One of our research goals is to pinpoint the elusive Noah Gene. We know it's there, and we have to find it in order to fine tune our employee screening process. Our rare plant research must remain a secret. We cannot take the risk of additional company security breaches. I was advised that a large amount of Vincent's work was done on a blood sample known as JA0001. The code number isn't too original. It stands for James, April and is most likely blood sample number 1. Apparently he was the only one that knew this blood sample was from his daughter. We have no proof he was able to crack the genetic code to verify the existence of the Noah Gene. If he did, he didn't share the evidence with any of the researchers working on the project now. At this point, we know Vincent felt compelled to write a document to his daughter disclosing highly classified Thornburg Genetics material. Apparently, he did not do so for his son or wife. I think Vincent determined that his daughter had the Noah Gene and his son and wife did not. With April's test scores being 98% on the first, 92% on the second and 90% on the third, I believe April has the Noah Gene and is able to discern others who have the Noah Gene. Do either of you have any comments on this?"

"How far has the research come on the Noah Gene genetic footprint?" asked Tanya.

"Progress is slow. Actually, since Vincent was last involved two plus years ago, we've gained only about 2% additional accuracy on our genetic mapping, topping us off at about 72% accuracy. As in all of nature, the deeper we dig, the better the genetic codes are hidden or masked. It's like fighting through a computer program firewall to gain every little tidbit of information. We just need the right genetic path to get us over the top, to make the secrets of Thornburg Genetics virtually safe forever. It would sure make life a lot easier for us if we could determine the Noah Gene status of an employee with a simple blood test rather than all of the written tests we put employees through."

"Here is another situation we can discuss. We know there is a breach of security by a Thornburg Genetics employee. Our greenhouse inspectors found four plants of one rare plant species in a college greenhouse at The University of Washington Botany Greenhouse. The aloe vera gold plant is only available in our research labs. Now somebody else has some of those plants. It scares me to think there may be more of our rare plant species out there in the hands of private individuals. Somebody has been able to avoid our security detection methods. We have been so careful administering our employees written tests and blood testing our higher security classified employees. Unfortunately, we know there is a potential for chemo or radiation therapy to alter the human physical genetics enough to disrupt The Noah Gene. In other words, we probably have an employee that does well on tests and ranks high on our list with their genetic makeup but can evade our security. He or she can gather information from higher-ranking Thornburg employees who are unaware it isn't safe to share with them. The Noah Gene does not block this transfer of information. As much as I hate to say it, we know Vincent had both chemo and radiation therapy near the end of his life due to lung cancer. Potentially he could have set up a system to remove classified information and plants from Thornburg Genetics."

"Do you think Vincent would divulge classified information to someone other than his daughter? I don't believe that for a minute," said Mark.

Tanya shook her head no as well.

"We have to look at every possible angle," said Lexis. "Nobody, and I mean nobody, is off the hook here until we get this security breach mess cleared up. This whole matter could take years to resolve, and we may never find the breach. Four out of our twelve worldwide facilities have become suspect due to the aloe vera gold plant. After discussing this entire situation with two level seven security consultants, we think we can use April to lead us to our rogue employee or employees."

Lexis could see the look of surprise on both Mark's and Tanya's faces.

"What do you mean by use April? She has only been with us for one year now," said Tanya.

"Let's just say this whole Noah Document situation and April requesting to meet The Keeper scenario may be a blessing in disguise. Numerous employees at our Philadelphia facility have seen April going to room 101. She has remained in room 101 under a cloud of secrecy for significant lengths of time. Some employee or several employees are watching every move made by fellow employees in Thornburg Genetics. Whether the breach of security is in the form of employees desiring to obtain more rare plants, rare plant compounds, classified research documents or other information, you can be sure the reason for the breach revolves around money. We will plan a couple more discreet, lengthy meetings in room 101. We want the meetings to look suspicious to any employee involved in the Thornburg Genetics security breach, but April will be none the wiser. We can throw a big party for her promotion and leak the amount of money and perks she will be making with her new contract. Even though April has a private office, she is in an area with almost one hundred other employees. In this case, we will attempt to turn office gossip to our advantage."

"What about April. Are we going to tell her about this situation?" asked Mark.

"This is all top secret. She will go on with life, helping millions of people and know nothing about this situation. Security will be in charge of the operation. The more I think about this, the more I think this is the break we need to flush out the culprit and close our security breach. I hope we don't have to wait long for results. The question is what form the results will take. We are talking about April being in the middle of a life-threatening situation, and I am quite fearful for April's safety, but my decision is for the good of Thornburg Genetics."

Chapter 23

Keegan shared some of his background information with April as they walked back to the motel room. He was originally from Ireland and moved to the United States when he was ten. An auto accident that claimed his parents' lives left him an orphan at age twelve. He had not been in the car when it was rear ended at a stop sign and pushed into an electric pole by a furniture truck with brake failure. He attended Michigan State University and loved martial arts. He had no brothers or sisters and had been raised by his grandparents. Keegan thought that was why he was promoted quickly through the security ranks at Thornburg Genetics. No relatives meant no complications should top secret or sensitive information become a security issue. In other words, Keegan was expendable.

April told Keegan all about her life. She was excited and enthusiastic when discussing her love for the people of Ecuador where she had lived for almost three years. She told him about her college background and the loss she felt when her father passed away. Not once did he ask about the meeting or why she was there. She wasn't sure if it was because he already knew or he was displaying his manners. When they arrived in the motel room, the door to the meeting room was closed. They continued to talk quietly and could hear voices coming from the meeting room. About ten minutes passed before the door opened. Lexis walked through and looked at April and Keegan.

"We are ready to reconvene. I have to say this is the most difficult promotion I've ever been involved in," Lexis said with a chuckle. "Normally employees just latch on to our promotion offers and go. You are quite a spectacular young lady, and we're glad to see that you think things through."

"Thank you," said April as she walked back into the conference room. "This whole situation has been a little awkward for me. I'm not trying to cause any problems, but I have to make sure everything is legitimate and planned out to the best of my ability."

April and Lexis joined Tanya and Mark at the table.

"Where shall we start?" asked Lexis.

Mark commented first. "Well, let's summarize our meeting. All of the ideas and proposals have been laid out on the table. At this point, April has agreed to accept the job promotion. She has met The Keeper as requested, and we have agreed to a charity. We need to obtain The Noah Document for obvious security reasons. We have agreed to keep the document intact and have it available for April to review. April, you have had some time to think all of this over. What are your thoughts?"

"I am ready to accept the promotion and turn The Noah Document over to you with the stipulation it not be destroyed and I have access to it as needed. I will continue to do my best at making Thornburg Genetics the top company in the world. I'm sorry for any aggravation I've caused getting us to this point, but I hope you understand my need for a cautious attitude."

"We are glad this has all worked out. Welcome aboard, April," said Mark.

"I for one am glad you are cautious," said Lexis. "You have shown great maturity in your decision making process."

"I'm very excited," said Tanya. "We know we will receive many years of quality teamwork from you, April."

"There is one more item to take care of this evening," said Lexis. "We need to know the location of the document."

"I have the document in a safe-deposit box at the Bank of America on Highbridge Street."

"Tanya wrote down the address."

"Do you know what time they open?" asked Lexis.

"I believe they open at 8:30."

"Tomorrow is Tuesday. Would you please drive to the bank and arrive at 9:00 AM sharp. Keegan will meet you at the front door and escort you in. Do you have an extra set of car keys?"

"Yes, right here in my pocketbook."

"Good. If we can get those now, I will give them to Keegan. One of our security staff will drive your car from the bank to an undisclosed location. Once you retrieve the document, stay with Keegan and he will escort you back to your car. Do whatever he tells you without question."

"This sure seems like a lot of work just to get this document out of the bank. There must be details that you aren't telling me."

"We can't explain all of the details now, April, but we will give you more information in the future. That's just the way it has to be for the moment," said Lexis. "Please trust my judgment as The Keeper."

At this point the conversation ended. April thought she was in the middle of something sinister and couldn't imagine what situation would demand so much security and secrecy.

"It's been a full evening. Is there anything else that needs to be discussed before we adjourn?" asked Lexis.

"When will I be able to see The Noah Library?" asked April.

"Soon my dear. We have a lot of things to work through, and I'm too tired to think straight right now. I need to see this document to determine what our next course of action must be. Let's conclude our meeting for tonight. Mark will escort you back to your apartment."

"Yes, ma'am."

"Good evening Miss James," Keegan said as Mark and April exited the meeting room. "I will meet you at the Bank of America at 9:00 AM."

"9:00 AM it is, and have a great evening, Mr. McGrath," April said in a make believe Irish accent as she nodded her head to Keegan. They both smiled at each other.

Once they left the room and were out of hearing distance, Lexis said to Tanya, "I can't wait to see the contents of that document."

Mark and April were escorted by Em back to the Ford Expedition. Em returned April's handgun, which April reloaded immediately.

"I love a girl that packs heat," said Em.

Mark drove April back to her apartment. There were no signs of anyone following their SUV other than the Thornburg security staff. Mark waited by the curb until April let herself into her apartment building. April had no idea there were several Thornburg Genetics security staff assigned to specific posts monitoring the building.

Chapter 24

Keegan was looking out of the meeting room window and following April's every step across the hotel parking lot when he heard Lexis speak to him.

"Keegan, will you come here a moment?"

"Yes, ma'am."

"I know you heard our conversation, but I just want to review the situation. Tanya, tell me if I miss anything. Our April James will be retrieving a classified document from the Bank of America on Highbridge Street. We have directed her to arrive at 9:00 AM. You are to meet her there, enter the bank with her, retrieve the document and immediately escort her to her car at the undisclosed location. You will deliver the document to our Thornburg Genetics location. I will be making an appearance there as Global Marketing Officer tomorrow. They already know I'm coming. Please make sure my office is scanned for bugs and is secure. Do not let this document out of your sight until you hand it directly to me. Here are the keys to April's car. Have one of your female security staff that looks similar to April pick it up from the bank parking lot. I consider this a top-level security issue. Any questions Keegan?"

"No, ma'am. I'm on it."

"Maybe we should make sure there are no bugs or cameras in April's office either," said Tanya.

"That's a good idea. Keegan, can you arrange that as well?"

"Consider it done, Lexis."

"I will see you both in the morning. Thank you, Keegan, as always your work is appreciated."

"Thank you, Lexis," said Keegan as he left the room.

"Tanya, I'll see you at 9:00 AM at Thornburg. It's been quite an evening hasn't it?"

"All last week was exhausting, and I don't think I've accomplished one thing that's been productive today. I'll see you in the morning."

After Lexis had been alone a few minutes, she chuckled to herself. April reminds me of me when I was younger, she thought. I wonder what other surprises she has for us.

Chapter 25

April saw the answering machine light blinking when she entered her apartment. There were two messages on the machine. She pushed the message play button and the machine responded; Message number one, eight eleven PM. "Hello, April darling. It's Jason. I just wanted to tell you I had a great time with you this evening, and I'm thinking about you. Talk to you later. Bye."

Message number two, nine seventeen PM. "Hello, April. It's me again. I guess you were tired. Must be you crashed for the night. I guess I'll see you at work tomorrow. Love you. Bye."

It was almost midnight and way too late to call Jason back. It had been an extremely emotional day, and April suddenly realized how exhausted she was. Within five minutes she was in her bed with her sheet and blanket pulled up and wrapped around her head. She found herself thinking about Keegan. He's kind of a neat guy she thought to herself as she drifted into a deep sleep.

What was that awful noise? What was going on? April sat up in bed. Oh, the alarm clock. She laid her head back down and hit the off button. It was 7:45 AM. April felt tired, yet rested at the same time. She couldn't remember the last time she had slept with such vengeance. As she slowly gained consciousness she thought about the day before her. She knew this was the day that would change her life forever. Why did they need so much security just to pick up The Noah Document? There had to be a ton of information that nobody was telling her. On the other hand, why should they? It had been less than a week since she had sprung the promotion addendum on them.

April drove into the Bank of America parking lot at 8:57 AM. She put on her best acting front and hopped out of the car like it was just a typical day. As she strolled toward the bank, Keegan met her on the sidewalk.

"Top of the morning to you, Miss James. I trust you are rested after last evening's events," Keegan said with a smile. Then he lifted his hand and covered his mouth. "Remember, there are surveillance cameras everywhere."

"I slept wonderfully, Mr. McGrath. Thanks for asking."

"I'm glad to hear it. Shall we proceed with the project at hand?" Keegan opened the bank door and let April lead the way. She went to the service desk and told the representative she needed to access her safe-deposit box.

"Your box number, please," said the representative as she looked up the information on her computer screen. "I need to see some form of identification, please." The representative looked at the ID and then at April. "Thank you, Maryanne," she said.

Keegan shot a questioning look at April, but said nothing. April just looked straight ahead and smiled.

"Do you wish to have this gentleman proceed with you, Miss Hogan?"

"Yes, please."

"Follow me, please. Right this way." The representative led them to the vault, which contained the safe-deposit boxes. She inserted her key and turned it, then said to April, "Let me know when you are finished so I can lock up again."

"Yes, ma'am."

Then the representative left the vault. Keegan watched as April inserted her key in the safe-deposit box and opened the small door. She took out a standard size manila envelope covered with packing tape and slid it into her dark green canvas bag. Keegan could see the envelope had been the only item in the box. April locked the box, and they left the vault and walked back to the service desk without saying a word.

"I'm done now, ma'am," said April.

"Thank you, Miss Hogan. Is there anything else we can do for you today?"

"No thank you. Have a nice day."

April and Keegan left the bank and walked into the parking lot. April noticed her car was already gone.

"This way please, Maryanne," Keegan said with a laugh. He opened the passenger door on a white Toyota Camry, and April slid onto the beige leather seat. Keegan closed the door, circled the car and hopped in the driver's seat. As they drove out of the parking lot, Keegan was the first to speak. "Well, my dear, everything went smooth as silk."

"Wasn't it supposed to?"

"One never knows in my job."

"Why does this involve so much secrecy and security? It's all a little overwhelming, and I'm not getting any straight answers."

"I'm afraid I can't discuss security issues with you, Miss Maryanne Hogan, and exactly where did the name Maryanne Hogan appear? You caught me off guard with that little stunt."

"Well, I decided not to use my real name at the bank, just in case."

"In case of what, Miss James?"

"One never really knows in my job."

"Hey. That's my line. Now where did this Maryanne Hogan alias come from?"

"It's kind of a long story."

"I have nothing but time, me dearie."

April paused for a moment. She wondered how much more of her life she should reveal to him. "When I went to my first year of college I may have been a little rebellious."

"You don't say."

"It's true. Naturally, I was not old enough to drink. However, for twenty dollars I was able to purchase a perfectly good Sheriff's ID card to show I was of legal drinking age. My name on the ID card was Maryanne Hogan."

"A forged ID card, April? I'm shocked."

"I'll bet you are. Somehow I don't think your name is found under the definition of perfect in the dictionary. Anyhow, not long after I purchased the ID, I was arrested for doing something stupid. I mean really stupid. I was under the influence of alcohol when it happened. Because it was a small town, the police department was used to dealing with college kids. After six hours, I sobered up and, wait a minute, why am I telling you all this? I barely know you. You promise me right now that you won't tell anybody about this conversation. I mean nobody!"

"I promise with all my heart. There's no way I'm going to miss the end of this story."

"You're security. I still don't trust you. You can't tell anybody. Say it again."

"I will tell nobody about the evil ways of Maryanne Hogan, alias April James."

"Okay, that will do. I sobered up and they let me out of my jail cell. I had to admit to them that my real name was April James. They kept the I.D. card and told me if I ever got into trouble again they would arrest me for, I don't know, I think they rattled off about ten different violations. They also told me my parents and the college would be notified. I was so embarrassed from the stunt I pulled and so afraid my parents would find out what happened that I was a wreck for days. I prayed ten times a day they would never find out what happened and thank God, to my knowledge, they never did. To this day, only a couple of my close non-gossiping friends know the whole story. They just wrote it off as one of those college things you learn the hard way. They weren't perfect either. I transferred to a different college for the spring semester.

You should have been there when I was trying to explain to my parents why I was transferring out of a college I had wanted to attend for a year and a half before I was accepted and now didn't think it was the right school for me after all."

"I know you're going to tell me what this grave act of stupidity was."

"I believe I'll save that for some other time or possibly never."

"That's not fair. You made me swear a solemn promise to tell no one, and I don't even get to hear the whole story?"

"That is correct, Mr. McGrath."

"You hurt me deeply, Miss James."

April laughed. She hadn't had this much fun talking to someone for what seemed like ages. Oh the memories. She felt a connection forming between her and Keegan.

"I can't wait to hear your deepest darkest secrets, Mr. McGrath."

"Me life has been nothing short of perfection, Miss James."

"Oh, I'm sure of that."

Chapter 26

April and Keegan were about ten blocks away from Thornburg Genetics, when Keegan flipped on his right turn signal and drove into a McDonald's parking lot.

"So, Keegan, you've decided to treat me to a fine breakfast this morning I see."

"Actually, we are here to pick up your car, Miss James. However, I would like to extend an offer for dinner some evening, rather than breakfast, if you are available of course."

"That sounds like fun."

"Great, I'll give you a call."

April spotted her green Honda CRV near the back of the McDonald's parking lot and Keegan pulled in next to it. April reached into her canvas bag and pulled out The Noah Document. She handed it to Keegan. When he reached out to take it, his hand accidentally clasped onto April's hand. April felt a rush of adrenalin. Their eyes met for a brief moment before Keegan removed his hand and took the document from April.

"Miss James, I don't know exactly what's in this document or exactly what you are into, but please be careful."

She smiled at him and said, "Okay, Keegan. Thanks. By the way, would you please call me April, not Miss James?" Then she opened the car door and scooted into her own car. She had known Keegan for less than twenty-four hours, but she didn't want to leave him right now. She wasn't sure why. He seemed like such a rebel and was not at all like Jason. She gave him a quick wave as she backed out of her parking space. Jason was so refined, a great communicator and blended into her lifestyle. April was pretty sure Keegan wasn't all that worried about blending in. Now she had agreed to go out to dinner with Keegan. What was she thinking? Jason and she had been seeing each other regularly for a few months now.

"Must be I need more sleep. This whole matter has clouded my judgment," April said to herself.

Keegan walked into McDonalds and purchased a medium coffee. Then he made the short trip to Thornburg Genetics.

April's thoughts turned to work. She had a pile of paperwork on her desk. She hadn't even managed to get through her pile from the vacation week yet. What would today bring? What reason would she give Jason for not answering the telephone last night?

It was 9:35 AM when April arrived at Thornburg Genetics. She pushed open the large glass front door and walked directly to her office. There was a big banner hanging over her door with one word on it: Congratulations. "Wow, the news sure got out fast."

As she approached the banner she heard Larry say, "Hey, April. Good going."

"Congratulations, April," said Cal.

"Thanks, guys."

"Will you bring me along?" asked Paula.

"I don't know that I can."

Then she heard, "She doesn't deserve this. Here one year and getting promoted. I've been here three and there hasn't been a promotion for me." It was Jeff. At least you always knew where you stood with him. If he thought it, he said it. Jeff was on the bottom of the heap when it came to team players. For some reason the company kept him around. Thanks, Jeff, I love you too, April thought to herself. April ignored him and entered her office.

As she sat down at her desk she heard, "Hi, April." It was Kara.

"Hi, Kara, how are you today?"

"I'm fine, and I have to say just a little jealous." Kara sat down on the soft fabric chair in front of April's desk. "We all hear you've been promoted, but nobody really knows what you've been promoted to. We would sure like to know more."

"Sure, Kara. I've been promoted to North and South America Public Relations Specialist. Now, you have to understand this is a new position, and I don't even know all of the details yet. I'll let you know more as things begin to take shape."

"Will you still be working here or at some other location?"

"I will be here at times, but I believe the new job will require some travel."

"You won't forget us will you?"

"Not at all, how could I forget my best shopping buddy? Besides, everybody here is such a hard worker. I promise I won't forget that."

"Thanks, April. I have to get back to work now. I'll see you soon."

"Okay, Kara, thanks for stopping in. It's always fun."

I work with such great people, April thought. Even Jeff can be decent when he's not in one of his mood swings. I guess we all have them on occasion. April opened up her computer and rifled through her inbox. There was a mandatory meeting at 11:00 AM.

"I guess I'm still in the loop for now," she thought.

Then she listened to her voice mails. One of them was from Jason. "Call me as soon as you can." The other important one was from Mark, "We have a meeting at 1:00 PM in conference room 2."

April picked up the phone and called Jason. "Hi, Jason."

"Hello, April. Congratulations on your promotion."

"Did you hang this big banner over my door?"

"Big banner? No, that wasn't me. It was probably Henry. Immediate supervisors are usually the first to be told about promotions from within their departments. I'll have to stop down and check it out. Hey, April, I have two things to mention. First, I have several pieces of paperwork for you to sign. This is Tuesday and your promotional job will start tomorrow. Second, I left a couple of messages on your answering machine last night. Is everything okay?"

"Everything is fine. After you dropped me off last evening, I got a telephone call from Tanya. Her, Mark and I met last night to further discuss this promotion. We came to an agreement and by the looks of this congratulations banner you must have received all of the paperwork this morning."

"Yes, Mark delivered it to me just after 8:00 AM. It seems that a celebration is in order. How about dinner this evening? Some place really nice. Let's say, Anthony's Ristorante."

"Oooh, how can a girl refuse an offer like that? What time?"

"I'll make reservations for 7:00 and pick you up at 6:30."

"Great. I'm looking forward to it."

"Wonderful. I'll be over in a few minutes to check out the banner and have you sign more paperwork. See you shortly."

April hung up the phone. It hadn't hit home before, but now the excitement, anticipation and fear of a new position hit April all at once. She had doubts as to whether or not she could handle the new job, and it started in less than 24 hours. What was she going to do with all the paperwork backed up on her desk? She didn't even know all of her new responsibilities yet, and she had guaranteed that she would maintain a 15% annual sales increase. That depended more on the sales force than her. Again she wondered why she was offered a promotion over so many other qualified candidates. April started to tear up with the immediate moment of stress.

Chapter 27

Keegan drove into the Thornburg parking lot and entered the side door. In his hand was a laptop case with the Noah Document in it. It was a short walk to Lexis' office.

"Good morning, Keegan," said Lexis. "Did everything work out as planned?"

"Everything went smooth as silk. Nobody tailed us and nothing out of the ordinary took place that we are aware of. We are on the bank camera videos, but I have someone taking care of that. It appears that no one is the wiser about Miss James, though I have to say I was a bit surprised about one piece of information."

"What's that, Keegan?"

"It appears that our Miss April James has a name she uses as an alias."

"Really, and what is that?"

"I made a promise that the secret would be ours until the grave, Miss Lexis."

"Well then, you had best be true to your word. I know you will check everything out properly!"

"Of course I will, ma'am."

"You like April very much, don't you, Keegan. I've never seen your face glow the way it does when you are around her." Keegan could feel his face turning red rather than glowing.

"It shows that much?"

"It does to me."

"There may be a hint of interest, Miss Lexis. I can't deny it. It's hard to resist a young lady that packs a handgun."

"I'm sure that's the main draw item. It has nothing to do with her bubbly personality or good looks of course."

"That may be part of the attraction too, now that you mention it."

"Just be careful, Mr. Keegan McGrath. You know any breach of security protocol could endanger April's life as well as your own. Let me know if you feel you need to be reassigned for any reason."

"I fully understand, Miss Lexis."

"Well, are you going to deliver the package to me or stand there all day with that laptop case in your hand?"

"Sorry, ma'am. I was slightly distracted. Here is the package, signed, sealed and delivered." Keegan laid the black laptop case on the desk and reached into his left front pants pocket for the key. He unlocked the case, unzipped the top and retrieved the manila envelope April had given him. It was covered with brown packing tape with the words 'April James only' written in bold magic marker. Keegan handed the envelope to Lexis. "Here you go, ma'am."

"Thank you, Keegan. Why don't you stop back in a couple of hours? In fact, we have a meeting at 1:00 o'clock."

"Thirteen hundred hours it is, Miss Lexis." With that, Keegan zipped up the laptop case, picked it up and left the room.

Immediately Lexis opened the envelope and started reading. The first sheet of paper was the letter to April from her father. Vincent was such a great, hardworking guy, Lexis thought to herself. She briefed the letter then set it aside. Underneath the letter was the item she was waiting for.

"The Noah Document," Lexis said out loud and gave a little smile. It took Lexis about half an hour to read the document. It was very intriguing. "I wonder why Vincent wrote this? Must be he felt we could do more to save people with the medical knowledge we possess here at Thornburg. It appears he felt the research work just wasn't making its way into medications as quickly as he thought it should. He knew most of the reasons for the delays."

Lexis picked up her telephone. "Hello, Tanya."

"Hello, Lexis."

"Shall we take a walk around the facility?"

"Sure, I'll be right there."

"Thank you, Tanya."

Lexis locked the Noah Document in the bottom drawer of her desk and then locked her office door. She walked down the hallway to meet Tanya. They toured the entire facility stopping briefly at different departments to talk with supervisors and employees. Lexis was always on the lookout for quality employees that could be advanced in the company. She also wanted to keep on top of employee morale and pharmaceutical advancement. Most of the employees recognized Lexis as the Global Marketing Officer of Thornburg Genetics and they knew Tanya was a vice president of marketing. It was a little over an hour before they reached the sales department. Lexis saw the congratulations sign over the door of April's office.

"It looks deserted around here," said Lexis. They stopped at the secretary's desk, and Tanya asked where the sales staff was.

"They all had an eleven o'clock meeting. Is there something I can help you with?"

"No. Not right now. Maybe we'll be back later," said Tanya.

"Meetings, some days I think meetings will be my death," chuckled Lexis.

"I know what you mean," said Tanya.

"Why don't we have an early lunch in the cafeteria," said Lexis. "Then we will see what surprises our Miss James will come up with at our 1:00 PM meeting."

"She certainly does keep things interesting," said Tanya as she and Lexis smiled at each other.

Chapter 28

It was 1:00 PM. Tanya, Mark and April were seated in Lexis' office. Lexis walked into the office followed by Keegan. Keegan closed the door behind them, and they both took a seat.

"Good afternoon," said Lexis. "This is without doubt one of the most important meetings we will have in the history of Thornburg Genetics. This room has security clearance and everything we discuss is of the utmost confidentiality. I have requested that Keegan join us, because there has been a major change of plans since last night, and he needs to know additional information."

"This morning I read the document April's father, Vincent James, left for her when he passed away. He appropriately titled the document, The Noah Document, and laid out several bits of information only a limited number of people in Thornburg Genetics know. At this point, the five of us possess knowledge of certain elements portrayed in this document, while only April and I know the overall content. Everything discussed at this meeting will stay between the five of us unless I personally authorize others to become involved. You each have a pad and pen in front of you. If you have any questions, please write them down, but let me finish talking before you say anything. Okay. Let's start at the beginning."

"Vincent apparently wrote The Noah Document to April, because he thought the medications from the research he was involved in were not made available to the public fast enough. April, you know most of what I am about to share, but the others here only know bits and pieces."

"April's father was diagnosed with stage 3B colon cancer at the age of thirty-three. He was prescribed an experimental drug designed by Thornburg Genetics called C1 Extraction (nicknamed The Blue Mule, thanks to our research staff). We officially call the pill Constellation Blue. It was designed to treat numerous forms of cancer. After taking the pill for seven days, he was completely healed with no side effects from the medication. We know much more about this medication now thanks to advances in genetics and computer science not available at the time of his cancer. Unfortunately, there is no cure for the type of lung cancer that took his life. Also, the drug that cured him over thirty years ago has still not been introduced to the open market."

"At first I was extremely angry when I read The Noah Document. Vincent wrote about classified Thornburg Genetics information. However, I believe Vincent was totally frustrated about people dying every day from the same cancer he was cured from thirty years ago. From a researcher's emotional stance, I can see why he felt the way he did. A researcher expects to create a life-enhancing pharmaceutical and have it brought to market for the good of the people. That is their job. However, Vince was not aware of the overall picture. There were pieces of the puzzle we did not share with him. These pieces dealt with tricky political and security issues that only a select few employees knew then and continue to know now. I will explain the security issues in more detail and only touch on the topic of politics, but first I need to share more background information."

"Mark, Tanya and I have visited and are aware of The Noah Library. This information is new to Keegan. What is The Noah Library? As you know, floodwaters destroyed the entire living earth in Noah's time. After the flood, the earth was a devastated mess. The pre-flood and post-flood earths were completely different. The environment had changed, resulting in the extinction of who knows how many plant species. Many of the plants Noah was familiar with were missing from the new environment. Other surviving plants were yellowing and dying. Noah and his son Japheth gathered plant specimens and took what steps they could to preserve as many of the disappearing species as possible. From the tablets we have, we know many species are extinct. We have searched the world for every rare and exotic species of plant we could find. To date, Thornburg Genetics researchers have found and preserved exactly ninety-six species that, to our knowledge, cannot be found in the wild. Noah's son, Japheth, was gifted in the subject of botany. He knew the fauna of the area were extremely important for manufacturing medications. Though their technology was nothing like today, a number of Japheth's lineage turned into well-advanced druggists. They amassed numerous records, mostly in the form of written tablets. The tablets are like pages out of a medical encyclopedia. They have engraved line drawings showing the plant's replica, name, and healing properties. Over time, additional plants were added as the world was repopulated. I'm talking hundreds of plants overall. These tablets comprise two thirds of The Noah Library. We are using these records today to conduct research on plant compounds to provide tomorrow's pharmaceuticals. This is a wonderful gift left to us as a result of Noah's son, Japheth."

"The knowledge contained in this library is guarded by a select few. In our inner circle, we simply call them protectors. In Noah's time, the original protectors were determined by lineage that started with Japheth. Over the decades and centuries, it became much more difficult to determine who in Japheth's lineage should be selected to guard and protect the secrets of Noah's library. We know that additional manuscripts and tablets have been added to the library over the years. With all of the bloodshed and land conquered in the Mesopotamia region throughout time, we truly believe the only way The Noah Library survived was by the hand of God. Think about it. If you know any history about that region, you know that Babylonians, Assyrians, Alexander the Great, Parthians, Romans, Persians, and others ruled Mesopotamia. Prophets, never royalty, knew The Noah Library's purpose but did not disclose its location or contents to the world. From what we can tell, only a limited number of people even knew it existed over the centuries. We know the exact location of the original library was in a cave in what is now Iraq near the Turkish border. The library protectors decided The Noah Library would not always be secure in its existing location. Copies of the tablets were made, and the entire library was moved to an even more remote mountainous region in Iran. We have both the original tablets and copies in our possession. The Noah Library was never lost, never forgotten, and protected in strict confidence."

"At that time in history when the library was moved, many records of Japheth's lineage were destroyed. With a fragmented lineage, it was impossible to know which heirs should be the select few considered protectors of the library with its plant knowledge. The most influential protectors devised a plan in an attempt to keep the line of protectors intact. We have the written historical records in our possession. The plan was not entered into lightly. There are numerous mentions of prayer to God, fasting, dedication of life and secrecy. One section of the plan was to devise certain written elements a true protector would instinctively know and be able to respond to in a favorable fashion. April, I believe you have recently become quite familiar with part of those written elements. The tests you recently took contain many questions designed by the protectors. That is why many of the questions seem odd and obscure. Another section of their plan outlined the creation of formal businesses and using the money generated to mask the true intent of keeping The Noah Library a secret. A third section of the plan was to have the governments of numerous countries as allies. You can't fight government so why not work within its confines? A fourth product of their planning was the implementation of The Keeper. Today, The Keeper and Global Marketing Officer of Thornburg Genetics are synonymous. Thornburg Genetics is a thriving pharmaceutical and research business, as well as a front to protect The Noah Library and its secrets. By using the written tests and watching the growth of select employees, we know almost 100% of our employees with knowledge of The Noah Library have what we call The Noah Gene."

"What is The Noah Gene? The Noah Gene dictates protector status. Our theory is that The Noah Gene is a genetic information filter found in only a limited number of people worldwide. These people are descendants of Japheth."

"Those who have this physical attribute cannot share certain information with others unless those people also have The Noah Gene. The information I am referring to is the written content within The Noah Library and related Thornburg Genetics research. We have had our researchers working on The Noah Gene theory for years now. We have to unlock its secrets in order to maintain protection of The Noah Library."

"Why do we have to protect The Noah Library and its contents? Here are the security issues I was referring to earlier. Let's talk about plants for a moment."

"We have plants that have never been seen by anyone other than a small group of Thornburg employees. These are all enclosed in temperature and climate-controlled Thornburg Genetic facilities throughout the world. Many of these plants are slow growers, growing only one or two inches per year. Others may flower and produce only a dozen seeds once every few years. To say the very least, most of these plants are fragile beyond belief. The diversity is unbelievable. The only individuals allowed in facilities housing these plants are long-term Thornburg Genetics employees with a 99.9% protector status determination. In other words, they have The Noah Gene and cannot reveal secrets pertaining to our operations."

"Even with advancing computer technology, it takes years of research to determine the compound relationships of these 96 species in relation to other well-known plant species. This is one reason why our C1 Extraction cancer drug developed thirty years ago is not on the market yet today. The other major reason is due to volatility. Thornburg researchers involved with these rare plants are handling volatile compounds."

"Let me give you two examples that show this volatility. First, twelve years ago, two of our top chemists mixed two of these rare plant compounds together as part of their research project. To keep things simple, five drops of compound A were added to five drops of compound B. After a ten second delay, we had a lethal chemical reaction. The reaction between those ten drops of two compounds blew out a chunk of our lab building way too big to explain to the public and resulted in two dead top chemists. As a result, we had to either move upper level security research operations away from metropolitan areas, or design explosive-proof labs in our buildings."

"Example number two: Again, another top biotechnology researcher was working with volatile compounds. The employee did not know there was a slit barely a millimeter long in his rubber glove. Suddenly his hand started throbbing. He looked at his hand and saw blood inside his glove. He rushed to the sink in a secure wash area just outside the lab door. When he took his glove off and rinsed the blood off, he literally watched as flesh slowly started to dissolve from his hand. Fortunately, a coworker sprayed a special biological disinfectant on the open wound that counteracted the compound. Unfortunately, the employee lost part of the back of his hand and part of his little finger. Vincent knew about these incidents but felt they should not hold back release of the Constellation Blue drug. He felt the good effects greatly outweighed the drug's potential dangers. We now have six major Thornburg Genetic research facilities throughout the world set up solely for volatile compound research. We also have several environmentally controlled greenhouses that contain our rare plant species."

Lexis paused and took a sip of ice water.

"With a couple hundred Thornburg researchers working with volatile plant compounds, I suppose accidents will happen, but we do all we can to avoid such catastrophes. We are in the business of saving lives, not losing them. We want our research to make a difference by healing, improving and lengthening people's lives. We have to balance the great positive medicinal effects with the volatile drawbacks. I have to say not one day or night goes by that I don't wish some of these healing products were on the open market. Then I read about genocide in Rhodesia and the Sudan. I read about dictators that let their citizens die from starvation. Our world is filled with power mongers. Allowing known volatile compounds into the hands of such people is asking for even more problems than we already have. I wish world circumstances were different."

"Here's the clincher. We have known for four or five years that information is somehow being smuggled out of Thornburg Genetics. Bits of our research have shown up in competitors' pharmaceutical companies. We know this because we have a limited number of employees working undercover in the top world pharmaceutical research companies. To summarize, we believe there is a security breach through either our American or Mexican research facility. We are not sure whether we have one or several employees involved. We think the problem is miniscule, but who knows how far it extends. We don't know if the motive is an employee wanting fast money, another drug company wanting formulas to advance their product line, or a company power play to offer explosives or biological weapons. We aren't even sure if whoever is involved knows how volatile these compounds can be. This much I do know. We have to find out."

"On a very sad note, we have four cases where Thornburg Genetic research employees have vanished, only to turn up dead. Evidence shows they were tortured, most likely in an attempt to obtain classified Thornburg Genetics research. We believe they were killed by covert operatives, though their deaths are not listed as such. The research they were conducting appears to be safe, because to our knowledge it has not surfaced outside Thornburg. Torture is not a pretty picture, and we hope to avoid it at all costs in the future. However, this does support our Noah Gene theory that these employees could not divulge their research information even under torture. We also have five employees who are currently missing persons."

"April, I want you to know that finding The Noah Gene and interpreting its characteristics was part of your father's research in addition to his cancer research. Did you know your father had blood samples drawn from you in his possession and had used them in his research projects?"

April shook her head no.

"We didn't know either until two days ago. I am assuming Vincent knew you have The Noah Gene we are searching for. He was searching your genes and his own in an attempt to make a connection. However, at this point in time The Noah Gene is still considered a theory."

"So where is all of this taking us? Enter April James. April, as of our meeting last night, unbeknownst to you, we were going to allow you to help ferret out our problem employee/employees; our covert operatives. We had hoped your quick promotion, your meeting with us after hours, and the multiple tests taken so close together would raise a red flag somewhere in the Thornburg organization. We believe the undercover operative, or operatives, are gleaning as much information as possible about our research programs and employees at all times. I hate to admit this, but we were basically going to put you out there like a sitting duck waiting for pot shots. However, after reading The Noah Document, I've decided you know many of the Thornburg secrets. While I feel a little uncomfortable letting a one-year employee infiltrate so deeply into our network, I feel I have no choice. I also have a lot of faith your father considered you a carrier of The Noah Gene and pretty well knew he could trust you. Based on what I know about you, I am almost positive you have The Noah Gene. Your test score results were very high. We know Vince didn't choose your brother to share The Noah Document with, and you chose not to share it with him even though the two of you are close. Also, you have had this document in your possession for over one year now and have not shared it with anybody else. That shows a statistically high probability you are a protector."

"April, we hope someone is watching your every move. Whether or not you like the situation, The Noah Document has put you in the middle of our Thornburg Genetics security breach. You may be our only answer to eliminating this breach. You need to know that by exposing this document, your life is potentially in grave danger. Someone in our organization wants classified information. We hope they approach you. As of this moment, you need to be on constant alert mode and be afraid of the unknown."

There was silence as all eyes were trained on April. April couldn't believe what she was hearing. So this is why there was so much secrecy about security issues and now she was in the middle of a mess. What a wonderful way to start a promotion. She rehashed the words and background information provided by Lexis.

"Thanks a lot, Dad! I hope you can hear this conversation," she thought.

Chapter 29

"I'm sure there must be questions," said Lexis.

"Can you tell us more about the breach in security?" asked April. "You said research from Thornburg facilities has shown up elsewhere. Are there any specifics you can share with us?"

There was silence for a moment.

"I'm not trying to avoid the question. I just want to make sure I explain significant details correctly," said Lexis. "First, discussing any of the research we believe has been pirated is not feasible at this meeting. The research is all chemical analysis and math equations that I can't attempt to explain. My staff informs me the research should be exclusive to Thornburg Genetics. It is information no other drug company could come up with through their own efforts. Most of the researchers hired are for lower security level projects. We do job out certain research aspects to other laboratories, depending on the project. No laboratory is all inclusive when it comes to research. Biotech equipment is highly complicated, specific for a very narrow range of tasks, and expensive. Maybe sensitive information was jobbed out in error. However, only employees scrutinized carefully and believed to carry The Noah Gene handle top level research, so this seems improbable."

"We do have a breach of security in our rare plant division. In the past two years, three separate incidents have occurred where plant species controlled only by Thornburg Genetics have shown up in college-controlled greenhouse facilities. When the first two incidents occurred, Thornburg Genetics employees removed the plants from those facilities immediately."

"My security team guaranteed me we had a sure fire plan to capture the culprit when the third event occurred." Lexis looked at Keegan. Keegan shrugged his shoulders and raised his eyebrows. "One of our inspectors notified us he had discovered four aloe vera gold plants in a college greenhouse. Aloe vera gold is a rare plant known only to Thornburg Genetics. We set up numerous security cameras and monitored the plants around the clock. We were ready to apprehend whoever was involved with the plants the moment they showed up. To make a long story short, we have a video tape showing a person walking into the greenhouse on Christmas morning, placing the four plants in what appeared to be a special climate-controlled box, and exiting the greenhouse never to be seen again. Our security staff notified Campus Security immediately that a thief was in the greenhouse. Campus Security personnel were on the scene within 3 minutes of this person showing up on the security cameras. They found a full-cover head and face mask only a short distance away from the back of the greenhouse.

The operative was nowhere in sight. The controlled plants in question look exactly like regular aloe vera, with a gold dot on the underside of the leaf being the only way to distinguish them. They would never be noticed by anyone in the college setting who didn't know exactly what to look for. With numerous professors and students using designated greenhouse spaces, it is impossible to track how these particular plants were placed in the greenhouses involved in these three incidents. We cross-referenced college students, instructors and anyone who had access to these greenhouses with former Thornburg Genetic employees. Nothing unusual showed up. The only thing the three greenhouses involved in the incidents have in common is their climate control systems were set up by the same company. We expect the thief is a highly advanced botanist. Thornburg has only one hundred and twenty employees with access to these plants worldwide. Some of the employees are general greenhouse staff and others are research staff. Again, all background checks on staff turned up nothing. Researchers were following their protocol when handling the rare plant species. Somehow plants or seeds were stolen, and we are unable to detect how or by whom."

"I guess I'll ask the obvious question. How do you know the plants weren't found in the wild somewhere and then brought into the colleges?" asked April.

"Obviously we couldn't ask college personnel about the plants. How would it sound to ask: 'Did you know you have super rare plants in your greenhouse? Oh, by the way, whose plants are they, and where did they get them?' The only thing we could do was set up an undercover security staff in the area to collect information. No professors or students complained about having their plants missing or stolen from the greenhouses, so we can only assume they were illegitimate. I can't say a rare plant will never be found in the wild. We live in a vast world and anything can happen. It's just the chances of finding these plants in the wild are almost impossible, as the plants we deal with require a specific environment with very narrow parameters to stay alive. At this point in time, there is no environment in the world, other than a controlled facility, which is not too hot, cold, moist, dry, polluted, etc. to sustain these plants for any extended period of time."

"How have they survived this long then? There are a limited number of micro ecosystems throughout the world where these plants were cultivated on a small scale for centuries. Protectors cultivated the plants. As greenhouse technology progressed, these plants were moved into the climate-controlled facilities and eventually Thornburg Genetics was formed. The company has had different names over the years. We still monitor the known cultivation sites to see if these plants will somehow regenerate. Many of the sites have been altered completely and aren't monitored. For example, some sites now have towns or cities built on them while some have changed from wetlands to farmland. Forests have been harvested and cleared. These sites will never host a rare plant again. We also have botanists exploring for new plant species throughout the world. New species are discovered now and then, but there have been no new species related to the tablets in The Noah Library. The whole process of how and why these plants existed over the centuries is extremely complicated. Every plant we monitor has its own story, and even I don't know many of them to the extent I should."

"Exactly how were these plants discovered in separate greenhouse facilities if nobody knows what they look like except Thornburg Genetics employees?" asked April.

"I did mention that an inspector found the plants. These are official government inspectors that monitor greenhouse operations throughout the world. They pretend to look for disease, mold, insects and such, but their real intent is discovering rare plant species. There are only forty countries that have research facilities sophisticated enough to grow these species on what we call a level A basis. These facilities are inspected annually. Other facilities such as colleges and universities are considered level B sites and are in about one hundred countries. These are inspected every two years. Level C sites are simply retail nurseries and green houses that are open year round. These are inspected once every three to five years."

"The official government inspectors are really international government inspectors from a division of Thornburg Genetics sanctioned by the United Nations. We have twelve full-time inspectors on the go constantly. They are on the road for two months and then home for two weeks. Yes, they are known protectors and, as such, do not divulge what their true job is. One inspector was involved in two of the rare plant findings and a second one was involved in the third incident. They are highly trained botanists and have extensive rare plant training as part of their jobs."

"What is stopping someone from setting up a private laboratory or greenhouse facility?" asked Tanya.

"We have thought of that. It is possible. Probably one to two dozen of our controlled species could flourish in a relatively simple climate-controlled greenhouse setting. The only problem is it would take a considerable amount of money to start up and operate the type of facility required for the rarest plants in the Thornburg collection. Complex water and air filtration systems are expensive. The operations have to be rodent and bug free. Available sunlight has to be controlled. There is little chance such a facility could tap into the necessary research grant money or private funding required without the word getting out. Word like what research scientists are being hired, what expensive equipment is being built, etc. would find its way into the rumor mill. It would be virtually impossible not to be detected. Without cooperation between companies, any small operation would only get farther and farther behind in any type of research. A large amount of information dealing with plant compounds, I would say seventy percent, is originated through Thornburg Genetics. We have to be a leader and stay at the top in this area of research."

"With all of that said, a small hobby type operation is plausible. The plants found by our inspectors have all been aloe vera gold. This plant, while rare and not found in the wild, does not require nearly as much pampering as most of our other species of rare plants. It is likely someone is cultivating it in a home-style greenhouse. The aloe vera gold requires only limited air and water filtration systems in a semi-sterile environment. It might even survive in a natural microenvironment, but it would have to be near a dryer desert region far away from pollutants, though our field botanists have never located any. Again, we don't know whether the breach of security is for significant financial gain or some type of power move."

"Let me talk for a moment about government involvement," said Mark. "We receive a limited amount of funding from the United Nations through an account earmarked as world security issues. This is a no questions asked fund. World powers are only aware of enough information to know there is a potential for world imbalance or a major crisis without proper funding. Our sponsor is the United States, but nobody knows about our operation with the exception of four government officials who are, of course, protectors. Government funding accounts for only a small portion of our annual budget and is used for expenditures such as the greenhouse inspectors. Some of our high security risk research facilities are guarded by the military. We cannot let any of these volatile compounds fall into the wrong hands."

"I know very little about The Noah Library, but why are the documents kept secret? Why not release them if they aren't a security risk?" asked April.

"This matter has been discussed numerous times, April. About seventy-five percent of the tablets deal with issues we consider security sensitive, such as plant descriptions and Noah Gene lineage. If we declassify certain tablets, it will be hard to keep the rest private. At this point in time, we just think it is inappropriate to release any of the tablets. I will say we are also constantly monitoring any new tablets and documents discovered by archeologists. Because our influence is viewed positively by most foreign countries, we are allowed to examine any newly discovered manuscripts, tablets, hieroglyphs, etc. to determine if they are sensitive to our classified research projects. No additional tablets concerning rare plants have been found in recent years; however, four additional gold tablets of interest have been discovered."

"How is The Keeper selected?" asked April.

"Tanya, will you field that question please?"

"Well, I've only been through one selection, which was Lexis of course. Basically, department heads from thirty-five areas within Thornburg Genetics were brought together for a meeting. To be brief, Lexis' name just kept surfacing in several different key areas of expertise during that selection, and she was elected unanimously as The Keeper. The Keeper's generic title is Global Marketing Officer of Thornburg Genetics. I believe somebody always surfaces who is a natural selection for the position. There doesn't seem to be any major competition. Why do you ask that question, April?"

"Could jealousy over The Keeper position lead to a security breach?"

"I don't think we ever considered that angle. I don't know the answer to that question. What do you think, Lexis?"

"We would like to think we exist in this nice company where everyone and everything is perfect, but who knows. I'm open to any and all ideas."

"You said that my father was working with my blood sample in his research projects. Where did he get a blood sample?"

"Did you ever donate blood for any reason?"

"Of course, he must have obtained a sample after I donated to the Red Cross."

Then the room was silent. The five people looked back and forth at each other.

"I guess there are no more questions," said Lexis. "Let's think up some strategy for our next course of action in stopping the security breach. Good luck with your new job, April. Keep your eyes open and let us know if you see or sense anything at all that seems even remotely suspicious."

Chapter 30

"Hey, big brother, how's it going?"

"Are you on a secure phone line?"

"You always ask me that even though you know that's the only way I operate."

"I know that and guess what; I'm still going to ask. Where are you calling from?"

"A pay phone in Timbuktu, come on man."

"So, what have you got for me?"

"Our Miss April James signed her contract last night at a special meeting with Mark and Tanya. I wasn't even invited to the party. Can you imagine? Now here's the real deal. Guess who's wandering around Thornburg Genetics today? It's our favorite Global Marketing Officer, Lexis. I'll bet you any amount she was at that meeting last night too. I don't think April is sharing all of her life's experiences with me. It doesn't seem fair for her to hold out on me after I treat her like such a lady. I told you about all the perks April will have with this promotion. Are you ready for this? She also requested and was approved to start up and operate a cushy little charity to help the people of the world obtain more medical supplies or something. Thornburg will donate two hundred thousand dollars to start the charity. Her contract states she does have sales goals to meet, but you know how it is in these big companies. Who knows whether the bigwigs ever really meet their goals or not? It's always some poor schmuck at the bottom of the food chain that gets axed if sales goals aren't met. I'll tell you this; she definitely has something on Thornburg Genetics. April is getting way too much for an employee who has been here only one year."

"I thought you told me that company sales are increasing significantly due to April? Give me a good reason this isn't just a legitimate contract designed to keep a top-notch employee at Thornburg."

"You didn't see Tanya's face when she read the request April handed her in that envelope at the interview. I'm telling you, the word SHOCK didn't describe it. I was bounced from the room so fast it felt like greased lightning. They didn't bounce me because of some charity request, my brother. Trust me on this one."

There was silence for a few moments. "You definitely have my attention. What next?"

"I have a nice dinner date planned with April in about half an hour. I will put on my perfect gentleman profile once again and see what I can find out."

"This isn't some type of sting operation is it? We've been looking for a break for four years now and nothing has happened. All of a sudden we are handed the goose that lays the golden egg. I don't like it."

"Relax, will you. If I hadn't been in that room at just the right time as Human Resources Director, we never would have known about this whole situation. You think everything that happens is a conspiracy. This is an unexpected break, not a conspiracy. I know how to handle this."

"Keep me posted and don't get too cocky. I know you're smart, but there are a lot of smart people in the world and Thornburg Genetics is loaded with them. We have to get insider information as soon as we can. I could have Mark and Tanya followed, but I'm sure it would be a waste of time. There's no sense in bugging April's apartment, because I'm sure she has been warned not to discuss anything outside a secure setting. I'm also sure she couldn't discuss anything because of that Noah Gene snafu. It's up to you to dig deep, Jason."

"I have a plan in mind, but I have to do some more research to determine who all the players are. I'll be in touch soon."

Chapter 31

"Once again you whisked me off to a wonderful dinner date, Jason."

"I'll do anything for you, April. Big promotions don't happen every day. Besides, you are the special girl in my life. I love our time together. So, how does it feel to be the North and South America Public Relations Specialist?"

"I'm still totally in shock. I can't believe this is happening to me."

"Have you decided where your home office will be?"

"I'm staying right here for now. I love Philadelphia, and I'm getting to know more people every day. Besides, you're here."

"Whew, that was a close call. I sure don't want to see you leave. How would I live without seeing your smiling, beautiful face every day? So, how do you like your scallops?"

"Mine are great. They taste like they're fresh from the sea. How are yours?"

"I can't get enough scallops. They're my favorite meal and these are the best. So, what is this charity you're working on? You never mentioned anything about it to me. I feel a little left out."

"I was going to tell you tonight. It was kind of a last minute thought, and I didn't want to say anything until I saw whether or not it would become a reality. I'm so excited. You know how I love to help people. This charity will allow me to help people all over the world. I haven't given the charity a name yet. Would you like to help me name it?"

"I will be honored to help, but I have to laugh. You should have seen the look on Tanya's face when you sprang this charity idea on her. I don't really know why she had me leave the room. Must be she was totally frustrated."

April paused, looked down, and started playing with her glass of water. "Yeah, it's not a request Thornburg Genetics gets every day."

"Well, they went for it. Congratulations! I know you have considered some names for the charity. What have you come up with?"

"I have some ideas, but why don't we work on it together?"

"I have a note pad right here. Should we start now?"

"Sure, I didn't think you would be that interested."

"Why would you think that? If it's of interest to you, it's of interest to me. I do work in a pharmaceutical company, out saving the world. I like the whole charity idea a lot. In fact I would like to volunteer to promote the charity to our fellow employees."

"Really?"

"Yes, right after we get it named."

April reached across the table with both hands and grasped both of Jason's hands. "I love you, Jason."

There was a pause as Jason studied April's face. "I didn't know if I would ever hear those words from you, April. I love you too. I have since the first day I set eyes on you and getting to know you made my desire for you even greater."

"That's a sweet thing to say. I have wanted to tell you I love you many times before, but I just had to make sure it was true in my own mind. I had to make sure everything fit right in the different areas of our lives."

"Do you have a dating checklist of criteria or something? You haven't been reading some kind of how-to date book, have you?"

April laughed. "I'll never tell. It could be that I just know what I'm looking for in a man."

"Could I interest either of you in some dessert?" asked the waitress.

"No thank you," said April. "I believe we are finished." Jason nodded his head in agreement.

"I'll bring your check then."

"Let's go back to my place, Jason. I'll put on a pot of hazelnut coffee, and we can work on naming the charity."

"That sounds like a plan. Let's see, how about the April James Charity of Life."

"Yuck, I can see we have a long ways to go."

Chapter 32

"Hey, big brother. It's me and yes I'm on a secure line. I just have to tell you about my little dinner date last night with April. Guess what?"

"I can't imagine. What now, Jason?"

"I am now a crusader for the new Thornburg Genetics charity. April thinks I'm the best guy on the planet, and she told me she's madly in love with me."

"And you woke me up at six in the morning to tell me this. I'll send you a fresh, crisp, one-dollar bill for your charity fund. How's that for a special moment."

"Come on, Max. Don't be so sarcastic. You haven't heard the best part. I trapped her. Here's how it went down. We were talking about the new charity that Thornburg agreed on. I was looking directly at April's face to catch any reactions. Then I said, 'you should have seen the look on Tanya's face when you sprang this charity idea on her. She was totally flustered.' And guess what?"

"I don't know. What?"

"She immediately looked down and started playing with her glass of water. I looked away to avoid direct eye contact, because then I knew. When you look away from a person the way she did, it means either you're lying or there's more to the story. She's not lying, because we have a full fledge charity on our hands. That means she knows more. There's more to the story. April is, without a doubt, our ticket inside."

"You and your psychoanalysis. You read too many books."

"Psychoanalysis always worked with you, big brother."

"That's what scares me. You seem to have the gift of observation and interpretation of people."

"I have some sweet ideas for executing a plan of attack. I know April won't be able to resist helping us."

"Go easy, Jason. We don't want this opportunity to get away from us. A year from now we can be sitting on a nice white sandy beach, waiting for our next margarita to be served. What about Sheila?"

"Sheila is on the back burner for now. It's April only. Sheila will understand."

"Your sense of commitment goes above and beyond the call of duty."

"Mr. Commitment, that's me," Jason said with a laugh. "I'll be in touch soon."

Chapter 33

Within ten days, April had selected four employees to assist her with her new job duties. It was a difficult selection process, because April didn't want to alienate friends and coworkers, but both Mark and Tanya insisted the transition proceed quickly. April's new job had the same duties except she was now in charge of promoting Thornburg Genetics in both North and South America. April made a decision to leave her office set up at the Philadelphia Thornburg location. Due to limited space, an office area was leased in the building across the street. April and her four employees were on the second floor of a ten floor building. The office space was in the front corner of the building, and April could see the spring greenery of the Thornburg building gardens from the office she chose. Her employees each had a window office as well and could see either the Thornburg building gardens or the adjacent front street. The reality was they were all too busy to spend much time enjoying the view.

Jason had taken April out to dinner several times and had surprised her with home-cooked meals in her apartment on two different evenings when she had to work late. April loved the attention and pampering Jason was giving her. The promotion and office move required long grueling hours during the week, and she spent her first two weekends working to get the office set up to her satisfaction. She told Jason how much she loved him and appreciated his support while she was so busy. Jason's newfound interest in helping set up the Thornburg charity also made April feel special.

April hadn't seen Keegan since the last meeting with Lexis a little over two weeks before. He was probably keeping Lexis safe. She thought about his Irish accent and adventurous spirit. He was interesting to spend time with and funny.

"I just get through telling Jason I love him and here I am daydreaming about Keegan. Why am I thinking about him? Jason is so much more refined. He's always on an even course, always happy, and always positive. He has never screamed or yelled at me and nothing seems to bother him. What do I really know about Keegan? I think Keegan is more, what's a good word, safari-like. He seems used to getting his own way. He is easy to talk to though, and it's not like I'm engaged to Jason yet or anything."

April reprimanded herself for thinking about Keegan. It wouldn't be right to tell someone you love them and lead them along while thinking about another guy.

Chapter 34

"Hi, April. This is Tanya."

"Hello, Tanya. How are you?"

"I'm fine, thanks. Is everything progressing well with your new job?"

"All of the pieces seem to be fitting together nicely. We are super busy putting together information for distribution to all of our sales and marketing staff, along with jump-starting the new charity. Are you sure there are twenty-four hours in a day? It doesn't seem like it."

"I know you're busy. Make sure you delegate to lighten your load. I read the resumes of the employees you selected to work with you, and they are excellent."

"They are exceptional employees, and we work well together. I've given them lots of assignments. We just have to get everything lined up in the right order."

"April, the reason I'm calling is to see if you are ready for some traveling."

April cringed at the thought. She wanted to travel, but she was so involved in numerous projects she didn't have a minute to spare. She knew travel was expected as part of her new promotion but hadn't had time to think about it. There was no choice. The answer had to be yes. She tried to answer in as positive a manner as possible. "Of course, I am looking forward to it."

"You sound very positive, but I'll bet you haven't even given travel a thought. I know how busy you are, but you have good employees working with you. Don't worry about your projects and the office. Everything will work out. We would like you to give a presentation in our Quito, Ecuador Thornburg Genetics branch. Now that we have had success promoting the Body-New Pharmaceutical line in the United States, we want to go global. We want you to share your approach for making the Body-New Pharmaceuticals a household name. Why don't we plan on a ten day excursion? I'll be in town, and we will leave next Sunday afternoon at 1:00 PM. Bring whatever you want for luggage. We have one of the small private company jets reserved."

April was thrilled at the chance to travel, but she was skeptical about leaving the office after only two weeks of preparation time with her new staff. This gave her five working days to get the new office in some semblance of order. She hoped her staff wouldn't feel neglected, but she decided she couldn't worry about things she had little control over. Her computer and cell phone would keep her in touch with staff. This meant she would have to dress up her digital presentation.

"What will our agenda be in Ecuador? I have a longtime friend I would really like to see while we are there."

"You can plan adequate free time to visit a friend."

After discussing a few more details, Tanya and April said goodbye and ended their telephone conversation. As soon as April hung up, she called Jason and told him the exciting news. He said it sounded like fun and wondered if there was room for an extra passenger. After assuring him this was purely a business trip, she told him about the itinerary and her intention to see an old friend while in Ecuador.

April worked long hours every day preparing for her ten days out of the office. She only saw Jason two nights that week and was exhausted by Friday. She went to the office again on Saturday morning and decided to call it quits at noon. With suitcases to pack and a presentation to polish up, she decided she just couldn't see Jason that afternoon or evening. It had been a while since she had attended a church service, and she felt like she was neglecting God. She called Jason and invited him to go to church with her the next morning. Jason declined the offer to join her. This seemed rather out of character for Jason as he rarely missed an opportunity to be with April. She asked him why he didn't want to go. He said he was planning on having breakfast with a college friend he hadn't seen in a while. In reality, Jason didn't want April around that morning, but he knew he had to ask her if she would like to go with him. She declined and told him to go ahead and have a good time. Under his breath Jason gave a sigh of relief. She didn't even ask him who he was going to meet. If April ever found out he was seeing Sheila, things wouldn't go well. He was sure April would never go out with him again, and Max would kill him if he found out Sheila was still in the picture. If he botched the use of April as the needed Thornburg Genetics insider for their mission, he decided he might as well catch a plane to Siberia and go into hiding. He probably should have let Max know he had changed his mind and was still seeing Sheila, but Max didn't need to know everything in his life. He knew April would ask him about the breakfast rendezvous, and he would probably have to lie to her.

Jason asked April if he could pick her up and take her to the airport instead. April accepted the offer and asked if he could pick her up at eleven fifteen. He said that would work out well, and he was glad he would have a chance to see her before she left.

April enjoyed the 9:00 AM Sunday church service. The choir selection was inspiring, and the pastor talked about serving God in foreign countries. It was a topic April could relate to, and her concentration on the sermon slipped as she started to think about the planned trip to

Ecuador later that day. It had been over a year since she left Ecuador, and she missed the many people she had worked with.

April arrived at the airport at noon. Jason stopped the car at the front entrance of Continental Airlines.

"I have a little surprise for you before you go."

"What kind of surprise?"

Jason reached under his seat and procured a small blue velvet box. He opened it, and April saw a yellow gold band with a sparkling diamond in the middle. "I love you and I would like you to marry me, April."

April held out her hand and took the boxed ring as tears started rolling down her cheek. "It's beautiful, Jason. What a surprise. Of course I will marry you."

"Well, we better get you on your way to Ecuador."

"That's not fair. You can't hand me a diamond and then expect me to leave you." She put her arms around his neck and gave him a long, passionate kiss.

"It adds a level of suspense to our relationship, doesn't it?" asked Jason.

April did her best to stop crying and wipe away the tears. She knew her eyes were still red when Jason got out of the car to help unload her luggage. An airline associate was on the spot to pick it up. After a hug Jason gave her a special going away kiss. April slid the small box into her coat pocket.

"I'm going to miss you," she said to Jason.

"I'll miss you too, sweetie. Make sure you call me."

"I will, but it may be at some odd hour. I can tell there is a lot of work to do even though I only have a partial schedule. Tanya told me my time has to be flexible because there will be impromptu meetings."

"I understand. Bye for now. I'll see you sometime the week after next."

"Bye-bye, I love you."

"I love you too, April."

April turned and walked through the front door of the Philadelphia International Airport terminal. She looked back and gave a little wave to Jason who was watching her from his car. He waved back then pulled away from the curb. April carried only a small suitcase with her business information and her laptop inside. She stopped at the nearest restroom to check out her eyes. They were still red and mascara had run down her cheeks with the tears. After touching up her face, she proceeded through the security checkpoint with no delay and was escorted to concourse A east, gate A10. There were three small jets on the tarmac. One had the lettering Citigroup, the second was marked Exxon. The third was a Gulfstream with no visible markings on it. It was the only one with the steps lowered.

"Here you go, ma'am," said the escort. "Have a great day."

"Thank you, sir, you too." April handed the young man a tip. He thanked her and shuffled off as April boarded her flight. It was 12:35 PM. There were ten seats on the jet and only one was taken.

"Good afternoon, April."

"Hello, Tanya. It's good to see you again."

"It's good to see you too. Are you exhausted yet?"

"I'm only on the verge of exhaustion. The change to the new job, assignments to the staff, and getting organized quickly has been a challenge. Everything is falling into place though."

"I'm sure everything will be fine. Are you ready to see some of the world, make some presentations, and meet lots of new people?"

"I'm ready."

"The plane is scheduled to leave at exactly 1:00 PM. We still have a few minutes left. Why don't you relax a little? This week will be busy, but there will also be some time for rest and relaxation."

"It's just the two of us?"

"For now it is. We have to make a couple more stops. We do our best to maximize flight time, because it is rather expensive."

April slid into the beige leather seat across from Tanya. "These seats are so comfortable. The only flights I've ever taken have been crowded commercial flights."

"I guess you could say this jet defines luxury."

At 12:45 PM the captain and co-pilot walked through the hatch door. "Good afternoon, ladies; are we ready?" asked the captain.

"Yes we are," said Tanya.

"Let me run through the seat belt and oxygen mask instructions, then we will be ready for lift off in just a few minutes."

April looked at her watch. It was exactly three minutes after one when the Gulfstream lifted off the end of the runway. April laid her head back as the force of the jet pushed her back into the seat. All of a sudden she felt exhaustion set in and drifted into a deep sleep.

Slowly she regained consciousness and looked at her watch. It was two thirty five. She had been asleep for an hour and a half and felt a little groggy. She glanced across the aisle at Tanya, who was reading a magazine.

"I guess I was more tired than I thought."

"That was quite a nap, April. Do you feel a little more rested?"

"I feel more rested, but now I feel like a zombie. I don't have one ounce of energy."

"I know that feeling. It happens every now and then. Would you like to look at a magazine?"

"Sure, what have you got?"

"I have Better Homes and Gardens, Coastal Living or Nascar News."

"You read Nascar News?"

"I have been known to follow the Nascar circuit, but I believe the magazine was a bit of a prank by my husband. I found it snuck between my other magazines in my carry on. It looks as though he may have pre-read it."

"I think I'll stick to Coastal Living, thanks."

Tanya laughed.

April drifted in and out of sleep as the jet purred. The pilot's voice came over the loudspeaker. "It is now 4:40 PM, mountain time. We will be landing in ten minutes."

Tanya had mentioned to April it would be after dark before they arrived in Ecuador. Must be they were picking up more people, she thought. She glanced over at Tanya. She was reading her Nascar magazine.

"Where are we now?"

Tanya looked at April. "We are arriving at a scheduled, undisclosed location."

"What does that mean?"

"I told you we had to pick up more passengers. I believe that's what this landing is for. It's just at an undisclosed location only the pilots know."

April didn't really understand the whole undisclosed location thing but said nothing more as the plane descended. She looked out the window and saw another jet not too far away. With the flat olive green color, she knew it had to be a military jet. It was there for a few seconds, tipped its wings to the left and disappeared. As they touched down and approached the terminal, April could see olive green and desert brown camouflaged Hummers. They passed a row of large convoy trucks. It was obviously a military installation. She wondered whom they would be picking up here. The jet stopped at the terminal. April could hear the hydraulics groaning as the exit door opened and the steps swung down. Tanya unbuckled her seat belt.

"Let's go for a walk, April. Bring your pocketbook, but everything else can stay here."

"Sure, but what's going on?"

"Oh, I guess you could call it a little side trip," said Tanya with a smile.

"Is this...?"

"Shhhhhh," said Tanya as she lifted her finger to her lips.

"I can't believe I didn't figure this out long before now," whispered April. "I should have known when I saw all of these military vehicles."

"I did think you were a little more perceptive, but we'll let it slip this one time."

"You're really sneaky. I'm blaming my inability to figure this out ahead of time on jet lag and being overworked."

Tanya walked down the steps with April right behind her.

"Good afternoon, ladies. My name is Lieutenant Kenneth Mears. Please follow me."

April could see several military personnel watching her and Tanya as they walked the short distance to a black Lincoln Town Car. It made April feel like a dignitary of some sort. Lt. Mears opened the back passenger door, and Tanya let April slide in on the dark leather seat. Lt. Mears closed the door. Tanya followed him to the driver's side, where he offered her the same courtesy. Lt. Mears then sat in the driver's seat, started the car and drove due west. The afternoon sun highlighted a small mountain range in the distance. The road they traveled pointed directly at the mountain. As Lt. Mears accelerated the Lincoln, April couldn't help but peek at the speedometer. The arrow signaled a speed of eighty miles per hour. It didn't feel like they were even going forty miles per hour with the glass smooth road and only desert sand on either side of the car. The mountain range grew larger and larger as they approached. Then Lt. Mears slowed down and stopped at a chain link fence gate. The fence went as far as the eye could see in both directions. The top of the fence was covered with razor wire. It looked to April like it must have been twenty feet tall. From the adjacent guard booth, a military woman in fatigues carrying an M-16 approached the Lincoln. Lt. Mears handed her a paper, which she studied briefly. She looked at him, peered in the lowered window at the two ladies in back, turned and walked back to the booth. Slowly the chain link fence gate in front of them rolled sideways, and Lt. Mears drove through. There were two more identical fences at one hundred foot intervals. The gates had already been opened on these. Lt. Mears drove the remaining mile to a large parking lot at the base of the mountain. April could see a massive steel door built into the side of the mountain. Smaller entry doors were scattered on either side. Lt. Mears brought the car to a halt in front of an entry door numbered fifteen in large one-foot tall numbers. A man and woman dressed in Military Police fatigues stood on either side of the door. Lt. Mears opened the car door for Tanya and then April.

"Please follow me, ladies."

Both of the MPs saluted as the Lieutenant and visitors approached the door.

"At ease," Lt. Mears said. He pulled the papers with the written orders out of his shirt pocket and displayed them to the MPs. Each studied them. April looked around in every direction to see if she could determine where she was. There was nothing but desert and mountains to be seen. An occasional jet blasted through the air, and a helicopter could be heard in the distance. After both MPs reviewed the papers, the one closest to them said, "All clear sir." Then he took a security card the size of a credit card out of his pocket and slid it through a scanner next to the door. There was a buzzing sound as the door unlocked, and the MP pulled the door open to allow them entry.

Lt. Mears led April and Tanya through several doors and corridors. They passed only a few military personnel as they walked. April noticed all of the personnel had red armbands with black MP lettering on them. After several minutes of walking, they stopped at an unmarked door. Lt. Mears reached into his pocket and produced a security card similar to the one used to allow entry into the mountain fortress. He passed it through the scanner bolted on the frame next to the door. Again there was a brief buzzing sound as the door unlocked. Lt. Mears opened the door and stepped through, then held the door open for Tanya and April. They stepped into a ten-by-ten foot room that had solid steel walls and a concrete floor. The light gray walls and matching floor gave the room no personality. One wall was lined with four dull green metal, cushioned chairs. There was nothing else in the room. As the door closed and locked behind them, Lt. Mears stepped up to the next door and ran his security card through that scanner. Again there was a buzzing sound as the door unlocked. This time Lt. Mears held the door open for Tanya and April. As they walked through the door, they saw Lexis and Keegan sitting on additional dull green chairs. They both rose to their feet.

"Good afternoon, ladies," said Keegan. "I trust your flight accommodations were acceptable." Keegan winked at April.

"The flight was very smooth," said April.

Tanya laughed. "However, April really doesn't know, because she slept most of the way here."

"Things a little hectic with the new job, are they?" asked Lexis.

"They are, but I'm enjoying the work. I didn't realize how tired I was though. As soon as the plane lifted off, I was out cold."

"Well, the next few days shouldn't be quite as hectic for you," said Lexis. "Now let's proceed with our business. I think we all know why we're here this afternoon. Lt. Mears, will you do us the honor?"

"I will be glad to, ma'am. Please follow me."

Lt. Mears led them down a short corridor to an elevator. After once again scanning his security card, the door opened and all five of them stepped into the elevator. The elevator had doors on both sides. April looked at the floor designation control panel. The letter G was lit up. Apparently G stood for the ground floor she thought. There were two numbers above the G and four numbers below it. April wondered what the mountain compound was used for and how cavernous it must be. Was it measured in acres or miles?

Lt. Mears took a key out of his pocket and opened a small control box. He slid his security card through yet one more scanner, punched in a code, hit the enter button and shut the control box door. The elevator descended to the bottom floor and stopped. April expected to exit through the door opposite the one they entered, but the same door they had entered opened automatically. Lt. Mears waited as Lexis, Tanya, April and Keegan exited into a large waiting area that extended into what appeared to be offices. The room was much more inviting than the gray room they had just exited. At least the ten chairs and conference table were made of wood, and the floor was carpeted. There were half a dozen office dividers, most likely with desks or workstations behind them. Banks of file cabinets were scattered throughout the room. On one wall were two massive bookcases lined with well used books. April walked over to them and glanced at the titles. Most were biology, history and geography books. Some of them appeared to be very old and had faded leather covers. Suddenly, a short, thin man with silver wire-rimmed glasses popped out from one of the cubicles. His full head of solid white hair, which was slightly askew, the wrinkles at the corners of his eyes, and white lab coat gave the impression he was a scholar or professor.

"Good evening, Lexis. Good evening Tanya. I see we have a couple of new faces here."

"This is April James and Keegan McGrath," said Lexis.

"Hello, April and Keegan. My name is Charlie Mantz."

Charlie took a quick glance at April. "April James. They told me you were coming. You do have your father's facial features. Vincent was a fun guy to work with. I'm sorry about your loss."

"Thank you, Charlie. I appreciate your sympathy. Dad passed away over a year ago now, so I've moved on with my life. You know he wouldn't have wanted me grieving for a long period of time."

"I'm glad to hear everything is okay with you. How is Midge doing?"

"She's doing fine as well. It's a full time job for her trying to keep track of me."

Charlie laughed. "I believe your father mentioned that trait about you, but he wouldn't have changed it for the world. I have to say I'm glad to see you are now part of the Thornburg Genetics team. So, April and Keegan, are you ready for the most important and thrilling event of your life?"

"I already have goose bumps on my arms," said April.

"This has to be the neatest thing ever," said Keegan. "I just can't believe this library has been here all the time I've been employed in the Thornburg Genetics security department, and I never found out about it."

"Sometimes secrecy actually works," said Lexis.

"What other secrets are you harboring?" asked Keegan.

Lexis just looked at Keegan, smiled, batted her eyes a few times, and said, "None, of course."

"You know Lexis and I are ready for another library tour," said Tanya. "We never miss this opportunity."

"First, let me give you a brief history of The Noah Library. Lexis gave me a copy of the document your father left for you April. Since both you and Keegan have read that document and the information portrayed about The Noah Library is accurate, I won't bore you by repeating it. I do have an update though. At the time Vince viewed the collection we had 3221 tablets. Of those, only one was composed of gold. You will see that tablet plus four additional gold tablets in the special glass showcase in the library. The initial gold tablet had an inscription, which thanked Yahweh for allowing life to remain on earth after the great flood and allowing Noah the honor of passing knowledge on to future generations. The additional four are inscribed in Hebrew with praises to Yahweh for not destroying mankind and praising him for being the God of the universe. These tablets were discovered about five miles from the original Noah Library. We believe there are at least two more, because the number seven is significant as the number of perfection from Noah's time to present day. Why weren't they with the other tablets? Based on historical practices, we believe the Israelites did not want the praises to Yahweh mingled with the other tablets written about common items such as plants and medicines. For them, the word sacred had a death-defying meaning. They had a reverence for God we barely know today. Let me cover a few ground rules. Here is a pair of lint-free cotton gloves with a special rubber grip surface for each of you. Please place these on your hands as soon as I give them to you. You must keep them on as long as you are in The Noah Library. You are welcome to touch, hold, or view any tablet except the five gold tablets. I ask that you place each tablet back in the exact location where you picked it up. I am also going to issue a mask for each of you to cover your face in case of a cough or sneeze. We want to keep the library as pollutant and germ free as possible. Are there any questions?" Charlie glanced at each person in the room.

"Great, follow me for a look at The Noah Library."

Chapter 35

Charlie opened a side door and led the way into a well-lit ten foot by ten foot room composed entirely of dark wood panels. The panels were trimmed with carvings of pomegranates, olive tree branches, doves and palm leaves. April wanted to tell Charlie how beautiful the room was, but she was so awestruck she was unable to speak. It was similar to entering an ornate church sanctuary. The room demanded respect, peace and quiet. It was an intense feeling that was different than any April had ever felt before.

When they were all in the room, Charlie closed the door without making a sound. Carefully he chose his steps to the large, ornate, carved wooden door at the opposite end of the room. His hand flicked a well-camouflaged light switch. Charlie took his time opening the double doors. As the view widened, each of them could see row after row of tablets lined up on glass shelves. The reflective lighting in the room gave a rainbow hew of colors. Charlie could hear the gasps as they stepped into The Noah Library. As they moved about the room, the light reflections changed. First the tablets were bathed in a gunmetal blue color, the next moment it was a cadmium orange color. The lighting made the tablet inscriptions intense.

Charlie laughed out loud. "You are welcome to talk in this library."

April found an intriguing silver tablet with an engraved plant on it. She lifted it slowly and placed it in her left hand, admiring the beauty of the engraving. The engraver made the palm leaves look as though they were alive. She looked at the inscription but had no idea what it said. It was probably inscribed in Hebrew or Aramaic. She looked up and saw Keegan with a tablet in his hand as well. He was about ten feet from her in the same row of tablets. He looked up and caught her staring at him. He lifted his mask and gave her a big smile. April smiled back. Keegan placed the tablet back on the shelf and moved further down the row. April placed the tablet she was holding back on the shelf and moved over to the next row. She picked up a clay tablet engraved with hieroglyphics. Then she noticed an alcove to the right. She stepped in and saw the five golden tablets in a showcase. Each tablet was placed against a solid black cloth background. They were flooded with unusual silver-colored lights that accentuated their beauty. The gold tablets almost appeared to project their own light. It was so bright April had to squint. Even though Charlie had told them they could talk, the library was quiet. Each of them was engrossed in the tablets of clay, stone, bronze and silver. April wondered how many visits Lexis and Tanya had already made to The Noah Library.

After an hour Charlie came to each of them and touched them on the shoulder. Without any words spoken, each of them knew it was time to leave the library.

April felt like all of the energy and emotion she had in her body had been extracted. She looked at Keegan, Tanya and Lexis. Their faces looked pale and drained. Then she observed Charlie. Even his countenance was altered from the experience.

After they had been escorted back to Charlie's office, they all sat down. There was silence in the room. They each looked back and forth at each other without saying a word. Then Charlie spoke. "April and Keegan, you will feel like normal again in about fifteen minutes. Lexis and Tanya have been through this before. Everyone who remains in The Noah Library for any length of time departs with the feeling that all of his or her strength has been sapped. It's a type of trance-like state. We don't have any idea why. It may be the historical value of the tablets. It may be we feel a connection with Noah from centuries ago. I personally believe it is a connection with God himself. God ordained the creation of the tablets. The Noah Library is the only place on earth I have ever felt this way."

As April began to revive, she suddenly smelled coffee. Charlie was pouring her a mug full. "Drink this," he said. "The caffeine will help perk you up." April watched as Charlie passed everybody a mug full.

After a few minutes, Charlie said, "I see your father didn't mention the trance-like feeling in the Noah Document. I'm glad he left some element of surprise."

"The whole experience was amazing," said April. "There are no words he could have ever used to describe it."

"It is a unique sensation, isn't it?" said Tanya. "I figured it was a first-time experience that wouldn't happen again, but I feel the same way every time I leave the library."

"I sure wish I could harness that energy flow," said Keegan. "It was unbelievable."

After a few minutes of small talk, they were on their way back to the plane. Lexis had already told them she would not be flying with them. She said goodbye to April, Tanya and Keegan as they walked up the steps and disappeared into the waiting jet. Tanya and April sat in the same seats they arrived in. Keegan chose a seat behind April. The captain spoke over the loudspeaker. "Good evening. We will be departing shortly. Our destination is Quito, Ecuador. The weather forecast indicates we will have clear skies. Our arrival time is 4:30 AM. Please buckle your seat belts and prepare for liftoff."

Chapter 36

The plane arrived in Quito at 4:30 AM as announced by the pilot. Due to the late hour and mesmerizing effects of The Noah Library, there was no conversation during the flight. As they stepped from the plane onto the tarmac, a baggage handler arrived from the terminal.

"Welcome to the lovely city of Quito, Ecuador," he said.

"Thank you," said Tanya. She turned to April and Keegan and said, "Follow me."

April was quite familiar with the terminal. Her job in the Peace Corps had required her to fly in and out of the Quito airport at least six or seven times, and she had also met visitors here on several occasions. She figured she probably knew the airport as well as, if not better than, Tanya; but since this was her first trip to Ecuador under the auspices of Thornburg Genetics, she decided not to mention it. Maybe there were special procedures she didn't know about.

"Have you ever been here before, Keegan?" asked April.

"I have been in this airport a few times. I've tried to memorize as much of it as I can, but I didn't have a lot of time to scope it out. From my experiences in general, you will find traveling arrangements through Thornburg Genetics are very well organized. I can almost guarantee you there will be a Thornburg representative ready to greet us and transport us to a hotel as soon as we clear customs. Everything moves along like clockwork whenever we show up. How many times have you been here?"

"Several times. Ecuador is where I was stationed with the Peace Corps, but you already knew that, didn't you."

"It may have been noted in your background information."

"I hate to think what else is in my background information. Anything good?"

"I can't discuss it. It's top secret."

April looked at Keegan and rolled her eyes.

"What kind of a look was that?"

"That was a, you are a pain in my neck kind of look."

"I'll have to store that one in my memory banks."

Moving like clockwork was an understatement. There was a VIP line that took them swiftly to the passport counter. As soon as their passports were reviewed, they stepped up to the security counter. After declaring they had smuggled no drugs, alcohol, live plants or fruit with them, they were on their way to retrieve their baggage. The same man who had unloaded their baggage at the plane was waiting for them just past the customs counter. Security personnel didn't even look through their baggage, but waived them through.

Keegan looked at April, shrugged his shoulders and raised his eyebrows as if to say, I told you so. April smiled and looked at her watch. It took exactly eighteen minutes from the time they left the plane to the time they passed through security and customs.

"You were right, Keegan. That was fast."

Tanya walked over to a gentleman who was waiting just beyond the security checkpoints. April and Keegan followed her.

"April and Keegan, I would like you to meet Sebastian. He is one of my friends and colleagues at Thornburg Genetics here in Ecuador," said Tanya.

"I'm pleased to meet you, April," he said as he shook April's hand gently and gave her a quick kiss on the cheek.

"Me alegro encontrarme con vosotros," said April.

"Thank you," said Sebastian.

"I am pleased to meet you, Keegan," he said as he briskly shook Keegan's hand. "The three of you must be tired. Let's get you to your hotel room." Sebastian led them out the front terminal door and opened the back passenger-side door of a Mercedes parked just outside.

"Señorita April, if you please." April slid in and Sebastian closed the door. He then opened the passenger side front door for Tanya. Keegan opened the driver's side rear door. April and Keegan both smiled at each other as he slid into his seat. The baggage handler stood patiently near the trunk of the Mercedes waiting for the guests to get comfortable. Then Sebastian opened the trunk, and the baggage handler proceeded to load the luggage. After giving him a tip, Sebastian jumped in the drivers' seat and sped away from the terminal.

April's thoughts drifted back through time. When she worked for the Peace Corps, it took anywhere from forty-five minutes to an hour and a half to get through customs. Her suitcases were always searched and sometimes left in shambles. Her main goal then was to help villages in need of food, medical supplies, clean water and other life improving necessities. Marching through customs in eighteen minutes and traveling in a Mercedes was like a dream. Just over a year ago travel from the airport would have been in a crowded bus, and she would have been carting her own luggage. The inequality just didn't seem fair. April knew she must never get to the point where VIP treatment was expected. No, a better word was demanded. I love the Ecuadorian people she thought to herself. I have to keep the Thornburg Vision of Hope Charity in mind and concentrate on helping those I can through the charity and my job.

The Thornburg Vision of Hope Charity was the name created by April and Jason after several sessions haggling over a proper name for the new, approved charity. April thought about Jason and the fun they'd had swapping words in and out of the title to arrive at the final name.

April felt a nudge. Keegan was looking at her. "Sebastian asked you a question," he said quietly.

"I'm sorry," April said. "I was deep in thought, and I'm a little tired. Could you repeat the question?"

"Yes, Tanya said that you used to work in Ecuador through the Peace Corps. Will you tell me more about that?"

"I will be glad to. It was a great time in my life. For three years I called the village of Alshi my home. I helped many of the small adjacent villages improve their agriculture practices, including better soil fertilization, soil erosion protection, and increased production of coffee, cacao, papaya and banana crops. I also helped them improve their product marketing, so they could obtain the highest price possible for their labors. We worked many hours creating clean water supplies and arranging for improved medical treatment in the villages."

April wasn't sure how well the idea of improved crop marketing would go over. Oftentimes there were middlemen who didn't care how much money the growers made as long as they grew the next year's crop. Sometimes the middlemen even loaned money to the growers just to get them started for another growing season. Of course, this left the growers indebted to the buyers. April helped the growers form a type of agricultural cooperative, and her life had been threatened several times because of it.

"I also spent a lot of time in the jungles with the Shuar."

"I would like to thank you personally for all of your work, Señorita James. Even with our good intentions, oftentimes we are not so good at helping our own countrymen."

April wasn't sure what to say. She didn't know if Sebastian was legitimately thankful or if this was a formality. He seemed sincere enough, so she responded with a simple thank you. The conversation ended as they pulled in the main driveway and stopped in front of the Hotel La Casa Sol. April was amazed at the beauty of the hotel with the spotlights reflecting off its entryway. She couldn't wait to see what it looked like in the daylight. She had heard of the La Casa Sol when she worked with the Peace Corps but had never been to the hotel in person. A nicely dressed gentleman was already waiting at the front passenger door. He opened the door for Tanya, then April. Keegan had already let himself out and was surveying the property. Sebastian popped the trunk from inside the Mercedes, and the gentleman unloaded the luggage, placed it on a carrier and pushed it into the front lobby.

"Thank you, Sebastian," said Tanya.

"You are welcome, Mrs. Jefferson. It was good to meet you, April and Keegan."

"Thank you. It was good to meet you as well," said April.

"Yes, it was good to meet you," said Keegan.

With all of the formalities over, Sebastian drove out of the driveway into the sparse traffic.

April and Keegan followed Tanya to the front desk. It turned out the front desk manager was the same gentleman who unloaded their luggage from the car. After checking in, the desk manager pushed the cart with the luggage to the bottom of the lobby steps. There were two floors at the Hotel La Casa Sol, and they were staying on the second floor.

There was no elevator and April and Tanya followed the desk manager up the steps. The desk manager had luggage in both hands. Keegan waited at the bottom of the steps and watched the luggage on the cart while the desk manager made a second trip and finally followed him up the stairs on the third and last trip. Keegan would have preferred to carry his own luggage, but he didn't want to insult the hard working desk manager. Tanya had reserved three rooms adjacent to each other. The desk manager waited as each of the three guests pointed out the room where their luggage was to be placed. Tanya gave him a tip. He smiled, said thank you, and disappeared down the steps.

"I'm exhausted, and it's after 5:00 AM," said Tanya. "Why don't we meet for a late breakfast or lunch in the café at noon? That should give us plenty of time for your presentation at 2 PM, April."

"That sounds good to me."

"I will work around both of your schedules," said Keegan. "Just keep me posted."

They said goodnight to each other, and Tanya and April went into their rooms. Keegan stayed in the hallway. He could hear their doors being locked. Keegan waited to make sure nobody else was around, and then he tapped on April's door. April looked through the security bubble and could see Keegan standing there.

"Who is it?" she asked.

"'Tis Keegan McGrath," he whispered, mimicking her voice.

She opened the door. "What did you do, forget your toothbrush or something?" April said with a smirk on her face.

"That's funny, but no. In fact, I am about to demand a security switch."

"What does that mean?"

"The desk manager knows you are in this room and I am next door. For security reasons, I want you to swap rooms with me."

"I don't suppose arguing will do any good. The bags are very heavy, and I don't want to break a nail. You wouldn't mind moving them next door for me, would you?" April asked as she batted her eyelids at Keegan.

"I can see everything with you is going to be difficult, isn't it."

"I'm just trying to be realistic, Mr. Security."

"I have an idea you could haul these bags twenty miles if you had to, but since I want to get some sleep tonight, I'm hauling your bags next door at this very moment. Would your highness like me to carry you as well?"

"I don't think that will be necessary, but thanks for the offer."

"You are something, April James."

April performed her nightly shower, tooth brushing and hair routine in record time, slid into her pajamas, pulled back the covers and hopped into bed. She set her travel alarm clock for 11:30 AM, shut the lights off and fell asleep.

Chapter 37

When the alarm sounded the next morning, April felt refreshed. Tanya and Keegan perked up after a hearty breakfast and a strong cup of coffee in the hotel café. Her afternoon presentation to the Thornburg Genetics Ecuadorian Marketing and Management team was flawless. After the presentation she received numerous compliments about her Body-New Pharmaceutical brand name recognition idea and implementation procedures. She was introduced to several of the Thornburg Genetics employees she would be working with.

The next evening, April gave a speech and presentation portraying the Thornburg Vision of Hope Charity. It took place in the small auditorium at the Thornburg Genetics facility and was by invitation only due to limited seating. A reception was held afterward at a restaurant adjacent to the facility. At the reception, she saw a familiar face while she was talking with a group of businessmen and women. She excused herself, ran the few steps to Miguel with open arms, and they embraced. Miguel kissed April on the cheek. April stepped back and looked Miguel in the eyes.

"How are you, Miguel?"

"I am fine, Señorita James."

"What brings you here tonight? I didn't expect to see anyone I knew."

"As you know, I too am interested in helping my fellow Ecuadorians achieve higher standards of living. My main interest is in the field of health. I wanted to attend college and become a pharmacist but just couldn't afford the curriculum price. Instead, I am obtaining a degree in health, nutrition and education. This way I can at least train some of the villagers close to home to take better care of their own bodies as well as their families. This is my second semester, so I have a long way to go. Sometimes I volunteer at the local hospital. I saw a notice posted on the bulletin board there that said April James, from the USA Thornburg Genetics Company, would be giving a speech at a fundraiser to promote a new charity. It said the charity was designed to benefit underprivileged towns and villages throughout the entire world by distributing medical supplies and providing health education. I only know one April James, and your last letter to our village stated that you had a job with Thornburg Genetics. I knew it had to be you. I'm sorry I couldn't dress better, but these are the best clothes I have."

"Don't be silly, Miguel. You look fine. I'm so glad to see you again!" April gave Miguel another hug. "I'm glad to know you are attending school for such a worthy cause. I think this is right for you. You've always had such a tender heart."

"Thank you, Señorita James. I appreciate the encouragement. I must be honest though. My visit tonight is twofold. There is another matter I must bring to your attention, but it must be in private."

"What is it, Miguel?"

"It must wait until I can talk with you alone, Señorita James."

"I don't like the look I see on your face, Miguel."

"It is not good news."

"Well, I'm sure this function will last well into the night. I am staying in a hotel not too far from here. Could we meet for breakfast?"

"I have class from eight to ten in the morning. I could meet you after that."

"If I have any meetings, I'll reschedule them."

"Which hotel are you staying in?"

April looked in her purse and found the business card with the hotel information on it and handed it to Miguel. "Do you know where the Hotel La Casa Sol is located?"

"Si, Señorita James. I can be there in a very short time after class."

"Why don't I meet you at twenty minutes after ten in the hotel lobby? Do you need some money?"

"No. That is not necessary, but thanks for asking. I am going to leave now, but I will see you tomorrow morning."

"I would consider it an honor if you will let me buy you breakfast tomorrow morning."

"If you insist, Señorita James."

"I'm so glad you came tonight, Miguel. Tell everybody hello."

"I will, and it is good to see you again. Goodbye until tomorrow."

Miguel turned and walked into the crowd. He had barely disappeared when two couples cornered April to discuss how they could be involved in the Thornburg Vision of Hope Charity. This was the part April hated the most. She knew many of the people that attended events like this all over the world had lots of money and viewed this as an opportunity to flaunt it. Others attended with a hidden agenda in mind, probably political, or because any contribution would be a nice tax write off. It was hard to sort out the people with genuine feelings for those in need. She sure would like to see some of them spend a few weeks in the Peace Corps. They would view the world in a different way after a stint in a foreign country. They probably tripped over some homeless person just to get in the door tonight, she thought to herself. Then she caught herself and knew she had to have a more positive outlook. The main objective of the charity was to help underprivileged people. Finances were needed to accomplish this. Did any preconceived notions beyond that really matter?

It was almost midnight. Most of the crowd had dispersed, yet April knew many of them would converge in the bar area and socialize into the early hours of the morning. She looked around to see if she could spot Tanya or Keegan.

"Good evening, Miss James."

April turned and there was Keegan. "I was just looking for you."

"I know you were. That's why I came over."

"What do you mean, you know?"

"Haven't you ever taken the time to study faces? Faces are a wealth of information. Sometimes they say more than even I want to know."

"What is my face saying at this moment, Mr. McGrath?"

"Right now it's saying, 'I'm standing here chatting with a handsome man. Where has he been all of my life?' A few seconds ago your face was saying, 'Help me, I'm sick of mingling with the upper class, my feet hurt, and I would rather be anyplace but here.'"

"Your 'I need help' analysis is right on, but the 'handsome man' analysis is way off base."

"Hmmm, maybe I need a refresher course in analyzing case specific people."

"For some reason I don't think that's necessary. What about Tanya, where is she?"

"Tanya left about two hours ago. She said something about having to work tomorrow."

"Very funny."

"Maybe you can tell me a little more about Miguel on our way back to the hotel."

"What do you know about Miguel?"

"Nothing really. I just observed the reunion you had with him. I knew you would fill me in with all the details later. It's important security information, of course."

"I know. Everything is about security now, isn't it?"

Keegan looked at her and nodded his head up and down. "Shall we go? Sebastian will give us a ride back to the hotel."

After arriving back at the hotel, Keegan asked April what the game plan was for the next day.

"Tanya was gracious enough to let me sleep in. She thought I would be exhausted, and she was right. I can hardly function. I'm supposed to meet Miguel at ten twenty tomorrow morning for breakfast at the hotel. He will be attending college classes from eight until ten. He said he had some bad news and wanted to meet me in private."

"How do you know Miguel?"

"He was a teenager in a village I was helping through the Peace Corps. I've known him for four years now. He is a very thoughtful, caring young man. Anyhow, he's coming here after his class in the morning. I offered to buy him breakfast. I am guessing he is barely scraping by financially and probably doesn't get very much to eat. Would you like to join us?"

"Are you sure I won't be interfering?"

"Not at all."

"In that case, I accept, Señorita James."

"Now, Señor McGrath, no more questions. I have got to get some sleep."

Keegan said goodnight to April at her hotel room door and walked the short distance to his own room, unlocked the door and stepped in. He waited a few minutes for April to get settled in her room. Then he slipped on a jacket, quietly opened his door, stepped back into the hallway and headed for the hotel courtyard.

The courtyard was empty as Keegan strolled to the outdoor steps that led to a veranda. He sat down on the steps and took his cell phone out of his pants pocket. After punching in the telephone number he only had to wait for one ring before he heard a voice on the other end.

"Hello."

"This is Keegan. What did you find for me?"

"I've been waiting for your call, sir. His story checks out. He is a student at Pontifica Universidad Catolica del Ecuador. He is twenty years old. His hometown is a place called Alshi. He has no arrests on record and appears to be squeaky clean."

"He will be arriving here in the morning. Keep the tail on him until his arrival, then discontinue."

"Ten-four, boss."

With that the telephone clicked dead. Keegan liked telephone calls that were short, sweet and to the point. He felt a little more at ease after being briefed on Miguel's background check knowing Miguel was going to arrive with bad news for April the next morning.

Chapter 38

It was 10:00 AM. Keegan was sipping his first cup of coffee and thumbing through the newspaper. USA today was the only newspaper written in English he could find at the hotel. He could speak and understand most spoken Spanish, but making sense out of written Spanish was time consuming. He looked up and saw April bouncing towards his table. She was a gorgeous young lady. He liked the shine of her slightly damp, straight brown hair. Sometimes he had to remind himself his role was security and he was not on a date. He knew she was seeing a coworker named Jason. Sometimes things just don't work out he thought. Even if he pursued a relationship, he was on the go so much it probably wouldn't work out. However, the hope and dream of finding such a wonderful young lady to share his life with couldn't be passed up. What was life without dreams?

"Good morning, Keegan. I thought I might find you here. How do you like the real Ecuadorian coffee?"

"To be truthful, you just never know how strong they are going to serve it. I must be at about half coffee and half cream at this point. Must be you slept well. You have quite a bounce in your step, and last night you were barely dragging your feet across the floor."

"I feel great. I feel on top of the world this morning."

"I slept until 9:00 myself. I can't remember the last time that happened."

April stared at Keegan. "Some security guy you are. You left me to fend for myself while you slept. What if someone had abducted me? You probably slept so late because you're getting old." April laughed and Keegan could see a teasing twinkle in her eye.

"That's very funny, Miss James. Maybe your shenanigans have driven me to the point of exhaustion."

"Somehow I find that hard to believe."

"Would you like a cup of coffee while we wait for your friend Miguel?"

"Please."

"I can't wait to see what a little caffeine does to you," he said as he motioned to the waiter.

The waiter automatically picked up the coffee pot and walked to the table. "Señorita, would you like coffee this morning?"

"Yes, please."

"More coffee for you sir?"

"That would be great. Thank you."

As the waiter was leaving, Keegan saw Miguel enter the cafe area. "Your friend is here, April."

April turned and looked. There were only a few people in the cafe at this hour. Miguel spotted April and then glanced at Keegan. He hesitated before starting to walk towards the table.

"I don't think he was expecting a third wheel," said Keegan.

"He'll be fine once you're introduced."

Miguel approached the table with caution.

"Good morning, Miguel."

"Good morning, Señorita James."

"I want you to meet Mr. Keegan McGrath. Keegan is a coworker of mine."

"I am glad to meet you, Señor McGrath."

"I'm glad to meet you too," Keegan said as he stood up and stuck his hand out in Miguel's direction. Miguel shook hands with him.

"Here, Miguel, sit next to me," said April.

"Thank you, Señorita."

"Did your class go well this morning?"

"It did go well. I learn more and more about things I must share with the people in my village. Today we learned several advanced first aid and CPR techniques."

"That's great. Do you like the studies?"

"More than I can say."

"I expect you'll be a mayor someday soon."

"That's very flattering, but I'm not so sure about that," Miguel said with a snicker.

"Let's get something to eat. I want you to get whatever you would like. My company will be honored to pay for it."

"Thank you very much, Señorita. I am rather hungry today. I shall repay your hospitality sometime in the future."

The waiter poured Miguel a cup of coffee and took the order for their meals. Keegan couldn't help but wince as he watched Miguel drink his coffee black.

"While we are waiting, why don't you tell me the bad news, Miguel?" Miguel glanced at Keegan and then back at April. "It's okay. Keegan is a close friend of mine. I asked him to come with me this morning."

"Very well." Miguel paused and tears formed in his eyes. "Señor Quinonez is very sick. He went to the hospital here in Quito one month ago and was told he had cancer. He is not well. The doctors told him he would live for six months at most."

Keegan looked at April's face. What ten minutes ago was a bubbly, vivacious April was now an April with a look of pain and shock.

"He is only forty-eight years old. Are they treating him with chemo or radiation?"

"As you know, our village does not have much money. We do not have enough money for expensive cancer treatments."

"Where is he now?"

"He is staying with a relative here in the city. I don't like to ask this question, Señorita James, but is there any way your charity can help Señor Quinonez?"

"I have to go see him. How far away is he if we take a cab?"

"His relative lives in an apartment between here and the airport. It is only about ten minutes from here."

"I will need a copy of his medical records."

"He has a folder with all of his medical information."

"Why didn't somebody write and tell me about this?"

"We knew you had a new job, and we didn't want to burden you. Señor Quinonez said that things would work out according to God's plan. That's what you used to tell us all of the time."

"Yes, I know, Miguel."

The waiter arrived with the meals and distributed them as ordered. He filled each coffee cup to the brim. "Is there anything else I can get for you?"

"Not now, thank you," said Keegan.

"Let's eat our meals before we go see Señor Quinonez," said April.

April wasn't at all hungry after hearing the report on Señor Quinonez. She tried her best to concentrate on eating, knowing that Miguel would not want her to be upset. April looked at Keegan. He saw her looking and shot a smile at her. He certainly had not lost his appetite. He was taking large strides at clearing the food from his plate. Miguel, on the other hand, appeared to be savoring each bite and was taking his time. There was little talk and only the clang of silverware and coffee cups as they ate.

"That was a fine meal," said Miguel as he cleared the last morsel of food from his plate.

"It was excellent," said April.

"Indeed it was," chimed in Keegan.

"Miguel, I want to go see Señor Quinonez right now. Does your schedule allow you time to go?"

"Si, Señorita. I have another class at two."

"I would like Keegan to go with us."

"A friend of yours is a friend of mine and is always welcome."

"Thank you, Miguel. I was supposed to be back at the Thornburg office at noon, Keegan."

"Let me make a telephone call for you and let them know you may be late. Did you have any specific appointments?"

"Not that Tanya told me about."

"I'll go make a call now and meet you in the lobby."

"Thanks, Keegan. I'll talk to the waiter and have him put our meal on the hotel tab, then be right out. Miguel, would you write down the address for me on this sheet of notepaper and the address where you are staying as well in case we get separated?"

"Si, Señorita, I will do that right now."

In less than ten minutes, April and Miguel met Keegan in the lobby.

"I called Tanya and briefly explained the situation," said Keegan. "Whatever time you arrive at Thornburg is fine."

"Thank you, Keegan. I appreciate it."

"You know I will do anything I can to help you out."

"Let's go catch a cab," said April. She negotiated a price of twelve dollars for the three of them to travel to the apartment where Señor Quinonez was staying. April gave the address to the cab driver as she and Keegan slid in the back seat. Miguel hopped in the front passenger door. Keegan reached out and took hold of April's hand. She could feel shivers rush up her arm and she turned and looked at Keegan.

"Everything will work out," said Keegan. Then he released his grip on her hand, but continued to smile at her.

April considered Keegan to be more of a rough and matter of fact type of guy, and she enjoyed seeing this caring and gentle side of him. She wanted to know more about him, but didn't know how to tell him that.

The cab driver pulled into traffic and headed east.

Chapter 39

In just a few minutes the surroundings went from modern high-rises and office buildings to single family homes on suburban streets. Then these faded into apartment houses and duplexes with narrow streets. There were only a few single-family homes scattered here and there in this neighborhood. The streets were busy. Cars, motorcycles and small trucks jockeyed in and out of traffic, always looking for the next space to squeeze into. Sidewalk vendors were in abundance on major street corners. While the overall cosmetic appearance of the neighborhood was a little run down, it still had a cared for appearance and was kept neat and tidy. National flags were proudly hanging from almost every porch and balcony.

The driver pulled up to the curb in front of a whitewashed, stucco finished apartment building. Two small boys were at either end of a jump rope, flicking it up and down as a young girl in the middle jumped again and again in perfect rhythm. It looked like she could go on forever. Miguel hopped out of the taxi and the three children ran over to greet him.

"Buenos días," said Miguel.

"Bien," the children replied in unison.

Keegan was already out of the car and April watched him scan slowly in every direction. She wondered what he was looking for in particular. She would have to pick his brain sometime to see what his security training and experiences over the years had taught him.

April paid the cab driver and gave him a tip. "Gracias," he said. She stepped out of the cab, closed the door, and watched the cab speed off. It was lost in traffic in a matter of seconds.

Keegan joined April and they watched as Miguel sent the children back to play on the narrow sidewalk.

"Follow me," he said.

They walked up the five steps onto the landing at the front entryway of the apartment building. April could see a basement apartment on both sides of the steps. They walked in the entryway door, passed eight mailboxes on the wall just inside the door and started up the stairs. Eight mailboxes meant eight apartments. April knew Keegan had noticed this. He didn't miss anything.

They followed Miguel to the third floor. The forest green colored door had a number six painted on it in white. Miguel knocked on the door.

"Que est ce?" came a female's voice from inside.

"Es Miguel."

There was a loud clicking sound as the door was unlocked. The door swung open, and a cheery, smiling, round face appeared. As soon as she saw Miguel was not alone, April could see a slight hesitation.

"Hello, Maritza. This is April James and Keegan McGrath. They are friends of mine and Señor Quinonez." Maritza gave each of them a hug.

"Please come een. Carlos ees a very seek man, but he ees holding hees own right now."

Then Señor Quinones appeared through a doorway from a side room. "Señorita James, what are you doing here?"

April ran over and gave Señor Quinonez a gentle hug and kiss on the cheek. She noticed the cane he was holding and how frail he looked. His complexion was gray and ghostlike; nothing like the tan, healthy outdoor look she had seen him with just over a year ago.

"You have lost a lot of weight, Señor Quinonez."

"Yes, I know. It's cancer, Señorita James. You are looking at a dying man. But don't stand there staring at me. Come in and sit at the table. Maritza, will you prepare some coffee please?"

"Si, Carlos."

"Hello, Miguel, how are you this fine day?"

"I am good, Señor Quinonez."

"And how are your classes going?"

"Very well, gracias."

"Who is your friend, April?"

"This is Mr. Keegan McGrath."

"Good morning, Mr. McGrath. Señor Quinonez held out his hand. It is a pleasure to meet you."

They shook hands. "It is an honor to meet you, Señor Quinonez."

"Come, come, have a seat."

"Why didn't someone write to me or call me about your cancer?" asked April. "You knew it would be of interest to me."

"We knew you had just taken a new job and would be very busy. We didn't want to intrude in your life. I thought to myself, this is cancer. The doctors told me I was going to die. What could April do for me except feel sorry for an old man? No, contacting you and getting you all worried was not the right thing to do. Remember what you told us? Things always work out according to God's plan. And look, I prayed to God that I would see you again before I died and here you are. I am ready to meet God."

"But, you aren't an old man. Your village needs you. Why did you pray to see me?"

"I wanted to see you one more time to tell you thank you. Thank you for helping us grow more food. Thank you for showing us that hard work and better care of our livestock pays off with surplus animals. Thank you for helping us with our school and the medicines you brought us. I did not say thank you enough when you were here helping us."

Tears came to April's eyes as she listened. Memories of one person and then another from the village flashed through her mind. Memories of the projects they had worked on together popped up one after another. She didn't realize how much she had missed the village. She felt guilty that she had ignored them since she started working for Thornburg.

"Thank you, Señor Quinonez. We shared a lot of new experiences together, didn't we?"

Maritza served them coffee and a piece of sweet cornbread. April and Carlos talked about all they had been through together. Occasionally Miguel would inject a comment. Keegan just sat back and listened. He was hearing about the real April James for the first time. They all roared with laughter when Señor Quinonez told the story about April's first day in Alshi.

"We were told someone would be coming to help us in our village. Of course, being the proud people we are, we didn't think we needed any help. But important people told us we did. The day arrived, and we waited patiently for the worker to show up from the Peace Corps. Everyone in the village wanted to be there when Señorita April James arrived. We didn't want her to think the village was a mob, and she was on display, so a small greeting committee of ten people was formed. The committee waited on the porch of the village office. The village office was my house porch as I was the mayor. Finally, about noon we could hear a vehicle. It had to be our worker. Then a jeep pulled into view and drove up to my house. The driver got out and introduced himself. He was an Ecuadorian, from Quito, who was hired by the Peace Corps to drive a young lady to our village. The young lady, Señorita April James, was in the jeep looking at us. She looked around the village and then back at us. The driver told April this was Alshi and invited her to come meet some of the people. We had stepped off the porch by now. She jumped out of the jeep and introduced herself to us. Her Spanish wasn't too good and our English was even worse. So, here's this scrawny little girl with a giant smile holding her hand out to shake ours. We looked at her hands. We didn't say anything directly to her, but later that day we were all laughing amongst ourselves. Her little hands were so smooth and dainty, and our hands were big and calloused. How was this little girl going to help us? We decided someone was playing a joke on us. At least she did have a strong grip for someone with such little hands."

"The driver unloaded a few bags of luggage and a couple of small trunks, said adios, and drove off. There was April, just standing there and probably thinking; what have I gotten myself into? We were standing there looking at her and thinking, what next? Then it happened. Most of the kids in the village have a great time chasing Nubia. Nubia is the ugliest goat you have ever seen. He is this yellow straw-colored goat with big brown spots scattered across his entire body. The greeting committee and Señorita April watched as ten or twelve kids chased Nubia. Nubia ran back and forth in the street and then in our direction. He ran right up to April and stopped. All eyes were on April and Nubia. April stood there like a statue, looking down at the goat. The children had stopped just a few feet away. There was silence in the whole village. Nubia took two big sniffs of April and looked up. Their eyes met for a moment. Then smack. Nubia butted April with his horns. April was on her back looking up from the ground. Nubia gave one blat and ran off as the kids all gathered around April. April was still on her back on the dusty ground, gasping for breath. We asked her if she was okay. Then she started to laugh. She laughed and laughed, so we laughed too. Then one of the small boys went over to her and held out his hand to help her up. Did April let him help pull her up? No, she took hold of his hand, pulled him down on top of her and started tickling him. The next thing you know here's all of the kids and April rolling around in the dust and dirt trying to tickle each other. After a few minutes, April stood up. She tried to dust herself off, but it was useless. Her clothes were dirty, her hair was dirty, and she looked like she had been farming all day. We were all staring at her, and she raised both hands high in the air and hollered, 'I'm here.' By now the whole village had gathered. Everyone laughed and gave her a hug and a kiss on the cheek. At that very moment, we knew she would be a part of us and would help us."

Keegan was still laughing when he said, "You were bested by a goat. I didn't see that on your resume."

"Don't you tell one person, Keegan or you're in big trouble."

"But that whole story was hilarious. I'm sure that hundreds would love to hear a story like that."

"I'm warning you, Keegan. Don't do it! Though I have to say, the experience gave me a lasting impression. I'll never forget looking up from my back at that clear blue sky and saying to myself, these people must think I'm one big loser. A goat that's running away from four year olds knocked me down. It can only get better from here."

Then there was silence as April started crying.

"What is the matter, April?" asked Carlos.

"I'm thinking happy thoughts about the village I spent so much time in, but I'm thinking sad thoughts about your illness."

"Don't cry for me, April. My prayer to see you again before I died was answered."

"Miguel said that you have papers from the doctor and hospital. Would you allow me to see them?"

"Of course, Señorita James. Let me get them for you." Carlos ambled off with his cane to retrieve the papers.

"He is very sick," said Miguel. "Can you help him, April?"

"I don't know, Miguel. I will do all I can."

Carlos came back to the table with a few well-worn sheets of paper in his hand and held them out to April. "This is the diagnosis and recommended treatment."

April looked the papers over briefly. "May I take these with me? I will make a copy and have them returned to you."

"Si, Señorita James. You may keep them. They will be of no use to me."

"Please don't say that, Señor Quinonez. You must stay positive."

"I am a dying man, April. I understand reality."

"I haven't even asked how your wife and children are handling this."

"They are doing well. We have talked everything over. Thanks to your help in the village my family will be fine after I am gone."

"I have to go now, Señor Quinonez. I am so glad to see you again. I am going to do all I can to help you."

"Thank you Señorita James. You have already done so much for my family, our village, and me. I am glad I have this opportunity to see you and tell you thank you."

Miguel and Keegan shook hands with Carlos and said goodbye. April gave him a hug and kiss. They left the apartment and walked back out onto the sidewalk. A bright yellow cab responded to Miguel's gesture, and the driver eased the three of them into traffic for their return trip.

Chapter 40

It was almost one o'clock when April, Keegan and Miguel arrived back at the hotel. Miguel excused himself and said he wanted to get back to college for his two o'clock class. April wrote down his address and told him she would be in touch soon. She gave Miguel a big hug and thanked him for finding her and telling her how sick Señor Quinonez was. Miguel again thanked April for breakfast and then headed back to class.

"What do you think about lunch?" asked Keegan.

"After this morning's events, I'm really not hungry. I think I'll head up to my room and change. I need to get to Thornburg Genetics and meet more of the employees I will be working with. Why don't you go get something to eat and we can meet here in the lobby in twenty minutes. Will that be okay?"

"That works for me. I am at your service, as always. Twenty minutes it is."

April walked to the door leading to the hotel stairway and walked up the steps to the second floor. Her eyes started tearing as she thought about Carlos Quinonez, his family, and the village of Alshi. She knew things wouldn't be the same after his death. As soon as April walked into her room, she started crying uncontrollably. It wasn't fair. Why should a man as nice as Carlos be facing death? He was only forty-eight, which was too young to die. The world needed more people like him to be a better place.

April said a short prayer. "God, I know I don't pray as often as I should. When I do pray, it's often because I want something. I pray now for the life of Señor Carlos Quinonez. You are the great healer, Lord. Please heal him. If not for my sake, please heal him for the sake of his family and village. I pray this in Jesus' name, amen."

April slipped her clothes off and headed for the shower. She was able to stop crying and pulled herself back from her moment of uncontrolled emotions to prepare for her job. This was not how she had planned to spend her time in Ecuador.

April walked down the hotel steps to the first floor. She saw Keegan seated in an overstuffed chair where he could observe both the steps and street through the hotel window. He smiled at April and stood up as she approached. He could detect some remnants of redness in her eyes and knew she had been crying.

"This is hard for you, isn't it, April?"

April just nodded her head up and down.

"Is there anything I can do?"

"Maybe, let's talk on the sidewalk."

Keegan followed April out the front door and onto the sidewalk. There was a small café just up the street, with colorful tables and chairs arranged on the sidewalk. April chose the most secluded table, pulled out the bright orange colored chair and sat down. Keegan followed suit and sat directly across from her. A waiter appeared immediately. It was after lunchtime and most of the seats were empty.

"How may I help you?"

"One large coffee to go, with cream please."

"Si, señorita."

"How much coffee do you drink every day?" asked Keegan.

"Usually I drink a cup or two. Today I'm drinking more because my nerves are a wreck."

April looked at Keegan and leaned forward. She placed her elbows on the table and cupped her hands around her mouth. Keegan leaned forward. April whispered to Keegan, "This is what I have to do. I don't know enough specifics about cancer and the cancer drug treatments being produced by Thornburg. We both know about the miracle drugs that have never been released to the general public. I have the doctor's diagnosis with me. When we get to the Thornburg building, I have to call Lexis. I have to ask her if I can fax this diagnosis to someone who can determine if those drugs can be used to treat and save Señor Quinonez. If the Blue Mule healed my father, I believe it can heal Carlos too."

"Oh boy, this is going to get complicated," Keegan whispered back. "What do you want me to do? I know even less about this situation than you do."

"You're Lexis' right hand man. You can talk her into releasing the medication I need for Señor Quinonez. She'll listen to you."

"I don't know how much help I can be, April. My job is security. This whole scenario may be a conflict of interest."

"Please, Keegan. You've got to help me."

"I can't say yes or no right now. The first thing you have to do..."

April interrupted. "You mean WE have to do, right?"

"The first thing we have to do is talk with Tanya. This whole situation will have to be worked out one step at a time."

April and Keegan waited in silence until their coffee arrived. Keegan knew April's brain was working at fast forward speed. When the coffee arrived, April paid the waiter, left a tip on the table, and they walked to the curb to search for a taxi. It was just a few minutes before two o'clock when April and Keegan arrived at Thornburg Genetics, Ecuador. The business was housed in a three-story building and took up one small city block. This location was the main headquarters for all of the Thornburg Genetics operations in South America. A noted feature of the property was its immense, well-manicured front garden. Roses and lilies thrived in the fifty plus degree weather and were all in bloom. The rose bushes looked like cascading waterfalls of color. April had seen pictures of the garden, but was taken aback by its true beauty.

"This is too beautiful for words," said April as she paused to enjoy a trellis full of bright red roses. "I could spend a whole afternoon just meditating here in this garden. It's unfortunate that reality has arrived. I have to get to work."

"It is an extraordinary garden, isn't it?"

As they reached the front door April said, "I guess you'll have to lead the way, Keegan, since my first visit to this building was only yesterday."

"Don't tell me. The first stop is to see Tanya."

"That is correct."

"She is most apt to be four doors down on the left, Miss James."

The fourth door was open when April and Keegan arrived. There was Tanya with papers and a laptop spread out on a small conference table.

"Good afternoon," said Tanya. "Come in and have a seat. How is everything going, April? Keegan gave me a brief synopsis this morning about a friend of yours that has taken ill. How is he?"

"To be truthful, he has cancer and is not expected to live much longer. He is a man I worked with from day one through the Peace Corps. I feel so sorry for his family, his village and him. He's only in his late forties. I would like to ask you some serious questions Tanya. Is there a secure room we can talk in at this Thornburg location?"

April could see the look on Tanya's face change from the usual self-confident look to 'oh no, what now.'

"You know, April; I used to love my dull boring life. I came to work, talked about pharmaceuticals, and went home. Day after day, year after year, it was the same routine. I liked my life that way. Then, along comes April James. April James, the hiker and shooter who makes every day an adventure. You're killing me, April. I never know what will be next. Please don't force me to take my own medications."

"You know," said Keegan, "I have a couple of security issues to tend to. Just page me if you need me for anything."

"I don't think so," said Tanya. "I have an idea you're in the thick of this, Mr. Keegan McGrath."

"I can't believe you are insinuating such a thing, Mrs. Jefferson."

"Well, I am, Mr. McGrath."

Tanya rose from her chair. "Follow me. I already have a good idea where this situation is going."

April and Keegan followed Tanya to a nearby stairway. They went down one flight of steps to the basement. Tanya led them down the hallway, stopped at a room that had a placard stating 'command center', took the keys she had been carrying in her hand, and unlocked the door. She held the door open as April and Keegan walked inside and then closed it. April looked around the room. There was a conference table with twenty chairs. In the middle of the table were ten telephones. The far corner of the room housed a large bookcase with numerous office supplies. There were pads, pens, pencils, markers, file folders and numerous other items. It looked like a small office supply store.

"What is this room used for?" asked April.

"Right now this is a secure room for discussions," said Tanya.

April knew this was the only answer she was going to get at the moment.

"Have a seat anywhere. I have to make a telephone call." Tanya picked up the headset of the nearest telephone and spoke into the mouthpiece. "Hello, this is Tanya Jefferson. I am in the basement command center. Is this room secured and may I have a secure telephone line please? Thank you. Okay, April, we're secure."

"I'll try to make this brief. I have a friend here in Ecuador whose name is Señor Carlos Quinonez. At the charity reception on Tuesday, another friend of mine, Miguel, was in attendance. He told me he had some bad news for me. I found out the bad news this morning. Señor Quinonez has cancer. That is why I went to see him immediately. He gave me a copy of his medical records showing his diagnosis and recommended treatments."

"I already know where this discussion is going, April. You want Thornburg Genetics' experimental cancer medication, don't you?"

"Yes, for Señor Quinonez."

"It's a decision I can't make. I have a secure line set up, and I'll dial Lexis' number. Only The Keeper can make a decision like this." Tanya picked up the telephone again and dialed a number. There was a pause, and then finally, "Hello Lexis, this is Tanya. How are you today?"

"I'm fine, Tanya. The weather is sunny and nice. The work today is great. You're not going to change all of that, are you?"

"I wouldn't dream of it, Lexis. Let me put you on speakerphone. Sitting here with me in the Ecuador command center is one Miss April James and one Mr. Keegan McGrath."

"April and Keegan. Those names sound familiar. To what do I owe the honor of speaking with you today?"

"Go ahead, April. It's all yours," said Tanya.

"Well, I'll try to make this brief. As you know, before I came to work for Thornburg Genetics, I was involved in the Peace Corps. I spent three years in Ecuador in the village of Alshi. The mayor of the village is Señor Carlos Quinonez. On Tuesday night at the charity reception, I was approached by a friend of mine from the village whose name is Miguel. We met for breakfast this morning, and he told me Señor Quinonez is very sick. He is staying at a relative's house here in Quito. Keegan and I went to visit him this morning. Señor Quinonez has terminal cancer. He is only in his forties and an honorable man. He was like a father to me while I was in Alshi. I have his doctor's diagnosis with me. He cannot afford conventional treatments and is just sitting at his relatives' house waiting to die. I know we have medication that can cure him. He was a father figure to me, and I'm not willing to lose him if it can be avoided. Not yet. Keegan thought it would be a good idea to talk with you." April turned and smiled at Keegan, who had an astonished look on his face. "Will you help me save his life, Lexis?"

There was a pause, and April knew Lexis was thinking about the situation she had just portrayed.

"I understand your feelings, April, and I wish we could save everybody in the world. You know the security issues involved with the drug we are talking about. I can't make a snap decision. I will have to think of all of the ramifications of a yes or no decision. You said you have his diagnosis with you?"

"Yes I do."

"Take a look at the diagnosis and read it to me."

"It says stage III melanoma with a high probability of stage IV melanoma."

"Okay. He has a severe form of skin cancer. What other facts are listed in the description? It should give the location of the cancer and other tests."

"Yes. The location is upper back, shoulder and neck area. There are several spots ranging in diameter from three millimeters to two centimeters in diameter. Biopsy depths are from one millimeter to four millimeters. The doctors conducted a Sentinel Node Biopsy. The cancer has moved into his lymph nodes."

"Is there any mention of cancer in any specific organ?"

"No, but I don't see where any tests of specific organs were completed."

"Okay, and finally I need the name of the physician and medical facility."

"The form says Dr. Emilio Delgado from Quito Cancer Research Center."

"The diagnosis will be correct then. I believe this is a curable cancer with Thornburg Genetics experimental drugs. Scan a copy of the diagnosis and send it to me as an email attachment. I will have to run it by research and then decide if I want this volatile drug out on the streets. You understand I can't get into the habit of taking phone calls every time someone I know has a friend or family member that contracts cancer. Please don't get me wrong April. I don't want to see anyone suffer. I just know how volatile this drug is. It cannot fall into the wrong hands. I will let you know what my decision is. Is there anything else before we say goodbye?"

"That was the reason for my call, Lexis," said Tanya.

"Very well. We'll talk later. Goodbye."

Tanya reached over and pushed the telephone off button.

"What do you think Lexis will do?" asked April.

"I never try to second guess Lexis," said Tanya. "She has a mind of her own, and she reasons in a way I will never fully understand. She is very intuitive and methodical in her thought process and is good at leaving emotions out of the equation."

April looked at Keegan. He just shrugged his shoulders and raised his eyebrows. Some help he was, thought April.

After the telephone call with Lexis, Tanya gave April a full tour of Thornburg Genetics, Ecuador. April met many employees and spent a considerable amount of time with six employees she would be working closely with on a regular basis. The six suggested they go to a restaurant and have dinner together. After the day's activities and bad news about Señor Quinonez, April was exhausted both mentally and physically. However, she did her best to spend quality time with the team of employees. It wasn't until she and Tanya arrived back at the hotel that April realized Keegan wasn't with them. She was so exhausted she didn't bother to ask Tanya where he was. After a quick shower, April barely made it into bed before she fell asleep. The next thing she knew, the alarm was beeping. It was already 6:30 in the morning.

Chapter 41

April left her hotel room at 7:15 and happened to meet Tanya at the top of the stairway. "Good morning, Tanya."

"Good morning, April. Did you sleep well?"

"I slept great. I didn't wake up once last night, and I didn't hear a thing until the alarm went off this morning. How did you sleep?"

"I didn't sleep that well and now I'm starving."

Tanya and April walked into the hotel cafe and sat down.

"Where's Keegan? I haven't seen him since yesterday afternoon," said April.

"I have to be honest with you. I never get involved in his assignments or business. He reports directly to Lexis and receives his assignments from her. He may not even be here in Ecuador. Who knows?"

"Really? Things change that fast for him? Does he ever get a day off?"

"I think he gets blocks of time off here and there. Knowing him, he's probably bored if he does take time off. If he's not here, there is most likely another Thornburg security employee watching us even as we sit here."

"Do you think so?"

"I'm pretty sure."

April looked around at the people in the cafe but couldn't pick out anybody that looked like security. Tanya was watching her.

"Good luck trying to find them. On occasion I see a familiar face, but overall they play their undercover role well."

After breakfast, Tanya and April were picked up by a Thornburg employee and arrived at the Thornburg building just before 8:30.

"I love these gardens," said April as they walked toward the main entrance.

"Aren't they beautiful? They seem to be in bloom year round."

After a morning of intense work, Tanya and April decided to eat a quick lunch at the Thornburg cafeteria. As they were en route, Keegan walked up from behind.

"Good afternoon, ladies. It's a beautiful day in Quito. Did you miss me?"

"Of course we missed you," said April.

Tanya just smiled.

"May I have a word with Miss James in private?" asked Keegan.

"Yes you may. I'll meet you in the cafeteria in a few minutes, Tanya."

"I'll save you a seat."

April walked with Keegan to the front door and out into the garden. A handful of people were seated in various spots enjoying the shrubs and flowers during their lunch break. Keegan led April to a small, secluded area with a bench. "Why don't we sit down?" He looked around to make sure nobody could see them and then whispered to April. "The first of seven C1 Extraction cancer treatment pills was delivered to Señor Quinonez this morning. The medication is actually called Constellation Blue."

"Delivered! I thought Lexis was going to tell me what her decision was."

"She asked me to tell you in person. The medication arrived at the airport very early this morning. I personally have to deliver one pill per day for the full seven-day treatment. Now here is the situation. Obviously, Mr. Keegan McGrath with the bright red hair can't waltz into Maritza's apartment every day without looking rather suspicious. I have to meet Carlos at a different location every day. It will be hard the first couple of days, because he is in tough shape. After that it should get easier every day. Throughout all of this, I want you to remember you are a security risk."

"Do you have to put it that way?"

"Okay. There are security concerns surrounding this operation. How's that?"

"Much better. Is this medication guaranteed to work?"

"I didn't get into that type of discussion. Will you let me finish?" There was a pause of silence. "Due to these security concerns, here are your directions, April. Under no circumstance are you to contact Señor Quinonez during the rest of your stay here. I have already explained this to him, and he understands the situation. He also said he would inform his family and Miguel that they should not contact you. Have you told anybody else about his illness?"

"I did talk with Jason. He knows about Carlos."

"I need you to think real hard and tell me exactly what you told Jason and how he responded."

"Why? Is there a problem with Jason?"

"My job is to trust no one and question everyone. If I had known you were calling Jason, I would have coached you on what topics to discuss or avoid. There is no harm done, and we will work through this matter."

"When Jason and I talked, I told him I was approached by my friend Miguel who told me Señor Quinonez had cancer. I told Jason Señor Quinonez was staying in Quito because of the cancer, and that I went to visit him."

"Did my name come up? Did you say; WE went to see him?"

"No, I told him that Miguel and I went to see him."

"That was good planning."

"I told Jason that Señor Quinonez didn't have enough money for cancer treatment, and I was going to donate some money for pre-scribed chemo, radiation and experimental treatments."

"Did you give him money yet?"

"No. We just saw him yesterday, and I was waiting to see what response Lexis would give me."

"How much money did you plan on giving him?"

"The treatments here would cost about eight thousand dollars. I figured it would total about ten thousand by the time everything was done."

"Did you give Jason an exact amount?"

"I told him the treatments would cost about ten thousand dollars."

"What else did you tell Jason? Think April, it's very important."

"Just how much I love Señor Quinonez and didn't want him to die. The rest is private."

There was silence for a few moments, and April watched Keegan press his lips hard together and wrinkle his eyebrows. She knew his mind was processing the conversation trying to determine what security issues were at stake.

"Okay, April. Here's what we have to do. I am going to arrange an electronic exchange of funds from your bank account to a special Thornburg account. Since the ten thousand dollar figure came up when you talked with Jason, that's what we'll go with. Do you have your bank account number with you?"

"I have it right here in my pocketbook. Let me write it down for you."

"You won't get any of the money back. It will go to the Quito Cancer Research Center. I will make arrangements to have Dr. Delgado administer the treatments. First, I'll have to make sure it doesn't interfere with the Thornburg C1 Extraction treatment we just gave him. Here is my dilemma. Dr. Delgado is a well-known cancer research specialist. What explanation will there be when his terminally ill patient is healed in one week with an experimental drug treatment? His research results will be skewed. We certainly can't reveal the fact he is taking the Constellation Blue medication. I don't like this whole scenario."

"If I tell Jason I paid for cancer treatment and don't see Señor Quinonez again, he'll know something isn't right."

"That's a good point. I guess you will be visiting him again after all. I've got to put more thought into this whole situation. Just don't say anything more to Jason than you have to."

"Not a word more than I have to. I can't anyhow because of the Noah Gene."

"That should be a fact. I guess that concludes our conversation for now. Tanya Is waiting, and I have a lot of work to do. I'll see you later Miss James."

"When?"

Keegan looked at April's face. She was staring at him. She is one beautiful young lady Keegan thought to himself. It's a shame she's seeing Jason on a regular basis. I guess that's my selfishness taking complete control of my body.

"I'm not sure. You have my cell phone number if you need me." Keegan kept looking at April. He couldn't force himself to look away. He knew the question he was about to ask was a bad idea, but... "April."

"Yes, Keegan?"

"Would you like to go out to dinner tonight?"

April didn't hesitate, "I would like that very much, but you seem to be very busy. Do you think it will work out?"

"It should. I'll call you."

"Okay."

April and Keegan both stood up.

"You may not want to mention our potential dinner date to Tanya."

April laughed. "I'm a big girl. I'm not required to report everything I do to Tanya." Then April turned and walked toward the entrance door. Keegan stood in the garden and watched April disappear.

"Wow, I have to be careful. I may be getting too personally involved."

Keegan took his cell phone and dialed a ten-digit number. "Hello. Is this private investigator, Samantha?"

"Keegan, how are you, honey? I haven't talked with you in a while."

"Yes, it has been a while, hasn't it?"

"Indeed. I assume you have an important assignment for me or were you calling for a date?"

"Let me think a minute. Do you still have that fluorescent pink hair?"

"No, I had to dye it black for an undercover bit I was doin."

"Oh darn. Well, I guess it's an assignment then."

"You like my bright pink hair do you, honey? Are you going to offer me some overtime? I can use the money."

"More than likely."

"Well then, tell me whatchya got goin, honey."

"Jason Otis works in the Human Resources Department at Thornburg Genetics in Philadelphia. I'm going to email a picture of him to you. Let's tail him a few days. Keep me posted."

"Any specifics?"

"None in particular."

"That's what you always say. I know you're lying to me."

"General surveillance."

"Honey, if there's a hair out of place, I'll find it. You know I'm the best."

"That's why I called you. Thanks, Samantha."

April met Tanya in the cafeteria. Tanya was seated near the door, reading a medical journal. She looked up as April approached. "I waited for you so we could eat together. I trust your discussion with Keegan went well. Was it a thumbs up or down decision for Señor Quinonez?"

"How did you know that's why he wanted to talk to me?"

"Lexis isn't a procrastinator. It either happens or it doesn't."

"It was thumbs up."

"I'm glad to hear that, April."

After lunch, April called Jason and told him she was having the money transferred from her account to Ecuador. Jason was his usual congenial self.

"How can anyone set a financial value on the life of a friend?" he asked.

"The treatment is experimental, but I pray his life will be spared by utilizing it along with chemo and radiation."

"It's the right thing to do. I'm so glad I have a fiancée like you, April. You are so thoughtful and caring."

If I'm so thoughtful and caring, April thought, how come I can't wait for a chance to go out with Keegan? "Thank you, sweetie," she said.

"When will you be back?"

"It will probably be the middle of next week. I'll let you know as soon as I have a flight itinerary."

"I can't wait to see you again, April. I really miss you."

"I miss you too, Jason. Here's a big hug and kiss. Bye-bye for now."

"Bye, April."

April hung up the phone. She was mad at herself for agreeing to go to dinner with Keegan. She didn't want to admit there was an attraction she just couldn't say no to. What was the attraction? Several other men had asked her out since she started working for Thornburg Genetics. They were handsome men with money and power, but April wasn't interested in any of them. She couldn't say no to Keegan, and she couldn't say no to Jason. She could feel her life getting complicated, but had no idea how to change her feelings.

Within two hours of their discussion, Keegan had ten thousand dollars electronically transferred from April's bank account in Philadelphia to a special Thornburg account in Ecuador. Then he called Lexis and told her about the situation. She contacted one of the level seven Thornburg Genetics research teams and told them that Carlos Quinonez would be receiving experimental drugs from the Quito Cancer Research Center in addition to the Thornburg C1 Extraction drug. The team was familiar with much of Dr. Delgado's research and decided there would be little, if any, side effect if the C1 Extraction and Dr. Delgado's drugs were dispensed at the same time. The chemo and radiation would be the toughest treatments to work through.

Keegan had Carlos set up an appointment with the Quito Cancer Research Center for the following morning. He had the money transferred from April's account to the Research Center. He gave Carlos strict orders not to tell anyone where the money came from or that he was taking the Constellation Blue pills. He explained to Carlos it could lead to security problems for Thornburg Genetics and put April's life in danger. Carlos agreed that no one would be told about the special pills. Then Keegan called April.

"Hi, April. It's Keegan. Can you talk for a minute or are you in the middle of something?"

"I can talk."

"I'm calling you about dinner arrangements for this evening. What would be a good time for you?"

"To be truthful with you, I'm having second thoughts. I feel guilty about going to dinner with you while Jason is home without a clue. He is my fiancé after all."

"What do you mean, fiancé? You aren't wearing a ring."

"Jason surprised me with an engagement ring just before I flew out of Philadelphia."

"I didn't know that. Why aren't you wearing it? Have you told anyone?"

"I haven't told anyone, and I'm not sure why I'm not wearing it. I said yes to his proposal."

"It appears you're not sure if being engaged is the right decision. Maybe you should find out for sure. How about joining me for dinner at six?"

April paused as she tried to decide what to do. She felt a tugging sensation in the bottom of her stomach. What if she liked Keegan more than Jason? Could she ever break off an engagement? The best option would be not to go out with Keegan. The silence on the phone remained. "Forgive me if I seem hesitant. I don't know what to do, Keegan."

"Listen. You have to take some risk in life, and it appears you have some soul searching to do. Maybe a discussion over dinner would help clarify some things. If you feel uneasy at any time, we can call off the rest of the evening. You just say the word."

There was a pause again. "Okay. Let's have dinner at six. Do you know where I'm staying?" April laughed.

"I have a pretty good idea. I think you're still in the hotel room next door to me."

"I'm looking forward to dinner. I'll see you then."

Risk! Maybe that was the calling card that separated Keegan from the others. Keegan was willing to take risks, and April liked certain elements of risk as well. April knew Tanya was having dinner with some of her friends from Thornburg. Tanya had asked April if she would like to go with them, but April had declined. At least this way she wouldn't have to explain anything to Tanya. She hoped Keegan didn't take her to the same restaurant Tanya was going to. That was a risk she was not interested in.

Chapter 42

At six o'clock sharp, April heard the knock on her door. She had taken extra time selecting a black skirt and white blouse that emphasized her figure. The slight amount of mascara and blush highlighted her facial features. She had sprayed a thin mist of cherry blossom perfume on her wrists and rubbed them together. The silver dangly earrings were her favorite, and she was sure Keegan would like them. They matched the necklace which flowed from her neck and accentuated her long brown hair. He had better notice how good I look she thought as she walked to the door in her black heels. She looked through the peephole in the hotel room door. It was Keegan. April opened the door. Keegan was wearing a navy blue sport coat over his light blue shirt with thin white stripes. A dark blue and silver print tie drew color out of his charcoal colored slacks. April stared at Keegan, and Keegan stared at April. Keegan was the first to break the awkward silence.

"You look stunning, April."

"And you look very handsome, Keegan. Did you have any trouble finding my place?"

"No trouble at all. Your directions were perfect. Shall we go?"

"I'm ready."

April picked up her fitted black jacket, stepped through the doorway and took hold of Keegan's arm.

The taxi pulled up in front of La Terraza Del Tartaro restaurant in the business section of Quito. Keegan escorted April inside. They took the glass front elevator to the penthouse level. Keegan told the maître d' his name and they were escorted to a window seat. The restaurant offered a panoramic view of Quito. Keegan knew the sunset from this location would be beautiful. The fading sunlight would be replaced with the shimmering city lights. Keegan showed his manners by pulling out a chair at the table for April. A single red rose lay on the table in front of her. After seating April, he pulled out the chair across from her and sat down.

"I think this is the most beautiful view I have ever seen, Keegan. It seems like we can see to the end of the world from up here."

"I'm glad you approve. You look positively beautiful tonight, April."

"Thank you. Is this rose from you?"

"It is indeed. What is a candlelight dinner without a rose?"

"It's quite romantic." April lifted the rose to her nose and smelled the blossom. "This smells so nice. Thank you, Keegan."

"The perfume you're wearing smells wonderful as well."

"Thank you."

"May I get you something to drink," asked the waiter?

"I would like water with lemon, please," said April.

"I'll have the same, please."

"Very well," said the waiter as he handed both April and Keegan a menu and then disappeared.

"Do you come here often?" asked April.

"I only come here for special occasions. This is my fourth time here."

"And does special mean with three other women?"

"No. It means on business for Thornburg Genetics."

"I can't get over how beautiful it is here." April took a moment to relax and scan the view, studying the city architecture and skyline. Then her mind drifted back over the last few days.

"Do you mind if we discuss some of the events of the last couple of days?"

"I don't mind. What would you like to talk about?"

"Is everything all set with Señor Quinonez?"

"Yes. All of the details have been arranged. He will be meeting with the doctors at the Quito Cancer Research Center tomorrow morning. They will be giving him an experimental treatment, along with the chemo and radiation. I have to laugh. I'm afraid the results of the treatment will skew their research statistics. I'd like to see the look on their faces when he's fully healed in one week. They'll think their experimental drug is a miracle drug. Anyhow, when your workday is finished tomorrow, I told him you would come to visit him. He's looking forward to that. Make sure you let Jason know you went to see him."

When Keegan mentioned Jason's name, April could feel guilt creeping up inside her. Here she was engaged to Jason and sitting in a five star restaurant with Keegan. "God, please help me to know what to do," she thought. It was such a romantic place, and April didn't want the night to end. She picked up the red rose and took another big sniff. She was in her own little world when the waiter carefully set a glass of water in front of her and then Keegan.

"May I take your order now?"

"Could we have a few more minutes, please?" asked Keegan.

"Yes, you may, sir. I will come back in a few minutes."

Keegan stared at April. "Would you care to share your thoughts with me?"

"No. They're warm and happy thoughts about tonight and this place. I want to immerse myself in them." April stared out the window at the distant mountain peaks. "I guess we should order," she said after a few moments. "What would you recommend?"

"They prepare beautiful steaks here, and their filet mignon is the best."

"Why don't you order for both of us, Keegan?"

"Really?"

"Really."

"I've never had that request before. Now the pressure is on."

"I'm not so hard to please. You think Jason is involved in the security breach somehow, don't you?"

"Actually, no. He hasn't been ruled out, but there is no indication whatsoever that he is involved in the Thornburg security breach."

"Are you ready to order now?" asked the waiter.

"Yes. We would like two filet mignon dinners, medium rare with brown rice."

"Thank you, sir."

"And will that be served with fresh local vegetables?"

"Yes, sir. They will be served in a side dish for you to share."

"Thank you."

After the waiter left, April continued the conversation. "So tell me again why I'm supposed to be super careful with every move I make. You said someone was probably watching my every move because of the Noah Document."

"That is entirely possible. However, we have zero indications of anything suspicious at this point in time. That may be a blessing or a curse, and we may not know which for some time."

"So, I have to live the rest of my life wondering if there's a big round target on my back?"

"Relax a little, April. Let things sort themselves out. You've been super busy lately. Concentrate on your work and let me concentrate on security. All I am asking you to do is to be aware of your surroundings and let me know if anything unusual appears."

"I guess I'm a little hyper. Let's avoid any more business talk tonight. I want to enjoy our sunset meal and time together."

April and Keegan topped off their scrumptious dinner with a cup of the strong Ecuadorian coffee with cream. Then Keegan escorted April back to her hotel room. They paused at the door.

"Thank you for the special evening. It was wonderful," said April.

"I enjoyed every moment tonight," said Keegan.

"I would ask you to come in for a while, but I have to get some paperwork in order for a presentation at work tomorrow."

"Thanks for thinking about it, but I have several loose ends to tie up as well."

Keegan slid his arms around April and drew her close to him. She put her arms around him and looked up into his eyes. Their lips met in a gentle, long, enticing kiss. Then Keegan loosened his grip and held April gently. "This evening was wonderful, April. I'll see you tomorrow." He smiled at April as she took her arms from around his shoulders. She took a deep breath and then a sniff from the red rose Keegan had given her. She looked up and smiled at him again.

"Goodnight, Keegan," she said as he walked down the hall to his room next door.

Keegan glanced back and winked. "Goodnight, April."

Chapter 43

The next morning, April met Tanya outside her room, and they walked to the hotel cafe for breakfast. There was no sign of Keegan. After a quick breakfast they were on their way to Thornburg.

"Today is Friday," said Tanya. "My goal is to finish up here on Monday and fly out on Tuesday. What do you think, April?"

"I can work with any time frame you want me to. I can complete any unfinished business using the telephone or computer after we leave. It's been a pleasure working down here. All of the employees are so friendly and interested in their work. Will we be flying back on the company jet?"

"That's the plan. I have to make sure one is available. What time shall we request?"

"If there's time, I would really like to see my friend Señor Quinonez again before we leave. Would 11:00 AM be workable?"

"Eleven will work. That would put us back home about 8:00 PM. I don't plan on doing much that day. It can be a sort of rest and relaxation day. We should leave the hotel by ten."

"That sounds good."

Just before noon, Keegan found April working in an office cubical. "Good morning, April. Did you sleep well last night?"

"I had a great night's sleep, and you?"

"Actually, a couple of security issues came up, and my night's sleep consisted of about four hours. In fact, after I talk to you I'm going back to the hotel and catch a nap."

Keegan leaned over close to April and whispered. "So here is the situation. Carlos went to the cancer research center this morning and started his experimental treatment. The treatment is given once per week for six weeks. He is supposed to report back in one week for his second treatment. He thanks you for financing his treatments." Keegan leaned back and winked at April. "According to Tanya, you two will be headed back to the U.S. on Tuesday at eleven hundred hours."

"Yes, I want to see Miguel and Señor Quinonez that morning before we leave."

"That's fine. I will be seeing Carlos every morning. I'll make the arrangements for a visit. Is there anything else before I go back to the hotel and crash?"

"No, I'm just working away here as fast as I can."

"Okay. I'll catch up with you later. Have a great day." With that said,

Keegan turned around and walked out of the office.

"That's exasperating. Yesterday we had a perfect evening together and today he's all business. He didn't even give a hint of a special time together last night. I guess he really is tired, but I don't think that's a good enough excuse. Let me see what happens. I won't judge him too harshly just yet."

Keegan went back to the hotel. He was more tired than hungry and decided to skip lunch. He went to his room and thumped down on the bed. He was thinking about April as he drifted off to sleep. He woke up to the sound of his cell phone ringing. He checked the caller I.D. It read as an unidentified caller.

"Hello."

"Hello, Keegan, honey. How are you?"

"Hello, Samantha. It was a long night and I'm in the middle of a nap. Other than that I'm fine. You can't have info for me already."

"I wouldn't call it just any old info. I would call it juicy info!"

"Juicy? I'm not going to want to hear this, am I?"

"Of course you are, honey. At approximately twenty two hundred hours on Thursday, Jason Otis met a Miss Sheila Smith at the airport. I discovered that Sheila works as a stewardess for Empire airlines. If her name is really Sheila Smith, I'll give up a month at the hairdresser. A background check showed she has been a stewardess forever. I don't believe it, but I didn't bother to dig any deeper than that because I knew you would be on her trail like a hound dog. I'll leave the nitty-gritty background stuff to you. Anyhow, she and Jason spent about an hour at the hotel airport bar and then trotted off to hotel room 303. Sheila is scheduled on an outgoing flight at seven AM. I assumed the little rendezvous was going to be an all-nighter, but Mr. Otis left just after midnight. Your man Jason seemed to be somewhat nervous out in the open like that. He kept looking around and fidgeting with his drink straw. There didn't seem to be a care in the world with Sheila."

"He didn't spot you, did he?"

"What! Pleeease, Keegan honey, give me some credit. What do you think I am, a rookie or something? This isn't my first stakeout, you know."

"Okay, okay, I'm sorry."

"I accept that apology, but now I'm going to reveal my strategy. I followed Jason to the airport bar, and then grabbed a booth. I called a couple of my girlfriends, and they hustled over to the airport bar as well. We had a great time celebrating our fake birthdays, which allowed me to take numerous photos of Jason and Sheila. You know, some smoothie-coo bar photos." Samantha chuckled and then said, "I think they're madly in love."

"I'm sure they are, Samantha. Email me the pictures, and as always, this is our little secret."

"It always is, honey."

"Good work. Why don't you stay on Jason's trail until Tuesday night at nine, then your assignment is complete."

"Okay, boss. He's in my sights."

"Thanks, Samantha."

Keegan hit the off button on his phone. "What a dirt bag Jason is. So now I know Jason can't be trusted, and I can't say a word about this to April. If their relationship blows up it may affect the chance of discovering the Thornburg security breach. He probably couldn't wait for April to leave town so he could have his little fling, and he sent April to Ecuador with an engagement ring. I can't see this whole scenario going well at all. I have no idea if Jason is involved in the security breach or if he's just cheating on April, but Jason just moved toward the top of my suspected security breach list."

April didn't see Keegan again until Tuesday morning. After a seven AM breakfast with Tanya, April excused herself and met Keegan upstairs at his room. From there they hailed a taxi in front of the hotel. April told the taxi driver the address, and the two of them were on their way to see Miguel and Carlos.

After the taxi pulled away from the curb, April turned in her seat and faced Keegan.

"I haven't seen you since Saturday. Have you been busy with security issues or trying to avoid me for some reason?"

"I've been very busy, April. Why would I want to avoid you?"

"I don't know. I've thought of a hundred different reasons, but none of them make sense. We had a great time together last Friday night and then you just dropped out of my life. Something is wrong."

"Yes, April, I guess something is wrong. My Friday night with you was the best night of my life. I never thought I would meet anybody like you. Every time I'm near you it feels so right. That presents problems. First, part of my security role is protecting you and keeping you out of harm's way. I don't want to give up that role. I'm afraid if I don't control my emotions for you I will have to excuse myself from protecting you. Then I will be worrying about you all of the time and won't be able to concentrate on my other job functions. That brings me to my second point. You are engaged to Jason. Am I correct?"

"Yes, I am engaged to Jason."

"Then how can you kiss me the way you did the other night. Was it only a 'thanks for the evening kiss?' It felt like a lot more than that to me. I wouldn't want you kissing some other guy like that if I were engaged to you. You must have thought it through. What did it mean?"

"I have to say that I have some strong feelings for you. I can't tell how deep they are."

"Was it the heat of the moment? Do you think about me when I'm not with you? Are you bonding with me because I'm in a security role and a protector of sorts?"

"Keegan, I know it's not just a sudden infatuation with you. I've been out on many dates. I feel different when I'm with you. You bring a liveliness that I don't often feel. Do I love Jason? Yes. The two of you have different personalities. He is easy going. He does his best to please me. We seldom argue, and he is a gentleman. You are more of an adventurer, a take it one day at a time kind of guy. Could you make a commitment to a lady or are you going to get cold feet and run back and forth across the world forever?"

"I certainly couldn't sit behind a desk all day, greeting people as they walk in the door and checking hand bags. Correct me if I'm wrong, but aren't we in this car now because we are meeting an old friend from your stint in the Peace Corps? Let's see now. I think it was only a little over a year ago that you were meandering through the villages of Ecuador. Now you have a job that's going to require weeks of travel every year, and you're talking to me about commitment to a partner. I don't know Jason well, but he seems to be a bit of a wussy boy. I sure can't see you being married to a guy like that. I can hear it now. April, do these sheets match this pillowcase? Call me and let me know what you want me to make for dinner."

"Stop it now, Keegan!" April said in a loud voice. "I won't let you talk about Jason that way. He doesn't deserve it. At least he's a professional. That's more than I can say about the way you're acting. You're just jealous."

There was silence for a few moments. Keegan could see the cabdriver look nervously in the rear view mirror again and again.

"Por favor mire la calle!" said Keegan in a normal tone of voice to the driver. The taxi driver adjusted his rear view mirror to a different direction and looked straight forward.

"I didn't know you could speak Spanish," said April.

"I would appreciate it if you wouldn't tell anyone. It helps me maintain my status as a dumb American. I guess my conversation with you just proved that point. I'm sorry I talked that way, April. I don't know what came over me."

Keegan so wanted to tell April about Mr. Nice Guy Jason meeting up with Sheila Smith at the airport hotel, but he knew for security reasons he couldn't share that information. He knew he had to control himself better.

"I accept your apology. But, I have to say I kind of like a guy getting that upset over me. You must have been thinking in overdrive for the last two days. Is there anything else you would like to share with me?"

"Do you have to practice being annoying or does annoying come natural to you, April?"

"Annoying? First you're totally in love with me and now I'm annoying. I think you're a little confused."

Keegan laughed and then laughed again.

"You are something, April James. I'm not even going to attempt a comeback for that statement."

"You're giving up kind of easy, aren't you?"

"Maybe I know when to change topics."

"Are we almost there?"

"We'll be there in just a couple of minutes."

"Are you going to ask me out again?" April whispered.

"No. You're engaged. Stop teasing."

April whispered again, "I thought you liked being competitive."

"I have a great idea, April."

"What's that?"

"Let's move on to a different topic," whispered Keegan.

April gave Keegan a big smile and stared at him. They rode in silence for the remaining three blocks. Then the taxi pulled up in front of the same whitewashed apartment building April had visited seven days before. The greeting committee of children from the previous visit was nowhere in sight. As they stepped out of the cab, Keegan paid the fare and handed the driver a five-dollar tip. "Thank you," said Keegan.

"Gracias," said the cab driver as he sped off.

April and Keegan walked in the front door of the apartment building. As soon as Keegan shut the door behind them, he heard Señor Quinonez.

"Greetings, Señorita James and Señor McGrath, I've been waiting for your arrival. It is so nice of you to stop by."

"Señor Quinonez, you look much better. How are you feeling?" asked April.

"I feel like a new man, thanks to you and Señor McGrath, and the new medication. I owe my life to you. What can I do to repay you?"

"Seeing you healthy again is all I wanted Señor Quinonez. There is nothing to repay. You would have done the same thing for me if you were able."

"Someday and somehow I will pay you all back for your generosity. Please, come upstairs to our apartment. Miguel and Maritza are waiting."

Chapter 44

It was just after ten when April and Keegan arrived back at the hotel. Both of them knew enough not to broach the subject of the Friday night date again during the taxi ride back. Tanya was seated in one of the overstuffed lobby chairs waiting for their trip to the airport. Part of her baggage was on the floor next to her and the rest was on a cart. She stood up when April and Keegan walked in. "Good morning. How was your visit?"

"It was great," said April. "Señor Quinonez looks like a new man. He's full of energy again and his smile is back to normal."

"I'm glad to hear that. Maybe I can meet him sometime. We will probably work together here again at some point in time."

"That would be nice. I know you will like him."

"He sounds like an interesting fellow. Right now we have to concentrate on getting to the airport. Our ride should be here in a few minutes."

"I'm all packed," said April. "I have to run up to my room and I'll be back shortly."

"I'll escort Miss April to her room and see you in a few minutes, Tanya."

Keegan dropped April off at her hotel room door.

"I'll meet you back here in a couple of minutes," said April. "I have to check on something in my room. Will you arrange to have my luggage picked up? Just wait a couple of minutes for me."

"Okay, I'll be waiting."

It seemed like April had barely gathered her belongings when she heard a knock on the door. She walked over and looked through the security peephole in the door. "Who is it?"

"It's Keegan McGrath, my dear, as promised."

April opened the door. "Where's your luggage?"

"I have to finish up some business here. I won't be flying back with you."

"Oh. When will I get to see you again?"

"I can't answer that question. I don't always get to schedule my own assignments. I'm sure our paths will cross again in the near future. You have my cell phone number. If you want to talk about anything at all, just call me anytime, day or night. It's kind of tricky to reach me sometimes due to security issues, but leave a message and I will get back to you. Anyhow, I've enjoyed our brief time together, and I will be escorting you and Tanya to the airport."

"I don't want to leave here feeling the way I do right now, Keegan. I feel like there is a big empty spot in my emotions, and I feel like you should be there."

"April, I can't bear to tell you all of the feelings I have for you. You have to decide if Jason is the man you want to spend the rest of your life with. If he is, then I have to stay out of the picture. If not, well, I really want to see you again."

The ride with Sebastian to the airport was a quiet one. Keegan escorted April and Tanya to the Thornburg jet, said professional goodbyes and watched them as they boarded. As soon as the hatch was closed, he turned and walked away.

The flight back to Philadelphia was quiet. Tanya seemed to be huddled in her own little zone, busying herself with paperwork and occasionally drifting into short naps. All April could think about was Jason and Keegan. Just a few weeks ago it had all seemed so easy. Jason was mister right and April knew she had fallen in love with him over time. Then along comes mister adventurer. Keegan looked at every day of life as a special project, a challenge. He was way too sure of himself, yet he knew himself. He was right, there was no way he could ever sit behind a desk and not travel, and April knew she wouldn't expect him to. Thornburg Genetics security was his life. What exactly did he do anyhow? He was always shrouded in a cloud of mystery. He was always waiting for the next bit of security info. April thought about their date at La Terraza Del Tartaro. The night was perfect. The ambiance and rose he had given her sure made her feel special. April smiled. On the other hand, so did Jason. She knew he would be at the airport to greet her. He would want to take her to a special restaurant to welcome her back and who knows what else he might have planned. He was so sweet. Predictable was the word. He would be home every night to pamper April if that's what she wanted.

"Wussy boy," April said out loud.

"Wussy boy?" asked Tanya.

"Oh, sorry, I guess I was day dreaming."

"It sounds interesting. Am I going to hear the rest of the story?" asked Tanya.

"I don't think so."

"That's too bad."

As they entered the greeting area at the Philadelphia airport, April could see Jason near the front of the crowd of friends and relatives who were there to meet the arriving passengers. She slid the engagement ring on her finger, then waved and threw him a kiss as they made their way to each other. When they met, April dropped her bag and threw her hands around Jason's neck. They embraced and kissed for a moment. Then Jason took the bouquet of roses he had hidden behind his back and held them out for April to admire.

"Oh, Jason, these are beautiful. You are so nice to me."

"I enjoy being nice to the future Mrs. Otis. I missed you and couldn't wait for you to get back."

"It wasn't fair to have you hand me an engagement ring on my way out of the country."

April felt a tap on the shoulder. She turned and saw Tanya standing next to her. She did her best to conceal the engagement ring so Tanya wouldn't see it.

"I would like you to meet my husband, Brandon. Brandon, this is April James and perhaps you remember Jason Otis."

"Hello, Brandon. It's a pleasure to meet you," said April.

"It's a pleasure to see you again," said Jason as he reached out to shake Brandon's hand.

"It's nice to meet you, April," said Brandon. "Jason; It's nice to see you again as well. Are you keeping everyone in line at work?"

"I am doing my best, sir. Sometimes it's a challenge."

"Well, Jason," said Tanya, "I'm not as young as you and April are. I'm sorry to cut the conversation short, but I'm tired and ready to head home. I'll see you both at work tomorrow."

"Goodbye, Tanya," said April. "I'll see you tomorrow. It was a pleasure to meet you Mr. Jefferson." April and Jason watched as Tanya and Brandon walked toward the airport baggage claim area.

"Are you hungry, April? I thought we could grab a quick bite to eat."

"I'm not really hungry, but I would love to go spend some time with you. I haven't seen you in ten days."

"Let's go pick up your luggage, then off to dinner. Let me carry your computer and bag for you."

"Sure. I'll swap those for these lovely roses any time. I missed you, Jason."

"I missed you too, April."

April and Jason held each other's hand as they waited for the luggage. Brandon and Tanya were nowhere in sight, and April figured they had already claimed theirs. April's luggage was hand carried to the V.I.P. corporate jet baggage section and in a matter of minutes they strolled to Jason's car. Jason signaled and made his way out of the parking garage. He glanced at April and she smiled at him.

"Let's go to Randy's."

"We haven't been to Randy's in ages," said April.

"It just feels like a hamburger kind of night, and if you want to eat light they have that scrumptious salad selection you like. I'm sure you're tired after your busy work schedule in Ecuador."

"I didn't think I was hungry, but the thought of a 'Randy Burger' is pretty appealing."

It was after 8:00 PM and booths were plentiful. Jason chose an end booth far away from the entrance. A waitress was on the spot as soon as they sat down.

"Here is a glass of water for both of you. What else would you like to drink?"

"I'll have a medium root beer," said April.

"Make that two, please," said Jason

"Are you ready to order or would you like a few minutes?"

"I would like a 'Randy Burger' with slaw, but no french fries please," said April.

"I'll have the 'Randy Burger' deluxe with American cheese, and I do want the fries please."

"Coming right up folks. I like serving people that know what they want," said the waitress as she hurried off towards the kitchen.

"So, April, tell me about your trip. Don't leave out anything."

"I can't believe it's over already. I was on the go every minute. There was the fundraiser for the Thornburg Vision of Hope Charity one night. I had no idea how exhausting that would be. Meeting so many people and trying to keep names and faces together is hard and trying to remember if they attended the charity function or were coworkers was another chore for the rest of my time there. I think the charity event alone tired me out for three days, but I don't want to sound like I'm complaining. All of the people I met were very nice and showed concern for the goals of the charity."

"So, did you make a million for Thornburg?"

"That's funny. You always say that and of course the answer is yes. Tanya and I had several meetings with sales and marketing executives and staff. We have to continue to advance the Body-New Pharmaceutical line so it becomes a standard household name."

"So, I guess your new job agrees with you."

"So far, so good."

"How is your friend, Señor Quinonez doing?"

"Well, I saw him just before I left. He's had one cancer treatment at the Quito Cancer Research Center with five more to go. The treatment is experimental, so only time will tell how effective it is. It's all in God's hands at this point in time. At least his spirits are higher than they were. It's really a miracle the way this whole situation came together. I could just as easily have heard nothing about his illness until after he died and then the bad news letter would have arrived in the mail. I don't know why they didn't write or call and let me know there was a life or death situation."

"When it all came together the way it did, what more could you ask for. We'll keep Carlos in prayer."

"He is such a fine, caring man."

"Here you go, folks, one 'Randy Slaw' and one 'Randy Deluxe' with American. Would you like a refill on those sodas?"

"Yes, please," said Jason.

As the waitress left, Jason reached across the table and grasped April's hands. April looked straight into Jason's eyes, knowing that something was up.

"I have a surprise for you."

"A surprise?"

"Yes, are you ready?"

"I am."

"I've put a lot of work into this, April. I told you that I wanted to support the Thornburg Vision of Hope Charity here in the office, so I coordinated a fund raiser for Saturday night."

"Really? How nice. Tell me about the plans. It must have taken you hours."

"I reserved the whole banquet room at the Holiday Inn. It will be a formal event. You know; tuxes and gowns. Dinner is scheduled for six. At seven fifteen we will have a keynote speaker. That would be a Miss April James. Then, a small local band will play a variety of music until eleven. I decided to keep the ticket cost down with the anticipation of some major donations."

"Wow, you put a lot of effort into this. It sounds absolutely wonderful. Thank you, honey. You're the best."

"Anything for the one I love. I know the goals of the charity mean so much to you."

"I'm in shock. Does my face show it?"

"Maybe a little."

"Maybe a lot. So who's coming?"

"For this event, I decided to invite mostly big names. I talked with Mark and Tanya. They gave me some names of upper level executives in the medical field that they thought would be sympathetic to the cause. They also gave me the names of some major pharmaceutical representatives, and I invited most of the executives from our Thornburg location. There should be about two hundred and fifty people total."

"That sounds great Jason, but what about our co-workers and other friends?"

"I knew you would ask that and I agree they need to be included. I thought they might feel a little out of place at this event, so I plan on having another open house type of event for Thornburg employees and friends in a couple of weeks. I'm still working on the details. They should be completed by close of business on Friday."

"Wow, you are just great, Jason. I love you."

"I love you too, April. Well, our burgers are getting cold. Shall we?"

"Let's eat. I'm going to steal a couple of your fries. You arranged a Saturday night formal charity ball. I'm still in shock."

Chapter 45

"Good morning, April. This is Keegan. How are you this fine day?"

"Hello, Keegan. I think I'm great, but I just got up. How are you doing?"

"I'm on top of the world, me dearie."

"Should we be talking on my cell phone?"

"I've run a security check, and we are all clear. I'm calling for two things; first, I understand there's a big charity function this evening."

"Yes there is. Jason set the whole thing up while I was in Ecuador. Isn't that amazing?"

"Yes, Jason is amazing, isn't he?"

"I'm sorry. I didn't mean it that way."

"That's okay, April. Life is too short for game playing. I just wanted to let you know that a few of my best security staff will be in attendance."

"You guys are really worried about me, aren't you?"

"To say the least, April."

"I don't feel threatened at all. This seems like a lot of fuss for nothing. If something was going to happen to me, why wouldn't it have happened in Ecuador instead of here?"

"Your trip to Ecuador was sort of last minute. I can only guess that any plan from a conspirator will be cold and calculated, not off the cuff, not rushed. Past security history doesn't support anything different. We don't know what we are dealing with. You are the sitting duck, and we just don't know what moves may be made or by whom. Maybe nothing will happen, but for now you are our main ticket to detecting the Thornburg Genetics security breach. Anyhow, the second thing I called about is our friend, Señor Quinonez. He finished the C1 Extraction treatment Wednesday. He looks and feels like a new man. Today he will be receiving a full battery of tests to determine the effectiveness of the experimental treatments he has received at the cancer center. He will get a copy of the paperwork. I've made arrangements to receive a copy. I'll let you know the results."

"Thank you for letting me know, Keegan."

"You are welcome, Miss James. I have to go for now. Good luck at your event tonight."

"Goodbye, Keegan."

As the phone clicked off, Keegan thought about the pictures in his possession. Samantha's assignment had produced some useful information. Jason was seeing some airline stewardess named Sheila. The name fit the golden haired, primped up trophy girl. Could Jason be involved in the Thornburg security breach? It didn't seem likely since he let himself be spotted out in the open with another woman when he was engaged to April. That would be a move made by an amateur, not a professional. Keegan laughed at the picture of Samantha and her two friends celebrating a birthday that wasn't. She was his favorite undercover sleuth.

"That Jason is a sleaze bag, and April has no idea," Keegan said to himself. "I can't say a thing to her right now, but she will know all about the real Jason Otis before she ever walks down the wedding aisle. This really stinks."

April stood at the Holiday Inn banquet room door and greeted everyone as they entered. Jason stood next to her and briefed her on some of the guest's names and positions. His job as Director of Human Resources was an important link for the success of the event. Most of the people they weren't familiar with came from medical centers and corporations outside Thornburg Genetics.

"You did such a wonderful job of planning this. The room set up is perfect and everyone seems to be happy they were invited."

"The truth of the matter is that some people love these events because they can show off their jewels and money. Others hate these events, but come and put on their happy faces for the cameras and their corporations."

"I know," April laughed. "I just tell myself they are all glad to be here. It makes looking at them from up on stage a lot easier when I'm speaking."

"Either way, if it generates funds to help others, it has to be a good thing. Besides, that's why I planned less talk and more entertainment."

"Your idea is a crowd pleaser."

At seven fifteen sharp, Jason stood on the elevated stage in front of the microphone. The guests had just been served a top of the line slice of cheesecake, with fresh black cherries in sauce dripping over the edge, after a five star meal.

"May I have your attention please," said Jason.

It took a couple of minutes for the guests to end their conversations and focus on the podium.

"While you are finishing this fine dessert, I have asked the chef and those who provided this wonderful banquet tonight to allow us to recognize them. If you look over to my right," and Jason pointed, "by the double doors, you will see Chef Craig and his staff. Let's give them a round of applause." The room echoed with the sound of hands clapping topped off by a couple of shrill whistles from the crowd. "Thank you for creating a wonderful meal, Chef and staff."

There was a pause as the guests once again focused on Jason. He looked down at his pre-written introduction. "As you know, there is a purpose for this evening's event. There are many charities worldwide set up with the goal of helping those people less fortunate than us. Our research makes Thornburg Genetics a major player in providing medications to save and improve people's lives and lifestyles. Recently, one of our employees, Miss April James, requested this charity be set up to improve the standard of living for impoverished people. Since we at Thornburg Genetics immerse ourselves every day in helping others, the idea was embraced with open arms. Specific, important projects have been set up for immediate funding within the charity. At this time, I would like all of you to join me in greeting Miss April James, Chairwoman of the Thornburg Vision of Hope Charity."

Jason started clapping, which enticed the crowd to applaud as well. April stood up and approached the podium. A screen was lowered behind her, the lights were dimmed and the first slide from April's presentation appeared on the screen. It was a picture April had taken just before she left her Peace Corps assignment in Ecuador and returned to the United States. The picture showed a group of small children gathered around a Doctor. The children's gazes were fixed on the woman in the white lab coat with a stethoscope on a small boy's chest. The background showed a small white concrete block building. It was obvious the building was a makeshift medical unit. April took in a panoramic view of the audience before she spoke.

"Before I started with Thornburg Genetics, I spent twenty-seven months in the Peace Corps. This picture was taken just over one year ago in the village of Alshi, Ecuador. The village is twenty miles away from a real, fully staffed medical clinic. In our world that means little. We can drive twenty miles in twenty minutes. Unfortunately, there are no paved roads leading to Alshi. Alshi is up in the eastern mountain ranges. Life is much different there than it is here in Philadelphia. Approximately four hundred people live in this village. Doctor Helen Stafford, pictured here, arrives at Alshi once each month. She takes time from her own busy schedule and uses her own finances to treat the people in the village and surrounding area, because most of the people here can't afford medical help. They grow their own food or trade goods for the food they eat. They make hand woven blankets and hats to earn a little extra money. They have a roof over their head and gather firewood for heat. The mean income in Alshi is one thousand dollars per year. Yet these are some of the happiest people I've ever met.

Thanks to the Peace Corps, they have improved crop growing practices, water systems and general sanitation methods. There are thousands of villages like this throughout the world." April paused a moment and clicked to the next picture.

"I want each of you to concentrate on the cute little brown-eyed fellow the doctor is holding on her lap." April paused again to allow the crowd to focus on the screen. "This is four year old Fortunato. He had a severe cough and high temperature for two weeks before Doctor Stafford made her monthly trek to Alshi. Little Fortunato was diagnosed with pneumonia. I was visiting another village at the time and came back to meet with the Doctor. Doctor Stafford did not have the necessary medication with her, because she can procure and transport only limited quantities each trip. Time was not on his side, and he died from the pneumonia just two days after this picture was taken. I had the unfortunate honor of attending his funeral." April paused again. "With more consistent medical treatment available, he would still be alive today. This is just one example of a premature loss of life. I can share dozens of stories about sick children, pregnant women, parents and grandparents all requiring medical attention. Often the medical needs are simple, but proper medication is not available. Their world and our world are completely different, yet we are all humans struggling in the same world."

The room was silent with the exception of several sobs and gasps. April knew many people in the room were trying to bridle their emotions, and it was all April could do not to burst into tears. She went on to explain the initial charity goals for Ecuador, Mexico, Republic of the Congo and Sudan. All of the goals were medical related.

"In conclusion I want to say this. I know all of us lose loved ones, and I know the world will never be perfect. I'm not asking one person here to become a martyr or give up your lifestyle. God has given each of us a place and task on this earth. I just want each of you to be aware of the situations surrounding fellow human beings. Thornburg Genetics has been gracious enough to back the Thornburg Vision of Hope Charity, which is designed to reach out and help fellow human beings where we can. I ask you tonight to assist us in this mission. I guarantee that helping others in this way will bring an abundance of joy into your own life. Thank you for allowing me to share this information with you this evening."

April turned around and met Jason ascending the stage steps. Applause broke out as the lights slowly brightened again. The audience continued to clap, and they all rose to their feet as April left the stage. April glanced at the crowd, raised her hand and waved. She could see red eyes and knew that many of those in attendance had been crying.

Slowly the people sat back down as Jason spoke into the microphone. "I thank you, April, for your heartfelt and sincere message of hope. I believe your presentation touched each of us in a different way. This evening folks we invite you to reach out to others in the world with a generous gift. On each table are a number of cards with the Thornburg Vision of Hope Charity name at the top. These cards are for contributions to the charity. Please take a moment to fill out that card. Contributions can be made as one-time gifts or in monthly installments. All gifts are tax deductible. There is also a box to check if there is some other way you would like to contribute. Envelopes for your donations are next to the beautiful lavender-colored boxes at both rear exits. Place your card in one of the envelopes and drop it in one of those boxes. We must ask ourselves what we can do to help make the world a better place. Please take some time to think about this matter as you enjoy the band. I want to personally thank each of you for attending tonight's event. Please enjoy the rest of the evening."

Jason reached up and turned off the microphone, departed from the stage and walked toward April. The band started playing a slow quiet piece as the sound of people talking again started to fill the banquet room. Jason reached out and took hold of both of April's hands. "You were absolutely brilliant, April. I think everybody in the room was crying. I am sorry to hear about the tragic events you have witnessed. You never told me about them before. It really does make one reach into their heart."

"Thank you, Jason. That whole scenario was so sad. It's a topic I have tried to avoid. I had all I could do not to bawl like a baby up there on stage."

"Well, I'm going to let you mingle with the crowd, my dear."

"Thanks again for putting all of this together, Jason. I love you."

April went from table to table and talked to as many people as she could. Some congratulated her on the charity she had set up, others thanked her for sharing her experiences, and others told her they would be making future contributions for such a worthy cause. April wondered why this type of information seemed so new to affluent people. You could read about world poverty in any newspaper or news magazine. She decided either people just didn't take time to think about it or avoided the issue unless directly confronted. As April was walking between tables near the rear entrance, a young man approached her.

"Hello, April, my name is Nadish Patel. I represent a wealthy benefactor who is willing to contribute a sizeable amount of money to the Thornburg Vision of Hope Charity. I would like to talk with you in private tomorrow. This matter must be discreet. Here is my business card.

Please call me tomorrow morning around ten. I have to say your presentation was very powerful. I will relay all of the information to my employer. Please do not share this information with anyone. Have a good evening, Miss James."

April looked at the business card the stranger had just handed her. When she looked up again, he was gone. What a peculiar fellow and odd request she thought, but she knew that wealthy people sometimes handled their business transactions with secrecy. April continued to converse with people until well after midnight. Jason finally joined her and suggested they leave.

It was a little after ten the next morning when she dialed the number on the business card.

"Hello, this is the office of Nadish Patel. How may I help you?"

"Is Mr. Patel available? He asked me to call this morning."

"May I ask who is calling, please?"

"This is April James."

"Thank you. Please hold."

Soothing background music played on the telephone as April waited. She thought she recognized the tune, but couldn't name it.

"Hello, April. Thank you for calling. How are you this morning?"

"I have to admit I'm a little tired after last night's event. I didn't get home until way after midnight, but I'm up and ready for the day."

"Did you make out well with contributions last night?"

"I truly don't know at this point. Since today is Sunday, we decided to wait until tomorrow to tabulate the results."

"I'm sure an abundance of money will be pouring into the charity. Your vision of hope was perfect. So, let's talk business. As I said last night, I represent a wealthy benefactor who may wish to donate a substantial sum of money to your charity. I would like to meet with you to discuss this matter. As you pointed out, today is Sunday. Would you be available for a meeting later this evening?"

"I don't want to sound ungrateful, but is there any way we could meet on a week night?"

"I wish I could say yes, but my schedule is very full during the week. I have tonight free, but if I wait to meet during the week it will probably be two weeks out. My benefactor is anxious to contribute now. I know what you are thinking. Why the rush? The answer is, when my employer gets something in his mind he wants it taken care of immediately. It's just his style. My job is to see that his wishes are carried out with precision. Believe me, April, a meeting tonight will be worth your time."

"Okay, Mr. Patel. You've convinced me."

"Great. Why don't we meet for dinner at 7:00 PM at The Golden Mast Yacht Club? I will make reservations under my name. Now, I know this sounds a little strange, but would you please come alone and under no circumstances should you share this information with anyone. My benefactor hates publicity and is, shall we say, eccentric. I don't want to disappoint him. You understand."

"Discreet it is, Mr. Patel."

"Please call me Nadish."

"Okay, Nadish. Would you give me the address and some directions to The Golden Mast Yacht Club and their telephone number if you have it handy? I'm not familiar with that location."

Nadish gave her the address and simple directions. He thanked April for agreeing to meet with him on such short notice, said goodbye and hung up the telephone. The more April thought about this proposal, the more uneasy she felt, but people with significant wealth probably do demand their privacy. April wondered who the unknown benefactor could be. Was it some movie star? Was it a company CEO? Maybe it was somebody who had to get rid of some money for a tax write off. At least Nadish had chosen a very public place to meet. April walked over to her side table and picked up her telephone book. There it was, The Golden Mast Yacht Club. It sported a half page ad in the yellow pages. Maybe the benefactor owned it. She decided to keep the whole matter confidential as she agreed. She would have her cell phone with Keegan's number ready on speed dial if needed, and her handgun in her pocketbook.

Chapter 46

April left early for her evening appointment at the yacht club. The time spent that afternoon with Jason had been enjoyable, but the only way she could convince him to leave was by telling him she had work that had to be done by the next day. She hadn't lied to him because she did have work to do. She just didn't mention the planned rendezvous. The Sunday evening traffic was very light, and April had no problems locating the well-lit club. April had lived in Philadelphia since birth, but had never seen this exclusive yacht club. It looked like a scene from a Better Homes and Gardens magazine. She was fifteen minutes early, but decided to ask about the reservations just in case Mr. Patel was already there.

"Good evening, ma'am. Do you have reservations?"

"Yes, sir. Reservations should be made under the name Nadish Patel."

The maître d' glanced at the book on his podium.

"Ah, yes. Right this way, ma'am."

The maître d' led April past several picture windows. The sky was overcast, and lights from boats and the marina docks were starting to reflect off the water. There were only a few occupied tables, and with the dimly lit seating area, nobody seemed to notice as they glided by. As they approached a secluded corner table, a man with his back to the wall stood up.

"Your seat, ma'am," said the maître d'. He then turned and left.

"Hello, April. Thank you for coming."

"Hello, Mr. Patel. It's good to see you again."

"Please call me Nadish. Mr. Patel seems too formal."

A waiter appeared and asked if they would like to order a drink.

"Would you like a glass of wine or a mixed drink?" asked Nadish.

"I would like a cup of coffee, please," said April

"Make that two please."

April attempted to analyze Nadish Patel. She had been so tired on the night of the charity event she had a hard time remembering what he even looked like. Now she remembered seeing his dark hair and well-trimmed mustache. The dark pupils of his eyes matched the color of his hair. The black suit he was wearing made his whole being appear intense. He would have fit in any corporation's top executive echelon. The next hour consisted of ordering a meal and discussing in depth the Thornburg Vision of Hope Charity. Mr. Patel asked April several questions about her stint in the Peace Corps. Finally Mr. Patel said, "It is time to meet my employer, April. I assume you are ready."

"I am meeting him tonight? Will he be joining us here at the table?"

"Here is the situation. We will be going to the benefactor's yacht. As I said before, everything we say and do must be discreet. The meeting will be short, which is why I am enjoying this meal with you now. He will be discussing the donation of a sizeable contribution to the Thornburg Vision of Hope Charity. I must repeat this again, please understand that the benefactor hates publicity. You will be talking to him, but you won't be able to see him as he will have a screen set up between him and you."

Nadish could see April's facial expression change to one of doubt. "Don't worry, April. I assure you this matter is legitimate. I know it seems out of the ordinary, but this is how he operates."

"I think I need to know who I'm dealing with, Mr. Patel. This whole thing is really getting out of hand. I don't know him, I don't know you, and I'm not sure what is happening here, but this situation is way beyond normal in my book."

"All I can tell you, April, is my employer is a well-known person. I can't give you his name."

"Why doesn't he just donate money the same way our other contributors do? They send a personal check or their company sends a check. Why all of this secrecy? I mean you could have brought a check with you tonight. This whole thing is on the edge of creepy. If I weren't sitting in a fancy restaurant, I would have been gone long ago."

"April, all I can tell you is I have worked for this gentleman for some time now. He has always treated me fairly, and he just completes his business in a different manner than most people are used to. I don't know why he operates the way he does and I don't ask. All I know is that he wants to make a sizeable donation, and he wants to meet you in person. He is his own boss and works in his own way. I ask you not to back out, and I ask you to trust me. If you are afraid of something bad happening to you, don't be. He chose this place because it is very public."

April thought through the evening's events in silence as Nadish watched her. It was definitely a high-end restaurant in a public location. She had her handgun in her pocketbook and knew she could retrieve it in less than three seconds if need be.

"Okay, I will meet with him. I have to go to the restroom first."

"Believe me, April, you are making the right decision."

April strolled to the women's room. She was the only one in there.

While she was sitting on the toilet she pulled out her cell phone and sent a text message to Keegan. It said, "I am at The Golden Mast Yacht Club in a meeting. I will call you in 1 hour." April put the cell phone ring tone on silent and slid it back in her pocketbook. After washing and freshening up, she headed back to the table. On her way back, she again started having second thoughts about the meeting. The whole approach was way too crazy. She said a short prayer to herself.

"God, please protect me. I feel like I'm headed for the lion's den."

When Mr. Patel saw April approach, he rose from his chair. "There is one last thing I have to ask. Do you have any type of recording device on you?"

April smiled and chuckled, partly from being nervous and partly because of the question.

"No. Why would I have a recording device?"

"It's standard operating procedure for me to ask. Okay, that's it for the formalities. Let's go meet the benefactor."

The breeze was chilly and there was a slight smell of seaweed as they walked out on the docks. It was on the edge of dark. The over-cast sky and dimly lit docks gave April an eerie feeling. After walking past a dozen large boats they stopped at dock number twenty-seven. The yacht was backed into the slip and the lettering on the back read, The Jolly Roger. Doesn't look like a pirate ship, April thought to herself. There were four steps leading from the dock to the boat deck. April followed Nadish up the steps and into a dimly lit cabin. Even in the dim light, she could see the exquisitely carved mahogany door and window casings. The light was coming from sconces mounted on the walls, and a small ornate chandelier. The cabin trimmings reeked of wealth.

"Have a seat here please, April," said Nadish as he turned and de-parted through the same door they had just entered.

There was silence and April waited for something to happen. She could see a small screened partition fifteen feet in front of her. At last a voice said, "Good evening, April."

April knew the benefactor was behind the screen. "Good evening, sir."

"Thank you for meeting with me this evening, April. First, let me apologize for all of the secrecy. The events that led to this meeting probably raised your level of doubt and suspicion to new highs. I hope Nadish was able to convince you my sincerity is legitimate. Confiden-tiality is such a pain some times; however, it is necessary due to my lifestyle. Just so you know, I had your background researched and you have an impeccable reputation. I am a generous person, and I want my contributions going to organizations that are up front with their intentions. From past experience if the leader has strong moral and ethical values, so does the organization. I donate to several worthy causes and your charity intrigues me. However, I wanted to talk with you in person before making a commitment. First, do you have strong morals and ethics?"

"I was brought up in a family with strong ethics and morals through my religious background. I am not a perfect person, but I do my best to follow Biblical principles in all aspects of my life."

"Would you please tell me in your own words, what you expect the Thornburg Vision of Hope Charity to accomplish?"

April thought for a second. "Initially, I expect the charity to donate financial assistance to people in foreign countries that live tough lives with inadequate food supplies, few medical services and poor health standards. Financial donations will be used for health education, improved farming and trade practices and actual, meaningful, medical treatment."

"I see, and where does Thornburg Genetics come into play?"

"Thornburg Genetics will be donating or discounting many pharmaceuticals for use in medical clinics and by transient medical staff."

"Are you personally monitoring the donation disbursements?"

"Yes, sir. I am making sure every penny possible goes to those in need. My goal is to keep administrative costs at approximately eight percent. I will also monitor all attempted misuse of funds and supplies by foreign governments."

"That sounds very reasonable, April. I like what I hear, so this is my proposal. Of course, everything discussed tonight is strictly confidential. Is that understood and agreed on?"

"Yes, sir. I understand completely."

"I need you to guarantee me in your own words that everything is confidential."

"I promise that everything discussed tonight will be confidential."

"Thank you, April. I believe you to be a young lady who will keep a promise."

There was silence for a few seconds and then the benefactor spoke again.

"For the next ten years, I am set to contribute two million dollars per year to the Thornburg Vision of Hope Charity, and I wish to give you one hundred thousand dollars per year to properly administer the funds."

April gasped. She couldn't believe what she had just heard and didn't know how to respond. "That is very generous sir. I'm speechless."

"I feel that the Thornburg Vision of Hope Charity is a worthwhile cause."

"Thank you sir, however, I already have a fulfilling job for which I am well paid. I don't feel it is necessary to receive an additional hundred thousand dollars per year to administer the donation. Perhaps you would consider contributing that amount to the general charity fund as well?"

"I thought you might say that, and admirably so, but I insist that you receive it personally. What you decide to do with the money is up to you. I want you to understand this offer fully, April. Over a ten year period, you will receive twenty million dollars for the Thornburg Vision of Hope Charity and one million dollars personally."

"I have no adequate way to thank you for your generosity, sir. Thousands and thousands of people will have better lives thanks to you. Thank you very much. May I ask you what your name is sir?"

"I prefer to remain anonymous, but thank you for asking. There are two envelopes on the table in front of you. Both have checks in them. One is for two million dollars and the other is for one hundred thousand dollars. Please pick those up and place them in your pocketbook."

April did as she was directed.

"Now, April, there is one stipulation that you must adhere to in return for my generosity. For years now, Thornburg Genetics has had the ability to produce a drug that will effectively heal numerous varieties of cancer. It has not been made available to the public. This drug, in the form of a blue pill, will knock out most types of cancer in seven to ten days. Why it has not been made available for purchase by the general public, I have no idea. Here is the situation. I have had these pills in my possession. They have been broken down into components by chemists and attempts have been made to duplicate them. There is apparently one compound in these pills we cannot duplicate. We need you to obtain the formula for us. Think of it this way. Your real passion is to help people by giving them a more productive life. My passion is exactly the same. What could be better than receiving a new lease on life by having a deadly cancer eradicated from your body in seven days? There would be no chemo and no radiation treatments to suffer through, and your body would have a complete healing. You can play a vital role in this April. You can help save millions of lives."

"I work in marketing sir. Even if there were such a pill..."

"STOP NOW," the benefactor shouted. "You know there is such a pill. A Carlos Quinonez in Ecuador, your personal friend, just started experimental cancer treatments. He was scheduled to die. His progress was monitored. After two weeks he was fully healed. The rest of the study group of patients showed no similar gains. Lucky doesn't work in medicine. He received special treatments. He received them from Thornburg Genetics, and he received them because he was your friend. If I am wrong, call me a liar, April."

There was silence. April knew the man behind the screen was letting his words sink in. She couldn't lie. April felt her stomach churning and was afraid she would throw up. He knew. How did he know?

"Please God, help me," she whispered.

The silence was broken. "I am a man who jumps on opportunities. So here is what I want you to do for me, April. I want and demand the formula for this medication from Thornburg Genetics. I also want one hundred of the special blue cancer pills immediately. At one million dollars per pill, I will make one hundred million dollars short term and possibly more. It's all based on supply and demand. As soon as I have sold all of the pills, you can have the formula back. I'll have moved on to another challenging project by then. I am going to give you the name of a man who works at Thornburg Genetics in the research and development division. I am sure it will take some persuading, but he knows the formula. I need it and the pills as soon as possible. I am a powerful man, April. If I don't get this formula, you can be sure things won't go well for you. But at heart, I'm a gentle kind of guy. I don't want to talk about threats. I want to talk about reality. You know this medication should be made public. You know that millions of people die from cancer worldwide every year when they could be healed. Thornburg Genetics is a company on the edge of murder because of their refusal to provide available cancer treatment to the public. April, you must obtain the formula so we can save people together. Take the twenty million dollars for the charity. Take the one million dollars you will receive and spend it any way you like. Bringing this drug public is a lifesaver, not a detriment. Thank you for meeting with me tonight. I expect you to abide by your moral obligation of secrecy. There is one last order of business before I ask you to find your way back to the dock and restaurant. The person you will contact at Thornburg Genetics is Raymond Hoffman. I will be in touch, April. You may leave now."

April pushed her chair back from the table, rose and walked to the back of the boat. She gently walked down the steps to the dock and turned towards the restaurant. She walked past two boats, grabbed hold of the aluminum railing on the dock next to the third boat and threw up. The splash of water beneath her was the only other sound on the quiet dock.

Chapter 47

A smile came to the benefactor's face. From the back of The Jolly Roger, he could see April bent over the railing just three boats down, and he heard her gag as she threw up. She didn't deny one thing. Their gamble had paid off. April was the break they had been waiting for. It had to be planned carefully. He didn't really need the money, but hey, a few more million couldn't hurt. The pleasure of this project was the challenge. It would be worth giving April a measly two million dollars for the charity and one hundred thousand for herself. If she delivered the hundred blue pills, they were worth at least a million apiece. There were lots of rich people with cancer that would pay at least that for more time on planet earth. The formula would be worth even more. Once he had the pills and formula, he could stiff the Thornburg Vision of Hope Charity for the rest of the donations he had promised.

He watched April leave the dock area. His hands were sweating profusely from the rubber gloves he had been wearing all evening to avoid leaving fingerprints on the yacht. Quickly he descended the steps to the dock. He bent over and pulled the two tabs on The Jolly Roger logo. It peeled off the boat easily and revealed the true name of the boat, Empty Nester. Nadish had selected a great yacht for the occasion. It gave a big, powerful, luxurious and demanding appearance. The true owners were out of town for two weeks. Despite the overcast sky, it was a beautiful night. The benefactor wadded The Jolly Roger decal into a ball and stuck it between his knees. He took the black ski mask out of his front pocket, slipped it over his head, and stuffed the wadded up decal in the same pocket. He turned and walked down the dock in the opposite direction from the restaurant. At the end of the dock, Nadish, still in his suit and tie, was sitting in the rowboat the benefactor had commandeered earlier. The benefactor laughed at the sight. The light from the dock highlighted the orange life vest wrapped around him. The benefactor gracefully slid onto the back seat. Nadish pushed them away from the dock and started rowing. "Where to?" he asked.

"Due west, stay just beyond the docks and make no noise. I'll tell you which dock to pull into."

"What about lights? I can hardly see where I'm going."

"No lights."

They left the yacht club and started passing the expensive waterfront homes. Some were well lit while others were dark and looked abandoned. They could hear the sound of a boat motor in the distance. It was probably a fisherman in search of that huge bass or pike. Nadish had no idea how far he had rowed. His armpits were starting to chafe from the suit jacket and dress shirt rubbing against his skin. He wished he had taken off the jacket, but the benefactor had demanded he wear it. Finally the benefactor spoke again. "Over there, pull up at the end of the dock with the small blue light. You row back to the restaurant and retrieve your car. I borrowed the boat from one of the docks at the marina. Just pick any dock there and tie it off. The owners will find it. There's a gallon of Clorox, rubber gloves and a sponge back here. Wipe the boat down good. Dispose of everything after you finish, including your suit. Make sure nobody sees you with the boat or when you leave the marina. Don't worry about the screen on the yacht. You'll receive your pay in a few days. You did a great job, Nadish. I'll keep you in mind for future assignments."

"Thank you, sir."

The benefactor stepped out of the boat onto the dock. He picked up the small flashlight lying on the dock, took off his rubber gloves as he walked up the dock, and disappeared in the dark. Nadish pushed away from the dock and started rowing back east to the marina. After he had rowed a hundred yards or so from the dock he stopped, unbuckled his life vest and took off the suit coat. The trip back to the yacht club was a long one.

The benefactor picked up the vehicle he had stashed behind bushes at the vacant camp. He started down the road before he turned on his headlights and called Jason. Jason's cell phone rang. "Hey, Jason, it's me. I'm on a secure line."

"Just a minute. Okay, this line is secure, Max."

"Don't let this go to your head, Jason, but your plan worked perfect. Have you ever thought about working for the CIA? We discussed the pills, formula and money. It's a good thing I know Dr. Delgado. I went right for the throat and dragged Carlos Quinonez into the middle of it. She didn't deny a thing. We've got our Thornburg contact. We just have to play her like there's no tomorrow."

"Remember your advice to me, big brother. Don't get too cocky. April is very smart. We have to be careful. I'll monitor every move she makes."

"I have to say that I felt kind of sorry for her. She was so upset after our meeting that she didn't get thirty feet down the dock before she was throwing up."

"That's no way to treat my future wife and lover, you ruffian. Since when have you felt sorry for anybody? You're not getting soft on me are you?"

"Like I said, I felt bad. It even brought tears to my eyes."

"If you had tears, it was from laughing, not sympathy. I suppose you told her what a gentle, caring guy you are too."

"Of course, that's me. I care for those less fortunate than myself."

"You are so full of it, Max. Listen, it's the sixth inning of the Phillies and Mets game. I've got to go. I'll call April in a little while and see what story she conjures up to cover her night's outing."

"You should have been a psychologist, Jason."

"That may be my next career."

"Okay, enough with the small talk. Mission Golden Mast successful."

There was a click and the phone went dead. Jason hated it when Max did that. A goodbye, see yah or something would be nice. Max knew Jason hated it and did it on purpose. Jason called April at the end of the next inning.

Chapter 48

April drove home as fast as she could. She kept glancing at her dash-board to make sure she didn't get picked up for speeding. She knew the man she had just spoken with was literally dead serious. As much as she hated to admit it, he was right in so many ways. People were dying from cancer every day, and she knew the drug called C1 Extraction, alias Constellation Blue, alias The Blue Mule, could save millions of lives. Even though the drug was volatile, there had to be some way to produce and distribute it without causing a security breach. April slammed on the brakes. She'd almost run a stop sign. Her stomach still felt tender, and her whole body felt jittery. She was glad she had an unfinished soda in her car to rinse out her mouth.

"Composure, April," she said to herself. "Keep this all under control. Stay strong."

April arrived back at her apartment building and went to pull into her designated parking space. "Jerk!" she hollered. Somebody else was parked in her space. She found a free space, made sure she had her pocketbook, and checked it for her handgun, wallet and cell phone.

"Oh, no, I forgot to contact Keegan." She knew she didn't want to talk to him if she could avoid it, so she sent him another text. "Forgot to call you. Hope this didn't cause a problem. Sorry for the delay. Had a great dinner with an anonymous guest I met at the charity event. He contributed a large sum of money to the charity. I'll talk to you later."

She turned the ring tone back on and slipped the phone back in her purse. It rang immediately. The caller I.D. said Keegan. She sent him another text saying she would talk to him tomorrow and slipped the phone back in her purse again, locked her Honda and walked to her apartment, acting as though nothing out of the ordinary had happened. After locking her apartment door behind her, she set her pocketbook on the coffee table, sprawled out in the overstuffed brown leather chair, and started crying.

"This guy is dangerous. What will I do? I promised to keep our meeting and conversation confidential. On the other hand, I had no idea he was going to threaten me."

After the evening's events, April's body shut down and she fell asleep. She woke up startled. The telephone was ringing. She looked at her wall clock. It was ten fifteen. She had only been home fifteen minutes. It rang again. April reached into her pocket book and pulled out the phone. It was Jason. "Hello, Jason."

"Hi, April. I wanted to tell you it was fun spending the afternoon with you. How is your work going? Are you getting caught up?"

"I'm getting a lot of work done, but I don't think I'll ever be one hundred percent caught up."

"I'm sure of that. That's the world of marketing and sales."

"So how are the baseball games unfolding? Did the Mets win?"

"They are just starting the eighth inning. The Mets are ahead by one."

"What's the score?"

"Six to five. It's been a real slug fest."

"The game sounds like a thriller, Jason."

"I better let you get back to your work so you can get some sleep tonight."

"It sounds to me more like you want to get back to your game."

"I must confess I don't want to miss the finale. Anyhow, I love you and I'll see you tomorrow."

"I love you too, Jason. Thanks for calling. Good night."

Jason laughed as he hung up the telephone. April was without a doubt one of the toughest girls he knew. Max made it sound like their meeting left her in a trauma, yet she sounded as though she had been through no trauma at all. He didn't detect one quiver in her voice. He hoped Max didn't underestimate her. April was very cool and calm. Jason decided it was too bad they had to use April as a pawn. He could really get used to having her around on a permanent basis.

As soon as they hung up, April got out of her chair and took her sweater off. After a hot shower, she boiled water and made herself a cup of mint tea in hopes it would soothe her stomach.

"I have to think this through," she said. "What am I going to do? I'm dealing with a man who is powerful, rich, most likely dangerous and apparently not afraid of using any tactic necessary to get his way. He wants, no he demands, that I somehow obtain these pills with the formula. I barely talked Lexis into providing the treatment for Señor Quinonez. Now I'm supposed to contact a Raymond Hoffman. I have no idea who he is. Wait a minute. How could I even talk to this benefactor? He must have the Noah gene or I couldn't have even talked to him. Now he knows I have it, because I talked to him without refuting anything. Of course, I didn't really say anything. I think all I did was listen. I have to do a better job of thinking this scenario through. There has got to be a way to distribute this medication and get it out to the public. Maybe distribution through a military base would work. The problem is the C1 Extraction would become a rich person's drug due to the security expenses. Well, I can't go down that road now."

"I've always done my best to keep my word. Now I opened my mouth and made big promises of strict secrecy and no publicity to Mr. Benefactor. Sure, sir, everything you tell me will be held confidential. I swear it on a stack of Bibles. You are an idiot, April. What were you thinking? I know what you were thinking. You were thinking this guy was on the up and up. It turns out he was the world's biggest deceiver. Sure, I've got lots of money to give you. I just need a little favor from you, April. Maybe you could destroy your whole life and everything moral you've ever stood for so I, Mr. Benefactor, can benefit. We're on the same page, April. We both want to help others, April. It's a great plan for him and destructo for me. Well, Lexis, Tanya and Keegan should be happy. I, the sitting duck, am now off my seat and standing out in the open. Maybe, if I'm lucky, I'll live through this and have a great story to tell my grandchildren. That is, of course, if they have this Noah Gene, and I even have the capability to tell them. What next? I can't make a telephone call from here. They, whoever they are, probably have my apartment bugged and are watching my every move. How did they find out about Señor Quinonez? This means that if I don't cooperate with the benefactor, I, as well as my family, Señor Quinonez, his family, and village are all in danger. This is the second time I've said this. 'THANKS A LOT DAD. I HOPE YOU ARE HAVING A GOOD LAUGH. THANKS A LOT FOR SHARING THE NOAH DOCUMENT WITH ME.' I guess I'll leave a little early in the morning and call Lexis from a pay phone on the way to work."

Chapter 49

The warm tea helped relieve April's upset stomach, but she could not get to sleep. Her mind kept going over and over the scenario on The Jolly Roger. She hated herself for being so stupid and falling under the influence of the benefactor's slick ploy. She didn't know what time it was when she finally fell asleep, but she didn't stir again until 6:45 AM when her alarm went off. April decided to follow through on her plan to leave early for work and make a telephone call from a pay phone. She knew there would be a pay phone in the lobby of the Quality Inn about eight miles away. She decided that should be secure enough for an initial call to The Keeper.

April left her apartment fifteen minutes earlier than usual. She drove directly to the Quality Inn. Overnighters were already leaving the motel. A parking space was open just five slots from the main entrance. Numerous glances in the rear view and side mirrors all the way from her apartment led April to believe no one had followed her. She hopped out of her car and walked quickly into the motel lobby. The desk manager was in the process of helping a guest check out. Nobody seemed to notice as she walked down the short hallway and discovered the bank of pay phones. She chose the telephone farthest from the front desk, lifted the receiver off the hook, and punched in the emergency telephone number she had memorized just weeks before.

"Hello, this is Lexis."

"Good morning, Lexis, this is April."

"Where are you calling from?"

"A pay phone in a Quality Inn lobby."

"Are you on your way to work?"

"I am."

"And what is the nature of this call."

"The sitting duck has been contacted."

"Go to work and continue with your normal routine. I'll be in touch."

There was a click on the other end of the line. April placed the phone back on the hook. Nobody paid any attention to her as she walked out of the motel and drove to Thornburg Genetics.

"Hello, Keegan. This is Lexis."

"Good morning, Lexis."

"April has been contacted. I want you to do a face-to-face interview and keep me posted. Check her car, computers, telephones and apartment. Make sure there are no bugs. See if the plan we talked about will work."

"I'm on it, Lexis."

These were the kind of days Keegan hated. He had a five-hour drive in front of him to get to Philadelphia. The only tidbit of information he had at this point was that April had been contacted. He figured she had been contacted at The Golden Mast Yacht Club since he received a text from her the night before stating she was going there. There was no way of knowing how serious the situation was. Was somebody tailing her? Was her apartment bugged? Was some whacko after her? Was her life in immediate danger? The unknowns in his security position were the hardest hurdles to jump.

The traffic cooperated and Keegan arrived in Philadelphia with his dull gray Ford Taurus rental car. He had already run external tests on April's cell phone. At the moment there was no bug or other monitoring device, but that could all change in a matter of minutes. He could route her calls through a scrambler system, but a sophisticated tech person could detect it. That would send up a big red flag and complicate the situation a great deal. That was the problem with technology. Every day a new product hit the market. Even with his two research personnel, it was hard to keep up on innovative products that could breach security systems, and hackers were always trying to break into the new software.

Keegan decided he did not want to be seen at the Thornburg Genetics office, so he went directly to April's apartment. He studied her apartment entrance and the surrounding block for several minutes before getting out of his car. Nothing looked out of place. He walked nonchalantly up to the entryway door. It had an electronic code device so those entering just needed to push the right numbers. Keegan had no idea what the numbers were, but he had the emergency lock picked in less than ten seconds. He paused outside April's third floor apartment door. He knew once he was inside he had to move quickly and quietly. If there was some type of surveillance equipment in the apartment, he would have to rush and get April out of Thornburg immediately. It could be a set up with a motion detector, a sound detector or any other form of bugging device. He would probably have some time, because the odds of someone monitoring her apartment while she was at work would be slim. Keegan slipped on the rubber gloves he brought with him. There was only a click as he picked the apartment lock and slid into the apartment, making no noise. First he hit the electrical outlet boxes. There was no evidence of a bugging device. An electrical box was a favorite location for placing bugging devices, because electricity often provided enough interference to avoid detection. Keegan knew his expensive detection equipment wouldn't be fooled by a little electricity. Suddenly he felt something brush against his leg. It was an orange striped cat. "You scared me, kitty." Keegan took a second to pet the cat and run his bug detection unit across the cat's collar. From the outlets he went to the light fixtures and combed the rest of her apartment. After a thorough search that lasted an hour, Keegan verified that April's apartment was clean. He wasn't surprised. If he were dealing with real professionals, they would have anticipated this move well in advance. Keegan installed a micro-wireless camera under April's side table. The pencil-sized camera took only a small piece of duct tape to secure it. The lens was focused on the entry door. He made sure it was angled high enough to avoid any movement of the cat if it went by. Anybody entering or exiting the door would set off a motion detector. When this happened, a signal would be sent to his remote computer and immediately to his cell phone. When he left the apartment, it was almost four o'clock. Keegan decided it was time for a meal.

April arrived at work on time. It took her a little while, but she was finally able to focus on her work. Jason called and invited April to eat dinner at his apartment. She told him she had to work about an hour later than he did. He assured her that was fine, because it would give him time to prepare a nice meal and everything would be ready when she arrived.

All day long, April was tense as she waited for Lexis to call back. The call never came. April had no idea what was happening, and she could feel her anxiety level elevate. At five thirty April left work and drove to Jason's. She didn't want to be at Jason's apartment right now, and she had to talk herself into relaxing. April took the key out of her pocketbook and let herself in.

"Good evening, April. You're just in time. I'll get everything on the table."

"What can I help you with?"

"Why don't you sit down and relax, honey. We'll eat in just a minute."

"It smells so good. What are we having?"

"I picked up choice filet mignon on my way home, and we have fresh green beans with a baked potato."

As soon as Jason mentioned filet mignon, April's mind flashed back to her dinner date with Keegan in Ecuador. She could remember the fragrance of the red rose and the orange sunset. It was such a comfortable feeling.

"I made you a surprise for dessert."

"What kind of dessert? I'll bet it's yummy."

Keegan ate a light supper and started his waiting game. He read the newspaper and browsed the news channel at the restaurant. He drove to the Putney Street Quality Inn and made reservations. He watched more news and checked his emails for an hour and then he left. A nearby Starbucks beckoned him. There were only two people in line, and the young lady behind the counter had his medium-sized black coffee poured in no time. Keegan was familiar with a large section of Philadelphia, but he decided to drive around and familiarize himself with the numerous side streets. After an hour of driving, he started to worry. It was 7:00 PM and April hadn't been back to her apartment yet. Keegan went to a nearby mall and walked for an hour. It was eight o'clock and still no April. Was she working late? Was she in trouble? Was she with Jason? The thought of her being with Jason made him cringe. Jason was a two-timer. Keegan decided he would drive back and park where he could see the entrance to April's apartment. It was about nine thirty when April finally pulled into her well-lit parking spot. He watched her pause at her apartment building door, look both directions, and punch in her code to allow entrance to the building. In less than two minutes his cell phone rang. The micro camcorder and motion detector were working. There was April walking into her apartment. Keegan decided to wait fifteen minutes before following her. He monitored the street and windows in neighboring apartments and homes. Nothing appeared to be out of the ordinary. He got out of his car and walked to April's Honda. His electronic detectors showed no signs of bugs in the car's interior or anywhere on the frame.

April heard her doorbell ring. She slipped on her bathrobe, wrapped her wet hair in a towel and trotted to the door just as the doorbell rang a second time. She peeked through the peephole and saw Keegan.

"Who is it?" she hollered as she laughed to herself.

"I'm pretty sure you know who it is."

"Are you alone?"

"I am."

"Why should a girl let a suspicious looking character like you into her room at this hour of the night?"

"Because I brought the pot of gold from the end of the rainbow just for you."

April opened the door.

"In that case you may enter my humble abode."

"Thank you so much. I didn't think you were ever going to get home."

"I don't recall any prior notification of a visit."

"No, there was no prior notification, but I'm sure you know why I'm here."

"Lexis sent you, didn't she?"

"That's the reason."

"I apologize for looking half drowned, but I just got out of the shower."

"That's okay. You actually look kind of cute in your bathrobe and hair towel."

"What do you mean kind of cute? Wouldn't beautiful be a better description?"

"I think we need to change subjects, so moving right along to the contact. I assume the contact happened at The Golden Mast Yacht Club?"

"I have to get my hair dry Keegan, give me five minutes. Make yourself at home. There's soda or juice in the fridge. Help yourself, I'll be right back."

Keegan took off his coat and walked to the refrigerator. "Do you want something to drink April?"

"No thank you."

Keegan found a glass, placed two ice cubes in it and drew water from the tap. He could hear the hair dryer start up as he walked to April's sofa and sat down. Ten minutes later she emerged in a pair of blue jeans, a white T-shirt and pink fuzzy slippers. She looked gorgeous, but Keegan knew he had to keep this situation on a professional level.

"You look nice, April."

"Thank you. It's been a while since we've seen each other. Have you been busy keeping Thornburg safe?"

"I'm always busy. That's why I like this job. So, it sounds like you've been busy too." Keegan pulled a small pad and pen out of his shirt pocket. "Tell me all about the contact. Make sure you include every detail, no matter how insignificant it seems."

"I didn't sleep well last night and I'm very tired, but I'll do my best. It all started Saturday night at the charity ball. As I was making my way around the tables and talking with the guests, a man came up to me and introduced himself. His name is Nadish Patel. He said that he represented a benefactor who was interested in donating a large sum of money to the Thornburg Vision of Hope Charity. The benefactor wanted to meet with me in private. Nadish gave me his card and asked me to call Sunday morning to make arrangements. That was yesterday."

April told Keegan the whole story about meeting at The Golden Mast Yacht Club for dinner. She started thinking about her meeting on The Jolly Roger and then she paused. She told Keegan she wasn't sure if she could continue, because she had promised the benefactor that everything they discussed would be kept confidential. It wasn't right to make a promise and then break it.

"April, I understand how you feel about breaking a promise. You are an above-board, moral person. I haven't heard your story yet, but I'll bet you are dealing with a person full of greed, anger and deception. I know you can't take a promise lightly, but you have to weigh the facts. Truth will prevail in the end, but in the future you have to think hard before making a rash promise. Your intent was innocent. I am sure this benefactor's intent was treacherous. When you are contacted again, guess what this benefactor's first question will be? Did you keep your promise, April? Did you talk with even one person about the things we discussed? How are you going to respond?"

"I don't know."

"April, right now you have to dig down deep and tell me everything that happened at the meeting. You know this guy is being deceptive. If not, why is he making you jump through hoops? He could have simply written a check and handed it to you or mailed it, said have a nice day and it would have all been over. This guy is dangerous, and he is preying on your outstanding moral reputation. That's even worse than you breaking a promise. He's a leech, April."

There was silence. Keegan knew April was churning all of the information around in her head. There was silence for several minutes.

"April, we are talking about a major breach of security at Thornburg Genetics. We told you something bad and ugly might happen. It happened. Do you think this person cares one bit about you?"

Finally, April spoke.

"You're right. He's using me. As much as I know I shouldn't break my promise, I have to. He went way out of bounds discussing things not related to the charity function. Now he's making me feel guilty for discussing those things with you. Mr. Patel took me out on the docks to boat slip number 27. The name on the back of the boat was The Jolly Roger."

Keegan laughed. "The Jolly Roger? That sounds original."

April continued with her account of the meeting. After she finished, there was silence from Keegan. He had written several notes. She knew he was mulling over all the information she had given him. Then he leaned over and took her hand.

"I'm sorry you had to go through this. It must have been terrible. You did the right thing by contacting Lexis and describing this event to me. I think you know this person is not interested in doing things right. The whole idea of making you feel guilty with the anticipation of getting the cancer drug to the public is total deception."

"I know the benefactor is only interested in himself."

"He is throwing you sympathy crumbs and hopes you will take the whole piece of bait. I guarantee you if he has his way he will profit big and you will end up ruined in the end. Be extremely careful from this moment forward. We're dealing with a dangerous, evil foe, April. When he contacts you again he is going to ask if you have kept your promise. You have to have the right answer."

"I don't know what to say."

"You'll think of something, April. Now, let me work through a few security issues with you. First, I was in your apartment this afternoon and scanned the entire apartment to see if there were any bugs."

"You were in here and didn't even let me know ahead of time?"

"I can't divulge everything that happens in the security world ahead of time. There is a lot of sophisticated surveillance equipment on the market. You have to trust me to do my job, and I can't tell you everything I do. I didn't want to violate your personal space without letting you know, but I had no choice. Sorry, April. Second, there are no bugs on your cell phone at this time. Third, there are no bugs in or on your car at this time. Well, there may be a few bugs on your windshield."

"Very funny. Is there anything left that's sacred in my life now?"

"Absolutely nothing, as you will know with the next tidbit of information. Are you ready?"

"I can't wait."

"Taped on the underside of your nice cherry lamp table nearest the door is a miniature camera. It is set off by motion. Every time you walk in front of it or the door is opened, the camera starts recording and runs until the motion stops or for a minimum of three minutes. A transmitter sends a signal to my cell phone. I can view everything the camera is picking up between the table and door. So, before you go prancing through here in your underwear, keep that in mind."

"Is this some kind of sick humor to get even with me for something? I can't see all of this being necessary."

"After your meeting with The Benefactor, you're asking me if this is a joke? Come on, April, this guy and whoever he's working with, or for, is dangerous."

"I'm sorry, Keegan. I'm really nervous."

"Well, look at it this way. You have a commodity that somebody wants. At least you aren't expendable at this point in time."

"That gives me a big feeling of relief. So what's the next step?"

"The next step is for me to leave and jump into some research. I need to see you tomorrow night. I'll bring the surveillance DVD from Saturday's charity event. My staff should have captured your contact with Nadish Patel. Call me tomorrow and let me know what time you can come over to the Quality Inn on Putney Street. It's the same one you called Lexis from this morning."

"How did you know that?"

"Every time Lexis is contacted I receive a notification of the caller's telephone number. I looked it up. You made the call from the Quality Inn."

"I should have been able to figure that one out."

"Anyhow, do you still have the business card this Nadish Patel gave you and the checks from The Benefactor?"

"Sure, they're right here in my purse."

"Why don't you jot down the information off the card? That way you'll have it if you need it."

April got up and walked to her kitchen counter where she had a pad and pen. Keegan got up and followed her. After she retrieved the business card and checks from her purse, she wrote the name and number on the pad and handed Keegan the card.

"I'm afraid I can't give you the checks. I can only hand those over to a reputable person. I don't think The Benefactor would approve."

"Thanks a lot. I can assure you he wouldn't approve, but I promise to take good care of them. I have one more order of business before I go." Keegan reached in his pants pocket and handed April a cell phone. "Here is a cell phone similar to yours. Use only this phone to contact me and do not contact The Keeper again unless it is set up through me. Do you have any questions, April?" She shook her head, no.

"Then I must be on my way." Keegan walked to the door. As he approached it, his cell phone rang. He looked at the cell phone caller ID and glanced back at April. "Calling so soon my dear?"

"Very funny," said April as they both laughed.

"Remember, April, you have to handle every day like it is business as usual."

Keegan said good night and drove back to the Quality Inn.

Chapter 50

It had been a long day, but Keegan knew he had to move on several security issues before he could get some sleep. He opened his laptop and fired off several emails to his assistants.

Email 1: priority one – discreet - boat named The Jolly Roger, dock number twenty seven at The Golden Mast Yacht Club, Philadelphia.

Email 2: priority one – discreet - background check on Nadish Patel, see business card attachment.

Email 3: priority one - copies of surveillance DVDs from Saturday night Thornburg Vision of Hope Charity event between the hours of 7:30 and 9:00 PM.

Email 4: priority one – discreet - background check on Dr. Emilio Delgado, Quito, Ecuador.

Keegan had hand selected his security team and knew he had one of the best, if not the best, teams of any major corporation. The assignments he had just distributed would be completed as soon as physically possible.

After he sent out the emails, Keegan concentrated on Raymond Hoffman. Raymond was a level seven, security clearance pharmaceutical researcher. He had just completed twenty-nine years of service with Thornburg Genetics two weeks ago. His last three years of state and federal income tax records appeared to be in order with no abnormalities. His last three years of credit card use also appeared to be normal.

Raymond wasn't married. Keegan made a note to check for any girlfriends. "Oh, he has one sister with the same address, Elizabeth Hoffman. Apparently she doesn't use credit cards. She doesn't appear to be working anywhere and hasn't filed any tax returns for the last two years. There's no obituary posted. If she were an invalid in any way, it's likely she would be receiving social security disability. That's a negative. Huh. Something doesn't add up here. I think I need to have a talk with Raymond in the near future."

It was 2:00 AM. Keegan was exhausted and decided his work was complete. It was time for some sleep. He hated to go to bed without a shower, but he couldn't keep his eyes open. A shower would have to wait until morning. He called Lexis and briefed her on the day's events, then slipped under the fresh white sheets.

Keegan woke up to the ringing of his cell phone. He picked it up off the table next to his bed. The time on the cell phone read 7:10 AM. He checked the caller ID. It was the camcorder from April's apartment. He pushed the talk button, and there was April standing in front of the apartment door with a big smile on her face. She was holding a piece of paper with handwritten words in bold letters. It said, "Good morning, off to work, did I wake you?" and then there was a smiley face. Keegan watched as she held the sign. Then she waved, turned and walked out of her apartment door.

"She can be such a pain, but she is funny," Keegan said to himself. He set the phone on the night stand and drifted back to sleep.

It was 8:30 when Keegan woke again. He made a cup of Maxwell House coffee supplied for the room and poured it into a Styrofoam cup. After a quick shower, he put on a pair of jeans and his khaki colored, two pocket shirt, then went straight to his computer. "I see the crew has been busy," said Keegan.

Email 1: response - No boat named The Jolly Roger docked at The Golden Mast Yacht Club. Boat at dock #27 named 'Empty Nester'. Owners Robert and Marsha Folts are out of town for two weeks. Round trip airline tickets to Bahamas. There is evidence of glue residue on back of boat. Probably a temporary sign saying 'The Jolly Roger' adhered to boat covering the true 'Empty Nester' name.

"So, must be our benefactor borrowed the boat for the evening. That means he either knows the owners or knew they were going to be out of town."

Keegan sent an email back: good job - assignment complete.

Email 2: response - the telephone number on the Nadish Patel business card has been disconnected. It was a throw away cell phone number in existence for four days. Number is not traceable. Name is fictitious.

Keegan sent an email back: good job - assignment complete.

Email 3: response - copies of charity event surveillance DVDs available. Call for package delivery.

Email 4: response - working on background check on Dr. Emilio Delgado, Quito, Ecuador. I will contact you when information is complete.

"That's right, let's find out everything we can about this guy."

Keegan picked up his cell phone and punched in the numbers to one of his security research assistants. "Hi David Chung. How is everything?"

"Everything is great. Don't you ever sleep boss man?"

"Sure, I sleep while you're working. How soon can you get me those DVDs from the charity event?"

"Where are you?"

"At the Quality Inn on Putney Ave."

"Just a minute. Okay, you're not too far away. I can have them to you in fifteen or twenty minutes."

"I know you're a night owl. Have you had breakfast yet?"

"Breakfast? I just got to bed."

"Why don't you meet me next door at the Putney Street Diner? I'll have your coffee ordered and ready."

"I can't wait. Can you ask for a little extra caffeine? You know my wife is going to kill me."

"Take it easy. She understands the importance of security. Besides, would you rather dine with a cute, snuggly wife in the comfort of your own home or with a good looking Irish kid with red hair?"

"That's some choice when there is no choice."

"I'll see you in twenty minutes. This shouldn't take too long."

"Famous last words, that means I'll be home for lunch, if I can keep my eyes open that long."

"Where's that proud sense of spirit and self-sacrificing mentality you used to have?"

"I'm coming, boss. I'll see you soon."

Keegan chuckled as he heard a click on the other end of his cell phone. David Chung was the best technology guy alive. He probably had the suspect all picked out, and he didn't even know the details. His innate sense of piecing puzzles together was uncanny.

Twenty minutes later, David made his way into the Putney Street Diner. He could see Keegan in a booth staring at him. Steam was rising off two cups of coffee sitting on the table. Keegan ordered a large breakfast, and David ordered a bagel with cream cheese. In thirty minutes they were back in Keegan's motel room. The 'Do Not Disturb' sign was still on the door. After entering, Keegan locked the door behind them, and David turned on the portable DVD player he brought with him.

"Just so you know, the guy you are probably looking for came through a kitchen door into the charity event. He enters part way through April's speech, listens for a few minutes, then leaves. A while later he enters the conference hall again through the kitchen door. He locates April, talks with her briefly and then departs the same way."

"How do you know who or what I am looking for?"

"You gave me a period of seven thirty to nine PM. This is the only event of interest that I can see. We're looking for a 'who' aren't we?"

"Correct. How do you know this is him?"

"He's the only one not eating cheesecake, drinking coffee and pretending to have a good time."

Keegan laughed. "You're a funny guy, David."

"Well, what do you want me to say? He looks so out of place that it's pitiful."

"This is why I give you all of the top assignments."

"Top assignments huh? When I leave here I need twenty four hours off so I can get some sleep."

"Maybe, let's see what you have."

"Okay, here he is entering the charity event through the kitchen door at exactly eight thirty-eight PM. Look at his face. I think this is the first time he ever wore a tuxedo. Here he comes and boom, off the screen. Twelve minutes later he approaches April. Get ready. Now, I couldn't catch much of his side of the conversation with April because his back was to our camera most of the time. April didn't say much and for the most part listened to the guy. He handed her a business card, which she glanced at. She looked back up and he had turned and was disappearing into the crowd. Now back to camera one. Here's our guy less than two minutes later. He walks back to the kitchen door. Then he turns around and leans with his back against the wall, looking at the crowd. He scans for a minute and then slides through the kitchen door. End of story, except I know who it is."

"You know who it is?"

"Of course, his real name is Atal Maqbool. He's a local private investigator."

"How did you hunt him up? I wasn't sure whether Nadish Patel was an alias or a real name. I could see he was of Indian descent on the DVD you created."

"It took me all night to ferret him out, Keegan. I used the telephone number you gave me from his business card, the now disconnected number. No number is ever really disconnected without leaving a trace. You don't really want me to spend an hour explaining the hows and whys of my background work do you?"

"No. Never mind. Thanks for identifying him, David. Now I know where this is going. I guarantee that Mr. Private Investigator was hired for a week, paid a decent sum of money in cash, never met his employer, and will claim it was just another day of confidential work for a client. Best of all, I'm sure he will say it was all above board."

"It's a tough world out there, Keegan. You have to survive somehow. Cash is a great means of survival."

"I know. It's probably not even worth paying him a visit, unless he shows up somewhere else down the line. Every move he made will be shrouded with a cloak of confidentiality. You did a great job, David. Take your twenty-four hours. You deserve it."

"Thanks, boss."

Keegan called April and told her it would not be necessary to meet concerning her contact with Nadish Patel. The DVD recording was brief and no further information was required. It was eleven thirty when Keegan checked his email again.

Email 4: response-Dr. Emilio Delgado background check clean. No suspicious action. Note: Scoured the long distance telephone calls to Dr. Delgado's cell phone, house phone and cancer clinic. They receive hundreds of telephone calls per week. It would take hours to research each phone call completely. Please advise. Found two interesting calls. First was a telephone call from Philadelphia. A tracer showed the number was disconnected with no further information. It was one of those throw away phones. Buy the cell phone, buy the minutes, use it and toss it. Second was a telephone call from a land line inside Thornburg Genetics. The phone is on a desk vacant of personnel at this time.

Keegan sent an email back. Good job. Thanks for the information. Assignment complete. He recognized the first telephone number immediately. It was the same disconnected number on the Nadish Patel business card. Keegan doubted that Nadish Patel, the alias for Atal Maqbool, would have called Dr. Delgado in Ecuador. It had to be a phone call made by the benefactor before he gave the phone to Atal Maqbool. Keegan then typed the Thornburg Genetics telephone number into his security systems software. The computer screen showed the exact location of the telephone in the building. Then he typed in Raymond Hoffman's name. Keegan gave a light, shrill whistle. The vacant number used as a contact to Dr. Delgado in Ecuador was only two offices down from Raymond Hoffman's office. Keegan thought about the situation for a minute. Either Dr. Hoffman didn't have enough common sense not to use a phone so close to his office to call Ecuador or this was a setup from someone else inside Thornburg Genetics.

"Looks like we are dealing with a pro," said Keegan. "The benefactor contracted a private investigator for a short-term assignment, which by now is finished. He commandeered a yacht that wasn't his and set it up for a conference with April. He set up a cell phone number for ten days, had it disconnected and no owner information was available other than Atal Maqbool. The whole Ecuador scenario isn't quite clear though. How did the benefactor find out about the C1 Extraction pills disbursed to Carlos Quinonez? How did he know to contact Dr. Delgado? There has to be other contact numbers if we can just ferret them out, and I wonder if Mr. Jason Otis is in the middle of this. At this point I have to concentrate on our own Dr. Raymond Hoffman. The benefactor specifically named him. I wonder how he fits in the picture. I better call Lexis and brief her."

Chapter 51

There was a screech of car tires as Keegan deliberately slammed on the brakes in front of the Toyota RAV4. With no place to go except the ditch, the driver of the RAV4 slammed on his brakes and almost rear-ended Keegan's car. The driver of the RAV4 then laid on his horn, his face turning red with anger. What was this idiot in front of him doing? He didn't notice another car had pulled up tight behind him and stopped, leaving no place for his RAV4 to go. A muscular, giant man jumped out of the driver's seat, ran to the RAV4, slid a key in the driver's side door and opened it. It happened so fast the RAV4 driver didn't have time to react.

"Put your vehicle in park now, Dr. Hoffman."

Raymond was looking into the face of a huge bearded man that looked like an NFL lineman. Ray was afraid, but he detected an air of professionalism about the man. He reached for the shifting lever and felt the man grip his left wrist. Ray knew the only option was to follow the stranger's directions. All he could think about was his sister, Elizabeth. He put his car in park.

"Do you have any weapons?"

Raymond shook his head no.

"Release your seat belt, Dr. Hoffman."

Raymond did as he was told.

"Get out of your car now and go to the driver's side of the car in front of you."

Raymond could feel the pressure on his wrist and knew it would easily be broken if he made one wrong move. Raymond slid out of the seat and the mountain of a man put handcuffs on him and escorted him to the driver's side rear door of Keegan's car. A motorist drove by, but paid no attention to them. The stranger opened the door and Raymond slid onto the seat. The large man shoved Raymond across the seat and slid in next to him. He barely had room to squeeze in and get the door closed. Raymond had never been so scared in his life. He trembled as sweat rolled down his forehead and drenched his eyebrows, eyelids and cheeks. His shirt was also wet from the sweat. He had hoped and prayed this day would never come, but it was inevitable. He knew this was the day his life would end. As the car sped away with Raymond held captive, he looked back and saw his RAV4 following them. His captors didn't say a word. Ray glanced behind him again and his RAV4 was gone.

After driving up and down several streets in the suburbs, Keegan's cell phone rang.

"Yes?"

"The coast is clear. Nobody is following you."

"Thank you," said Keegan as he hit the cell phone disconnect button. Keegan took an immediate left. He went three more blocks and took a right. Just down the road was a large public city park. Raymond could see adults and kids engaged in various activities. Some were walking, walking dogs, jogging, or riding bicycles. There were several swing sets and kids' small rides in use. Why would his captors bring him here to torture him? It was too public. As they pulled into a vacant parking spot, Ray felt the handcuffs being removed from his wrists. The driver then spoke. "Dr. Hoffman, please get out of the car and go sit on the metal bench by the two shrubs over there. I will join you in a minute."

Ray was embarrassed. His hair, shirt and pants were soaking wet from sweat, and he smelled horrible. He reached for the door handle and pulled himself out of the car. As he got out, he looked in both directions. The bench was several yards from the biking and walking trail, as well as the playground. It was quite isolated. He hoped nobody would notice him as he walked to the bench. People seemed to be in their own little world and barely gave Ray a glance. Ray thought about running but decided he wouldn't get far, not being in great physical shape; so he did as he was told and ambled over to the bench, turned around and sat down. It was actually a beautiful, sunny, spring day. A handful of small white clouds that looked like popcorn drifted slowly to the east. If only he could enjoy the moment.

Keegan turned around and spoke to his accomplice in the back seat. "Good job, Justin, keep an eye on things. When I come back to the car with Dr. Hoffman, please join us."

"You got it, boss," he said as he opened the car door. "By the way, boss, do you think you could rent a bigger car next time?" They both laughed as Justin squeezed out of the Taurus and scanned the area for a good surveillance location.

Keegan hopped out and walked to the bench where Raymond Hoffman was sitting. Raymond looked every day of his 62 years; he was in misery and appeared to be on the verge of passing out.

"Dr. Raymond Hoffman, my name is Keegan McGrath. I am the head of security for Thornburg Genetics. I am sorry for the rough car swap. However, due to recent circumstances in the company, I felt this action was necessary."

"Then you're not them?"

"Who are 'them'?"

Raymond started to cry. Keegan had not expected Dr. Hoffman to fall apart and was surprised at the flood of tears. He looked from side to side to see if anybody was watching. The only person paying any attention to them was Justin, his assistant.

"Dr. Hoffman, you need to tell me what is going on. Please try to pull yourself together."

Ray pulled a hankie from his left back pocket and wiped his face. His eyes were red and tears oozed down his cheek. He blew his nose and slowly settled down.

"Yes, I guess you found out. Well, I'm probably better off talking to you than them, even if it lands me in jail."

Keegan noticed Dr. Hoffman retained a slight German accent even though he had been in this country for years after attending college at Harvard.

"You need to tell me what is going on Dr. Hoffman. I mean everything. We have a serious security breach at Thornburg Genetics. Your name has surfaced as a major potential security threat. I need information. I am going to record our conversation."

There was silence for a moment, and then Raymond started to talk.

"Yes, it all started a little over two years ago. Do you have identification, Mr. McGrath?"

Keegan pulled out his wallet and handed his Thornburg Genetics Security ID to Dr. Hoffman.

"Is this real?"

"Yes, Doctor, it's real."

"Yes, thank you. Are you familiar with the Noah Gene?"

"I believe it allows us to communicate right now. If I didn't have it, you wouldn't be able to tell me a lot of top secret issues you are about to reveal, because you would have a massive mental block."

"Yes, it's something like that, but much more complicated. I wish we could isolate the gene. It's still only a theory. We can observe how it functions so we know it's real, but we just can't trace it to its roots."

"Do you mind, Doctor? It all started two years ago and....."

"Yes, a little over two years ago I received a telephone call from..., what security level are you?"

"Seven, Dr. Hoffman."

"Yes, a little over two years ago I received a telephone call from The Keeper. Are you familiar with our research at Thornburg Genetics?"

"Doctor, you have to stay focused."

"Yes, well this is relevant. We have a drug called C1 Extraction, also known as Constellation Blue, which is in the form of a small blue pill. The C1 Extraction pharmaceutical cures numerous types of cancer. I don't mean shrinks cancer cells or puts them into remission; I mean it destroys cancer cells. The healing takes place in seven days. A little over two years ago, I received a telephone call from The Keeper. She told me not to write down the instructions she was about to give me, but to memorize them. Are you familiar with The Keeper?"

"I am familiar, Raymond. The Keeper is my direct supervisor."

"Yes, The Keeper gave me precise instructions to produce fifty C1 Extraction pills and deliver them to a specific clinic in Baltimore. I was directed to deliver them to a man who remained nameless, but he would have a tattoo of a pink ribbon on his left forearm. You know the pink ribbon that shows your support for breast cancer research?"

"I'm familiar with the pink ribbon, Doctor."

"Yes, well it seemed like a strange request. I do get an occasional request from The Keeper for these pills, but it has always been an order for seven pills and two times she ordered twenty-one pills. In the past, she never asked me to deliver them, but I would never question The Keeper. So, I manufactured the pills, put them in a plastic bottle and delivered them to the clinic. A man greeted me just outside the door. He was wearing a white doctor's smock and had a stethoscope around his neck. I had never seen him before and have never seen him since. He said hello and thanked me for coming. Then he displayed the pink ribbon tattoo on his left forearm."

"What did he look like?"

"Yes, he was a medium height Caucasian man. He was slightly bald-ing and had brown hair with just a speckle of gray. One thing I will never forget was his dark, thick unibrow. It seemed to make his eyes bulge. He was thin. That's all I remember about his physical features. He thanked me for all of my research work as I handed him the bottle of pills. He never went back inside the clinic, but walked past me, down the side-walk and disappeared out of sight. I was sure then I had made a grave mistake, but he must have had the Noah Gene or I wouldn't have been able to make the transaction. It probably wouldn't have mattered, be-cause I'm sure he would have taken them by force. I didn't know what to do. The Keeper had given me the orders, and I followed through. Exactly three weeks later, I received another telephone call. It was The Keeper again directing me to take fifty more C1 Extraction pills to the same clinic."

"I had a gut wrenching feeling that something wasn't right. I'm sup-posed to be in the research department, not in the pill delivery service.

My mind started working overtime. Was there some special mission necessitating the release of all these pills? Was the phone contact person really The Keeper? Was she on the take? The C1 Extraction pill had already been around for thirty years. Why was I being required to deliver such large quantities in such a short time frame? I wanted to call The Keeper back to verify the order, but I decided that would expose my first pill distribution blunder. Yes, therefore, I decided to play the slightly forgetful doctor and not show up. After I was an hour late for the scheduled delivery, I received another call from The Keeper. She asked me where I was and if there was a problem delivering the pills. I told her I was in the middle of a research project and it would be a problem to leave. I asked her if someone else could pick them up and deliver them. I suggested that somebody from security might be available. She told me that would not be possible and that I needed to follow her instructions and deliver the pills within the next hour. I felt bad, but I held my ground and told her the research I was involved in would take several hours. There were other staff available and I could send one of them. The whole situation was not adding up. Then The Keeper told me I must follow her instructions or there would be dire consequences. The pills had to be delivered within the hour by me. She sounded angry. I had never heard her angry before. Then she hung up. I didn't know what to do. I wanted to follow The Keeper's instructions. I had never let her down in the past, but something just didn't feel right."

Raymond started crying again.

"What happened next, Dr. Hoffman?"

The crying became bawling. Ray sobbed and sobbed. His face was red and tears soaked the front collar of his shirt. His hankie was dripping wet. A couple of joggers stopped a ways off and looked at Keegan and Ray to see what was happening.

"It's okay," said Keegan. "I'm just trying to help a friend through a bit of a hard time."

Ray nodded his head up and down indicating everything was okay. The joggers looked at them suspiciously, then slowly started on their way again.

"Dr. Hoffman, you have to tell me what happened. I can't help you if you don't."

After several minutes, Ray stopped crying. From the stench of sweat, wet clothing, red face and watering eyes, Keegan knew Dr. Hoffman was in misery.

"Yes, well I was right. It was not The Keeper. I made up a research question as a reason to call her emergency number. She mentioned nothing about the fifty pills, and I never delivered the second order.

Somehow, somebody was able to duplicate The Keeper's voice. I live with my sister Elizabeth. Neither of us was ever married. We lived with our parents. As they grew older they both had medical problems. We took care of them until they passed away. I have focused on my work at Thornburg Genetics and Elizabeth maintains the house. She has held a few part time jobs as well. We enjoy each other's company and everything was fine until I didn't deliver the pills. When I arrived home about four hours later, my sister was gone. There was a note on the kitchen table. It said that I would be contacted the following day. If I did not do as I was told, my sister would be killed. The note said to tell no one about the situation and go about my business in a normal manner."

"I couldn't sleep that night. All I could envision was Elizabeth being restrained in some moss and rodent infested basement somewhere. I went to work the next day and did my best to act normal. I couldn't concentrate on my work. About noon, I received a telephone call. It wasn't The Keeper this time; it was a robotic sounding man's voice. The person on the telephone gave me an address and instructed me to deliver the fifty cancer curing pills to that address and leave them in the mailbox. The drop would be observed. I was to come alone and my sister would be held for insurance purposes."

"The location proved to be just ten blocks from the Baltimore clinic. It was an old, vacant, run down, two-story house. A dented metal mailbox was attached next to the boarded up front door. I placed the pills in the mailbox and left. My sister didn't come home. I am still terrified, Mr. McGrath. I felt terrible and didn't dare to tell anyone for fear they would kill my Elizabeth. The next contact was a telephone call two days later. It was the same robotic voice. He told me I would deliver 100 of the cancer curing pills to them per week. I was also to bring the formula for the pill with the next delivery. They would hold my sister for one year and then they would release her. I told the caller I could not do that. He told me that I could and would provide 100 pills per week and the formula if I wanted my sister to be safe and keep my job. The man told me to make the next delivery to the same location as the last one in five days. I couldn't do it. Two days later I received a small package in the mail. There was no return address on it. Inside the package was a DVD. I was hesitant, but placed it in my DVD machine. The DVD showed my sister sitting behind a table. The background was dark and my sister was sobbing. She begged me to give them what they wanted. If I didn't she said they would kill her. Then the screen went blank, but the audio was still on. I heard my sister scream. It was horrendous. I can still hear her cry of pain."

Ray paused. He looked as if he would cry again, but he seemed to be out of tears. His face lost all expression. Keegan was afraid he might go into shock or pass out.

"That was over two years ago. I receive at least two phone calls per month from the man who is holding my sister. I recognize the robotic voice. I hang up the telephone as soon as I hear it. I also receive one un-marked package in the mail every month. Though the box sizes change, the contents are always the same: one homemade DVD. The thought of somebody torturing my sister is more than I can bear, so I destroy the DVDs as soon as they arrive without watching them."

Ray started crying again. "I hate myself, Mr. McGrath. I'm on strong anti-depressants. Every day I consider suicide, but can't do it because I imagine what would happen to my dear Elizabeth. Until now I couldn't tell anybody about the abduction. What if The Keeper took my research position away? My research is all I have, Mr. McGrath. I'm so selfish. Please help this to end. I want everything to end. I'm tired. I'm so very tired. Do what you want with me, but find Elizabeth. Save Elizabeth. I love her more than anyone on earth."

"Dr. Hoffman, why don't these people make their own pills?"

"No chemist can duplicate these pills. It is senseless to give them the formula. The formula contains a compound they cannot repro-duce."

"Why is that, Dr. Hoffman?"

"I'm sorry, Mr. McGrath. I won't tell you."

"It's because the compound is from an ancient, rare plant that only exists in secure Thornburg locations, isn't it Dr. Hoffman?"

Raymond had a surprised look on his face as he stared at Keegan.

"Yes, I know, Dr. Hoffman. I'm the head of security for Thornburg. It's my job to know."

Keegan was stunned by the account just portrayed by Dr. Hoffman. He knew the poor researcher's soul had been tormented for at least two years. Keegan wasn't sure if he himself could have handled that amount of pressure day after day without some physical or mental breakdown.

"You are a brave man, Dr. Hoffman. I'm sorry to hear about the events you have had to endure. I'm going to help you get your sister back, and I will do my best to help you keep your research position."

Raymond grabbed Keegan by the hands and gripped them hard. "You'll get Elizabeth back?"

"I will do my best, Dr. Hoffman. Now, in order to get her back I will need your help. I know you are going through an emotional time. Can you help me?"

"What can I do?"

"Answer this question for me. How were you able to communicate with them considering the Noah Gene factor? Shouldn't a mental block have happened somewhere in the communication or transaction stage?"

"The answer to your question is yes, but no mental block occurred at any time. I have a theory. My theory is the person I was communicating with may actually have had cancer and received chemo and/or radiation treatments. The treatments may affect the capability of the Noah Gene to block communications with those not having the gene."

"I have been advised of this theory. Do you know how many people in the world have had chemo and radiation treatments? Hundreds of thousands and maybe millions of people have had one or both treatments, Dr. Hoffman."

"Yes, but there are less than 50 of us that know about the C1 Extraction pill, and we communicate with a limited number of people other than Thornburg researchers. We do not come into contact with many outside people who have had chemo or radiation treatments other than family members or friends."

"I'll have to spend more time thinking this through. We have an enemy to stop, Dr. Hoffman. I have a lot to plan. Can you drive yourself home? You have to get home, get cleaned up and get some rest."

"Yes, I can do that."

"Okay. Listen carefully now. You have to carry out your daily routine like nothing has changed. Pretend this meeting never happened. Nothing has changed. Can you follow through your daily activities with no change of habits?"

"Yes, I will follow my daily routine."

"I have to form a course of action. I am sure you will be involved, but I don't know to what extent. The plan may be life threatening. Will you do everything I ask you to?"

"Yes, I will. Please help me get Elizabeth back."

"We will. I want you to promise me you will tell nobody about our encounter today. I do apologize for the abduction, but I didn't want to have a formal meeting at the Thornburg offices, and I didn't want to show up at your home in case it's being watched or bugs have been planted. I'm going to have your car brought here. Can you get home from here okay?"

"Yes, my sister and I used to come here frequently."

Keegan pulled his cell phone out of his shirt pocket and made a call.

Then he pulled a second cell phone out and handed it to Dr. Hoffman.

"Here is a cell phone that calls me, and only me, directly. Have it on and keep it with you at all times. To contact me, flip it open and push any number. Here is a charger. Keep it plugged in by your bed at night."

In a matter of minutes Dr. Hoffman's RAV4 pulled into the parking area.

"Let's get you home Dr. Hoffman. Are you sure you can drive yourself home?"

"Yes, I'm alright now. I feel like a huge weight has been lifted off me. It's the best I've felt in months."

Keegan watched as Dr. Hoffman pulled out of the park. "He is just another victim of the predators of this world, and these are very dangerous predators with large stakes looking for easy prey." Keegan walked over to his associate.

"Do me a favor will you, Justin?"

"What's that, boss?"

"Call our other driver on your cell phone and have him pick you up. I've got a thousand things to take care of."

"The old man looked in rough shape, didn't he?"

"Yeah, but he's tough. He'll be okay. He got caught up in a bit of a scam and now we have to work through it. I'll see you soon, Justin. Thanks for your help."

"Anytime, boss."

Keegan turned and walked back to his car. As he pulled out of the park, he started reviewing the recording of the meeting that had just taken place with Dr. Hoffman. The intensity of the situation had elevated. Not only had April been contacted, but a hostage situation was now also in the mix. To top that off, highly classified pharmaceuticals had been smuggled out of the Thornburg Genetics research laboratory by an involved high-level researcher. Keegan wondered who monitored the compound inventories at Thornburg and how had the culprits singled out Dr. Hoffman as the go-to man. Was Jason Otis involved? He knew about cancer treatments being given to Señor Quinonez at the clinic. Keegan knew he had to formulate a plan to shut down the Thornburg Genetics security compromise. It had to be simple, yet quick and effective. There were way too many variables for a perfect plan. April was involved, Dr. Hoffman and Elizabeth were involved, and who knew how many culprits were involved or what level of violence they would use.

Chapter 52

Keegan drove nonstop back to his motel. As soon as he closed and locked the door to his room, he turned on the television to mask his words. Then he called the emergency telephone number on his cell phone.

"Hello, this is Lexis. I'll call you back in five minutes."

The telephone went dead. Keegan knew Lexis was in a location that was not secure. While he was waiting, he went back over the information he had received from Dr. Hoffman. There had to be an inside connection, but who was it and how were they obtaining classified information? Keegan suspected Jason, but he worked in the personnel department. Someone in research and development would be a more likely suspect. However, Jason would have access to all employee personnel records and would not be out of place in any area of the Thornburg facility. As he mulled over each scenario his cell phone rang.

"Hello, Keegan, this is Lexis."

"Hi, Lexis, I have information for you."

"I'm ready."

Keegan explained the whole conversation with Raymond Hoffman. Then the brainstorming started.

"Things won't just go away if we take Dr. Hoffman out of the picture will they?" asked Lexis.

"No. These thieves will simply focus on a different employee. We have to use Dr. Hoffman to find out who they are."

"Why haven't they kidnapped Dr. Hoffman? Then they would have the formula they are demanding."

"I'm making a guess here, but I think there are two reasons. First, they kidnapped Dr. Hoffman's sister and are holding her hostage. Nobody even noticed she was gone. She disappeared off the radar, nobody noticed, and Dr. Hoffman could say nothing for fear of jeopardizing her life and his research job. With that move, they have a man inside Thornburg Genetics with a reason to cooperate. Second, if they had kidnapped Dr. Hoffman it would have been all over the television, in the newspapers and in the forefront of every law enforcement personnel's pre-shift briefing. That's too much publicity. I am guessing they have a chemist working with them. They can't duplicate the C1 Extraction. If they kidnap Dr. Hoffman, he doesn't have the research at his fingertips. Somehow they would also have to retrieve his research information, and without an inside person, it might take them years to compromise another employee. Their goal has to be financial gain, and the patience they appear to have will only last as long as they believe they can achieve their goal. It is my professional opinion the kidnapping and potential torture of Elizabeth Hoffman is the best means to a productive end result."

"You sound quite scary and over the edge, Keegan."

"I have to try and think like the criminals do. Speaking of these culprits' actions, you said employees had been kidnapped and killed or disappeared in the past. I looked into those cases a couple of years ago, but I'm going to take a fresh look. I will be looking at a complete list of names, addresses, dates, backgrounds, family information and any other pertinent information. I believe I have everything that was available at the time, but I want to make sure I didn't miss any valuable clues. Also, do you know of any employees who defected from Thornburg Genetics within the last ten years? By defected I mean somebody who said I quit and never showed up for work again, or went to another pharmaceutical company because of discontent over any peculiar situation."

"I will make sure you get another world-wide list of Thornburg Genetic employees that have disappeared or died of suspicious causes. Thank God the list has only about twenty names that we know of. You will have to check with the appropriate law enforcement agencies for any updates on the cases. As you know, they only tell us limited information on an open case. As far as defectors, I can't think of any disgruntled employee over a level four that has left unless it was for a medical reason or retirement. With thirty eight hundred employees we have a lot of ins and outs. You know the old grass is greener syndrome? We have research other companies want, and they have research we would love to have. Some of the other companies feel they can glean information if they can attract employees from their competitors. The difference is we don't want to obtain information by trying to seduce other companies' employees to jump ship. We do our best to promote from within and attract the best employees possible. So while we have some turnover, it's considerably less than our competitors."

"What are the odds an employee in a lower security level obtained classified information on the Noah Gene phenomenon, befriended a grade five or higher security level employee, and somehow manipulated his or her way into additional classified information?"

"Keegan, you are asking lots of hypothetical questions we will probably never be able to answer."

"I still have to ask the questions, Lexis. I am assuming you did not make the telephone call to have C1 Extraction pills delivered by Dr. Hoffman."

"As he said, I have called him in the past, I would say twenty times, to manufacture doses of the C1 extraction. However, security personnel made deliveries of the pills only as assigned by you and your predecessor. Based on the particular compounds used in the pill, I would never ask anyone other than security to make a delivery. Am I on the suspect list too?"

"Everybody is, Lexis. I can't dismiss anybody from my list until all evidence clears him or her. That's my job."

"Good. That's the right answer. You have to do everything you can to isolate these culprits and bring this whole security breach to an end. I have two more questions, Keegan. Why do they only call Raymond every two weeks and send him a DVD once per month? Why don't they keep pressing him day and night?"

"I think it goes back to what we were discussing a few minutes ago. Dr. Hoffman is on the inside. If the perpetrators push too hard and he cracks, no more inside man."

"Why do they only ask for one hundred pills, and not five hundred pills, or a thousand?"

"At this point it appears to be a random number. I'm sure the culprits are selling the pills for big money and don't want to overdo it. They may think that Thornburg's inventory system may somehow pick up on theft, not knowing the pills are custom made or how many are actually distributed. Speaking of inventory systems, how does Dr. Hoffman make pills and smuggle them out of the research facility without detection? That's an area of security I haven't been involved in."

"The security level six and seven researchers have free access to any drug or compound they need. They have access to the rare plant compounds and level seven employees even harvest some from the plants themselves. Because of the Noah Gene phenomenon, we have had no known security breaches until now. I believe this is an isolated incident, but we are going to have to check into this deeper to avoid another security breach."

"How do we know this is an isolated incident?"

"We test our competitors' drugs. No rare plant compounds have ever shown up in the samples we have tested."

"That's good. It appears I can focus on this isolated situation then."

"Do you have a plan in mind other than the one we discussed?"

"I've been considering multiple options. Forming a final plan is my next step. We aren't dealing with amateurs, Lexis. These people are smart and cunning."

"Well you have a lot of work ahead of you. I have confidence you will create a great plan that will be successful. For security reasons, I should not know what the plan is unless it is absolutely necessary. I'm counting on you to trap the culprits, keep Dr. Hoffman and his sister safe, keep April safe and eliminate the breach in security."

"I can only pray for a plan that will succeed in all of these areas. If nobody gets hurt, it's thanks to God, not me."

"Do you think Dr. Hoffman needs to see a psychologist?"

"Let's wait and see how things go. He's survived severe stress for two years now without cracking, and he's using hope as a pick me up right now."

"If anything changes, let me know. We'll talk later. I will in fact pray for this whole situation. Bye."

"Goodbye, Lexis."

Keegan pushed the off button on his cell phone. He took the hundred-pack of index cards off the desk in front of him and started writing down all of the facts he knew, all of his questions, and any information that seemed pertinent. After an hour, he checked his email. Lexis had forwarded information about missing and suspicious employee deaths. After reviewing the information, he saw nothing that suggested any relationship to the present case. The plan to end the security breach would have to come from the information provided by Dr. Hoffman and April.

Chapter 53

"Hello, Dr. Hoffman, this is Keegan McGrath."

"Yes. Good morning, Mr. McGrath."

"Are you holding up okay?"

"Yes. I feel better than ever. Before our, as you called it, encounter yesterday, I had no hope. Do you know what it is like existing day after day with no hope? Now I have hope."

"I'm glad to hear that, Dr. Hoffman. Is everything going well at work?"

"I'm in the middle of a project right now. My concentration is much better, but not perfect. Am I going to jail, Mr. McGrath?"

"I can make no guarantees, Dr. Hoffman. You smuggled classified drugs from our research facility. I understand the intent was honorable, and I believe you will not serve jail time and will remain in your research position if we can catch the culprits. I need your full cooperation though."

"Yes, I will cooperate fully."

"Okay. Right now you must concentrate on what I am going to tell you."

"Yes, Mr. McGrath. I'm ready."

"First, you must understand this. Everything I say to you is confidential and must remain confidential. Only you and I know about the complete details of the situation at this time. I talked to The Keeper and gave her a brief synopsis. If you reveal the facts of this situation to others, it can hurt Thornburg Genetics as a company, you, your research, fellow researchers and numerous other people. Do you understand?"

"Yes, I understand. Everything we discuss is confidential."

"Excellent, Dr. Hoffman, here is the plan. Again, there are no guarantees, but we will flush out the people holding your sister hostage if everything works correctly. We will be able to rescue your sister and keep the Thornburg Genetics research facility from being compromised further. You will be back to living a quiet life, and I am almost certain you will retain your position in the research department."

"Yes, I hate to sound like a skeptic, but are you authorized to make promises regarding personnel issues?"

"I work very closely with The Keeper. While The Keeper has the final say on any company decision, I assure you my opinion is valued. You have to trust me, Dr. Hoffman. I'm not one of the bad guys. You will understand this in a few minutes when I lay out my plan."

"Yes, I'm sorry, Mr. McGrath. I can't lie; I am on the edge about every move I make. I am fearful that any wrong move may bring harm to my sister."

"Then you have to work extra hard to stay focused, Dr. Hoffman."

"Yes, I know I have to concentrate. What happens if this plan doesn't work?"

"I'm going to be straight with you, Doctor. There are numerous variables to be accounted for in this operation. I believe the chance of complete success is about seventy-five percent. At all times, your life, Elizabeth's life, and numerous other innocent bystanders' lives are in danger. There is the potential for people to die. As you know, we are not dealing with nice people. In fact, I believe we are dealing with at least one person who is extremely intelligent and will stop at nothing to achieve his or her desired results." Keegan paused to let the information sink in.

"Thank you for being candid, Mr. McGrath. There is no other choice, is there?"

"I wish there were options, but there are none."

"Yes, I am ready, Mr. McGrath. Please place my sister's life before mine if there is ever a need to choose between the two of us."

"Elizabeth has to be proud to have a brother like you, Raymond. Stay strong. Are you ready for the plan?"

"Yes. I am ready."

"From this day forward this security operation will be called operation Gene Pool. Should you need to contact me for any reason, I will ask you for the operation name. If you do not respond, I will know the culprits are monitoring you, and I will not relay any information of value to you. Now repeat the operation name."

"Gene Pool, that is easy to remember."

"Good. Now listen carefully. When you leave for work tomorrow morning, you are to stop at the Holiday Inn on the corner of 12th Avenue and 10th Street. Do you know where that is?"

"Yes I do."

"At 7:30 AM, park your vehicle and walk in the front entrance. Walk directly past the front desk and straight down the hallway. On the left hand side is a men's restroom. I will meet you there with a recording device. I will set it up to record a conversation between you and another Thornburg Genetics employee. Are you familiar with an employee by the name of April James?"

"Yes, April is in sales and marketing. I have never met her, but I believe her marketing finesse has improved sales significantly for our company. Did you know I used to work with her father, Vincent James? Vincent was actually a recipient of the C1 Extraction treatment and..."

"Dr. Hoffman. You are getting off track. You must refocus."

"Yes, sorry."

"Our security surveillance indicates April James is somehow involved with the thugs who are demanding the C1 Extraction pills and holding Elizabeth hostage."

"Vince's daughter? I can't believe she would be involved in something like this. Why would she be involved?"

"We believe it is for financial gain. Our intelligence reports indicate she will be in contact with you soon. At this point we don't know exactly when or how. If she does contact you, we need a recording of the conversation. We anticipate that she will ask or demand that you give her a quantity of the C1 Extraction pills. I don't care what excuse you come up with, you must tell her no. She will probably use your sister as a bartering tool and anything else she can come up with to get those pills. You must tell her no. Do you understand?"

"Yes. I must tell her no. What if it is beneficial to say yes?"

"It is my job to plan the strategy Dr. Hoffman. I have been planning strategy for years. You are a researcher. You must tell her NO! Do you understand?"

"Yes, Mr. McGrath. I understand."

"Thank you, Doctor. If April James does contact you, call me immediately on the special cell phone I gave you."

"Yes, I will call you."

"Those are the instructions for now. Are there any questions?"

"I have no questions."

"Then I will see you tomorrow morning at 7:30 AM. Remember, your cooperation is vital to the success of operation Gene Pool."

"Yes, Mr. McGrath."

Raymond heard a click on his cell phone as the call ended.

Keegan had heard nothing back from Samantha since Saturday and decided to call her. "Hello, Samantha. Any more juicy news for my listening ears?"

"Hello, Keegan honey. I don't even get a good morning from you? What happened to your manners?"

"Sorry, Samantha. My mind is running through a hundred different scenarios right now, and I'm trying to focus on all of them at once.

Good morning."

"Sounds like lots of stress to me. I'll let it go this time, but only because I like you so much, honey."

"Thanks for the pardon. I guarantee I'll do better in the future."

"Excellent. Now back to your question about our friend Jason. There is no more information of vital interest. He spent most of his day Saturday and Sunday in his apartment with the exception of a jog and a few errands. He went to work on Monday and Tuesday and had a couple of dates with one April James. That's about it. There was no more evidence of extracurricular activities. In fact, with the exception of Friday night he seems rather boring. As always, you'll have a full report by the end of today. How did you like the pictures of our birthday party? I had the girls smile and pose just for you."

"The three of you looked great. The party was quite an undercover operation. Since you were having so much fun, do I still have to pay you for the evening?"

"Of course you do, honey. You saw the great photos of Jason and Sheila. Work like that doesn't come cheap."

"I know. Thank you for another well done assignment, Samantha. I'll stay in touch with you."

"You're welcome, honey. Bye for now."

Chapter 54

April hadn't heard from anybody in two days. It felt like a week. Keegan hadn't called, The Keeper hadn't been in touch, and the benefactor had made no further demands. Slowly she had drifted back into her publicity, marketing and sales requirements. The incident at the Golden Mast on Sunday night had moved to the back of April's mind. She had gone out with Jason the last two nights. His company relieved some of the pressure, but it was hard to stay focused and act natural. Jason hadn't mentioned anything to her about acting out of sorts, so she believed she was keeping up a good front.

April was sitting at her desk when the phone rang for the tenth time that morning. It was an outside line. "Hello, this is April James."

"Hello, April." Pressure instantly built up in April's head. There was silence for several seconds. "So you recognize my voice. That's good. I am calling to see how our arrangement is progressing. Have you contacted Mr. Hoffman yet, April?"

"Not yet, sir."

"I'm sorry to hear that. Is there a problem?"

"No, sir. I'm just not sure how to go about it."

"I'm sure you can create a plan. Well, I must keep this call short. I wouldn't want this phone number traced, now would I? So here is the situation. I expect results. I thought someone of your caliber realized that. It is apparent to me that you need a time frame to successfully complete the task assigned to you. You have until tomorrow evening to contact Mr. Hoffman and complete your mission. I'm sure you haven't told anyone about our plans as promised. We'll talk soon, April."

April heard the dial tone on her telephone. She pushed the off button and slowly set the cordless telephone on her desk. It was time for a break. April took the navy blue sweater off the back of her chair and slipped it on. She retrieved her pocketbook from her desk drawer, picked up her cell phone from the top of a stack of papers on her desk and walked to the garden in front of the Thornburg Genetics building. The garden was empty, as it normally was after the regular 10:00 AM scheduled company break. April opened her cell phone and speed dialed Keegan.

"Hello, you have reached the voice mail of Keegan McGrath. Please leave a message."

April slammed the cell phone shut and mumbled to herself, "Just call if you need anything, April. I could be dead by now, Keegan. Voicemail! Really?"

April opened her cell phone again and started a text message:

Keegan. Just received contact. Then her cell phone rang. There was no caller ID.

"Hello, this is April."

"Good morning, Miss April."

"Hi, Keegan. He just called me again."

"Hang up now and use the other cell phone I gave you."

There was silence on April's cell phone. She retrieved the cell phone Keegan had given her and dialed him back. "Hi, Keegan. Before you get mad at me, I forgot about the other cell phone. The benefactor called and I got rattled. It won't happen again."

"April, relax a little."

"Are you kidding me? I haven't relaxed since Sunday night."

"Okay, you're a little on edge. Take it easy. You have to be able to think clearly."

"I'm sorry, Keegan."

"It's okay, April, what did he say?"

"He asked if I had talked to Raymond Hoffman yet. I told him I hadn't. He said it would be to my benefit if I were given a time frame to complete my mission with Dr. Hoffman. He demanded that I talk with him by close of business tomorrow. The benefactor will call me back tomorrow evening. What am I going to do, Keegan?"

"Did he ask you if you kept your promise of confidentiality?"

"No, he didn't ask. He stated, I'm sure you haven't told anyone as you promised."

"I was going to call you a little later anyhow. I have a plan to draw these thugs out into the open. What are you doing tonight?"

"I have some work to do later this evening, but I'm going to Jason's for supper right after work."

"This is the third night in a row you've seen Jason."

"Thanks for keeping track of me on the apartment door camera system. He is my fiancé you know."

"I know. Sorry for the intrusion. Anyhow, this will work out well. Call me when you leave Jason's. I'll meet you on the way back to your apartment."

"This plan better be good. I think this benefactor guy is a nut job."

"We have to work through this one step at a time, April. That's why you have to stay focused and keep your mind clear."

"I know. I'll call you as soon as I leave Jason's."

It was 8:00 PM when April thanked Jason for another wonderful meal and said goodbye. She did have a project to complete for Thornburg and wanted to meet with Keegan as soon as possible before heading back to her apartment. She pulled out of the parking lot adjacent to Jason's apartment. She drove half a mile and speed dialed Keegan on the new cell phone he had given her.

"I've been awaiting your call, Miss James."

"I'll bet you have, Mr. McGrath. Where would you like to meet?"

"I'm right behind you. There's a Wal-Mart a couple of miles up the road. Pull in there and we'll discuss a course of action."

"What are you doing following me? Don't tell me my life is so endangered you have to follow me. You already have a camera in my apartment and now you're following me?"

"April, will you stop it. I'm trying to save some time here. I haven't had much sleep in the last five days. I'm not a stalker. We have a major security issue at Thornburg Genetics, and you are in the middle of it. You have to get a grip on yourself. I thought you were stronger than this."

"I'm sorry, Keegan. I'm really nervous. This whole situation has turned into an event I hadn't planned on."

"Again, it's okay. Pull over at the Wal-Mart and let's discuss a plan so we can try to get your life back to normal." April agreed and closed her cell phone. She was closer to the edge of a breakdown than she had realized. She also knew there was no one to vent her frustrations to other than Keegan. She pulled into the Wal-Mart parking lot and eased into a spot in the corner, away from the main entrance. Keegan pulled in between two cars about ten spots away. He exited his vehicle and walked to the front passenger door of April's Honda. Keegan was carrying a small canvas bag in his hands. He opened the door and slid in.

"I'm sorry for being so jumpy, Keegan. I decided there is no one else to talk to, so I'm venting all of my emotions and frustrations on you."

"Don't worry about it, April. I know you are under a lot of pressure. So, let's get right to the plan. Do you have Dr. Hoffman's telephone number available?"

"I have his work extension, not his home number."

"Good. Tomorrow morning you are to call Raymond and set up an appointment to meet him. As part of your job in marketing, it's always good to know as much as you can about the products you are marketing and the research behind them. Ask him for information about any new products that may be in the pipeline. You have to come across tough, so he knows you mean business. If he has been supplying pills or other contraband in the past, he should show some fear. Keep an eye on his body language and let me know what you detect. Dr. Hoffman is probably our only chance at closing the security breach at Thornburg."

Keegan reached into the bag he had sitting on his lap. He pulled out an electronic device.

"This is a recording device. It consists of two pieces. This is the wireless microphone. The battery is the size of a pencil eraser and the charge will last for half an hour to forty minutes. This is the recording device. The battery is bigger, and the charge will last much longer than the microphone. The microphone will function best if you clip it to your front bra strap. A colored, button down the front, lightweight blouse will help camouflage it. Slip the recording device in the pocket of a pair of slacks or hook it on the inside of a skirt lining. Under no circumstances are you to let him or anyone else know you have this device. It is voice activated. The switches are the same on the microphone and recorder. Just switch it on before you meet with Dr. Hoffman. The switch is one way and cannot be shut off. It will go off only when the battery is dead or by using a special tool. You must get Dr. Hoffman flustered enough to say something that gives us a clue about what he is involved in. Other than that, you have to be sharp and play it by ear. You are a smart lady, April, but from my background research I would say Dr. Hoffman is brilliant. He will be able to detect anything out of the ordinary. After you meet with him, continue with your mornings work as if nothing has happened. Work at the office until 1:30 PM, and we will meet back here for a debriefing. You also need to know I cashed the $100,000 check from the benefactor and put it in a special account. I can't believe it was real. The name on the check was not legible, and it was written on an offshore account that can't be traced. Do you have any questions, April?"

"I can't believe you cashed the check. What are you thinking? That's like stating I accept the benefactor's proposal. It's like stealing $100,000."

"We have to draw out our perpetrators. Cashing the check should do the trick. It's part of my plan, April."

"That's a great plan. 'Let me see if I can get April James killed.' Are you kidding me, Keegan?"

"It will all work out. You have to trust me. Let's focus on Dr. Hoffman right now. Do you have any questions about meeting with Dr. Hoffman?"

"What if he says no? What if he won't discuss the cancer pills and acts like he doesn't know what I'm talking about? What if, I don't know, just what if? I feel like such a snake."

"Come on, April. You're the victim. Use your female instinct. Dig those claws in and be demanding. You are a top notch, Thornburg Genetics employee fighting your way to the top. There is no such thing as no, only how."

Chapter 55

"Dr. Hoffman here, how may I help you?"

"Good morning, Dr. Hoffman. This is April James in Public Relations."

"Yes, April. I've heard your name mentioned several times. I'm sorry I haven't met you, but I don't get out of my research laboratory too often. I believe your father was Vincent."

"That's right."

"Yes, he was a great researcher. We worked together on several projects. He mentioned that you were always in a far off country helping less fortunate people. He said it was your passion."

"That's true. I was with the Peace Corps for over two years. That experience is actually what led me to Thornburg Genetics. I'm still all about helping people where I can."

"Yes, well what can I do for you, Miss James?"

"My role in marketing is to transform the Thornburg Genetics specific drug names into recognizable household brand names. It's like aspirin. Everybody knows what aspirin is. I have been on the job for over a year now and have spent no time in the research and development sectors. I am interested in obtaining any information that may be of use in giving Thornburg Genetics a creative edge in the marketing area. Knowledge of products is extremely important when marketing them. Up to this point, I have depended on other employees to educate me in this area, but I want to dig down to the basics. So, I'm calling to see if I can meet with you for at least half an hour to get a feel for the research division. My intent is to meet with you or others in your division several times over the next few weeks."

"Yes, I would love to meet you, April. Could I ask how you came up with my name? There are several brilliant researchers in our division."

"Whenever I talk with staff, your name seems to rise to the top."

"Yes, I see. That's rather flattering. I'm in the middle of a small project at the moment. Could you stop over at 10:00 o'clock?"

"That will work out well, Dr. Hoffman. I will see you then and thanks for taking time out of your busy schedule."

"Yes, I'm always glad to help. I will see you at ten."

As soon as they hung up, Raymond locked his office door, took the cell phone that Keegan had given him out of his pocket and punched the number one.

"Hello, Dr. Hoffman."

"Yes. Hello, Mr. McGrath. April James just called me, Mr. McGrath. She's supposed to come to my office in half an hour. I can't do this. This is Vince's daughter. Are you sure she's wrapped up in this extortion ring."

"Doctor."

"I can't do this. She will know something is wrong. My hands are shaking."

"Dr. Hoffman! Stop talking and relax for a second. First, I need to know the operation name."

"Yes, it's operation Gene Pool."

"Are you alone and is your office secure?"

"Yes, Mr. McGrath."

"I told you that our security surveillance indicated April James was involved in a Thornburg Genetics security breach. We had this discussion the other day. You have to get control of yourself and act normal. My background check shows April is a very smart young lady. We could even call her brilliant. Here is what we have to concentrate on. First, we must concentrate on obtaining any information we can to rescue your sister Elizabeth. Second, we must close the breach of security within Thornburg Genetics. Operation Gene Pool is in effect. You are the key to the operation, Dr. Hoffman. You can do this. Now get yourself under control. Divert your thoughts to something else until April arrives. Remember, Doctor; the answer to any request is NO. When you refuse to give April what she wants, we will find out more information about her true intent. I'll handle things after that."

"Yes, I'll do my best, Mr. McGrath."

"After the meeting you must act normal. Take lunch at 11:30 and meet me at a park called Liberty Park. It's only a few minutes from the office. Are you familiar with it?"

"Yes, Mr. McGrath."

"Don't forget to turn on your recording device, Doctor."

"Yes. I'm glad you reminded me. I'm very nervous."

"You'll be fine, Doctor. Just be yourself and concentrate on the task at hand for Elizabeth's sake. We have to rescue her. That's the intent of operation Gene Pool."

"Yes, operation Gene Pool."

Keegan closed his cell phone and let out a loud, nervous laugh. "This should be great. I have a brilliant geneticist with an inferiority complex and a brilliant, all around nice girl, forced to become a nasty witch. What's not to like about this plan. What could possibly go wrong?"

April kept glancing at the small crystal desk clock. At 9:50 she stood up and slid her hand in the right pocket of her black slacks. The tiny recording device was there. She decided to turn it on just before she entered Dr. Hoffman's office. She had attached the wireless microphone to her bra strap that morning when she got ready for work. The microphone was so small she hardly knew it was there. She was amazed that anything so tiny would work.

Dr. Hoffman was sitting at his desk waiting for April. Three times he had attempted to complete a log page in his journal. Three times he read what he had written, saw the entries made no sense and scribbled them out. "I have to stay strong for Elizabeth," he said to himself. He jumped when there was a knock on the door. He looked down on the desk at the full sheet of paper with the thick magic marker message on it, which said; ACTIVATE THE RECORDER.

"Yes, just a moment please."

Dr. Hoffman reached into his left hand pants pocket and pulled out the small recording device. His hands shook slightly as he flicked the switch on with his index finger. He slid the recorder back in his pocket, reached up under his shirt collar and turned the microphone switch on. Then he picked up the written reminder and placed it in the shredder.

"Come in, please."

April walked in and closed the door behind her.

"Hello, April. My name is Dr. Raymond Hoffman. It is so good to meet you. We aren't allowed too many visitors in this area because of the high security clearance required. You have a lot of your father's facial features. Vincent was a good man."

"Thank you, Dr. Hoffman."

"So what information can I help you with? I hope you understand a large portion of our research work is confidential and can't be discussed. It is the company's policy in order to avoid theft of trade secrets and genetic engineering. You understand."

"Of course Dr. Hoffman, I will be very discreet."

April paused for a moment; "I am here today to discuss a specific cancer pill that heals cancer in seven to ten days. From what I understand this is an experimental drug, yet the results are amazing. Do not deny this drug exists. I know you have access to it and that you can manufacture it. I believe you refer to it as The Blue Mule."

April watched the color drain from Dr. Hoffman's face. In seconds it was pale white. April was afraid he was going to pass out. "I need one hundred of these pills for a special project. The pills will be used to save some very important lives. You must believe in saving lives, Dr. Hoffman. That's what pharmaceutical companies do. I can barely sleep at night knowing this drug has been available for years, but has not been placed on the open market. Thornburg Genetics is allowing millions of people worldwide to die from cancer every year when they could be healed. Thornburg Genetics is a company that should be charged with murder because they hold back cancer preventing and healing drugs. We are killing people every day. You can help stop this massacre, Dr. Hoffman. You can wash the blood of millions of people off your hands. You must help me put an end to this. If I am wrong, I want you to look me in the face and call me a liar, Dr. Hoffman."

Dr. Hoffman was looking at the floor. He couldn't look April in the eyes. He could sense that April had the Noah gene. He could tell her everything, but he refused to. If she had the Noah gene, why was she acting so irrational? She should be protecting the C1 Extraction pharmaceutical at all costs, not trying to extort it.

"I need the supply of pills and formula, Dr. Hoffman. If Thornburg Genetics won't release the drug, I know many pharmaceutical companies that will be more than interested in it."

"Yes. How many others know about this?" he asked quietly.

April felt terrible. Raymond looked like he had lost every friend he ever had in the world.

"I can't answer that, Doctor. I don't know. What I want you to know is that I'm not here to scar your life. I'm here to help save millions of dying people from premature death. You can help. Why won't you help? Is it money? I can see to it you have more than enough money to last a lifetime. Is it your love of research? I can help you fund your own research facility. What is holding you back from saving millions of people?"

"Yes, it's not as easy as it appears, Miss James. You don't understand what I have to contend with. Thornburg Genetics is my life. I love the research aspect of pharmaceuticals. I don't have a say in what drugs are placed on the open market. Employees a lot farther up the corporate ladder make those decisions. From my perspective as a researcher, drugs are extremely complicated. My team and I may spend years developing a drug only to find a tiny problem that may affect a miniscule number of people when testing. Then it's back to the drawing board."

"You and I both know there are no problems with this drug, Raymond."

"Yes. There is a problem with the drug, though it's not a medical

227

issue. I will say no more about it than that. I'm sorry, but I have no authority to issue drugs or formulas. After working with your father, I would expect more integrity from you."

"Integrity is exactly what I'm talking about. Your integrity, mine and that of Thornburg Genetics is based on saving people's lives. Dr. Hoffman, I need one hundred pills and the formula, and I need them now. There are people I work with who are not as patient as I am. One of them may require this medication to survive. If this transaction does not happen, your life is in danger, Dr. Hoffman. Why don't you save us all a lot of trouble and let me have the pills and formula now. Name your price. Everybody has a price."

"The answer is no! You must leave my office now, April James."

April stared at Raymond without saying a word. She could see he was on the verge of collapsing and decided that nothing further would develop from this meeting. She slowly turned and walked out the door. Then she looked back at Dr. Hoffman.

"I'll be back in touch with you soon, Doctor! For your own sake, tell no one about my request."

April left the office and closed the door behind her. Her head ached, and she felt a knot in her stomach. She knew she couldn't start crying in the hallway. A few doors down, she found a restroom and ducked in, then locked herself in a stall. April was glad nobody else was in the restroom. Her emotions got the best of her, and she burst into tears. After a brief crying spell, she left the stall and looked in the restroom mirror. The face she saw looked pitiful. She retrieved some makeup from her purse and did her best to cover up her miserable feelings. It had been a lousy morning, and she had to be bright and cheery until her meeting with Keegan at 1:30 PM.

As soon as April left his office, Raymond lifted himself out of his chair and locked his office door. He pulled a white hankie out of his left back pocket. His crying was out of control for several minutes. Tears were dripping off the tip of his hankie and he grabbed a handful of paper towels sitting on the back of his desk. Raymond didn't dare call Keegan again. Operation Gene Pool was a failure. He felt like he had messed up everything. He knew he would never see Elizabeth again. He hated April James and all of the pressure she had placed on him.

Chapter 56

Dr. Hoffman had a small mirror he kept in his desk drawer and used it to scrutinize his face. It took half an hour before there were no left-over signs of red in his face from crying. At 11:30 Dr. Hoffman put on his happy face and left his office to meet with Keegan. As he started down the hallway, he heard a voice behind him.

"Dr. Hoffman. How are you today?"

It was one of his colleagues. She started talking about the weather and then asked him how things were going with his research today. Raymond couldn't concentrate on their conversation. The only thing he could think about was the meeting he had just finished with April James. After some small talk, he excused himself and continued down the hallway. He felt like he was a miserable failure. Why did he keep on living? He knew he could drug himself and be out of misery in a matter of minutes. Elizabeth, his sister, kept him going. He had to make sure she was rescued. Life would be back to normal if he could just work his way through this roadblock of demands.

Raymond barely remembered his drive to Liberty Park. He pulled into a corner parking space under a big maple tree. There were only three other vehicles in the parking lot. As soon as he shut his engine off and looked up he could see Keegan walking up the sidewalk toward him. Raymond opened his car door and stepped out.

"Good morning, Dr. Hoffman. I assume all went according to plan this morning?"

"Yes, Mr. McGrath. Good morning, I will say no, all did not go according to plan. My experience this morning with April James was horrible. I cannot believe that Vincent James' daughter is involved in criminal activity."

"I didn't know Vincent James personally, but I do know that criminal activity in Thornburg Genetics cannot be tolerated."

"Yes. That includes me, doesn't it, Mr. McGrath."

"You are trying to rectify a bad situation that was filled with good intent. That is an entirely different scenario. Do you have the recorder and microphone? I need to make sure everything you discussed with Miss James was recorded."

"Oh yes. I forgot to turn it off. Probably the battery is dead."

"There is no way to turn it off. Remember? We went over that."

"Yes. I do remember now. I'm not thinking straight, Mr. McGrath."

Then Raymond remembered all of the crying after his meeting with April. He knew it was all recorded. What difference did it make? It was just one more humiliating moment in his life. He took the recorder from his pocket and handed it to Keegan. Then he lifted his shirt collar.

"Yes. Would you mind unhooking this microphone?"

"Sure thing, Dr. Hoffman."

"I believe you are going to hear a lot of crying and blubbering at the end of the recording."

"Don't worry about it, Doctor. I know how stressful this whole ordeal is. Did Miss James ask you for anything?"

"Yes. She demanded 100 C1 Extraction pills and the formula."

"Did she use the term C1 Extraction?"

"No. She said she knew we had cancer curing pills that healed patients in seven to ten days and knew the nickname, Blue Mule."

"Did you tell her they were called C1 Extraction Pills?"

"I don't remember. Why? Is that important?"

"I will listen to the recording and see. If not I will ask you not to use the C1 Extraction name if there is a future meeting with Miss James. We may be able to focus on the drug name to ferret out the insider. What did you tell her when she asked for the pills and formula?"

"As you instructed me I told her no. I refused to give April James anything. I can't believe she's involved in criminal activity. Isn't there something we can do? Should I report her to the police?"

"Dr. Hoffman that is the last thing we need to do. We are executing a plan. We have to follow it to get Elizabeth back. Again, let me do the necessary security work. You stick to your research work. April James' day of justice will come. We have to give it time. Impatience on your part will only lead to trouble. Now listen to me. I need to review the recording of your meeting with Miss James. Step number one of operation Gene Pool is complete. I think you will find the meeting went better than you believe it did. Saying no to April will help draw more information out of her in the future. You must go back to work and pretend nothing out of the ordinary happened this morning. Do you understand?"

"Yes. I understand completely."

"Do you have any other questions?"

"What is going to happen now, Mr. McGrath. She said she would be in touch soon. What do I do?"

"I will call you later today, Doctor. Just hold tight."

"Yes. Hold tight. I will do my best. I don't know if I can be effective in this operation. I worry too much about Elizabeth. What if April calls me again before you do?"

"I do not think she will call you again today. She has to decide what her next course of action will be. Stay strong, Dr. Hoffman. I will call you back later today. Before you go I am setting you up with another recording device. If Miss James said she would contact you again, we want to be ready. Carry it with you at all times. Have the microphone attached under your collar and be ready to turn it on."

"Yes. I will be ready."

"Okay. Here is what I need you to do. Prepare one hundred of the C1 Extraction pills and make up a formula that looks real, but is not accurate. Make sure the formula will not give away any secrets about the real formula. Can you do that?"

"Yes, Mr. McGrath. I can do that, but I will not do so without authorization and direction from The Keeper."

Keegan reached into his button down shirt pocket and pulled out his cell phone.

"Here is my cell phone. You have The Keeper's emergency number. Call her now, please."

Dr. Hoffman hesitated. "She is probably busy. I do not want to disturb her."

"You need to know she is in favor of this operation. Dial her now, please."

Dr. Hoffman slowly tapped the numbers on the cell phone. He could feel Keegan staring at him. The phone rang twice.

"Hello, Keegan. How are you today?"

"Yes. Excuse me, please. This is Dr. Raymond Hoffman."

"Why are you calling from Keegan McGrath's cell phone, Dr. Hoffman? Is there a problem?"

"No, ma'am. We are working together on a project. I am sorry to take up your valuable time. Mr. McGrath has directed me to produce one hundred C1 Extraction pills and a false formula for these pills. I told him I would not do this without prior authorization from The Keeper. I am sorry for using the emergency number, but I feel I have no other choice."

"It's okay, Doctor. You are authorized to complete any assignment given to you by Mr. McGrath, and I want you to call me anytime you feel it is necessary."

"Yes. Thank you. May I ask you one other question?"

"Yes, Dr. Hoffman."

"How can I verify that you are the true Keeper?"

"That is a rather strange question. Why do you ask?"

"I prefer to be cautious at this time."

"I appreciate that, Dr. Hoffman. The last time I was in your office you showed me an oval piece of turquoise you had handcrafted into a ring. It was very smooth and had a beautiful background. Will that do?"

"Yes, thank you. Please forgive me for having mistrusted you."

"It's far better to be cautious than to guess, Doctor. How is everything going in the research department? I have to stop by again soon. Time seems to get away from me."

"Yes, time is a fleeting element. We look forward to a visit from you anytime."

"Thank you, Doctor. Would you please let me talk with Mr. McGrath for a moment?"

"Yes, here he is." Dr. Hoffman handed the phone back to Keegan. "The Keeper would like to talk with you."

"Hello, Keegan. This is a very interesting call. Aren't you full of surprises?"

"It's all in a day's work."

"I can't wait to see how this turns out."

"Thank you, ma'am. It's been a pleasure talking with you as well. Goodbye."

"Goodbye, Keegan."

"Thank you for calling The Keeper, Doctor. I wanted you to know that my business with you is legitimate. Now I have a lot of preparation work to do. I will listen to the recording you provided and will call you back later today. Are you set to go back to work?"

"Yes. I will go to the company cafeteria and then I will be in my office awaiting your call, Mr. McGrath."

"That sounds good. I will call you as soon as I can."

Keegan turned and retraced his steps down the sidewalk to his car. He watched Dr. Hoffman pull out of the parking lot. If it hadn't been a school day, there probably would have been a lot of people at the park. As it was there were only two moms and five children that Keegan could see. A couple of additional cars had pulled into the parking lot while he was talking with Dr. Hoffman. They were probably people enjoying some free time on their lunch break. It was now after noon.

Keegan plugged a cord into the recording device and plugged the other end into the car cigarette lighter. He slipped on earphones and plugged them into the recorder. The first thing he heard was Dr. Hoffman inviting April to come into his office. Dr. Hoffman said little during the ensuing conversation with April. Her statements to Dr. Hoffman were volatile. She plagiarized several ideas from her meeting with the benefactor. She told Dr. Hoffman he could save millions of lives and his integrity by handing over the cancer pills and formula. April really plowed into Dr. Hoffman's emotions. When he did talk, Keegan could detect a quiver in his voice. The worst part was the crying at the end of the recording. Dr. Hoffman was on the verge of a mental breakdown. Keegan knew that somehow he had to get him out of the picture. It would be less than an hour before April arrived at the Wal-Mart parking lot for her debriefing. That was enough time for a nice lunch. Keegan pulled out of the parking lot and drove to a nearby sandwich shop he located using his GPS system.

Chapter 57

April drove into the Wal-Mart parking lot at 1:40 PM. Keegan met her at her car. "Hello, April. How are things going? I assume everything went well at your meeting with Dr. Hoffman this morning?"

"I assume nothing went well. Raymond refused to give up any pills and wanted to hear nothing about giving up the formula. He barely said anything accept how much he owed Thornburg Genetics. Apparently his research is the only life he has. I can't wait for you to listen to this tape. Talk about an annoying habit. He starts every sentence with the word 'Yes'. Yes, I think so. Yes, I don't know. Yes, I can do that, yes, yes, yes, which is so annoying. But, moving along, now what am I supposed to do? This benefactor is going to call sometime soon. I have to tell him I have nothing to deliver to him. He's not going to be happy. Will they really try to kill me, Keegan?"

"Slow down, April. Relax a minute. I don't know what these people have in mind. We have to take this one step at a time. You can't be a quitter, April. Focus on the task at hand. Let me listen to the recording and see what I can extract. I'll call you as soon as I can after I listen to the recording."

April handed Keegan the microphone and recording device.

"That's it! I'm on the verge of a breakdown and all the support I get from you is, I'll call you later?"

"What else do you want me to say, April? I know this isn't easy, but I'm doing tons of behind the scenes work. You have to keep an even pace and pretend everything is okay. Can you do that for me?"

There was silence as April stared at Keegan's face. "I guess I have no choice. I'll wait for your telephone call. But don't wait too long or I'll be calling you. I better not get a 'leave a message' voice mail or I swear, Keegan, I'll hurt you."

"Don't worry. I'll get back to you. Here is another blank recording device. Use it to record the conversation when the benefactor calls you again."

"Thanks. I'm sure it will come in real handy."

"I have to go now, April. I'll be in touch."

"I want this to end, Keegan."

"I know. Keep smiling."

April left the parking area while Keegan was walking to his car. She revved her engine and squealed her tires lightly to let Keegan know she was aggravated.

Keegan turned and watched her leave the parking lot then finished the short walk to his car. He didn't have to listen to the recording April gave him because he knew it was the same conversation recorded by Dr. Hoffman. He decided to listen to what was recorded after April left Dr. Hoffman's office to see how she reacted after their meeting was over. Keegan plugged the device into the cigarette lighter and fast-forwarded to near the end of the recording. He located the spot on the recording where the meeting ended. Keegan heard the sound of a closing door as April left Dr. Hoffman's office. Then he heard a faint click of a door. It was almost a repeat of Dr. Hoffman's performance. There was the sound of uncontrollable crying that soon decreased to sobbing. Then Keegan heard April blow her nose. The sound of a toilet flushing caught Keegan off guard. Then he heard April speak into the microphone.

"Keegan. If you were here right now I would strangle you. Have a great day. You know who I am."

Keegan shut the recorder off. He decided no further plans could be made until the benefactor contacted April again. He called Dr. Hoffman.

"Hello, Dr. Hoffman. I am calling to let you know you did an excellent job this morning. April James is setting herself up for a big fall. We can already nail her for attempted theft, extortion and numerous other violations. She offered you money, a private research facility and the chance to save millions of lives. I am sure she will be back in touch with you soon as she indicated. That will be the next step in operation Gene Pool. When she contacts you again, tell her you have been thinking over the offer she made. Tell her you have worried about the millions of lives that could be saved with this drug. Then tell her you will call her back in a few days with an answer."

"Yes. I don't know if I can talk to her again, Mr. McGrath. April James is an evil woman. Why would I tell her I am considering her proposition?"

"Raymond. Listen to me. We have to get Elizabeth back alive and we have to trap April James and put her away forever. Your cooperation is the key to this. Don't fail me now. Dig deep down into your moral fiber. Operation Gene Pool will be complete before you know it."

"Yes. I will do my best, Mr. McGrath."

"That's the spirit. As soon as April James contacts you for another meeting, call me immediately and tell me what she said. I will give you the next step in the plan from there. Don't forget to turn on the recording device."

"Yes. Very well, Mr. McGrath."

"Goodbye for now, Doctor."

Keegan waited half an hour before he called April. "Hello, April.

Where are you?"

"I'm finishing a sandwich. I'm surprised you didn't have that on your radar too."

Keegan ignored the comment. He knew April was stressed out.

"You did a great job with the recording. I am, however, glad I wasn't there to get strangled." Keegan chuckled, trying to lighten up the situation.

"A great job! I thought Raymond was going to pass out or die on me or something. He looked like the most dejected person on the face of the earth."

"April. You did what you had to. Blame me. This had to be part of the plan to shut down our security breach."

"Okay, Keegan, I'm blaming you, but I don't feel any better."

"Listen, April, you have to let it go. We have to move forward. Here is our next step. Whether the benefactor calls you at work or at home, make sure you record the conversation. Call me immediately afterwards. Okay? We can work through this."

"Okay. What else can I do? I'm the sitting duck. Remember?"

April knew a call would be coming from the benefactor, but when? She hated this waiting game. How would he react when she told him Dr. Hoffman had denied her demands? She knew the conversation would be nasty.

Jason called April just before 4:00 PM. "Hello, April. I haven't heard from you all day. How is your day going?"

"You might say it's been a little crazy. I'm buried in paperwork."

"Can I interest you in a light dinner after work?"

"The offer sounds great, but I just can't tonight. Can I take a rain check?"

"You sound like you are on edge. What's going on?"

"I'm just a little backed up in my work, and I didn't sleep too well last night. I'll be okay."

"I don't think I can live a whole night without seeing you. I know how important your work is, but no time together at all?"

"I'm sorry, honey. I have to get caught up and get some sleep."

"Can I call you later?"

"Sure, an interruption would be wonderful."

"I guess that will have to suffice then."

"Okay, Jason. Thanks for understanding. I love you, honey. Kisses."

"Kisses. Bye."

The closer it came to the end of business hours, the more nervous April became. The benefactor said he was going to call, but it hadn't happened. April breathed a sigh of relief as she left her office for the day and did not have to contend with the benefactor. It felt like a fifty-pound weight had been lifted off her shoulders.

Chapter 58

April had just finished supper. She started working on her marketing material when her cell phone rang.

"Hello, April."

April froze. "How did you get this number?"

"You recognize my voice. That's good, April. You don't have an unlisted number. It's available to anyone. I see you cashed your $100,000 check. That makes us partners, doesn't it?"

April didn't respond. She walked over to her front apartment door and sat on the floor. She knew this would set off Keegan's cell phone and he would be able to see her on the camcorder he had installed.

"Did you contact Dr. Hoffman, April?"

"I contacted him this morning."

"Did you acquire the pills and formula?"

"Dr. Hoffman refused to give me anything. I tried my best. I thought he was going to have a breakdown. I told him we could..."

"April! How are we going to save millions of lives?" the benefactor interrupted. "I thought you could be more persuasive. What are your plans for obtaining the pills and formula? We need them now."

"I tried. I don't know what else to do."

"As usual, April, I must keep my call short. You are forcing me to push you to a higher level of motivation. I believe you have two nephews. I am sure you don't want anything to happen to them. Kevin and Korey desperately want you to obtain the pills and formula."

"You keep away from my family, you jerk. Who do you think you are? Don't you touch them!"

"I see I have piqued your interest, April. You have until Monday to obtain the items I have demanded. I will be in touch."

The benefactor hung up. April was raging mad. She stood in front of the door and looked directly at the camcorder. "You had better be watching this Keegan. If anything happens to my nephews, I'll, I'll, I don't know what I'll do! Something!"

April's cell phone rang. It was an unidentified caller. April hollered into the cell phone, "Hello. This is April James."

"Hi, April. This is Keegan."

"If anything happens to my family Keegan, somebody is going to get hurt!"

"Slow down, April. I only saw your movements on the camcorder.

I'm sorry you have to go through this, but you have to stay rational. I have to verify that the call was from the benefactor. Is that correct?"

"Are you for real? Who else would it have been? He threatened my nephews, Keegan! How did he get my cell phone number?"

"He probably got your number from Nadish Patel. Did you turn on your recorder?"

"As a matter of fact I didn't."

"What exactly did he say?"

"He said if I didn't have the cancer pills and formula by Monday he would hurt my family."

"I will have security staff watching your family as soon as I get off the phone with you. I tried tracing the incoming call, but no luck."

"I have to call David and Valerie and let them know what is happening. I have to call my Mom too."

"No, April. This has to remain a secret."

"Why Keegan? So Thornburg Genetics can keep their secret cures canned up? So a few million more people can die when they could have been cured of cancer? My family has to be sacrificed for that?"

"April. You know this is a dangerous drug. The perpetrators obviously know about its medical powers, but I don't think they know about its explosive properties. If the C1 Extraction pill falls into the wrong hands, it will only be a matter of time before a good chemist analyzes that feature. We are getting close to these people now. We have to continue with the plan. We have to put these ruthless thugs out of commission."

"What plan Keegan? You keep talking about a plan. I haven't been advised of any workable plan. Why don't you tell me all about this wonderful plan right now?"

"You have to trust me, April. I can't tell you the plan. If I do you might slip and reveal the wrong thing at the wrong time. Listen to how irrational you sound."

"Sure you have a plan. What's the next step?"

"I don't know if we will be able to nail Dr. Hoffman, but we have to try by talking him into giving you the pills and a formula somehow without blowing our cover. Then we have to get you out of this dangerous loop. The only way we can do that is by getting the bait to the perpetrators."

"Even if these people get the drugs and formula, it's never going to end, is it, Keegan? There will just be another call for another formula or another employee compromised."

"My professional opinion is, the demands will end for a long time and maybe forever when these thugs are caught. We live in a depraved world, April. There will always be someone out to conquer or enslave someone else. It's not fun for any of us, but it's still a fact. From all of the information we have, I believe the crooks want to score big once then disappear. My job is to catch them before that happens."

"I don't like any of this, Keegan. I don't even know the steps in your plan, and I can tell you ten places where this whole situation can unravel."

"April. You have to trust me. This whole thing will be over soon."

"Okay. So if I trust you, which I don't, what is the next move?"

"You have to arrange another meeting with Dr. Hoffman."

"What! Are you kidding me? That's the plan? He almost keeled over on me this morning."

"Listen to me. We want Dr. Hoffman to provide you with the pills and formula. That way we can hold him accountable for the Thornburg security breach. If he doesn't come through, we have to go through The Keeper to authorize releasing these items directly to us and circumvent Dr. Hoffman. This presents two problems. First, the benefactor may know that Dr. Hoffman did not cooperate. If he knows this and we tell him we have the pills and formula, your life is in grave danger. The second problem is we can't keep Dr. Hoffman employed at Thornburg Genetics, and he could potentially shift to the other side. He has too much research knowledge for us to allow that to happen."

"What are you saying, Keegan?"

"We can't risk his knowledge falling into the wrong hands."

"You're going to kill him? What about the Noah Gene that keeps the entire gambit of information secret except for a select few."

"There appears to be exceptions. Look April, I am not going down this path any further. We may not be able to snag Dr. Hoffman, but at least we know he is the employee who has been compromised in the Thornburg security breach. Since you contacted Dr. Hoffman, he most likely thinks you are selling out Thornburg Genetics in some type of get rich scheme. His devotion to Thornburg Genetics is uncanny. We have to get him involved so we can determine how he was compromised. We have to find out who the other players are in this game."

"So I'm just supposed to waltz into his office, and he is going to hand me cancer curing pills and a formula even though he emphatically refused this morning? Great plan, Keegan!"

"Listen to me, April. I am going to tell you the next step of the plan.

We are going to put severe pressure on Dr. Hoffman. Here is how I want the next step to go down. Don't contact him ahead of time. Just show up in his office early tomorrow morning. Tell him you are going to show up every day until he delivers the pills and formula. Tell him you are going to make his life as miserable as you can and that he has a lot more to lose than you do. With enough pressure, we hope he will crack and provide the pills and formula. He may even give up the names of his accomplices. Since you didn't use your recorder on the phone call from the benefactor, you can record the conversation with Dr. Hoffman tomorrow. Call me from your desk phone when you get back to your office after the meeting. Use your magic, April."

"What magic? This plan will never work."

"If it doesn't, I have other options."

"I'm beginning to trust you less and less. You're the one making my life miserable. Raymond and I should make a good pair. You make sure my family is safe, Keegan."

After April finished talking with Keegan she took time to mull the whole situation over in her mind. She felt alone and deserted. She didn't know if any of Keegan's plans would work and she was afraid for her family.

"Dear God," she prayed, "I know I don't pray as often as I should. I love my family, and I am in the middle of a situation I have no control over. I pray that you will watch over my family and keep them safe. I also pray this whole matter will end quickly, so I can get my life back to normal. I came to work for Thornburg Genetics to help save people's lives or at least give them a better quality of life. I want to continue doing that through my job and through the Thornburg Vision of Hope Charity. Watch over Keegan and be with him as he formulates plans and give him safety. I pray all of this in Jesus' name, amen."

Chapter 59

The man dressed in black followed the directions exactly as the benefactor demanded. For three thousand dollars, this job was a piece of cake. The bus stop was about a mile and one half from Dr. Hoffman's house. It was dark by the time the bus driver pulled over. The stranger was the only passenger exiting at this stop. He paid his fare in cash, thanked the bus driver and said goodnight. He watched the bus disappear and took a deep breath of the lightly falling mist. The smell of a fresh cut lawn filled his nostrils. He carried a small LED flashlight in his pocket just in case his job required it. But for now the streetlights were adequate. The walk to Dr. Hoffman's house would take less than half an hour. He met a young lady walking a dog up the sidewalk of the suburban neighborhood. He crossed the road to avoid her and continued up the sidewalk on the opposite side of the street. The German Sheperd whined and made a low growl. The young lady paid no attention and kept walking. The man laughed to himself. If she only knew his prior military training would allow him to snap the dog's neck in two seconds, her sense of security would have been shattered.

As he approached Dr. Hoffman's house, he stopped and looked around. The mist laid a good cover. There was nobody in sight. He had already scoped out the house and knew there were no pets or other people to contend with. The house had no alarm systems to foil his assignment. Dr. Hoffman lived here all by himself, just as his boss had suggested. The man's soft rubber soled, black shoes made no noise as he ascended the front steps onto the dark porch. He slipped the black ski mask out of his right front pants pocket and pulled it over his head. Then he peered in the front window. Through a crack in the curtain he could see Dr. Hoffman sitting with his back to the window in an overstuffed brown recliner. The television was on, and Dr. Hoffman was staring at the screen.

"Jeopardy," the man said. "What a waste of time."

He walked around the corner of the porch and tried the front door knob. It was locked. Probably the deadbolt was locked too. He took the pick set from his left front pants pocket. In less than a minute, he heard the click he was waiting for. He turned the knob slowly and pushed the door open. The deadbolt wasn't locked. Probably the old man locks it before he goes to bed he thought. At least he didn't have to kick the door in. The smoother the operation went, the better.

The hallway was well lit. The man in black could hear Dr. Hoffman answering Jeopardy questions out loud. Three in a row, four in a row, five in a row, it was time. The stranger pulled a small semiautomatic pistol from his ankle holster, walked into the living room and confronted

Dr. Hoffman.

"Mr. Raymond Hoffman! Do as I tell you and you won't get hurt."

Raymond jumped out of his chair in surprise and stood there staring at the man dressed in black, wearing a ski mask. The stranger could see the look of fear on Raymond Hoffman's face.

"Yes. Who are you? What do you want?"

"I have a message to deliver before I leave."

"What is the message?"

The man took a cell phone out of his pocket. With one hand he dialed a number and waited while his other hand directed the pistol at Dr. Hoffman's chest. "I am standing here with Dr. Hoffman." There was a pause. Then the man held out the cell phone and said, "It's for you, Dr. Hoffman."

Raymond slowly took six steps forward and took the cell phone out of the stranger's hand. The stranger stood sideways with a defensive posture, never lowering his handgun and never looking away from Dr. Hoffman.

"Hello?"

"Hello, Dr. Hoffman. Do you remember me?"

"Yes, I remember." Dr. Hoffman recognized the robotic sounding voice.

"You have been avoiding my calls, Dr. Hoffman. I hate being hung up on. Have you been viewing the discs I have been sending you?"

"No, I have not viewed any of them. I cannot look at them."

"I thought you loved your sister Elizabeth. I guess I was wrong."

"I do love Elizabeth. I can't bear the thought of how you are treating her."

The benefactor began to yell; "You don't love her! You are sitting in your nice little suburban home without a care in the world. Your sister is separated from you and in misery day after day from our torture. You can end all that torture, but you choose not to. You don't love Elizabeth."

"Please stop. Don't hurt Elizabeth anymore. She needs to come home. I'll do anything you ask."

"Anything, Dr. Hoffman?"

"Yes, anything. Please don't hurt Elizabeth anymore. Please send her back to me."

"Dr. Hoffman. This is your lucky day. I feel generous today. I believe a colleague of mine has approached you. Her name is April James. Does that name sound familiar?"

"Yes. I have spoken with April James."

"Good. Here is what I want you to do. She has requested one hundred of the cancer curing pills you have available and the formula for those pills. You have been uncooperative. As you know, I consider myself a reasonable man. You will give April James the pills and formula. I will give you a telephone number to call once she has those items in her possession. You are to tell no one about this call; no one Raymond, or the next visit from my assistant won't be as accommodating! Once I receive the pills, I will have them analyzed. I don't accept placebos, Dr. Hoffman. As soon as the pills are authenticated, your sister Elizabeth will be released. The formula will take a considerable amount of time to verify. I know where to find you if I need further information. I am growing rather tired of this cat and mouse game and your sister's company is boring me. Here is your chance to be the hero and save your sister. It is your last chance."

"Yes. I want to talk to Elizabeth."

"I thought you might, Raymond." There was a pause and Raymond could hear sobbing in the background, then a cry of pain. "Raymond, this is Elizabeth. Please do what they tell you. I miss you and want to come home. They are threatening to kill me if you don't cooperate. I don't feel well. Please help me, Raymond."

The captor snatched the phone from Elizabeth. The robotic voice said, "As you can hear, your sister is alive and well. But here is the situation. If you do not come through, death is too easy. I will sell your sweet sister into the slave trade market. DO YOU UNDERSTAND, RAYMOND?"

"Yes. Please don't hurt her anymore. I will do everything you have asked."

"Good, Raymond. My friend standing next to you will give you a telephone number. I will await your call."

The phone went dead. Dr. Hoffman slowly lowered it from his ear and handed it back to the stranger.

"Sounds like bad luck, Doctor," the stranger said and then laughed. He handed Dr. Hoffman an envelope, backed a few steps away, lowered his pistol, turned and walked into the hallway and out the front door. Dr. Hoffman walked over to the door, then closed and locked it. He locked the dead bolt as well, kneeled down on the floor and started crying.

Chapter 60

"Hey Jason, this is Max. Are you in a secure location?"

"My location is secure, Max."

"I just got off the phone with an old friend of yours."

"It worked?"

"Why do you sound so surprised. Of course it worked. It worked like a charm. Our friend Raymond assured me he will give the pills and formula to April when she connects with him again."

"You don't think he will back out again this time do you? He wouldn't do something crazy like turn himself in to the police or commit suicide or something."

"No, our poor Raymond wants his sister back. He loves her so much. He'll cooperate. Our mission should be completed within a few days. Do you have any questions about our plan?"

"No questions, big brother. I rented the DVD you told me about and I have to admit the getaway scene in that movie is a perfect fit for our needs."

"Yeah, you can never watch enough suspense movies to pick up some good practical ideas. Be ready to go at a moment's notice. I'll call you."

Chapter 61

At eight thirty the next morning, April knocked on Dr. Hoffman's door. She slid her hand inside her blouse and placed it on the microphone.

"Yes, come in," said Dr. Hoffman in a normal tone of voice.

April switched the microphone on, slid her hand in the pocket of her slacks and turned on the recorder. Then she turned the doorknob and walked in. Dr. Hoffman was sitting in his brown leather desk chair. When he saw April, the expression on his face turned to one of surprise. April hadn't called in advance, and she could see his face turn white as she closed the door behind her.

"Good morning, Dr. Hoffman. How are you this morning?"

Dr. Hoffman said nothing.

"I want to apologize for speaking so gruffly yesterday. It was quite out of character for me. I am just passionate about saving lives. However, I am here to ask if you have considered my requests. I still need to obtain the cancer curing pills and formula."

"Yes. I told you yesterday I cannot give you the items you requested."

"I know you said that, but I have no choice. You must provide these items. Here is the situation. I am only asking for this one small favor. I believe a higher level of motivation may be of value, so here is what I am going to do. I am going to walk down here every day and have a nice little visit with you until I get the pills and formula. I may even show up twice a day. I know you love your research job here at Thornburg Genetics. If you don't cooperate, I will guarantee to make your life the most wretched life on planet earth. I hate to do that because I offered you some great opportunities. I offered you money, a research facility and the ability to save millions of lives. You can have it all, Dr. Hoffman or you can have a hard way to go. The people backing me are ruthless and could care less about you. I, on the other hand, wish you would cooperate and avoid problems. What is your decision going to be? The time factor on this offer is limited."

"Yes. The truth is I've been thinking about our conversation. I love Thornburg Genetics, but even I am not blind to the fact my days here may be numbered. I need more time to think."

"How much time, Dr. Hoffman?"

"I will make a decision in a few days."

"That decision is not acceptable. I represent determined people in high places. They demand the pills and formula now. I really like you, and I don't want to see something bad happen to you. I am sure your cooperation is required, or your life is in danger. I will be back in two hours, Dr. Hoffman."

"I can't make a decision like this in two hours."

"You can and you will, Dr. Hoffman. There is only one decision to make." April turned and walked out the door. Her hands trembled as she walked down the hallway. "How was that, Keegan," she said, knowing the recording device was still on.

Dr. Hoffman stayed in his chair and fixed his eyes on the second hand of the wall clock. One minute, two minutes and finally five minutes passed. He pushed himself out of his chair and locked the door. After digging under a pile of papers on his desk, Dr. Hoffman found the cell phone Keegan had given him. He opened it, pushed the speed dial number one and Keegan's phone started ringing.

"Hello, Dr. Hoffman. How can I help you?"

"I am miserable, Mr. McGrath."

"What is the operation code, Dr. Hoffman?"

"Operation Gene Pool."

"Thank you. What happened to the cheerful, I have hope, Dr. Hoffman?"

"Yes. That beast of a lady, April James, was here again. She is pure evil. It makes me sick to my stomach just to talk with her."

"She met with you already? I thought I told you to contact me when she called to set up a meeting with you again."

"She didn't call ahead of time. She just appeared in my office. I was caught completely off guard. She left my office only five minutes ago. You have to help me, Mr. McGrath. I can't take this anymore. What am I going to do?"

"Did you make a recording of the meeting?"

There was silence and then Dr. Hoffman said, "I forgot about the recorder. There was a knock on the door and there she was. I could not turn it on. She was standing right in front of me."

"Can you remember what she told you?"

"Yes. She apologized for her rudeness when she talked with me yesterday. She started with such a sweet little voice today. She asked me for the pills and formula again, and I told her I could not give them to her. Then her voice turned demanding again. She said she would make my life the most wretched life on planet earth. I told her I had to think about the situation, and I would make a decision in a few days.

April James said that was not acceptable, because she worked for determined people in high places and I had two hours to make the right decision."

"That's everything?"

"Yes, that is everything. What am I going to do?"

"I have to get you out of the middle of this, Doctor. It sounds like she or one of her accomplices will do whatever it takes to obtain the pills and formula, including physical harm. I feel your life is in jeopardy."

"This evil woman has to be one of the people holding my sister hostage. I can feel the hate exude from her."

"She might be involved in some facet of your sisters' abduction, but let's move beyond that, Doctor. Do you have one hundred of the C1 Extraction pills made up?"

"No, Mr. McGrath, but I can have them completed within one hour."

"What about a formula, a fake formula?"

"Yes. I have a formula made up."

Keegan had an incoming ring on his cell phone. The caller ID said April was the caller. He decided to ignore the call until he could finish with Dr. Hoffman.

"Very well, Doctor. Our next step in operation Gene Pool will be to give the pills and fake formula to April James when she arrives again. You have to negotiate with her and tell her you don't want money or another job. She has to promise you that you can keep your research job at Thornburg Genetics."

"Yes. That sounds good, but can she make such a promise?"

"It doesn't matter whether she can or not. We are running a sting operation. We have to use April to get to the people holding your sister."

"Yes, I see. What happens when they find out the formula is a fake?"

"We have to find out who is behind their operation, locate your sister and wrap up this security breach before that happens."

"Yes. If we do not, then what?"

"We have to, Doctor. Now, you must also tell her that if she ever contacts you again, you will turn yourself in to the authorities, and she will be arrested with you. Don't forget to turn on your recording device. We have to have a recording of the transaction so we can nail her."

"Yes. I will lock my door and turn on the recorder before I let her in."

"Good thinking. This will all be over before you know it."

As soon as Keegan finished talking with Dr. Hoffman, he dialed April's number. "Hello, April, this is Keegan. You called?"

"Of course I called. You told me to call right after I met with Dr. Hoffman. Your plan may work after all. I told him I needed the pills and formula. He said he was considering the offer but needed a few days to get back to me. I told him I would make his life miserable forever if he didn't cooperate. He may be cracking. I gave him two hours to make the right decision."

"That will work. Don't be too easy on him, but don't send him over the edge either. If he gives you the pills and formula, make sure you thank him and let him know he is doing the right thing. Keep a good rapport with him. We may need him again in the near future."

"What do you mean a good rapport? We are on the verge of hating each other. Neither of us ever wants to see the other again if we don't have to. You have no idea how hostile these meetings are just from listening to a tape. This whole thing really stinks. I mean it, Keegan. How are my nephews and the rest of my family?"

"They are under constant security surveillance. They will be fine. The perpetrators aren't going to make any move against your family until they see whether or not the pills come through."

"They better be fine, Keegan."

"Listen, April, hopefully Dr. Hoffman will surrender the pills and formula. If he does, these are your instructions. Put the items in some type of bag, preferably something like a small tote. Text me, then start walking due west up Essex Street. Keep walking until I catch up with you. Did you record the conversation this morning?"

"It is recorded in its entirety."

"Good. I have to get you a fresh recorder. Walk out to your car in one hour and a fresh recorder and microphone will be in your driver's seat. Make sure you swap out microphones and recorders to get the transaction on record. I cannot stress enough how important this is. We have to have evidence against Dr. Hoffman."

"How are you going to put anything in my car without the parking lot cameras recording it? I thought everything was supposed to be top secret."

"Let me worry about the security details, April. That's my job."

"I can't wait for this to be over. You'd better not mess it up, Keegan."

"That doesn't sound very trusting."

"No! It doesn't!"

Chapter 62

At 10:30 AM, the knock on the door reverberated in Dr. Hoffman's ears. He had only met April James twice, but he was sure she was involved with the criminals holding his dear Elizabeth hostage. He hated her. It made him sick he had donated one hundred dollars to her Vision of Hope Charity. "Who is it, please?"

"It's April James. I am here to talk with you."

"Yes, please wait one minute." Dr. Hoffman stood up and, with shaking hands, turned on the microphone under his collar. Then he reached in his pocket and turned on the recording device. Slowly he walked to the door, unlocked and opened it allowing April to enter. He closed the door behind her and relocked it. April didn't like having Dr. Hoffman and a locked door blocking her only escape route, but Dr. Hoffman walked back over to his desk chair and sat down.

"Have a seat, Miss James." This was the first time he had offered her a seat. She slowly sat down in the brown leather chair adjacent to his desk. She could sense the tenseness of the situation.

"So, Dr. Hoffman, what is your decision?"

"Yes. I have put considerable thought into this matter. I will surrender one hundred cancer curing pills and the formula only if my terms are met."

"What are your terms?"

"Yes. I have decided I do not wish to accept any money or another research position. I love my research position at Thornburg Genetics. I want to keep my job here. I want you never to contact me again, and I never want to hear from your associates again. I also want my sister released immediately. If you do not agree to these terms I will turn myself in to the authorities, and I will turn you in as well. Do you accept these terms?"

"Your sister! What do you mean?"

"You and your associates have been holding my sister Elizabeth hostage for over two years now. Please do not play me for a fool, Miss James. You know all the details."

"I accept your terms, Dr. Hoffman."

"Also, nobody else will be told about this transaction."

"Who do you think I'm going to tell? It would be suicidal for me to tell anybody about this."

Dr. Hoffman retrieved a piece of paper from his desk and handed it to April. "I must insist you sign this before I will give you the pills and formula."

April took the piece of paper and read the hand written sentences. It was an agreement worded the same as his demands for giving up the pills and formula. April had no idea that Dr. Hoffman had a sister, much less what abduction he was talking about. She had no intention of signing an incriminating agreement. "I can't sign this, Dr. Hoffman. We are talking about a verbal agreement only."

"Perhaps I should call the police department now, Miss James."

"I don't think that would be a good idea."

"Then you will sign the agreement."

April wanted no part of signing anything. He had caught her off guard. She knew Keegan wanted her to get the pills and formula to set up Dr. Hoffman and end the security breach at Thornburg. Reluctantly she picked up a pen off Dr. Hoffman's desk, signed the agreement and handed it back to him. He laid the sheet of paper on his desk and opened his top desk drawer. He reached in the drawer and pulled out a brass-colored key. Then he proceeded to unlock a gray fireproof file cabinet at the end of the desk opposite April. He took out a brown plastic grocery bag and handed it to April. She opened the top and peeked inside. In the bottom were a dark amber bottle and a white business size envelope. She took out the bottle. It was unlabeled. April twisted the childproof lid, lifted it off the bottle and looked at the pills inside, they were robin's egg blue.

"They must remain out of any type of light as much as possible, Miss James."

April placed the lid back on and slid the bottle back in the bag. Then she took the envelope out. There was no writing on the outside and it wasn't sealed. She flipped the top open and lifted out the contents. The six sheets of paper had chemical jargon and notes on both the front and back. It meant nothing to April. "Thank you, Dr. Hoffman," she said as she slipped the formula back into the bag.

"Yes. Remember my terms, Miss James."

April didn't say another word. She couldn't wait to get out of Dr. Hoffman's office. She stood up and waited for Dr. Hoffman to open the door for her. As he walked toward the door April reached over and picked up the signed agreement he had left on his desk, folded it in half quickly, tucked it in her hand next to the bag, and followed him to the door. Dr. Hoffman opened the door, and April escaped. She couldn't wait to get as far away from his office as possible. She heard him lock the door as she walked down the hallway. She took the grocery bag with the pills and formula and stuffed it in the empty pocketbook she was carrying.

Dr. Hoffman went to his desk to retrieve the cell phone Keegan had given him. Then he noticed the agreement was missing. He rifled through the papers on his desk and then rifled through a second time. The agreement was missing. He knew April had stolen it. He could feel pressure building up in his entire body. He hated April with every fiber of his soul. Dr. Hoffman picked up the cell phone and called Keegan. It was all he could do to carry on a conversation.

"Hello, Dr. Hoffman. Was the transaction successful?"

"Yes, Mr. McGrath. Miss James has one hundred pills and the formula. I had her sign an agreement I formulated, then she stole it from me. I have never hated anybody in my life, but I hate that woman."

"What agreement is that, Dr. Hoffman?"

"It stated terms I required in exchange for the pills and formula."

"We never talked about a written agreement with April James. She actually signed something? I have already told you not to improvise. I hope you didn't raise some level of suspicion that will jeopardize the operation. I will remind you one more time that I am calling the shots as security personnel. You are not to change any plans on your own without my knowledge and approval. If you want your sister back, this is no way to do it. Did you record the transaction?"

"Yes. It is recorded."

"Call me before you leave work. I will meet you at Liberty Park and collect the recording device from you on your way home."

"Yes. That will work fine. I want Elizabeth back and April James in jail, Mr. McGrath."

"I understand. I believe the part you have played in operation Gene Pool is complete. I now have a lot of work to do on my end. I will stay in touch. You have the cell phone I gave you. If you encounter anything that seems at all strange, please contact me at once. Thank you for your help Dr. Hoffman and remember that everything we have completed and discussed is confidential."

"It is worth it all and more if I can get my sister back."

As soon as Dr. Hoffman was finished talking with Keegan he took the recording device off his collar and placed it under a pile of papers on his desk. Then he picked up his office phone and called the number he was given by the intruder the night before.

"Hello. This is Dr. Hoffman."

"Hello, Dr. Hoffman," answered the robotic voice. "Is the transaction complete?"

"Yes. It is complete. April James has one hundred of the cancer curing pills and the formula. She put them in a small black pocketbook after leaving my office just a few minutes ago. How and when will my sister be released?"

"Elizabeth will be released as soon as we analyze the medication and make an initial review of the formula."

"Yes. And when will that be?"

"I don't have an exact date. If everything is legitimate, we will release Elizabeth within ten days. Everything you provided will be legitimate, won't it Raymond?"

"Yes. The pills and formula are legitimate."

"Good. As soon as everything checks out, I will be in touch with you. I pride myself in being a man of my word. Remember, this entire matter is confidential. Nobody is to know about our arrangement if you value your sister's life. Do you understand, Raymond?"

"Yes. I understand completely." Dr. Hoffman heard the click as the conversation ended. He didn't want to deal with any of the people involved in his sister's abduction, but he knew Keegan's plan was far from foolproof. Raymond's main objective was to get his sister back whether it was by working with the abductors or by working with Keegan. At this point in time, it didn't matter which plan was successful. If he lost his job at Thornburg Genetics, but had his sister back, so be it.

Max made the phone call. "Hello, Jason. The goods are available."

"Ten-four, April is under constant surveillance until we initiate the next step of our plan."

After Keegan finished talking with Dr. Hoffman he waited for April to call. The phone rang immediately. The text message was short. "Have the goods." Keegan was five blocks away from Thornburg Genetics, sitting at a booth in the Essex Street Dunkin' Donuts shop. The smell of fresh brewed coffee held him captive. He was there less than twenty minutes when he spotted April walking up the opposite side of the street at a brisk trot. He let her continue to walk and observed the small wave of pedestrians moving in every direction. He determined that she was not being followed. It took him four blocks before he was able to catch up with her.

"Good morning, Miss James."

"Hi, Keegan. I'm not sure how good it is."

"Our plan is coming together nicely, April. I assume you have the goods with you?"

"They are right in my spare pocketbook as instructed."

"Let's keep walking, but maybe you can slow down a little. So tell me about the transaction."

"Dr. Hoffman said he didn't want any money, and he wanted to keep his research position at Thornburg. He told me he never wants to see me again and that his sister, Elizabeth, is to be released immediately. What exactly does that mean?"

"His sister? What is he talking about?"

"He said he knows that my associates and I have been holding his sister for over two years, and he wants her back."

"Really! That's a piece of information I hadn't counted on. Did you get that on your recording device?"

"As long as it's working correctly. It's probably still running."

"What else?"

"He wanted me to sign an agreement with him."

"You're kidding. What kind of agreement?"

"Something he could hang over my head if things went bad I guess. He turned his back to me, and I swiped it off his desk as I was leaving. I stuffed it in the pocketbook with the pills and formula."

"Okay. Here's the plan. I want you to keep everything in the pocketbook. When we finish our conversation, go back to Thornburg, pick up your car and take the items directly back to your apartment. I will have security personnel following you. Your apartment will be under surveillance until the benefactor makes arrangements for some kind of pick up. After you drop them off, return to Thornburg and finish out your day. Be careful, be observant and be strong."

"I know, and act like nothing happened."

"That's right. This will soon be over, April."

"Sure it will."

"What I need right now is the recorder you are wearing. Here is a blank recorder to replace it. Carry it with you at all times and have your microphone ready to turn on at a moment's notice, just in case."

"In case of what?"

"Plans don't always work out the way we want them to. I'm not sure how the end of the story is going to unfold. The benefactor is going to call you. Somehow a pick up or drop off arrangement has to be made. Just keep the recording device ready for that call."

"How is my family?"

"They are doing fine. My security net hasn't seen anything unusual. The culprits don't know we are there. My guess is when the benefactor finds out you have the pills and formula, he will care little about the threat he made towards your family."

"So I guess I have to wait for the Monday telephone call from the benefactor. I'm scared, Keegan. I thought I was tough, but I'm scared. If these people kidnapped Dr. Hoffman's sister, who knows if she is still alive or what other crimes they have carried out."

"They are dangerous beyond compare, April. Keep that in mind as I tell you the next step in the plan. I will have my cell phone line open at all times. My guess is when the benefactor contacts you and finds out you have the pills and formula, he will give you instructions for a drop, which you must follow at once. Don't be surprised if it happens before Monday. You have to call me and tell me exactly what was said. I will be a stone's throw away from you at all times. Use your judgment and don't get into a life-threatening situation. Abort the mission before that happens."

"But we have to catch these animals, Keegan. This has to end. I can't spend my whole life looking over my shoulder, running or wondering if the voice on my cell phone will be the benefactor."

"April! Make no move that is life threatening! If something goes wrong we can always go back and plan a different strategy. If you can't guarantee me you won't stand in harm's way, I will end the mission right now. I wasn't going to tell you this, but I have to. I know you are engaged to Jason, but I love you, April. It seems like I am always thinking about you. My reasons for not wanting you to get hurt are selfish."

"Don't, Keegan. Please don't say anymore. I think a lot about you too, but I'm engaged to a wonderful man. I can't think about this now. I promise I'll be careful."

"I'm sorry I said anything, April. It was out of line. This is terrible timing, but I don't want you to get hurt."

"It's okay, Keegan. I like what you told me." April put her arms around Keegan and gave him a hug. Then she kissed him on the cheek. "I had better get going. I promise I will stay safe."

"Call me for any reason at all, April, no matter how insignificant it may seem."

April grinned, turned and started the long walk back down Essex Street toward Thornburg Genetics.

Max received the call he was waiting for. "She still has the purse she left Thornburg with and no swap was observed with Keegan McGrath. She is heading back to the Thornburg office."

Chapter 63

April went straight to her car as Keegan directed. She set the pocketbook containing the pills, the formula and Dr. Hoffman's agreement on the seat next to her and sped off to her apartment. Her mind was preoccupied, and she didn't even remember the drive as she pulled into her parking space. When she walked into her apartment, she waved at the camcorder knowing Keegan would see her. She looked around her apartment trying to decide where to stash the pills and formula. What difference did it really make? Keegan had assembled some kind of surveillance team to watch her apartment and the camcorder would pick up anyone entering the apartment door. She took the small grocery bag with the pills and formula out of her pocketbook and placed it in the two-drawer stand next to her bed. She decided to leave the agreement from Dr. Hoffman in the pocketbook, and she placed it on the shelf in her closet with the rest of her pocketbook collection. April stood in front of the camcorder and waved again before she exited her apartment and drove back to her office. It was Friday. All she could do now was wait for the benefactor to call sometime on Monday.

Max received the next phone call he was waiting for. "April was carrying the black purse into her apartment building. Her car should be searched to make sure she didn't leave the medication and formula in it."

When April arrived back at her office she listened to the eight messages left on her voice mail. One of them was Jason. She listened to his message first. "Hello, April. It doesn't seem like we have spent much time together this week. It's Friday. I would love to come over this evening, create a stunning dinner and spend some time together. I have a surprise for you too. Call me back."

April drifted back to what Keegan had told her earlier that morning. He actually told her he loved her. She knew that Keegan and she connected well, but could she ever have a meaningful relationship with him? Jason was so comforting. Imagine Keegan offering to create a stunning dinner. April knew this was a terrible time to think about relationships. There was no way she was thinking clearly about anything. At least the pressure between her and Dr. Hoffman was over, but she had to work through the threats made by the benefactor. No decision that affected her personally would be handled in a rational manner. April reached for the phone and dialed up Jason.

"Hello, Jason, it's me."

"Hello, April. How is my favorite girl doing?"

"I had better be your only girl."

"You're the only girl in the world for me, sweetie. So you must have listened to my irresistible message."

"I did listen to the message. What surprise do you have for me?"

"You know I'm not going to tell you ahead of time."

"I know. You never do, but I still have to ask."

"How does six o'clock this evening sound?"

"Six is fine. I'll see you then. I can't wait. Bye-bye."

"See you tonight."

April finished her workday and drove back to her apartment. Her mind was in turmoil. As she drove she thought about Keegan and then Jason. Then the thought of waiting for the phone call from the benefactor slipped in. She hoped tonight's dinner date with Jason would take some of the pressure off her high strung emotions.

When she pulled into her apartment parking space she looked around to see if she could detect the surveillance crew. She didn't see anybody. She decided Keegan must have hired and/or trained some real professionals, but that wasn't a surprise. When she walked in her apartment door, she gave another wave at the camcorder. Then she headed off to take a shower. The warm water felt comforting as it massaged her body. Jason would arrive soon. She had the pills and formula in her possession and was finally able to relax a little. The water felt so good April hated to get out, but she knew Jason could show up any time. After she dried her hair, she slipped on a pair of designer jeans, a pink, short sleeve pullover and a pair of black high heels. She looked in the mirror. "You are one gorgeous girl," she said out loud.

She walked to the stereo and slid in a light classical rock CD. After dancing to the music for a couple of minutes she went over and looked out of her apartment window. The sun was already casting long shadows of the trees across the pond. She started to daydream but felt something brush against her leg. Her orange striped cat, Pumpkin, was looking for attention. She reached down and rubbed him until he got bored and walked away. Ten minutes later she heard a knock on the door. Even though Jason had a key to her apartment, he always knocked first and let her answer the door. April walked to the door and peeped through the security lens to make sure it was Jason, and then opened the door.

"Hi, honey," she said as she hugged him and gave him a long deep kiss.

Jason had one hand full of grocery bags and a small duffle bag was sitting on the hallway floor.

"Hi, sweetie, it's great to see you."

"Come on in."

April knew Keegan had just witnessed the whole event on the camcorder. She hadn't decided whether she liked making him a little jealous or whether he shouldn't be invading her private space with a camcorder. April took two of the grocery bags from Jason. He picked up the duffle bag, and they walked to the kitchen.

Keegan's cell phone rang. It was the camcorder in April's apartment again. He took the call. There was April giving Jason a hug and megakiss. Keegan was seething. April was treating Jason like royalty, and he was seeing this Sheila babe behind her back. What a double-crossing stinking louse. Keegan knew he had to tell her somehow. He also knew it had to be after the security breach at Thornburg had been shut down. There was still a good possibility Jason could be involved. He watched them move out of camera view and flipped his cell phone shut. Now it was time to sit around and wait.

"What's in the duffle bag?" asked April.

"It's the surprise."

"Oh, the surprise. You know how much I love surprises. When do I get to check it out?"

"You have to wait until after dinner."

"You're going to make me wait?" April asked in a girlish voice.

"Yes, honey, I'm going to make you wait."

"How unfair."

"I know, but you have to wait anyhow. Let's cook that stunning dinner, shall we?"

"Can I get another kiss first?"

"Let me look at you. You look like a super model and you're smart. I'm the luckiest guy in the world."

"That's sweet, Jason. Thank you."

Jason slowly put his arms around April's waist and drew her close. He looked in her eyes and smiled. Then he kissed her. It was a gentle kiss at first. Then the kisses were fuller and harder. They kissed for several minutes and then Jason released his grip on her.

"If I don't get started on dinner, I may lose my concentration. Then you will never get to your surprise, sweetie."

"Okay, dinner it is."

Jason showed April the contents of the grocery bags as he unpacked them; swordfish steaks, fresh green beans, two golden russet baking potatoes and two pieces of cheesecake with a maple syrup topping for dessert. He also brought his own spices for the delicacies and a four pack of wine coolers.

"Wow, Jason, this is going to be some meal. It's wonderful."

"Nothing but the best for you. Would you like a raspberry wine cooler to start our evening?"

"You know it's my favorite. What can I do to help?"

"Would you like to set the table and get out a couple of wine glasses?"

"It's the least I can do."

The light from the candles on the table bounced off the ceiling and seemed to make the table move ever so slightly. April had quiet classical music playing in the background. Both Jason and April ate slowly, enjoying the moment together.

"The meal was excellent, Jason. You are so nice to me."

"Would you like a piece of tasty cheesecake now or later?"

"Let's have it a little later."

"Sure, we can do that. You just sit right there, and I'll clear the table." He poured two cups of coffee, put a little cream in April's, and brought them back to the table.

"I feel guilty not helping you, Jason."

"Sometimes a beautiful woman needs to be pampered. Are you ready for your surprise?"

"Of course I am. You know it drives me nuts when you hold out on me. The pain has been excruciating."

"Okay. It's going to take me a few minutes to get it ready. I'm going to put a blindfold on you so you can't see it until the very last second."

"A blindfold? This must be some surprise."

"I'm not giving you any clues. Let's see. What can I use for a blindfold? I think this cloth dinner napkin will work. It's an extra one that's clean. Let's try it."

Jason stood up and walked around the table to April's side.

"Close your eyes and face forward, honey." Jason slipped the linen over April's eyes and tied a small knot behind her head. "It could be bigger. Can you see me, April?"

"A little bit around the edges," April said and then grinned. Jason leaned over and gave her a kiss on the cheek. "That's close enough. You have to promise to close your eyes when I tell you to."

"It's already kind of dark in here, but I promise I won't peek."

"Okay then. I have to go in the other room. Stay in your chair. I'll be right back."

Jason walked over and picked up his duffle bag and went into the bathroom just down the hallway. He shut the door and turned on the light. It took him only a minute to strip his deck shoes off and slide out of his dress shirt and jeans. He left them lying on the floor. He unzipped the duffle bag, pulled out a pair of black cotton pants and quickly pulled them on. Then he took a black T-shirt and pulled it over his head. Finally he pulled out a pair of eight-inch high black leather boots. He laced them up as fast as he could and tied a double knot to assure the laces would not come loose. He unzipped the side pocket of the duffle bag and grabbed the Glock 45 ACP and handcuffs. Then he reached for the bathroom light switch, shut off the lights and opened the door a crack.

"Are you ready, April?"

"Am I ready? I thought you left or something."

"Close your eyes. No peeking!"

"Okay."

Jason walked over to April and stood beside her. "Now keep your eyes closed and hold both of your hands out."

April opened the palms of her hands and slowly lifted them in the air. Jason could see the smile on her face. He felt bad for a moment. There was a ratcheting sound as April felt something cold on her wrists. Jason had both of her wrists in the handcuffs before April could move. He kept his right hand on the chain between the cuffs to control April's movements.

"What are you doing? Jason, what are you doing?" April had her eyes open, but could see little with the blindfold on.

"Now listen to me, April. Sit still. I don't want to hurt you."

"What are you doing Jason? You're scaring me! Take this blindfold off me! What are you doing?"

"You need to calm down, April. I'm going to take the blindfold off now."

Jason took his left hand and carefully dragged the blindfold up and off April's head, then dropped it on the floor. "Okay, April. Now listen to me. Today you received one hundred special cancer-curing pills and a formula to reproduce them. I am here to retrieve those items. Where are they, April?"

"What are you doing, Jason?"

"Stop asking me that!" Jason yelled. "I am here to pick up the pills and formula. I know you have them in your possession. My team followed you ever since you picked them up this morning."

"You're involved in this, Jason? But I thought..."

"Shut up!" Jason yelled as he took the 45 auto out of its holster and pointed it at April. "This isn't a game. Where are the pills and formula?"

"I can't give them to you."

"April. You're not getting it. I'm not leaving here without them. You can cooperate or I can destroy your apartment looking for them."

April looked up into Jason's eyes. They looked angry. She had never seen Jason in anger like this before, and she was afraid.

"I need the pills and formula now."

April just sat there staring at him. Her mouth wouldn't move.

Jason reached out with his left hand and grabbed April under the chin. He squeezed her right cheek with his thumb and the left with his fingers.

"Now, April! Tell me where they are now! Last chance!"

April searched her mind for a plan. She knew the camcorder would go off when Jason left the apartment. Maybe she could get to it sooner and get a message to Keegan somehow. She knew things would only get worse if she didn't cooperate. The pills and formula certainly weren't an equal exchange for her life. Keegan had told her to make no move that would be life threatening. She didn't understand why the Noah Gene didn't kick in unless Jason had it too. To think she had just told him how much she loved him and given him a kiss to prove it.

"They are in my bedroom in my night stand drawer."

"See how easy that was," Jason said as he relaxed his grip on April's cheeks. "We are going to take a little walk in there together, April. Please don't try anything stupid. I really do love you, but I will take any action necessary to obtain the pills and formula." Jason held onto the handcuffs and left the pistol pointed at her as they shuffled to her bedroom. He flicked on the bedroom light switch. "Get down on the floor, face down and put your hands out in front of you."

April did as she was told. She prayed to herself; "Please God, don't let me die. Don't let him hurt me. I don't know what is happening here, but I know you are in control and you are with me."

Jason gently kneeled on April's back and retrieved another pair of handcuffs from a black nylon pouch on his belt. He attached one end of the second pair to the pair April was wearing. Then he took the other end and handcuffed April to the steel bed frame. He stood up, keeping an eye on April, and took two steps to the nightstand. Jason pulled the single cherry wood knob and the top drawer slid open. He glanced back at April. She hadn't moved. He could hear her crying into the carpet, but didn't pay any attention. He was here tonight for one reason only. Jason set his pistol on top of the nightstand and pulled the brown plastic grocery bag out of the drawer. He reached into the bag and took out the amber colored bottle of pills. There was no label on it. After twisting the top, he lifted it off and looked inside. The pills looked right, blue and football shaped. Only their chemist would know if they were the real things. It looked like Dr. Hoffman had come through. Jason set the bottle on top of the stand and picked up the unmarked envelope that sat next to the pills. Quickly he shuffled through the papers. There were lots of handwritten chemical symbols and notations. He could only guess if it was the real formula.

"Are these the correct pills and the real formula?"

"That is all I was given."

"You didn't substitute them or swap them?"

"No."

Jason took the bottle of pills, brought them up to his lips and kissed them. "I think I'm in love yet again. Okay, April, now for the rest of the surprise." Jason took a cell phone out of his pants pocket and dialed a number. "Code word Night Hawk." He hit the off button, picked up his pistol, then sat on the bed. He looked down at April. She looked so forlorn, lying there, handcuffed to the bed rail, her face buried in the carpet. Her crying had turned to sobbing. She turned and looked up at Jason.

"What now? Are you going to rape me or kill me or something?"

"I'm surprised at you, April. Is that any way to think about your fiancé? Rape is a disgusting thought. I hate rapists. And murder is, well, it is just way too messy. Besides, you have been extremely cooperative. You are being rewarded for your good behavior."

"Then why are you doing this?"

"It's nothing personal, April. I actually do love you. This is all about money, one hundred cancer curing pills at one to two million dollars a pop. A three way split, soon to be a two way split, means I will net somewhere between fifty and one hundred million dollars. Then there's the formula. I'm set for life, sweetie. That is the end of our conversation. No more talking."

April thought about the explosive nature of the blue C1 Extraction pills. She wasn't sure how volatile one hundred of them could be. She thought about telling Jason, but quickly decided she would just as soon see Jason blow up at this point even if it meant she had to blow up with him.

Jason picked his handgun up and slid it back in his holster. April had a pair of running shoes by the foot of her bed. Jason picked them up and walked to the bathroom. He took two black sweatshirts out of the duffle bag and slid one on. Then he slid on a black ski mask. He picked up the pile of clothes he had left on the floor when he changed and stuffed them in the duffle bag. Next he put April's running shoes on top of them. From there, Jason walked out to the living room. He picked up April's pocketbook and found two cell phones, which he slid in his pants pocket. He continued his search and found her .357 revolver in the bottom. That was a good place to leave it for the moment. He took the pocketbook and placed it in his duffle bag, then zipped it shut. From the time he made the cell phone call, it took only eight minutes for the vehicles to arrive in front of April's apartment building.

Chapter 64

Keegan's cell phone rang. It was Cal, the head of his security operation at April's apartment site. Keegan answered the phone immediately.

"What's up, Cal?"

"We have a big problem, boss. Five huge black Chevy vans just pulled up in front of April's apartment building. At least six operatives, fully dressed in black clothing with ski masks, rolled out of the vans and entered the apartment building. There are at least a dozen more surrounding the vans. They have taken cover behind other vehicles parked on the street or behind the pine trees in front of the apartment building. My binoculars are picking up compact rifles in the hands of several of them. On the back of the operatives' clothing in large, bright fluorescent green letters is the word POLICE. Is there a drug bust or something going on?"

"Get license plate numbers and any information you can. I am sure they are not legitimate law enforcement personnel. Do what you can to stop them. They have to be after April."

"There are six of us, boss. We are outnumbered and outgunned. What if this is some type of drug raid by an official task force?"

"Stand down. Gather every bit of info you can. Take lots of pictures. Follow them if they leave. I'll be right there."

"That's affirmative."

After making his phone call, Jason went back into April's bedroom. "Here is the situation, April. We are going for a little ride. I have some people who are going to escort you outside to a vehicle. We do not plan on hurting you. We will be moving fast. Follow any instructions given, to the letter." Jason took a key out of his pocket, bent over and unlocked the handcuffs. Then he slid them off April's hands. They remained hanging from the bed frame. He handed her a black sweatshirt with the word POLICE on the back, black sweat pants and a black ski mask. "Put these on."

April stood up, lifted the sweatshirt over her head and put it on. Then she slipped the black ski mask over her head. As she took off her high heels to slide the sweatpants on there was a knock on April's apartment door. Jason ran to the door and knocked twice from the inside.

"Night Hawk," was all he needed to hear from the hallway. He unlocked the door and opened it.

"She is in the bedroom."

Four men in black fatigues moved quickly and silently into the bedroom. "Follow us now," one of them said to April. Two of the men grabbed April under her arms and ushered her out of the bedroom door. She had removed her high heels and felt clumsy in bare feet, but her feet barely touched the floor as she was hustled down the steps. April passed a small wave of people dressed in black at her apartment door entrance.

Jason grabbed his duffle bag. He reached in his pocket to make sure he still had April's cell phones. He locked and closed the apartment door as he exited.

Keegan heard his cell phone ring and tried to concentrate on driving while watching some sort of swat team accost April's apartment. The event was hard to see as April's apartment was almost dark. He had to slam on the brakes for a red light. There were three cars in front of him and there was no way around them. He had to wait for the green light. As he watched the screen on his cell phone he saw them lifting someone by their arms as they left the apartment. Even though everyone was dressed in black, he knew it had to be April. He watched the last person out lock the door and shut it. He was carrying a black duffle bag in his hand. Keegan figured it was probably Jason as it looked like the same duffle bag he had brought in earlier. Keegan hit speed dial number 9 on his cell phone.

"Cal, they have April! Be careful!"

"They are already on their way out the door boss. They're piling into the vans. Now they are leaving."

"Follow them. Did you get license plate numbers? Don't lose them."

"We only have two cars, boss. Here we go. I have to hang up."

Keegan sped down the street as fast as he dared. It was still five minutes to April's apartment. He called the security operations manager in charge of protecting April's family. "This is Keegan. We have an incident. Get April's mother, David, Valerie, Korey and Kevin out now and take them to the safe house. I will be in touch." Keegan knew that it would be next to impossible to catch the vans unless they happened to come in his direction. His cell phone rang.

"Yes, Cal."

"They road blocked us. We lost them."

"What do you mean they road blocked you!"

"Three blocks down from April's apartment the last van stopped. Two men must have already been staged to pull two cars in the street sideways to block it. The drivers got out of the cars, hopped into the last van and pulled away. There is no way to get around the cars."

"You couldn't push them out of the way?"

"Negative, boss, we didn't know if the cars were rigged with explosives or if a sniper had been left on the scene. We aborted the pursuit."

"Crap," said Keegan. "You made the correct decision, Cal. I'm not thinking clearly at this moment. Meet me back at April's apartment. Wait outside until I give you further orders. I don't know if anybody reported an incident at her apartment or not. We don't want to cause a scene that might raise suspicions."

"I haven't even heard a siren in the area, boss."

"With two cars blocking a street, you will soon. Get back to April's and wait for my call."

Keegan found a parking spot a block away from April's apartment. He could see a flashing light down the street and knew a police car was on the scene of the roadblock. They would have a tow truck there and have traffic flowing smoothly again in fifteen or twenty minutes. Keegan looked around him in every direction as he walked to April's apartment building. He saw one of Cal's cars just up the street. He went to push the numbers into the locking mechanism that allowed entry into the apartment building, but the door pulled open without unlocking it. He could see the duct tape holding the latch open. The duct tape must have been placed on the latch when Jason arrived to see April. Keegan ascended the steps two at a time and stopped in front of April's third floor apartment door. Had one of the thugs rigged some kind of bomb inside the door? Keegan remembered seeing the last person out lock and close the door in a purposeful manner. He pulled out his cell phone and replayed the camcorder recording. The crooks had left fast with no indication of tampering with the door. He put the cell phone back in his shirt pocket, took the key April had given him and opened the apartment door. The apartment was dimly lit. Keegan could see several candles on the dining room table. They were the only light source. He flicked the switch next to the entrance door and a burst of light filled the apartment. The smell of cooked fish lingered in the air. He looked at the dining room table and saw the two cups of coffee. He knew Jason and April had enjoyed a candlelight dinner, their last candlelight dinner.

"That dirt bag, I thought he was involved in this but not to this extent."

He walked over to the camcorder with the intent of removing it. Then he thought better and left it aimed at the door. Apparently there was no physical conflict between Jason and April as the apartment was not in disarray. No lamps or furniture were tipped over. Everything seemed to be in place. When he walked to the bedroom he saw the handcuffs hanging from the steel bed frame. What had Jason done to April? There was no blood or telltale signs of April being harmed.

Keegan thought about fingerprints, but already knew whose finger-prints were on the handcuffs. Keegan started blaming himself for not having better security around April's apartment, even though he knew there was no way he could plan on a small army infiltrating it. His heart beat erratically and he wanted to vomit. April was in danger, and he had failed her. Keegan made a phone call to Cal.

"How does it look out there?"

"The response personnel have one car out of the way and are flag-ging traffic by the other car at the blockage point. It's quiet around the apartment building."

"Okay. Come up to April's apartment. Post one person outside."

"Are you sure you want us up there, boss? It is a crime scene."

"I take full responsibility."

"Ten-four, boss."

Keegan's cell phone rang as his security team entered the apart-ment. Keegan knew the camcorder was still working and sent the sig-nal. He peered at the number on his cell phone screen just in case, then he hit the end call button.

"Okay, Cal, tell me everything."

"Remember, we were at a disadvantage. Everything we witnessed was under street lights and we used binoculars. At approximately 8:30 PM, five black Chevrolet vans rolled up in front of the apartment build-ing. Everything was quiet, and then bam they were there. All of the vehicles shut their lights off. Even before they had come to a complete stop, approximately six perpetrators, all dressed in black, jumped out of the vans and sprinted to the apartment building. Another dozen jumped out of the vans and scattered. None of them stood still. They ran behind adjacent cars and pine trees or up and down the street. They looked like ants scurrying about."

"Yeah, they didn't want to be standing targets. Sounds like major professional training."

"We were just far enough away we weren't detected, but it was close. There was just no way the six of us could have stopped that op-eration, boss."

"I understand. Then what happened?"

"In a matter of minutes, they were retreating from the building, piling back into the vans and leaving the scene."

"Did you see anything that looked odd or out of place?"

"It appeared that one person was being escorted, but it was hard to tell. It happened so fast, and we didn't have a perfect vantage point. We followed the vans up the street three blocks to an intersection. That is where the two cars were driven into the road and left parked perpendicular. We had to stop or hit the cars they left in the road. The drivers exited the cars on the side away from us. We saw them run up to the last van, which had stopped, and jump in as the van sped off and disappeared. There is one interesting note. From the time the vans pulled up in front of the apartment building to the time they left was less than five minutes."

Keegan whistled in amazement.

"That's fast. What about license plate numbers?"

"We managed to get four license plate numbers. I ran them while I was waiting for you to call. You are not going to like this boss. Two of the vans had Michigan plates. The plates were stolen. One van had a Pennsylvania plate. It was stolen. One van had a Florida plate. It was stolen."

"Were there any other markings on the vans?"

"No markings that we could see outright. We'll take a closer look at the digital photos, but I wouldn't hold my breath."

"Okay, ladies and gentlemen. You did the best you could under the circumstances. Send those digitals to the lab for processing. Cal, I want you and Heather to stay here a minute. I have one more assignment for you. The rest of you can call it a night."

Keegan gave Cal and Heather the address and directions to Jason's apartment. He told them to look for anything suspicious, but not to destroy the place. He told them to call him with any information, but expected none. They said goodnight as they left April's apartment. Keegan had turned his cell phone on vibrate so it wouldn't ring when the camcorder detected their departure. When he was alone he closed the apartment door, then walked over and sat on April's couch. Sitting on the end table next to the couch was a framed photo showing April and Jason embracing. Keegan picked up the frame and threw it towards the kitchen. He could hear the glass break as it hit the tiled floor. Pumpkin appeared and jumped up on his lap. "Hi there, kitty, I wish you could talk." He checked his cell phone and turned the ring tone back on. He knew what April would say now. It was all in God's hands. He wondered if he should have told April about Jason and Sheila. He knew the right answer was no and the momentary thought was strictly about revenge. The way things had turned out that bit of information could have been life threatening to April. At least she was still alive. What had triggered this event? Had April been contacted by the benefactor and decided to go it alone? Something was not right at all. This had been planned and planned well ahead of time by the perpetrators. Keegan knew it was a waste of time searching the apartment for the medication and formula. He was sure they were in one of the vans. Keegan's cell phone rang. The caller ID showed it was from April's cell phone.

"Hello, April?"

"It's me. Don't worry. I'm okay. I didn't see this one coming." Jason snatched the cell phone out of April's hand.

"Where are you?" asked Keegan.

"Hello, this is Jason. I'm sure you know who I am. April said you were the one to call. As you can hear, April is fine. I understand this is Keegan McGrath, head of security for Thornburg Genetics. I don't believe I have had the honor of meeting you in person. It really doesn't matter. I want you to listen closely to what I am about to say."

"I'm listening."

"April James volunteered to take a ride with me and spend some quality time with me. It's kind of an insurance vacation. April is the insurance that you will not attempt to track me down. You are to make no attempt to rescue her. If you make an attempt to rescue her, you are placing her life in jeopardy."

"Why should I believe one word of anything you are telling me?"

"Think about it, Keegan. I have no reason to harm April. I have the pills and formula in my possession. We have to do a chemical analysis to make sure the pills are legitimate and then April will be released. It's a very simple plan unless, of course, the pills are phony. You know the answer to that question."

"I have been assured the pills are real."

"Then there you have it. You will see April again within one week. No rescue attempts and no police agencies! Understood?"

"I understand."

"Good." There was a click and the telephone conversation was over.

Keegan had the information he needed. As soon as April told him she didn't see this coming, he surmised who did see it coming. He bolted from April's apartment to his car and punched 1224 Fiat Avenue into his GPS system. He got lost on a side street but managed to get redirected in a couple of minutes. "This dumb GPS system," he mumbled.

Chapter 65

It was almost 10:00 PM when Keegan pulled up in front of Dr. Hoffman's house. The lights were on inside. Keegan walked up the sidewalk and pushed the lit doorbell button. In a few moments the overhead porch light came on. Dr. Hoffman peeked through the small entrance door window.

"Wait just a minute, Mr. McGrath." There was the sound of a chain sliding and the deadbolt being turned. Then the door swung in. Dr. Hoffman was wearing slippers and a bath robe. Keegan could see the legs of long pajamas draped from the bottom of the bath robe to the tops of his slippers. "Yes. Good evening, Mr. McGrath. This is an unexpected visit. What can I do for you?"

"I need to talk with you, Dr. Hoffman."

"Yes. Don't you think it is getting a little late?"

"I don't believe this will take long. Aren't you going to invite me in?"

"Yes. Please come in."

"You seem nervous, Doctor."

"Yes. The last few days have been hectic, don't you agree?"

"They have, Doctor."

Keegan followed Dr. Hoffman into his living room. "Please sit here, Mr. McGrath." Dr. Hoffman motioned towards a beige leather couch. "Would you like some tea or coffee?"

"No thank you. Let's get right down to business. April James was abducted earlier this evening."

Dr. Hoffman showed no emotion. "Yes. I'm not surprised. She is an evil woman. She must have many enemies out there."

"It appears that her main enemy is sitting across from me. You see, Doctor; the people who abducted her were after the pills and formula you provided."

"She is one of them. Why would they abduct her to take something she was going to provide them with? Was she trying to double cross them?"

"They abducted her, because she doesn't work for them. They set her up through threats of bodily harm and treachery the same way the perpetrators are using Elizabeth to compromise you. April James is working for me!"

Dr. Hoffman looked stunned. "For you? So what does this have to do with me, Mr. McGrath?"

"It's this way, Doctor. I had a plan all set up. As you know, April took possession of the pills and formula. We were waiting for a telephone call from the thieves giving us delivery instructions. The call never came, but they knew April had the goods. You were the only other person that knew about the transaction. You informed somebody. Who was it?"

"Yes. I believe you are mistaken. April James must have been working with these people all of the time. She is evil and would stop at nothing to get those pills and the formula."

"April James works for me! You informed somebody she had those items. Who did you contact?"

"Yes, I only made arrangements to get my sister back. She should be home any day now."

"You made arrangements? Who authorized you to make arrangements with criminals that have jeopardized security at Thornburg Genetics? I was very specific when I told you to stay out of it and let me do the planning. Am I correct? Now who did you contact?"

"Yes. I have nothing further to say at this time, Mr. McGrath."

"If April James is harmed in any way, I will hold you personally responsible."

"My only concern is to get Elizabeth back."

"Are you looking forward to seeing her, Dr. Hoffman?"

"Yes, of course I am looking forward to seeing my sister."

"You may never see her again if you don't cooperate with me. I had a plan and you botched it."

"I have nothing more to say, Mr. McGrath. I believe our visit is over."

"Dr. Hoffman, I believe you will be talking with me very soon." Keegan lunged off the couch and walked out of the house. He slammed the front door behind him in a rage of anger. As soon as he was in his car, he pulled his cell phone out of his shirt pocket.

"Hello, Admiral Campanella?"

"Hello, Keegan. It's been a while."

"It has, Admiral. I apologize."

"That's okay. I know you are a busy man. What can I do for you?"

"I need a warrant for the arrest of a Thornburg Genetics employee. His name is Dr. Raymond Hoffman."

"Let me write this down. Dr. Raymond Hoffman. H-o-f-f-m-a-n?"

"Correct."

"Address?"

"1224 Fiat Avenue, Philadelphia"

"Charges?"

"The charges are theft of controlled pharmaceutical substances, theft of proprietary classified company information and espionage."

"This sounds serious. What else?"

"Please place a no visitation order on the warrant with the exception of me and especially no lawyers."

"Anything else?"

"That's all for now."

"Okay. So now what's the real deal? I'm not going to lose thirty-two years of Navy service time over some Mickey Mouse caper, you understand."

"Yes, sir. I understand completely. We have a breach of security at Thornburg Genetics. I was executing a sting operation. Dr. Hoffman was involved in the breach as well as two other employees. One of the employees was abducted. I need Dr. Hoffman out of the way for probably two weeks. It's basically for his own good."

"Sounds like you're having a good time, and I didn't get an invitation. Is there anything else I can help you with? A Navy Seal extraction team to rescue the abductee? Helicopters?"

"Just keeping Dr. Hoffman out of my hair will be sufficient for now, thank you, sir."

"Consider it done. Let me know what the next step is. Remember, two weeks."

"I'll keep you posted, sir."

Two unmarked black cruisers pulled up in front of Dr. Hoffman's house in less than an hour from Keegan's telephone call to the Admiral. Keegan watched as two Navy Military Police Officers walked to the door. Another MP stood outside the second car and observed while an additional MP remained in the driver's seat of the first car. Dr. Hoffman answered the door still wearing his pajamas, slippers and dark maroon, three quarter length bathrobe. Keegan could see the MPs talking with him. Then Dr. Hoffman held out his hands. One of the MPs placed cuffs on his wrist, and they escorted him to the first cruiser. Another MP went into the house. Keegan saw the lights go off and he knew the MP was securing the residence. As they drove off, Keegan wracked his brain wondering what the next move should be. He wanted to keep all of the evening's incidents as quiet as possible, but he knew there would be lots of questions at Thornburg Genetics on Monday when there was no April, Jason or Dr. Hoffman. Rumors would fly.

Chapter 66

The five black vans split up and took different streets just a few blocks from April's apartment. Each van had a pre-designated destination. Four of the destinations were strictly hiding places. The fifth van held Jason, April and four of the thugs. It was headed north out of Philadelphia. Their destination was a brick ranch house on the farthest edge of the suburbs. The house had been rented a week earlier, and the minor renovations for this operation had been completed. The house was nestled among numerous evergreen trees. The oversized metal garage on the property was almost surrounded by blue spruce trees, which limited viewing by any passersby.

As the driver of the van pulled in, he pushed the button on the remote control overhead garage door opener. The twelve foot wide garage door rolled up the track. He turned the van around on the blacktop driveway, backed into the garage and hit the remote control button again. The garage door followed the track back down to the floor. As soon as the door closed, the four masked thugs jumped out of the van. It was totally dark in the garage. Suddenly a light brought the surroundings into view. Jason slipped the blindfold off April's face and motioned for her to exit the van. As she got out and looked around, she could see they were in a concrete block garage with the windows covered to stop even a hint of light from escaping the building. Two of the thugs were holding black assault rifles. April recognized them as being colt military rifles. The thugs still wore their black ski masks. When she looked toward the rear of the garage, she saw a chain link fence enclosure. It appeared to be about ten feet wide and fifteen feet long.

"This is your home for the next few days, April," said Jason. "I could have made it a little fancier, but it will suffice. You have food and water in the refrigerator. There is a bathroom in the back corner. You have a cot and blankets."

April looked from the enclosure up to Jason's face. "You don't have to do this, Jason. You told me you loved me. Don't throw our relationship away. It's not too late. We can still have a nice life together."

"April, I do love you. You are a spectacular lady. The problem is that it is too late now. I have made an alternate commitment I must keep. In a very short time, I will be very rich. I have enjoyed our time together, but when I leave here tonight you will never see me again."

"So our relationship meant nothing?"

"Unfortunately, April, you are a victim of circumstance."

"Why me? Why did you target me?"

"Think about it. You're a smart girl. You will figure it out. Maybe I could get one last hug and a kiss."

"Don't touch me, you traitor!"

One of the perpetrators laughed. Jason snapped his head around and stared at him. The laughing stopped immediately. April could feel the tension.

Jason turned back and looked at April.

"You will be safe here. Do not try to escape. Do not cause any problems. Remember, April; I would hate to see any of your family hurt because you did something unethical. There is just no need for it."

"Stay away from my family, you jerk!"

"I do love it when you are feisty, April." Jason laughed, turned around and walked out of the garage side-entry door.

April looked at the four thugs remaining in the garage. It appeared that three of them were men and one was a woman. The one nearest her pointed the muzzle of his rifle at the door in the chain link fence enclosure and motioned at April. She could see they each had a holstered sidearm on their belts in addition to the rifles. April walked into the enclosure. The door clanked behind her. She turned and watched as a heavy padlock was snapped shut on the door. She knew a struggle would have been futile. One of them handed April a clean pair of sweatpants, t-shirt and hooded sweatshirt through a port in the chain link fence.

"We need your clothes back," he said.

April went to the bathroom in the corner, closed the door and changed her clothes as directed.

"God," she prayed, "I don't know why I am going through this. I guess it is to make me stronger. Maybe it is so I can see firsthand what greed does to a person. I pray I will come out of this alive and that you will protect my family. Please give Keegan wisdom in dealing with this situation. I ask all of this in Jesus' name, amen."

Chapter 67

This was one telephone call Keegan did not want to make. He was tense, his head hurt, and every muscle in his body ached as he dialed. "Hello, Lexis. This is Keegan."

"Hello, Keegan. This is a late phone call. Is it good news or bad?"

"It's neither. Let's just call it an update. By the way, your name has been taken off the list of suspects."

"That's nice to know."

"I'll get right to heart of the matter. April has been kidnapped and is being held hostage."

Lexis gasped. She had grown very fond of April and was not expecting this type of news. "What are the kidnappers demanding?"

"Their only demands are not to try following them and no police. If we follow these demands, they will allegedly release April in a few days."

"And what are your thoughts?"

"Jason called the demands in directly to me. He is heavily involved in this matter and may even be the mastermind. Even though he has betrayed April, I don't see him as a person who would inflict harm on her. He could have done so by now if that was his intent. Of course, there are no guarantees. Though I thought he might be a player, I didn't have him figured in the breach of security to this extent."

Keegan then relayed the entire chain of the evening's events. He told Lexis that Jason was one link to the security breach at Thornburg Genetics. He didn't know if additional insiders were involved with the exception of Dr. Hoffman. Under the additional pressure Keegan had created, Dr. Hoffman cracked. Lexis was still shocked that Dr. Hoffman never came forward with the information about his sister's abduction. Keegan assured her that everybody handles crisis situations in different ways. Dr. Hoffman chose to keep all of his emotions bottled up inside. It was a self-destructive move. Every day he could blame himself for the problem and carry the emotional burden. Keegan explained to Lexis that this had caused Dr. Hoffman to make poor decisions that, unfortunately, had been detrimental to Keegan's planned operation. He did not mention Jason's fling with Sheila Smith.

"So what is the next move, Keegan?"

"The next move is the one thing I hate the most. We wait. I'm going to the military facility to talk with Dr. Hoffman again. I need to see if I can squeeze more information out of him. I'm not sure how well that will go. My hunch is we can take Jason at his word when he said

April would be returned unharmed in about a week. To try and find the location where they are holding April would take a small army and way too much luck. They are going to do a chemical analysis on the C1 Extraction pills before they release April. Dr. Hoffman was directed to produce the real thing. He thinks his sister will be released if he provided the real thing, so I believe the pills are genuine. I could round up a huge number of security personnel and have airports, bus stops, train stations, taxis and every other mode of transportation under the sun monitored. I would have to include police departments. By the time I got everybody in place, it would be too late to achieve positive results, and everybody in the world would know Thornburg Genetics has a problem. This would jeopardize April's life big time. Besides, all of the maneuvers the thugs have executed thus far have been flawless. I'm sure an escape plan has been masterminded in an intricate manner. So what does all of this come down to? We wait."

"You are a smart man with a lot of experience, Keegan. I know you will do what is best for April, Dr. Hoffman and Thornburg Genetics."

"Thank you for your vote of confidence, Lexis. I have to admit I was blindsided by several of these events."

"You can't anticipate every move when an event this big happens. Think things through. We'll pray that everything works out for the best."

"That's a good idea. I have to go now, Lexis. I'll keep you informed of any major updates."

"Okay, Keegan. We'll talk later. Goodbye and God be with you."

After a sleepless night, Keegan dragged himself out of bed at 7:00 AM and brewed a cup of the standard in-room motel coffee. He reviewed the emails on his computer. The photos of the kidnapping scene had been downloaded. Keegan saw nothing out of the ordinary and there was no positive information from the staff analyzing them. The vans didn't have an identifying scratch on them. None of the thugs could be identified because of their black clothing and ski masks. There wasn't even a clothing tag showing. There was no evidence to trace and only a dead end.

Keegan left the motel and decided to stop and treat himself to a big breakfast. There was a diner about two miles from the motel. Traffic was light. It was a typical Saturday morning for most of the city of Philadelphia. After devouring four pancakes, three fried eggs, half a dozen strips of bacon, home fries and a tall glass of orange juice, Keegan drove to the Philadelphia Naval Station. He displayed his military ID card and explained his mission to the MP on duty at the gate. The MP made a telephone call. He returned shortly and pointed out the front gate to the brig where Dr. Hoffman was being held. It was close enough to be seen from the compound gate. Keegan left his Colt 357, Gerber folding pocketknife and cell phone out of sight in his car. At the front visitor desk, he filled out the visitor slip and handed it to the officer. Then he placed his wallet and car keys on a plastic tray. He removed his brown leather belt with the metal buckle and took off his shoes. The MP assigned to frisking directed Keegan to walk through the metal detector. The machine was silent. The MP took a hand-held metal detector and ran it over the heels of Keegan's shoes. The detector beeped loudly. The MP then looked inside the shoes and carefully slid his rubber gloved hand inside. When he was satisfied there was no contraband he handed them back to Keegan.

"You have steel shanks in your shoes, sir," the young MP said.

Keegan sat down in the provided chair, slid his shoes back on and tied them. He retrieved his belt, wallet and keys. The MP handed Keegan back his ID card.

"Sorry for the delay, sir. We will have Raymond Hoffman escorted to the visiting room shortly."

A female MP escorted Keegan through the two sets of security gates into a private interview room. The private rooms were used for lawyer-client confidential visits and other important meetings. They were in a separate location away from the general public visiting room. Each of the four private rooms had one window in the door for observation by an MP.

"Please sit in the chair on the far side of the table, sir," said the MP. Keegan followed the directions and moved to the far side of the single small table.

Dr. Hoffman had handcuffs on when he was escorted into the room. "Would you please remove the cuffs?" asked Keegan.

"Yes, sir," said the MP as he took a key off his key ring and unlocked the cuffs. "I will be right outside the door if you need anything, sir."

"Thank you."

Dr. Hoffman seated himself in the hard, low backed chair closest to the door. He wouldn't look directly at Keegan, but gazed down at the tabletop that separated the two of them. Neither of them said anything. Keegan thought Dr. Hoffman had aged ten years since he last saw him the night before. His complexion was gray, he had dark bags under his eyes, and what little he could see of the Doctor's eyes appeared bloodshot.

"Good morning, Dr. Hoffman." There was no response. "I want you to know having you arrested gave me no pleasure, Dr. Hoffman. So why did I do it? First, I requested information from you so I could pursue the criminals now holding April James hostage. You refused to cooperate. The second reason is just as important. Do you know what that reason is, Dr. Hoffman?"

Dr. Hoffman shook his head no without looking up.

"The second reason is to get you out of the way for your own good. The criminals have abducted April James, and they have abducted your sister. I believe they may abduct you as well if things somehow don't go their way."

Dr. Hoffman said nothing.

"Do you really think these people will release Elizabeth after more than two years?"

Dr. Hoffman looked up at Keegan. "Yes. They have assured me of her release, Mr. McGrath."

"And their word of honor is trustworthy why? But let's not dwell on that. My time here with you is limited. I need as much information about this scenario as you can give me. I have no idea what may pop up next in the chain of events. The better informed I am, the better the end results of this ordeal will be."

Again there was silence.

"I need information, Doctor! I am not the enemy! I am on your side! Do you understand that?"

"Yes. I have several thoughts concerning this whole matter, Mr. Mc-Grath. However, until my Elizabeth is returned, I have nothing further to say. When I see her face and know she is safe, I will cooperate one hundred percent."

"What happens if you don't see your sister again?"

"Yes. I was guaranteed she would be released within one week. If she is not, I will tell you everything I know."

"Very well, Dr. Hoffman. I can only hope for your sake that the outcome of this situation is positive."

"How long will I be here, Mr. McGrath?"

"Your length of time here depends on the outcome of the Thornburg security breach. It would be highly beneficial for you to tell me the information I need. When you change your mind, all you have to do is contact one of the MPs. I will be notified immediately. If this situation does not end in a positive fashion, I will see to it you are in this or another prison for the rest of your life. Our interview is over Dr. Hoffman."

Chapter 68

Jason hated to leave April sitting in a chain link fence enclosure like a dog. The look of betrayal on her face was almost unbearable. Then he thought about the pills and formula. Business was business. Keep looking forward. Don't look back, move on. Besides, Sheila was an exciting girl. He would just have to tame her down a notch or two, if that was even possible. Jason wasn't sure why, but Sheila would do anything he asked her, and Sheila's way of showing love was more deliberate than April's.

The plan was to make no more telephone calls until he reached Sweden. Max would be at the airport to pick Sheila and him up. Jason had allowed six hours to cross the border into Canada. He had a private Cessna Caravan lined up to fly him to Watertown, New York. From there he had a rental car reserved. It was a straight shot from Watertown up Route 81 and into Canada. He had another Cessna lined up in Kingston, Ontario to fly him to Montreal. If all went according to plan, Jason knew he would be at the Montreal airport Marriott Hotel between 9:00 and 10:00 AM. His flight to Stockholm, Sweden didn't depart until 9:40 PM. That would give him some time to sleep. He would be in Sweden at 2:05 PM the next day after crossing several time zones. The only problem that could pop up at this point was if Keegan McGrath did something stupid. He was told to do nothing, because it would endanger April's life. Jason knew he would have to monitor news stations as much as he could before attempting to cross the border into Canada. Sheila was also monitoring every bit of news she could at this point until she met up with him in Montreal.

It was 4:30 AM when Jason arrived at the Canadian border. Traffic was almost nonexistent from Watertown north. He had nothing to declare at the border, and his reason for entering Canada was business. His Thornburg Genetics ID card was legitimate and not questioned. The Pennsylvania driver's license and passport were both up to date. The customs officials requested to see inside the trunk of the Volkswagen Jetta rental car. He popped the trunk with the button release under the dashboard and pulled himself out of the car. The officials took a brief look through his suitcase and had him remove his laptop from the leather case. They found nothing of interest and told him he was clear. He thanked them, climbed back in the Jetta and they waved him through the checkpoint. Then Jason said goodbye to America forever.

Jason drove to the small airport terminal on the outskirts of Kingston. He found a parking spot close to the hangar from which he had arranged his flight to Montreal. Someone would eventually figure out the car was a rental and would return it to the rental company. He was thoroughly exhausted at this point. A small nap in the Cessna from Philadelphia to Watertown only put a dent in the twenty-four hours he had been on the go. The uppers he had taken before leaving Watertown were wearing off. He was glad the pilot handed him a large cup of coffee for the flight to Montreal. The flight was fast and Jason managed to stay awake and conversed with the pilot on occasion. As soon as they arrived, he thanked the pilot and gave him a tip. A courtesy van was waiting just outside the airport entrance, and Jason was transported to the Marriott.

Jason drifted in and out of sleep. He knew his body was over tired. He flicked on the television to see if April's abduction had made the news. Nothing was mentioned. Apparently Keegan had followed instructions and kept the situation private. It looked like the operation was a success. However, he didn't discount anything until he was in Sweden.

After picking up his British Airways ticket and clearing the security line, Jason started for gate number C-29. The aroma wafting from the Tim Horton's coffee shop lured him in. He purchased one large cup of black coffee and walked to the boarding gate. He found a seat where he could monitor the CNN news channel and the terminal aisle at the same time. Even if Thornburg security had figured out any of his plans, they would most likely want to keep the entire situation out of the eyes and ears of the public. There was little doubt in Jason's mind that Keegan McGrath would make no move to jeopardize the life of April James, one of Thornburg's up and coming star players. She would be released before one week as long as the cancer curing pills he was carrying proved to be genuine. The one hundred pills he was carrying would generate one to two hundred million dollars. Jason was mentally spending the expected money as he fell asleep in the airport chair.

In an instant, Jason jumped out of the chair as he felt someone kick his right foot. He had both fists clenched and then he heard the laughing.

"Sheila!" he whispered loudly. "What are you doing? You scared the heck out of me."

"Hi, honey. Were you having a nice snooze?"

People sitting nearby started laughing.

"I wish I had a photo of that one," Jason heard somebody behind him say.

He relaxed, gave Sheila a kiss and they both sat down. "I thought I told you not to do anything that would draw attention to us," whispered Jason.

"Relax, Jason. Nothing is going to happen here. We'll be on the plane in less than an hour."

"I know gorgeous, but I've had almost no sleep in the last day and a half, and I'm jittery. It's great to see you again, babe."

"It's great to see you too. We're together forever now, right, honey?"

"Forever, Sheila."

"See, I told you Thornburg Genetics would pay me what I'm worth, didn't I?"

"You truly did. As long as these pills are on the money, we are in the money."

"It won't take long to tell once we get to Stockholm."

British Airways flight 94 lifted off at 9:40 PM as scheduled. Jason wanted to fly first class, but he chose not to. Even though everything was going smoothly, this was one more way he felt he could avoid detection if someone were watching. Sitting in the semi-cramped general passenger seats seemed to prolong the flight. At least the stewardesses came by frequently with bottled water, soda and snacks. Jason felt Sheila elbow him when he winked at one of the stewardesses. "I saw that," she said smiling. Jason laughed then took Sheila's hand and held it.

After a brief layover in London, Jason and Sheila were in the air and on their way to Stockholm. At last Jason heard the words he had been waiting for, "The pilot has informed us we will be arriving in Stockholm, Sweden in approximately fifteen minutes. An attendant will be through to pick up any last minute items you would like to place in the trash. Please fasten your seatbelts and prepare for landing."

Jason hated long flights. Ten hours of flight time in cramped quarters with dozens and dozens of people was no fun. The smell of bad body odor reeked throughout the plane. The British Airways flight taxied to the designated Stockholm gate.

"I'm glad that's over," said Jason. "I can't wait for a breath of fresh air."

"These overseas flights are a little on the nasty side. I can hardly wait to take a shower after I do my stewardess thing," Sheila said as she laughed.

"That whole stewardess routine is a blast isn't it? I wonder if the Thornburg surveillance team will ever figure out that you changed your name and now claim to be employed as a stewardess. That was a great idea, babe. It will also look great on your resume if you ever decide to make a career change from a chemist."

"If they haven't figured it out they will eventually. They'll pump Raymond for information. My name will surface for sure."

"We never should have had our rendezvous at the airport hotel in Philly. It would have been too easy to blow our plans in acquiring the cancer pills."

"But I had to see you, honey. Besides, that lady sneaking photos of us was eating her heart out. She was as jealous as could be seeing you with the hottest looking chick on the planet."

"What are you talking about?"

"Remember those three gals that were celebrating a birthday party? They were sneaking photos of us. I'm sure they were hired by Thornburg to tail you. Who else would want your picture?"

"Why didn't you say something? That could have ruined our whole plan."

"You know how I like to live on the edge, honey, and it doesn't matter now. You aren't getting soft on me are you?"

"You are one crazy gal. That's why I love you so much." They both laughed as they worked their way through customs and moved with the crowd towards the baggage area.

"Hey, Jason, there's Max. He's here right on time."

As Jason and Sheila moved toward Max, they could see his hand waving in the air. They funneled their way through the patiently waiting travelers. Max held out his hand and gave Jason a muscular handshake. Then he hugged Sheila and gave her a kiss on the cheek.

"It's good to see you again, little brother. Welcome to Sweden."

"It's great to be here. Is this a secure line?" he asked as he looked back and forth across the crowd.

"That's a good one. You still have that sense of humor, little brother. You look tired. Were the last couple of days a little on the long side?"

"You could say that. I didn't get much sleep in the hotel. I got a little sleep on the flight over, but you know how comfortable those seats are on the airlines. Either your knees are cramped or your head is hanging over the back."

"Well, nothing but first class from now on. How was your flight, Sheila?"

"I'm fine. The airline seats don't bother me at all. Did you take good care of my home while I was gone?"

The three comrades continued their small talk as they waited for the luggage. After leaving the airport, their discussion changed to business.

"So Jason, I assume you have the pills and formula with you. Did Sheila have a chance to look the formula over?"

"No. We decided to wait until we arrived here."

"When would you like to test the pills and review the formula, Sheila?"

"I'll analyze the pills as soon as we get back to the house. That will only take me half an hour. Verifying the formula can wait. That will take a considerable amount of time and at this point, it's irrelevant whether the formula is genuine or not as long as the pills are. I think we can live quite well on a million dollars a pop minimum for the cancer curing pills."

"Thirty three million dollars apiece, and it's tax free. It took a few years, but we did it," said Max. "Team work is a beautiful thing."

During the short drive to Sheila's house, Jason handed the bottle of C1 Extraction pills to her. When they arrived, Sheila went directly to the laboratory in the basement. She walked over to the windowpanes of her controlled greenhouse area and looked inside. "How are you, my babies," she said to the hundred plants she maintained. The plants were comprised of four different species from seeds she smuggled out of Thornburg Genetics.

"I know you will help me duplicate the compound I need, won't you, honeys." She smiled and was proud of how lush and green the plants were. She would go in and spend some time with them the next day. Because of their delicate nature, she wore a special Tyvek™ suit and facemask to avoid introducing any pollutant that could harm them. "Tomorrow, my sweeties," Sheila said as she turned and walked over to her analysis workstation.

Sheila set the bottle of C1 Extraction pills on the tabletop at her workstation. She took an alcohol wipe and wiped down the surfaces of the bottle and the tabletop. She slipped into a sterilized aqua colored doctor's gown and placed a facemask on. After adjusting the straps behind her head, she walked to her two-bay, stainless steel sink. Sheila soaped and rinsed her hands, then pulled on a pair of sterile rubber gloves. Her entire basement was structured as a sterile environment. She kept it locked at all times and allowed no one else in. Carefully Sheila twisted the top off the plastic bottle of pills. With a pair of long tweezers, she reached into the bottle, selected one of the pills and dropped it into a sterile glass test tube.

"I choose you as our test tube, baby," she said. "You are our million dollar baby."

After placing the lid back on the bottle of pills, Sheila picked up a sterile glass rod and ground the pill into a fine powder. She took a special reagent and poured 20 milliliters into a separate test tube, then poured in the ground up pill. She swirled the mixture until it was fully dissolved. Next she took a syringe and drew a minute amount into the syringe. She inserted the mixture into the injection port of her gas chromatograph and waited for the analysis.

Sheila watched the computer screen as each element was graphed. When the process was complete, she brought up the screen showing the graph from the sample she had analyzed almost two years ago. The graph was an exact duplicate of the sample from the fifty pills Dr. Hoffman had provided at that time. Seven of those pills had saved Sheila's life.

"It's a match," she said out loud. "These are genuine, and there is my little unidentified compound. I'll figure out where you came from yet."

After placing the pills in a small fireproof vault, she took off her protective gown and other paraphernalia and ran up the stairs. Jason and Max were sitting at the kitchen table, each with a cup of coffee.

"The C1 Extraction pills are genuine. We are officially millionaires."

"Yes!" said Max as he pumped his fist towards the ground.

Sheila ran over and jumped in Jason's lap. Then she gave him a long tender kiss.

"We did it, babe. I don't believe it. Our plans worked to the letter. So what's next?"

"I have to make a couple of telephone calls," said Max. "I already have a potential customer." Max's first telephone call was to the United States. "Hello, this is Max. Code word Red Eagle. Release Elizabeth Hoffman and April James Tuesday night. That's Tuesday night." The second call was to North Korea. "Hello. This is Dr. Maxwell Curtis. I have reviewed the cancer diagnosis of your client. The potential experimental treatment we discussed has been procured. The supply is rare, to say the least, due to the complex manufacturing procedure. The price per pill is two million dollars, which brings the total treatment price to fourteen million American dollars."

Arrangements were made to have a personal jet flown from Sweden to North Korea at the expense of the North Korean Government. Max checked the bank account one half hour before he had to leave for the airport. "Look at this!" Max hollered. Sheila and Jason hopped out of their easy chairs in the living room and ran to the den. They stood over Max and stared at the laptop screen. Fourteen million dollars had been electronically transferred into their joint business account.

"That's almost five million dollars each, my comrades," said Max.

"Wow. Fourteen million dollars," said Jason. He turned to look at Sheila as she squeezed his hand. The smile on her face said it all.

Max drove himself to the airport. He had the seven pills in a secure travel wallet, tied around his neck and hidden under his collared, light blue shirt. As soon as he showed his passport to the VIP security booth personnel, his suitcase was processed and he passed through the metal detector. He was escorted to the small personal jet docked outside the terminal. Max decided this was the way to travel. Maybe he would buy his own personal jet with his share of the money. He had enough clothing and accessories to last him ten days. He had to stay with his client fifteen days. That was part of the deal. His client paid fourteen million dollars to be healed from cancer. Max guaranteed his client he would be healed in seven days. Max was required to remain on site for fifteen days as insurance that the treatment was legitimate. He didn't ask what the consequences of failure were.

It was just after four in the morning when Max's flight landed in Pyongyang, North Korea. Max was transported to a well-lit compound where his new client was housed. It was apparent the compound was a military compound as military vehicles and personnel in various uniforms were numerous. He had no idea of the exact location. After stopping at two check points, they arrived at a heavily fortified three story building. The building was surrounded by a twenty foot tall concrete wall with razor wire on top. The massive steel gate clanked behind them after they drove through. Max could see the thick steel bars on the building's windows. Upon entering the building, Max noted that security officers were everywhere. Several of them carried pistols and automatic rifles. Max was scanned with a handheld metal detector, and his luggage was searched. Then he was ushered to a room adjacent to his client. He took pill number one from his travel wallet and was escorted to his client's room. Max recognized his client's face immediately. It was the Supreme Leader of the Democratic People's Republic of Korea. He could see the weakened state of his body. His eyes were sunken with big black bags under them. His cheeks were drawn in and his complexion had a yellow gray hue. He was in a deteriorated state much worse than Max had expected. Max met with some resistance when he demanded he be allowed to complete a partial physical. His client waved off those around him, and Max went to work. His client's blood pressure was fine. His heart and lung functions appeared to be acceptable. His client said his bowel functions were fine, though he had eaten little in the last few days. Max knew his client's attending physician and trusted the cancer diagnosis one hundred percent. He was satisfied the pills would cure the liver and kidney cancer. He took pill number one and handed it to his client with a glass of water. His client swallowed the pill in anticipation of a quick healing.

Max was escorted to a plush room on the third floor with an eastern view of a mountain range. The windows in his room were all barred, and Max could see the top of the imposing thick concrete wall with the razor wire on top. Despite these surroundings, Max was treated like royalty. He could call for anything he wanted. He was given a menu that would meet the expectations of the most distinguished visitor. Max ordered a special egg dish with garden fresh vegetables. The meal came with several side dishes and a dessert. After partaking of the scrumptious meal, he sipped a cup of hot tea as he watched the sun rise over the mountain range.

After twenty-four hours, Max was escorted in to see his client again. His complexion had improved greatly and he was sitting up in bed. "This medication is superb. I can almost feel my body healing itself. Thank you, Dr. Curtis."

"You are welcome sir. It is now time for your second treatment." Max gave pill number two to his client and was again escorted back to the plush room. He hated the thought of spending fifteen days in that room, but he could watch television and order any book he wanted to read.

On the third morning, Maxwell was shocked when he saw the condition of his client. He could see a relapse was in progress and his client was doing poorly. This wasn't right. He had seen the drug in action before when he had obtained the lot of fifty pills from Dr. Hoffman. The health of the patients receiving those pills, including him and Sheila, improved significantly every day. He looked at the other six men and women standing in the room. They also knew that their leader's health had gone downhill.

"Is he being given any food or other medications that I specifically forbid?"

"We are following your orders as directed Dr. Curtis. Is there a problem?"

Max suddenly felt fear as he never had before. Either the pills weren't working or one of his client's advisors wanted the Supreme Leader dead and was poisoning him. "I need to stay by his bedside and monitor him. It appears there is some type of setback in his treatment."

"I am afraid that won't be possible," said one of his client's aides who appeared to be calling the shots.

"Then I cannot be held accountable for the results of this medication. I informed you ahead of time it was experimental in nature."

"You are already being held accountable, Dr. Curtis. You guaranteed positive results. We will know in seven days if you have been lying to us."

"Why would I lie to you and arrange to stay here fifteen days if a medication was ineffective?"

"It appears you would risk our leader's life to obtain a large sum of money, perhaps from some foreign dissident, Dr. Curtis. Perhaps you have arranged an escape plan from this location as well. I can assure you our building security is intense. You need to keep your end of the bargain Doctor."

"You know this doesn't make sense. If I wanted to scam you out of any money, I never would have traveled here to legitimately treat the Supreme Leader. Besides, my medication has been tested. It is an effective treatment for the type of liver and kidney cancer we are dealing with."

"You can't be insinuating that we are harming our leader in any way, are you, Dr. Curtis? We paid a large sum of money to have him healed. If there is a problem, you need to rectify it." Dr. Curtis then administered the third C1 Extraction pill. He could only hope for improvement in his client's health.

The patient's spokesman then turned to one of the other men in the room dressed in military uniform. In Korean he barked out an order, "I want the security on this building increased tenfold and two Special Forces officers in this room at all times." Then in English he stated, "Suddenly I do not trust Dr. Curtis. Escort him back to his room now."

Chapter 69

April had been locked in the garage pen since Friday night. Each time there was a shift change in those guarding her; she would attempt to carry on a conversation. Her jailers would not say one word. Their only task seemed to be to sit and observe her, often staring at her for twenty minutes at a time. Their black clothing with the black gloves and ski mask gave April an eerie feeling. It was obvious they had been given orders not to communicate with her.

April's feet were tender after being dragged from her apartment into the van in her bare feet. She discovered a first aid kit in the bathroom and rubbed antibacterial cream on the half dozen scrapes on her feet. Then she covered the scrapes with bandages and put on the socks and slippers they had provided.

Viewing the ten magazines that had been placed in the pen was already getting old, but at least thumbing through them gave April something to do. April had no idea what time it was. The lights in the garage had been on ever since her arrival on Friday. There was no clock in sight. She wondered what would happen if she faked a heart attack or seizure and then tried to escape when they came to help her. The odds were four trained operatives versus one marketing employee. Those were poor odds at best. The captors might not even respond. April decided a faked sickness was a lousy idea. As she was flipping through the pages of the Better Homes and Gardens magazine for the fourth time, she heard a clicking noise and looked up. She saw a person with a blindfold escorted through the garage entry door. April stood up for a closer look. She could see it was dark outdoors, even though the door was only open for seconds. It must be Monday night, she thought to herself. As soon as the door was closed, the blindfolded person was escorted to the chain link fence enclosure.

"You, go into the bathroom and shut the door," one of the captors snapped at April. April did as she was told. Once inside the bathroom she could hear the padlock click on the gate. After a minute she heard another click. April waited a few moments and then cracked the bathroom door for a peak. A woman was standing just inside the gate and looking from one side of the enclosure to the other. The woman had mostly gray hair, which was cut short, but stylish. She looked to be about sixty years old and had a slim figure. Her arms and face were slightly tanned, but her face looked stressed. April wasn't sure what to do. Was the new arrival another fatality of the cancer pill theft or some nut job brought into the enclosure to harm her? The woman didn't seem aggressive, and April decided she couldn't stay in the bathroom forever, so she exited with caution. The woman watched as April appeared. She seemed to be in a state of turmoil and didn't say anything to April.

"Hello. My name is April James." April held her hand out. The woman looked shell shocked. She slowly reached her hand out and shook April's.

"My name is Elizabeth Hoffman."

"You're Raymond Hoffman's sister?" April was shocked. This was the last person she expected to see in the pen with her.

"How did you know that? You must know my brother, Raymond."

"I work at Thornburg Genetics with your brother. However, I do have to tell you we are not on great speaking terms at the moment."

Elizabeth and April talked nonstop for an hour. They both drank bottled water and munched on snacks that had been provided in the pen. Elizabeth told April all about her experiences in her two plus years of captivity. She was never told why she had been kidnapped. She surmised it had something to do with Raymond's job at Thornburg Genetics. She was sure that since being kidnapped, her brother had been living his life in mental anguish. Elizabeth portrayed how close she and Raymond were as brother and sister. She told April that every month, Elizabeth's captors had produced a DVD showing Elizabeth being tortured. The torture wasn't real, but Elizabeth was forced to scream and cry to make it look real with the threat of violence if she didn't cooperate. She said her life in captivity had been bearable, though lonely and boring. She had her own room on the ground floor of a large house, and was given chores to do, but had very little contact with other people. She had no radio, no television and limited human contact with the outside world. To stay sane she would sing songs she could remember and make up stories. The house was in a compound with high walls and security guards on duty at all times. She told April she must have been held overseas, because the jet flight to her current location had taken hours.

April could see that Elizabeth was starving for affection, and they hugged each other and held hands frequently. April let Elizabeth talk as much as she wanted to and chimed in on occasion with a few select tidbits of information. As the conversation slowed down, Elizabeth told April she was exhausted and needed some sleep. There was only a single cot and April let her use it. She was snoring lightly in a few minutes. April rolled up in a blanket on the floor. After tossing and turning she was able to get into a position comfortable enough to fall asleep as well. The floor was so uncomfortable she kept waking up and had to readjust her body in order to fall asleep again.

April felt a tapping on her shoulder and jumped. Elizabeth was standing over her. "Why don't you sleep on the cot for awhile?" April

289

agreed and fell asleep in an instant. When she woke up she saw Elizabeth sitting in the canvas folding chair, reading a magazine. She watched April sit up and stretch.

"I must look like a complete mess, don't I, April?"

"You look fine, Elizabeth. I'm sure neither of us would win a beauty contest. I've been cooped up in here for two or three days. There is no shower, mirror or anything to primp with."

"You can call me Liz if you like, April. That's what my friends call me. So what's next? I have no idea why I'm here. Nobody has told me a thing."

"I was told I would be released within one week. I had no idea someone else would be involved in this. Must be you are going to be released too."

"Do you really think so?"

"I've been praying for a safe release since I arrived here. At this point in time, I don't know what day or time it is. The lights are on twenty four hours a day."

"I think it's Tuesday. I was flown here on Monday. I don't know if it's daylight yet or not."

"I would ask that person in black over there, but they won't talk to me. They haven't said one word to me since I arrived here and they put me in this pen. One of them is watching and listening to us at all times, though."

"Why are they holding you here, April?"

"It's very complicated, and it's probably best not to discuss it right now."

"It has something to do with Raymond, doesn't it?"

"It does, but I don't really know to what extent. Your brother is fine, though. We need to concentrate on us right now." April and Liz continued talking and sharing their life's experiences with each other. They talked about relatives and what foods they liked. April told Liz about her time spent in Ecuador, working through the Peace Corps. They had no idea how much time had passed when one of their captors walked up to the enclosure gate and spoke. By the tone of voice, they knew it was a female even though she was wearing the standard black ski mask.

"Ladies, we have been instructed to transport you. We will be leaving in ten minutes. Use the bathroom now if you need to."

Both April and Elizabeth decided to follow the captor's advice. After what seemed like a short ten minutes the captor walked up to the gate again. "We will be placing handcuffs on you. They will remain on you until we reach our destination. Please step forward and put out your hands."

"Where are we going?" asked April.

"I have nothing further to say. I am following orders."

April knew it was useless to try any further communication. She had no idea what their plans were and didn't want to agitate them, so she walked up to the gate and placed her hands through the small slot cut out of the chain link fence. The captor took her black leather gloved hand and slipped a cuff around April's right wrist. There was a click as she closed it. She put her index finger between the cuff and April's wrist to determine how tight it was. The captor gave the cuff one more click, then used the key to push a small pin which locked it in place. The captor followed the same procedure on April's left wrist. April then backed away from the gate. Elizabeth hesitated. She looked at April and then she looked at the captor.

"It's okay Elizabeth. We have to do what they tell us." Elizabeth walked over to the slot and slid her hands through. When her wrists were cuffed, she too backed away from the gate.

It was apparent the other captors had been watching the handcuffing procedures as three of them appeared on the scene immediately. April could see that two of the captors were still wearing holsters with pistols in them. One of the captors opened the double side doors on the van. The second disappeared through the doors into the van. The other two captors positioned themselves several feet back from the gate of the enclosure, one on each side of the gate. Both of them had shotguns pointed at the floor.

"One at a time ladies," the female captor said as she unlocked the gate.

"You first," she said as she pointed to April. April exited the pen and walked to the van.

"Stop at the van door before getting in. I have orders to blindfold you."

April stopped. She could feel the captor behind her. April saw the heavy black cloth drop in front of her eyes and felt it squeeze her forehead and cheeks as the captor tied the cloth in a knot behind April's head. All April could picture in her mind was being lined up in front of a firing squad. Then the captor helped April step into the van and she was guided onto the middle seat.

"Your turn," April heard the captor say. In a few moments she felt Elizabeth slide into the seat next to her.

"Are you alright, Elizabeth?"

"Yes, I'm fine."

The van rocked slightly as the captors were seated. April assumed there would be two captors in the seat behind them and two in the front seats. The van door was closed. April could detect some light with the blindfold on, but nothing else. One of the captors shut the lights off in the garage and then raised the overhead door. April assumed it was dark outside the building, as she could sense no light through her blindfold. Neither April nor Elizabeth knew it was a bright, clear, starry night.

The van driver did not turn on the lights, but pulled out of the garage and stopped until his comrade could close and lock the overhead door and join him in the front passenger seat. The driver then pulled down the secluded driveway, turned south on the suburban road and flicked on the headlights.

The captors had been assigned a specific route to follow. It would take three hours of travel time. Cutting back and forth over several roads, they arrived at their destination forty miles away. The only noise in the van was the humming of tires and an occasional thump from a bump in the road. April was mentally exhausted and nodded off for a short nap. She had no idea how long the van had been traveling when she felt Elizabeth nudge her. The van was slowing down. Then it stopped. She prayed a silent prayer. "Please God, protect Elizabeth and me. Please don't let our captors harm us in any way. I pray this in Jesus' name."

April heard the front passenger door of the van open. Then she heard the double side doors open. "We have arrived at our destination, ladies," the captor said. April knew this was a male speaking by his deep voice. The captor helped Elizabeth and then April out of the van.

"I am now going to remove the blindfolds and handcuffs. You are free to go. There are a few supplies here for you. I shouldn't have to say this, but do not make any foolish moves." The captor then removed the handcuffs from both April and Elizabeth and took off their blindfolds. A small flashlight was lying on the ground. Its beam of light was directed at two small sacks. The captor turned and walked toward the van.

"Where are we?" asked April. There was no reply as the captor who released them and a second captor standing next to the van holding a shotgun hopped in the van. They closed their respective doors and drove off into the night.

Chapter 70

April picked up the flashlight and pointed it at the two sacks. They were nothing more than oversized plastic grocery bags with the words 'Thank You' embossed on the side. Then April spotted her pocketbook sitting behind the bags.

"Are we really free?" asked Elizabeth.

"We are for now, but I don't think we should stick around here. We need to get away from this spot as fast as we can. Let me take a quick peek in my pocketbook before we leave." April rifled through her pocketbook. Her two cell phones were there, but the batteries had been removed. Her handgun was also there, but someone had removed the cartridges. She took a quick look through the bag closest to her. It contained one hooded sweatshirt, four bottles of water and prepackaged snacks. In the bottom was a pair of April's sneakers. She took them out, sat down on the dirt and put them on. After tying the laces, she stood up again. They felt good after having worn only socks and slippers on her feet since her arrival at the garage.

"I think we need to find some type of makeshift shelter and wait for morning," said April. "Who knows how long the batteries in this flashlight will last."

Elizabeth was looking through the second bag. "Here's a bigger flashlight," she said as she pulled it out of the bag and flicked on the button.

"Great. Flash it around and let's see where we are." Elizabeth slowly shined the light in a three hundred and sixty degree radius. There was nothing but the road lined with trees.

"Let's pick up this stuff and walk up the road a ways. Get ready to jump off the road quick if we see any headlights or hear a vehicle coming. Do you mind if I lead the way, Liz?"

"I wish you would, April. I'm still in shock at the thought of being free again."

April took the small flashlight and gave the large one to Elizabeth. "Leave this flashlight off for now. We'll use it for backup if we need to." They both slipped on sweatshirts to avoid a chill from the damp night air. Then they each picked up one of the bags, and April grabbed her pocketbook.

"The van pulled up from that direction, so let's go back that way."

They started walking down the road under the starry sky. The quarter sliced moon gave a small amount of light. After walking about a mile the surrounding trees turned into fields. Then a barn appeared in front of them. As they got closer the barn towered over them. It looked abused and abandoned. An attached shed had fallen in, either from a heavy snow load or neglect. Most of the wide boards making up the siding were dark brown in color with a weathered texture.

"This is way too convenient," said April. "The captors will know this barn is here if they decide to come back for some reason. Let's keep walking, Liz."

"I will do whatever you say, April." After walking another mile they came to a stand of evergreens. It looked like some type of reforestation project.

"I like this background a lot better. Let's get off the road and back in the pines. We can hide until morning."

"What about bears or wolves?"

"There may be a black bear around, but no wolves. I'm not worried at all about animals, Liz; I'm more worried our captors may come back."

"What about dogs?"

"Dogs?"

"Yes. What if they come back after us and have dogs to follow our trail?"

"We've walked quite a distance, and I haven't seen any sign of other human beings. I really think we have been set free, Liz. We can't walk all night. We don't even know what time it is. Let's just get off the road and into these pines. We'll find a spot that looks comfortable and pray for the best. My gut feeling is we will be okay."

Slowly they worked their way through the blackberry bushes lining the side of the road. Both April and Liz had small scratches on their hands and legs from the thorns on the bushes. Once they got a few feet off the road, the blackberry bushes disappeared and there was almost no undergrowth in the mature stand of pines. They came to a spot where a huge gnarled oak tree reached high to the sky and a pine tree deadfall laid on the ground next to it. More blackberry bushes surrounded the deadfall. "This spot looks good, Liz. We have a lot of cover and will be well hidden." April cleared out a few dead branches at the base of the oak tree and sat down. Elizabeth sat next to her. Nobody would be able to see them with the deadfall in front of them. April reached over and gave Elizabeth a hug. "Everything is going to be alright, Liz."

April took the big flashlight and started emptying her pocketbook piece by piece into the paper bag. They heard a noise from the direction of the road. A vehicle whooshed past. They could see the headlights bounce off a couple of trees between them and the road.

"I guess there's life out there after all," said Elizabeth.

"That's encouraging." April went back to her pocketbook. She found the cell phone batteries and handgun cartridges in the zippered side pouch. Must be Jason had placed them there. She held them out and showed Liz.

"Look, Liz. We have protection." April retrieved her handgun from the paper bag and loaded the six rounds into it.

"Do you always carry a gun in your pocketbook?"

"As often as I can. You never know when you may need one."

"I have to say I feel safer knowing you have that. Do you know how to use it?"

"Of course I do, Liz. I target practice frequently. Here, hold this light for a minute will you?" April handed the flashlight to Elizabeth. Then she opened the back of her cell phones, slid the batteries in place and turned them on. "There, I should be able to make a call in a couple of minutes."

The cell phones made their usual start up melodies and then they were ready for use. "Great! It doesn't look like there is any cell tower access out here, wherever we are." April speed dialed Keegan's number. Nothing happened.

"Well, Liz, the cell phones won't work out here, but at least we know what time it is. It is just after 2:30 AM and its Wednesday. Let's get some rest until daylight." April shut the cell phone off to conserve battery power. Then she leaned back against the towering oak tree. She offered Elizabeth her pocketbook to use as a pillow and Liz accepted the offer. April laid the handgun next to her where it was handy. She shut off the flashlight and laid it next to the handgun. It was dark under the oak tree and surrounding evergreen canopy and both April and Elizabeth fell asleep in a matter of minutes.

April was snatched out of her sleep by the sound of a branch snapping. She didn't move. Daylight was drifting through the thick canopy. Then she saw him. Twenty feet in front of her was a man, staring at her. April realized the downfall and berry bushes didn't provide as much cover as she'd thought they did when assessing the situation in the dark. She didn't take her eyes off him as she reached for her handgun on the ground next to her. She picked it up and pointed it at him. "What are you doing?" April hollered at the stranger as she jumped to her feet.

Elizabeth awoke, sat up and saw April with the handgun pointed in front of her. She realized that April was confronting a young man. The man had medium length, brown curly hair barely reaching the collar of his dark green parka.

As soon as April jumped up, he put his hands in the air and started to back up. "Hold on. Be careful with that thing. I'm not doing anything wrong. I have permission to be here."

"Who are you and what are you doing here. Don't move!"

"Relax, will you, please. My name is Aaron. I'm a college student, and I came here to take some photos of a waterfall back here in the woods. Would you mind pointing that thing in some other direction?"

April hadn't paid any attention, but now noticed a camera hanging from the stranger's neck. There appeared to be a camera bag sitting next to him. "Do you have a college ID on you?"

"I have one in my wallet. Do you want to see it?"

April thought for a moment. Even if he did have an ID it could be a fake. Besides from what she had been exposed to, if he were the enemy he would be wearing black fatigues, not a green rain parka and sneakers. And he looked way too scared to be a real threat. In a more relaxed tone of voice April said, "No, never mind. Tell me what you are doing again."

"There is a nice waterfall back in the woods. I try to get out here at sunrise a few times during the year to take photos of it. Sometimes when there is a light mist it displays a beautiful rainbow. I actually won seventy-five dollars from a photo of the waterfall that I entered in a local newspaper contest last fall. It's a beautiful spot. Would you like to see it?"

"It sounds wonderful, but not today. You can put your hands down if you would like to." April lowered her handgun.

"Anyhow, I was on my way back to the falls and saw the two of you. A path goes right through here." Aaron took his hand and pointed out the path. "I thought the two of you were dead or something, so I stopped for a closer look. There weren't any other cars up by the road. I didn't mean to disturb you."

"I wouldn't say you disturbed us. I would say you scared us to death."

"That was obvious. The last thing I expected to see this morning was somebody pointing a gun at me. You scared the snot out of me. What are you doing out here in the woods? Oh. Sorry. You don't have to answer that if you don't want to. My adrenalin is still flowing a mile a minute."

"No, that's okay. Let's just say we were out for a ride, and the people we were with dropped us off out here last night to fend for ourselves."

"They dropped you off out here? That sounds kind of weird."

"Yeah, well, you live and you learn. Where are we anyhow?"

"We're in the Blue Mountains just outside of Allentown."

"How close is Allentown?"

"About fifteen miles from here."

"Is there any way we could trouble you for a lift? I'll be glad to pay you."

"I'll take you back to town if you promise not to shoot me or something."

"If I were going to shoot you, I would have done so already, Aaron. We aren't criminals if that's what you were wondering. By the way, I'm sorry we are messing up your photo shoot."

"I can come back another day. Besides, wait until I tell my friends this story. They'll never believe it. Nothing exciting like this ever happens to me."

"I'll make a deal with you. How good are you at keeping secrets."

"You want me to keep this a secret? Are you kidding?"

"Only for a week or so. If you do, I'll come back if I can find this place again, take a little walk to the waterfalls with you, and you can tell all of your buddies. I'll even buy the crew some pizzas. This isn't a date, only a courtesy."

"It's a deal. What's your name?"

"I can't tell you right now."

"You're going to stiff me, aren't you?"

"Aaron, when we get to town, I'll take down your full name, address and telephone number, and I'll be in touch in a few days. That's a promise."

"Okay, I'll chance it. Are you two ready to go?"

April picked up her pocketbook and slid the handgun and flashlight in it. Then she and Elizabeth each picked up their plastic bags. They followed Aaron to his car. The small, four door, red Pontiac Vibe looked a little beat up, but April and Elizabeth would have caught a ride in anything that moved. Aaron had to clean out some empty soda cans and food wrappers from the back seat before April and Elizabeth could get in. April decided to sit behind Aaron so she could keep an eye on him. The Vibe started with the slightest flick of the key.

Aaron talked nonstop the entire trip. He talked about his buddies, college, family and food. April checked her cell phone after they had traveled a few miles. She now had cell phone access. She slid the phone back into her pocketbook and decided to call Keegan after they arrived in Allentown.

As Aaron started driving down a mountain road, a city appeared in the valley. "Welcome to Allentown."

"The view is great, and we are starving. There must be a McDonalds or something around here," said April.

"There's a McDonalds just down the road." Aaron continued to talk as he drove them to the McDonalds franchise. They both thanked him for the ride, and April offered to pay him. She had Aaron write his name, address and telephone number on a piece of paper and slid it into her pocketbook. He wouldn't accept any money for the ride, but he did reiterate his desire for April to keep her promise and visit the falls with him in the near future. He knew his friends were never going to believe the story about this crazy lady.

Chapter 71

The captors had taken nothing out of April's pocketbook. Her cash, credit cards, Thornburg Genetics ID and driver's license were all intact. She asked Liz what she would like to eat. They both ordered two breakfast sandwiches, juice, coffee and ice water. Both took turns using the restrooms. April told Elizabeth to go ahead and start eating while she made a cell phone call and then stepped outside the door. Keegan answered on the first ring.

"Hello. This is Keegan McGrath."

"Hi, Keegan. This is April."

"It's really you? Are you alone? Are you okay?"

"It is indeed me. We are okay, and we are back in civilization."

"Who is we?"

"Elizabeth and I."

"Elizabeth Hoffman?"

"That is correct."

"Is anyone else there? Are any of the thugs around?"

"Just the two of us are here."

"I don't believe it. I questioned if we would ever see you again."

"When were you going to fill me in on that positive little tidbit?"

"I don't need to now. Where are you?"

"We are in Allentown, Pennsylvania sitting at a McDonalds eating breakfast."

"Allentown; you're only a little over an hour away. How did you get there?"

"It's a long story. I'll tell you later."

"What is the address of the McDonalds?"

"It's near Woodlawn."

"I'll use my GPS. Stay right where you are. I'm leaving now to pick you up."

"Do you think we'll be alright here?"

"I assume they released you on their own. I don't foresee any problem."

"Okay. We'll see you soon."

April took a big bite of her breakfast sandwich and a large drink of orange juice. Elizabeth only had a bite of her first breakfast sandwich left. They both finished their breakfast sandwiches and juice and then started sipping on their water and hot coffee. They discussed their experience in the woods and the look on Aaron's face when April pointed her handgun at him.

"He looked so scared. The poor guy didn't know what to do," chuckled April.

"I felt sorry for him," said Elizabeth. "Are you really going to come back out here and go to that waterfall with him?"

"Sure thing, Liz. It sounds like a cool place. Want to come along?"

"I think I'm going to stay home for a while, if I ever get there."

"I hate to change the subject, but when I made a visit to the restroom I took a look in the mirror. I didn't even recognize myself. My eyes are bloodshot, my hair is a mess, and my clothes look like something I dragged through some kid's sandbox before putting them on. I haven't had a shower in days and I stink."

"We do look and smell like a couple of nasty people, don't we, April?"

"The worst part is nobody here but us seems to notice, and on top of that, I'm sticking to this vinyl seat. The bottom of my pants must be covered with pine pitch. I'll bet the seats in Aaron's car are sticky." They both laughed in unison.

"You haven't seen your brother in two years. How do you think the reunion will go?"

"It will be fine. We have always been very close. He is heavily involved in his work. He told me I didn't have to work, but I had a few houses I cleaned, and I volunteered my time at the hospital a couple of mornings each week. I guess we could be classified as an odd couple."

"If it works for the two of you and you're enjoying life, that's what counts."

They were both sipping on their second cup of coffee when they saw Keegan pull into the parking lot. They met him at the door with coffee in hand. Keegan gave April a big hug. "It is so good to see you, April." Then he turned and said, "You must be Elizabeth Hoffman. My name is Keegan McGrath." Keegan held out his hand, and Elizabeth shook hands with him.

"Yes. My name is Elizabeth Hoffman. Do you know where my brother Raymond is? I'd like to see him as soon as possible."

"I do know where he is. Let me grab a cup of coffee, and we'll get on the road. Would you ladies like to wait in the car?"

April took the car keys from Keegan, and she and Elizabeth walked to his car.

"Do you mind if I ride in the front, Liz?"

"Not at all. I'll sit anywhere as long as I'm headed home."

Keegan returned to the car with a medium coffee. April handed him the keys, and he drove out of the McDonalds exit lane. He had just started up the road when he addressed April and Elizabeth.

"Ladies, I know you two have been through a lot, but we really need to have a debriefing session. You have both been kidnapped and held captive. I need to find out as much information as I can about your captors as soon as I can."

"You listen to me, Keegan McGrath. Elizabeth hasn't seen her brother in two years, we've been kidnapped, we are tired and cranky and don't care about debriefing. We are alive and well, and we are going back to my apartment to get a hot shower. I hope you cleaned up all the food that was sitting on the table and in the kitchen so it doesn't stink in there. Liz and I are going to doll ourselves up a bit. In fact, why don't you stop at Penny's on the way back, so we can buy Elizabeth a couple of new outfits? I'm sure you have money in your expense budget for that. After we get Liz home, I can fill you in on our last few days' events. I assume you called Dr. Hoffman and told him his sister is safe."

"Well, er, no."

"No! Are you kidding me, Keegan? You didn't call and tell him?"

"It's a little complicated, April. He's being detained at a military facility."

"What exactly does that mean?"

"He is in military lockdown right now."

"He's in jail?"

"It's not exactly jail, it's a brig."

"What did he do?" asked Elizabeth.

"Like I said, it is rather complicated. Part of the reason he is there is due to the theft of goods from Thornburg Genetics. The other part is because I had him placed there for his own protection. The thugs that held you captive are unpredictable. I had a bad feeling Dr. Hoffman might be accosted if I didn't get him off the streets. Anyhow, you two gals do your thing, and I will get you an hour of visiting time with him. I'm not going to have him released until I'm comfortable this whole matter is behind us. You have to understand this is in everyone's best interest right now. Another thing I have to tell you, April, is your family is currently at a safe house. The sooner I can get things straightened out, the sooner I can get them back home."

"Okay, Keegan. Elizabeth and I need some adjustment time so

301

please bear with us."

There was silence in the car as Keegan drove back to Philadelphia. April and Elizabeth both fell asleep. Keegan woke them up after he parked in J.C. Penny's parking lot. "Here is a company credit card," said Keegan. "Please don't overdo it. I'll be the one paying the bill in the end." He handed the card to April.

"We will only be a few minutes. I think you should escort us in to keep us out of trouble, Keegan, don't you? You can check out all of the modern styles in women's clothing."

"Boy, is this ever a set up job or what."

April and Elizabeth laughed as Keegan followed them into the store. Elizabeth picked out a short sleeved blue knit top, a pink knit top and two colored t-shirts. Then she picked out a skirt that went with both of the knit tops and two pairs of jeans. April nodded her approval at the dressing room. Then Elizabeth picked out a pair of white Addidas sneakers with pink accents, a pair of blue flat bottom shoes and a pair of black high heels to go with her skirt.

"You are going to look like a million dollars, Elizabeth. What do you think, Keegan?"

"The outfits she chose look very nice."

"These are all the clothes she has that are in style. We can do some more shopping tomorrow. You'll probably want to come along won't you, Keegan?"

"Oh no you don't, Miss James. Not on your life."

After Liz tried on the clothing, she selected some new undergarments, and they moved to the checkout line. "It may be a few days before I can pay you back for these."

"Keegan won't mind paying for these, will you, Keegan?" Keegan knew he couldn't use the Thornburg credit card and graciously stated, "Not at all. It is my treat, Elizabeth. You deserve to look good after all you have been through."

After paying for the new clothing, Keegan drove them back to April's apartment. Keegan chose to wait in the car while the two ladies went in to primp. His cell phone rang. It was the camcorder inside April's apartment. There was April, waving away. She's such a delightful pain, he thought.

Keegan called the naval station and made arrangements for a visit with Dr. Hoffman. He was very specific in his demand not to tell Dr. Hoffman about his sister arriving for a visit.

In forty-five minutes, two beauties emerged from the front door of

April's apartment building. Keegan was standing outside his car, leaning against the roof. He straightened to full height and whistled as they approached.

"Wow. You two look gorgeous."

"Thanks," they both chimed together as they giggled. "We may be a little silly from sleep deprivation," said April.

When they arrived at the naval station, April opted to stay in the car. She knew a visit with Dr. Hoffman would be upsetting and not appropriate at this time. After being processed, Keegan and Elizabeth were escorted to the interview room. As soon as the room was secure, Dr. Hoffman was escorted in. He stopped short when he saw Elizabeth. His mouth dropped open with surprise.

"Is that really you, Elizabeth?"

"It's me, Raymond."

She looked down at his handcuffs and then back at Keegan. "Can I hug him?"

"Of course you can. He has to have the handcuffs on for security reasons, but you are welcome to hug him as much as you like."

Elizabeth ran over and embraced her brother around the neck and gave him a peck on the cheek. They both began to cry.

"I'll be back in an hour," said Keegan.

Once outside, Keegan and April drove to a mini market just outside the naval station compound gate. They each purchased a fountain soda, put a lid on it and sat at one of the four tables closest to the large paned glass front window. April described every detail of the kidnapping and release. She could sense Keegan was troubled about the event and knew it wasn't over yet. She wondered if it would ever be over. Keegan called the safe house and let April speak with her family to explain to them the limited amount of information she could without upsetting them. When she was finished, Keegan had the Thornburg security officers drive April's family back to their homes.

Keegan and April drove back to the naval station. April waited for Elizabeth in the reception area. Keegan told April he wanted her and Elizabeth to wait in the car until he was through talking with Dr. Hoffman. It was only a few minutes before Elizabeth appeared in the reception area. April led the way to Keegan's car.

Chapter 72

"Dr. Hoffman. I am elated to see the culprits released your sister Elizabeth. Did you have a good visit?"

"Yes, our visit was the best ever, Mr. McGrath. She told me pleasant information about April James. I believe I was wrong in my thinking about how evil she is. She treated my sister in a very gracious manner."

"April has a giving personality, Dr. Hoffman. Don't take too much blame for the way you felt about April. You had no way of knowing she was working for me through this ordeal."

"Yes. So what is the next step, Mr. McGrath? I have information which I am now willing to share that should be helpful in your investigation, but I will tell you this information only when certain conditions are met."

"What are the conditions, Dr. Hoffman?"

"First, you must assign someone to keep Elizabeth safe at all times. Second, I must be released from this prison immediately. Third, I must be reassigned to my research position at Thornburg Genetics."

"Let me be candid, Dr. Hoffman. YOU ARE IN NO POSITION TO MAKE ANY DEMANDS." Keegan paused to let the statement sink in. "This is reality. The plan I formulated went down the tubes when April was kidnapped. You provided information to the enemy that allowed this very ugly situation to occur. Your fault! Thank God both April and Elizabeth are safe. That problem is out of the way for now. However, my work is far from finished, and my life is not even close to business as usual. Now I am going to tell you my conditions, Dr. Hoffman. You will provide me with every piece of information you have. I need it now. If you don't provide any information, you will sit in this military prison until you do, you will not see Elizabeth again, and you will not conduct research again, because I will ruin your reputation. If another incident occurs that involves bodily harm to anyone at Thornburg Genetics and I can pin it on you, I will. However, if you choose to cooperate I will do my best to have you reinstated to your research position. If you are the team player you say you are, the time to talk is now. Thornburg Genetics security is still at risk. April's safety is still at risk. Elizabeth's safety is still at risk. The enemy is still at large. What is it going to be, Dr. Hoffman? Are you ready to talk or do I get up and walk out."

There was silence as Dr. Hoffman stared at the tabletop in front of him. He knew Keegan McGrath was staring at him, and he knew there was no compromise. The thought of sitting in a jail cell forever was torture. Even if charges of theft and espionage or whatever other trumped up charges Keegan had devised didn't hold up in court, it would take years to work through the court system. He would be broke from legal fees and have no chance of landing another research job. Besides, he really was a Thornburg Genetics team player. He couldn't leave a legacy that would hurt the company.

"Yes, I will cooperate in full, Mr. McGrath. The only thing I request is to have my life back. I love my sister. I love my research, and I don't want to spend another day in this place. Will you help me get my life back, Mr. McGrath?"

"I need your full cooperation. I will do my best to help you in any way possible if you will help me. You know the final decision to reinstate you to your research job falls on The Keeper. I will do my best to persuade her to reinstate you, Doctor. I need to know every detail about these thugs. Shall we get started?"

"Yes. I am ready."

"My concern is the enemy has one hundred C1 Extraction pills and a fake formula to produce the pills. What happens when the perpetrators discover the formula is phony? We could be back to square one again. The only upside is I now know at least one Thornburg Genetics employee other than yourself was involved in this incident. The operation flushed him out, but with nobody in custody, no leads and a volatile drug on the streets, the picture has not improved greatly."

"Yes. May I interrupt you for a moment? You should know the formula I provided was the real formula."

"No. You didn't!"

"Yes. Please let me explain the logic. I have a theory which I calculate to be ninety nine percent correct."

"I'm listening."

"I hadn't really thought too much about this situation until the last few days. I am going to pose a question to you, Mr. McGrath, and you tell me what you think. It is obvious the demand for the C1 Extraction pills and formula is driven by greed for money. The question is why someone would demand exactly one hundred pills. Why not fifty pills? Why not one thousand? What do you think, Mr. McGrath?"

"I have put some thought into that. My guess was the thugs thought it would be easy to obtain and smuggle out one hundred pills, but a larger number might be a problem and raise suspicions in your department. April told me one of the perpetrators stated they could sell the pills for one million dollars per pill. If they sold most of the pills, it would be a large payout with some pills remaining to analyze using the provided formula. However, they did receive fifty pills from you before. They obviously couldn't counterfeit the formula from those pills, so they had to demand the written formula. Also, the first fifty pills could not have produced sufficient money to suit the perpetrators' desires. My guess is they demanded small numbers of the medication so as not to raise suspicion and fly under the radar, so to speak."

"I believe your theories are only partially correct, Mr. McGrath. Here is my theory based on information you would not be privy to. I can only produce a limited number of the C1 Extraction medication due to a compound obtained from an almost extinct plant. The plants are under tight security control at an offsite Thornburg Genetics facility. I can almost guarantee this plant will never again be found in the wild. The plant is fragile. With all of the pollutants drifting around the world and the habitat this plant requires, I believe it will survive only in a specific controlled greenhouse environment. We only inventory a limited number of these plants for research. I am not able to extract enough of the plant compound to prepare one thousand C1 Extraction pills at one time. The plant is a slow grower. It could be mass-produced in the future, but not at the current time. Somewhere in the conspirators' network is a researcher that knows only a limited number of experimental pills can be produced at one time. I am sure this person analyzed at least one of the previous fifty pills I delivered. The C1 Extraction cannot be engineered without the rare plant compound. We have tried to copy the compound in our labs for years by using alternate plant compounds and genetic engineering. If we could use an alternate and eliminate the explosive capabilities, we could bring the C1 Extraction to the general public as the name brand Constellation Blue. Are you aware of an event that happened with an assistant of mine about three years ago?"

"I'm not sure. What event are you referring to?"

"On a Monday in May about three years ago, one of my research assistants did not show up for work. The young lady's name was Kendra Schlegal."

"As a matter of fact, I do know about Kendra Schlegal. She seems to have disappeared off the face of the earth."

"Yes. She hadn't missed a day's work in four years and spent many of her weekends in the laboratory as well. She was a brilliant researcher, but only at a security level four. We tried to call her house, but there was no answer. She did not show up for work again on Tuesday. Again an attempt to call her was negative. I drove to her apartment later that day. She rented the downstairs apartment and another family rented the upstairs. All the shades in her apartment were pulled down. Her car was in the driveway, so I walked up the steps onto the porch and into the front door foyer. The stairway to the upstairs apartment was inside to the left and the door to her apartment was to the right. I rang the doorbell. There was no answer, so I knocked loudly several times. It looked like someone had tried to force their way in the door, so I called the police department. A dispatch of two officers arrived in fifteen minutes. I told them I was Kendra's work supervisor, and her absence from work could not be explained. One of the officers knocked on the door, and the other climbed the stairs to the second floor apartment and knocked on that door, but there was no answer at either apartment. I was parked in Kendra's driveway, and they had me pull my car down the street and told me to stay back from the apartment. Another cruiser pulled up. I stood behind a tree and watched as those two officers slipped on bulletproof vests and helmets, then entered the front door. The first officer knocked several times, and there was no response. The second officer stood with his back against the porch wall next to the door with his pistol drawn. Then another officer walked up on the porch. She was very cautious. At that moment the first officer took this battering ram looking tool and hit the door once. The door flew open, and the officer standing next to the door entered quickly with the other two behind him. They were inside only a few minutes, and I feared the worst. When they exited the front door, all three officers had holstered their pistols. I approached them and asked what they had found. They told me they had searched the home and nobody was inside, but they were going to do some follow-up work. I asked if there was any blood. They told me no. They thanked me for my call and said they would contact me with any further questions. Two of the officers were cordoning off the area with yellow tape. By this time people were gathering, and I knew it wouldn't be long before news reporters appeared. I left and drove home. A few hours later I heard a knock on my door. It was a police officer from an investigation unit. He started asking questions about Kendra. He said there was evidence of a struggle in the house and asked if I knew of anyone that may have wanted to harm her. For the most part, my relationship with her was on a professional basis at the lab. She kept her personal life to herself. The officer showed me some photos of the inside of her house. Furniture was tipped over. Lamps and dishes were broken. Papers were strewn about. It looked like a burglary scene you see on the movies. I couldn't give the officer much information. Kendra is still listed as a missing person, but after this incident I believe she has to be involved."

"Why do you say that?"

"The only thing I could think of until the last few days was that Kendra had been the victim of a burglary and had been abducted and killed. Now I believe she may have acquired sensitive research information from Thornburg Genetics, tried to sell it and the plan backfired on her. I believe she may have been abducted along with that information. She may be hostage in some covert lab attempting to copy the C1 Extraction medication."

"Your theory sounds a little far-fetched, Dr. Hoffman."

"Think about it, Mr. McGrath. At the time of her disappearance, all of the upper level researchers at Thornburg Genetics were told our lives could be in danger. My colleagues and I are deeply entrenched in our research. Where else could we pursue research with rare and almost extinct plants and compounds? Where else could we pursue the Noah Gene? We are on top of the research world, Mr. McGrath. We would rather die than accept a position of lesser value. However, Kendra's philosophy was different. I hadn't paid much attention to it at the time, but she made this statement several times. She said she was worth more money than Thornburg Genetics could ever pay her. She was making one hundred sixty thousand dollars annually, Mr. McGrath. The rest of my colleagues and I enjoy our wages, but research is our life. That statement indicates Kendra was more interested in the money. Another issue to consider is the Noah Gene. You have been briefed on how the Noah Gene works. My mind locks up if I try to discuss certain research projects with people who do not have the alleged Noah Gene. My mind did not function that way with Kendra. I could have discussed any security level research project with her, though I selectively chose not to because of her lower security level. Even though I could have discussed any level research project with Kendra, it didn't feel right. My mind was not at ease. It felt like some of my brain's synapses had short-circuited. That is the only way I can explain the phenomenon. I did not feel that way at all when I talked to April. As much as I disliked her, I felt she had the Noah Gene. I now believe there was a malfunction in the genetic makeup of Kendra Schlegal. My theory, which I believe is about eighty percent correct, is Kendra had chemotherapy, radiation treatments or a combination of the two."

"She had cancer?"

"Yes. That is my theory, Mr. McGrath. I believe she had cancer and her treatment altered her genetic system enough so the Noah Gene did not come into play with any of the researchers that communicated with her. To make it simple, she is able to communicate with Noah Gene carriers without detection. I know it seems complicated, but she may have had access to enough research information through journals or hacking into computer software to know much more about Thornburg Genetics' secrets than she should have. If she is not the person masterminding this whole affair, I believe she is involved with someone who has also been on chemotherapy, radiation treatment or both. Whether she is involved of her own free will or not, I cannot say."

"Kendra has used the C1 Extraction medication herself hasn't she?"

"You are very astute, Mr. McGrath. That would be my deduction. Those first fifty pills probably went to her and others she knew who had cancer. That means they made no money off those pills."

"Wow. So I may be dealing with one or more potential recovered cancer patients. They may be former employees who have withstood chemo and radiation treatments and whose genetic makeup has been altered."

"Yes, that is my theory, Mr. McGrath."

"You aren't making my job any easier Dr. Hoffman. That would mean we have millions of people worldwide who could potentially fly under the radar when it comes to the Noah Gene."

"Yes. It may not affect as many people as you think. My guess as a researcher is that only a specific combination of chemotherapy and radiation therapy would be a problem. As morbid as this may sound, the odds of employees in the research field having cancer without anyone knowing and not being too ill to work are limited to maybe a few dozen employees. It could take years of employee background checks to track down the specific chemo and radiation combinations, if it could even be accomplished with all of the medical privacy issues prescribed by law."

"Great. Let's change subjects for a minute. How well do you know Jason Otis?"

"Yes. I have only talked with him on the phone a few times in the personnel department."

"He is involved in this matter. He is the person who kidnapped April James."

"Yes, I owe April James an apology. My sister told me what a wonderful person she is and how well April treated her. I had no idea she was a caring person from my dealings with her. I considered her pure evil."

"April is a first class young lady. She ended up in the middle of a scam the same way you did. It's unfortunate people can't live their lives without interference, but bad things happen to good people every day. Let's get back to Jason Otis."

"Yes. I know that meticulous employee background checks are performed at our company. I would venture something did not show up or was overlooked in his background. I only know him casually."

"Can you give me more information on Kendra? I checked out her background information just a few days ago. I was working for Thornburg in a different capacity when she disappeared. She kind of disappeared and never resurfaced, but I had nothing to tie her into our security breach."

"Yes. I haven't seen her in three years. I have a couple of photos of her from a picnic, and I have all of her research notebooks and computer records. We never discard any research information."

"So you feel she could have smuggled sensitive research information out of Thornburg Genetics?"

"Yes. I believe she could have. It's not hard to smuggle information out of a research facility if you are not a team player and nobody is expecting it to happen. We all sign documents saying we won't divulge any research information, but how are you going to stop it? In our case the Noah Gene comes into effect, but in less significant research it doesn't. Anyone can steal research information if they aren't afraid of the consequences of litigation."

"That's a security issue I'll have to work on. The photos of Kendra may be useful, but her notebooks wouldn't do me much good. When I was doing background work on this case Kendra's name did come up as a missing person, but there was no employee photo or fingerprints. I thought it was rather strange and my research staff has been working on it since then. They have submitted a request to the police department, but they are reluctant to share information as it is still an open case. Now I'll have to take a more thorough look at that situation. Someone must have hacked into the computer system and erased her photo and prints. Maybe our friend Jason took care of that. The thugs just released your sister, and you were in contact with them. Do you think they will attempt to kidnap her, yourself or anybody else in the future?"

"In the near future, my answer is no. They will sell the pills they have for a large sum of money."

"April told me that Jason mentioned a selling price of one million dollars per pill. What do you think?"

"Yes. If I had millions of dollars and contracted cancer, seven million dollars is a small price to pay for twenty, thirty or forty more years of life, but back to your question. I am sure these people will be happy with money for a time. They can live a life of leisure. However, they demanded the formula. That means someone will attempt to reproduce it. If it is Kendra, she will devote her entire life to an exact duplication of the C1 Extraction formula. The chances of her succeeding are much less than one percent because of the rare plant compound, but she will never admit defeat. She is stubborn. That is why we hired her. She must know Thornburg Genetics has rare plants, though I can only guess at the extent of her knowledge. Eventually a level of frustration will set in. Who knows what avenues she will take to accomplish her goals."

"I will have to dig deeper into her and Jason's backgrounds. April also mentioned that Jason said the money from the pills would be split three ways, but that would soon become a two-way split. Do you have any idea what that may mean?"

"Yes, I have no idea, Mr. McGrath."

"Thank you for your cooperation and insight. You have been a great help. Is there anything else you can think of that might be important?"

"I will let you know if I think of anything else."

"Great. I will arrange to have you released as soon as possible. You will have forms to sign stating nobody is responsible for your time spent in this facility and things of that nature. Are you okay with that?"

"Yes. I want to get back to a normal life, and I know you are doing your job, Mr. McGrath."

"I'm doing my best. Now listen to me. Do not go back to Thornburg Genetics until you have been cleared. I will contact you. Besides, you should spend a few days with Elizabeth."

"Yes. Thank you for understanding, Mr. McGrath. Now that I have seen Elizabeth and know she is safe, I feel like a new man."

Chapter 73

Keegan left the brig and walked quickly towards his car in the visitors' parking lot. He could see April and Elizabeth sitting in the back seat talking. Keegan stopped a few parking spots away and made a telephone call to Admiral Campanella. Dr. Hoffman would be released in two hours.

As he approached the car, April started giving Keegan a rough time. "You've been gone so long we thought they locked you up. Where have you been? Did you forget we were out here? We were here so long we had a couple of guys ask us out on a date. Not really, just kidding."

"Dr. Hoffman and I had a serious debriefing. He provided me with a lot of new information. It should help considerably in my investigation. I called and made arrangements to have him released. It will take a couple of hours. Why don't I take the two of you back to your house, Elizabeth? I can drop you off, drive back and pick up Dr. Hoffman."

"I don't have any money with me," said Elizabeth, "but maybe we could stop at a grocery store on the way home so I could pick up a few things. I'll be glad to pay you back. That way we could all eat supper together after you pick up Raymond."

"Aren't you two gals exhausted? You have both been on the go for hours now. Thanks for the offer, but why don't you two get some sleep. We can plan a meal together another time. Besides, I'm not sure Dr. Hoffman will be so thrilled to see April. They weren't exactly best friends, thanks to this security issue."

"We'll be fine," said April. "Liz said she talked to Raymond at great length about me. He couldn't believe they were talking about the same person but conceded that the security issue appeared to bring out the worst in both of us. Liz said it would be fine if we got together. The four of us can eat supper, then Liz and I can get to bed early."

"Just don't call me for anything tomorrow morning," said Elizabeth. They all laughed.

"Okay, gals. Here we go to the grocer."

Keegan waited in the car while April and Liz shopped. He mulled over the information he had received from Dr. Hoffman and wrote down a few notes and a list of things he needed to check. He spotted the girls pushing a cart full of groceries across the parking lot and checked the time. Half an hour had elapsed, and it seemed like only minutes. He hopped out of the Taurus and opened the trunk.

"This sure looks like a lot more than a few things."

"I had to stock up on cleaning supplies. Ray is very neat, but it has been over two years since I gave the house a good cleaning."

"Leave her alone, Keegan. She hasn't seen her house in two years."

"I only made a comment. I think you're a little cranky, April."

"I'll forget you said that," said April as she squinted her eyes and stared at him.

They loaded the groceries in the trunk and drove to the Hoffman residence. After unloading the groceries, Keegan drove back to the military base. The visitor parking lot was almost empty so Keegan chose a parking spot close to the brig reception area. The desk officer looked up when Keegan entered the front door. He told the officer he was there to pick up Doctor Raymond Hoffman. The officer made a telephone call and verified that Dr. Hoffman would be released at any moment. It was only a few minutes before Raymond was escorted into the reception area. He made a beeline for Keegan.

"Thank you for having me released so quickly, Mr. McGrath. Can we leave this place now?"

"We sure can. My car is right around the corner. I dropped Elizabeth and April off at your house. We picked up some groceries on the way. Elizabeth insisted that we come back to your house for supper. I know everyone is tired, and I'm not sure how you feel about April at this point since the two of you have been on bad terms with each other. Are you going to be alright with that decision?"

"Yes. Four days ago I never wanted to see the woman again. Now I know I owe her an apology. I just can't believe she is the person both you and Elizabeth portray her to be."

When they arrived back at the Hoffman home, Raymond hugged his sister again. He told April how much he had despised her and then apologized. April apologized for the way she acted and told Raymond how much she hated her role in stopping the security breach. Raymond thanked April for helping Elizabeth arrive back home safely. After a few minutes of small talk, Liz asked April if she would like to help her prepare the meal. Keegan and Raymond sat down opposite each other at the oversized oak dining room table. The two girls brought in a variety of deli meats and cheese. Each of them made their own sandwich. The mustard and mayo flew around the table. Then April said she would like to say a prayer. They all agreed it was an excellent idea after all they had been through.

"Dear Father in heaven, I thank you for putting a safety net around us. If it were not for you watching over us, we might not have been together here this evening. I pray that you will let us get back to a normal lifestyle and protect us from further evil. Please bless this food to our bodies now. I ask this in Jesus' name, amen."

They all said amen and thanked April for the prayer. As they were passing around the potato chips, carrots and celery sticks, Keegan's cell phone rang.

"Excuse me," said Keegan as he rose from his chair and walked into the living room.

"Hey, boss, check out the CNN news online. I think you will find it interesting. Look under the North Korean Leader headline."

"Okay. I'll check it out. Thanks for the information."

After finishing their meal, Keegan excused himself and walked back into the living room. He took his cell phone, connected to the internet and located the North Korean Leader CNN news article. It was a press release. Keegan could not believe what he was reading. 'Earlier today North Korean Officials held a news conference concerning the health of their well-known leader Kim Jong-Il. It was made public several weeks ago that he was diagnosed with terminal cancer. He has not been seen in public for almost four weeks. Today we are told an experimental drug has been administered in an effort to heal Kim Jong-Il. After only twenty-four hours of treatment the Supreme Leader of North Korea is sitting up in bed and joking with his staff and family. He appears to be on the verge of a miraculous recovery. Undisclosed sources say the seven day recovery time is unheard of. The recovery is in response to a series of drugs being administered under the watchful eye of Dr. Maxwell Curtis who is well known for his research in experimental cancer healing drugs and his medical care of high profile cancer patients. Updates to this story will be released as more facts are available'.

Keegan whistled. "It didn't take them long to find their first millionaire customer. Now we know where the first order of the C1 Extraction pills is located, and we know Dr. Curtis is definitely involved."

In Sweden, Jason had just seen the news release on television. He pulled himself out of the recliner and walked down the hallway to Sheila's bedroom. The door was open, and he walked in. Sheila was lying on her back, reading a book. "I thought you gave Max fake pills. How can Kim Jong-Il's health be improving on a placebo?"

Sheila lifted her book and peeked out. Then she smiled. "I couldn't help myself. I set up the pills in a day by day holder. The first pill I gave Maxwell to administer was the real thing. Let's call it a million dollar joke. The next few days probably won't go as well."

"You are a cruel, evil woman, Sheila."

"But you still love me, don't you, honey?" she questioned in a pretty, yet pouty voice.

"I still love you, babe."

Keegan went back into the dining room. "I have an up to date news flash for you. It appears the North Korean leader, Kim Jong-Il, has been given an experimental cancer treatment and his health is improving by the hour."

"You don't say," said Dr. Hoffman. "That is an unusual event."

Elizabeth looked back and forth at the faces of her brother and two guests. "Are you involved in this?"

"We really can't discuss the matter," said Keegan. He changed subjects and asked Dr. Hoffman if he had the photos of Kendra Schlegal available. Dr. Hoffman led Keegan to his den. "Yes, the photos are in this box." He thumbed through several well-marked envelopes and stopped at the one marked July 4th office picnic. Then he pulled the photos out of the Walgreen's photo envelope. "This is the photo. Kendra is standing next to me," he said as he handed the photo to Keegan. Keegan stared at the photo in disbelief. He kept a poker face, but he was positive the young lady he was looking at was Sheila Smith. He would have to have the picture enlarged.

"She is a very attractive young lady," said Dr. Hoffman.

"That's quite a hair style."

"Yes. Her hair was always cropped short and always a different color. One day it might be pink, the next midnight black and the next purple. But with personal appearances aside, she was a genius when it came to research. We miss her talents very much."

"May I borrow this photo? I would like to conduct a more thorough background check on her."

"Yes. You may keep it. I will have another copy made from the negative."

"Thank you, Doctor."

"Yes. You know, Mr. McGrath; I must tell you that April James is a delightful young lady. I am sorry I misjudged her."

"Under the circumstances you had every right to dislike her. I'm glad that whole set of circumstances is behind us now. I'm sure the working relationship between the two of you will improve."

"Yes, I believe you are correct."

"Well, Doctor. I don't know about anyone else, but I'm tired. I am going to try and gather up April and head out."

"Yes. I would like to invite you and April to our home again on Saturday night."

"The offer sounds great, but I will have to let you know for sure. I still have a lot of work to do. I'm not sure if I will even be in town on Saturday. Can I call you to verify?"

"Yes. That will be fine."

After a few minutes Keegan coerced April into leaving. Keegan wanted to discuss Jason with her. He knew she must feel awful about the way he treated her. As he drove back to the apartment he brought up the subject. She said she was too tired to think about Jason. All she wanted was a good night's sleep. Keegan walked April up to her apartment. His cell phone rang as soon as she opened the door. He looked at the phone. It was the camcorder in April's apartment. "And how much longer are you going to keep spying on me?" asked April.

"Not too much longer, my dear." He told her goodnight, left the building and drove straight to the motel.

Even though he was exhausted, he had one more task to complete before going to bed. He took the photo of Kendra Schlegal provided by Dr. Hoffman and scanned it into his computer. He enlarged the profile of Kendra's face. It has to be Sheila or a twin sister he thought. Keegan searched through his computer files and located the photos taken by Samantha. She had done an excellent job of capturing Jason's rendezvous with the blond woman at the airport hotel. Keegan arranged the photo of Kendra taken by Dr. Hoffman next to the photo of Sheila taken by Samantha. He used profiler software to determine if the ladies in the two photos were the same person. "Okay profiler, tell me what I want to know." In an instant the computer screen flashed the word he was waiting for. Match, one hundred percent probability.

"So Kendra is now Sheila. She's quite bold and sure of herself, isn't she? I wonder how deep her involvement in the Thornburg security breach goes. She may even be the mastermind. This means more background work in the morning."

Keegan rose at 6:00 AM, showered, shaved, tasted his cup of in-room coffee, which made his face crinkle, and went back to the computer. He now knew Jason was involved in the Thornburg security breach and suspected there was a high probability that Kendra, alias Sheila, was as well. Dr. Maxwell Curtis was a well-known physician and researcher. Would he be involved deep in this operation, or did Jason and Kendra just talk him into purchasing the C1 Extraction pills? This had to be the experimental drug he was administering to the North Korean leader. What were the connections here? Keegan had already exhausted his resources checking Jason's background after he abducted April. He decided to focus on Kendra and then Maxwell.

Kendra was at the top of her class in Biochemistry and Biomedical Sciences at the University of Oxford. Her grades were straight A's except in Medieval Literature, her only incomplete course. Keegan sent a quick email to one of his researchers to find out why only one course was incomplete.

Keegan's cell phone rang. He didn't like interruptions when he was completing background work, but when he saw April was the caller he picked up immediately.

"Good morning, Keegan."

"Top of the morning to you. How did you sleep last night?"

"I crashed. I can't believe how tired I was."

"I'm sure you were. You can only take so much emotion and stress before it gets to you."

"Guess what, Keegan."

"Do I dare?"

"I'm not going to work today."

"Skipping work huh? I have a notion to report you."

"You wouldn't do that, would you?"

"If you were to have a business luncheon with a top-ranked Thornburg employee, I believe your absence from work would go unnoticed."

"Would it now?"

"I do believe so. I'm in the middle of important security work right now. May I pick you up about noon?"

"If you insist, Mr. McGrath."

"I do insist. Please try to stay out of trouble until then."

"What do you mean? I never get in trouble."

"How well I know, Miss April James. I've got to go right now. I'll see you at noon."

"Noon it is. Bye-bye."

Keegan daydreamed about April for a few minutes and then went back to his computer. After attending the University of Oxford, Kendra attended graduate school at Columbia University. This information all coincided with the Thornburg Genetics records. Keegan decided to see if there was a college connection with Kendra, Maxwell and Jason. He typed in Maxwell Curtis in the University of Oxford alumni and student roster list. His computer hummed for a minute and a half. The results showed no match. Keegan then did the same search at Columbia University. The results showed that Kendra Schlegal and Maxwell Curtis had attended graduate school at the same time. Keegan dipped further into Maxwell's background. He typed in previous known addresses. A list of twelve popped up on the screen. Keegan looked down the list until he saw 111 Archer Street, Chicago, Illinois. He remembered seeing Archer Street on a list of previous addresses for Jason. After another half hour of research Keegan was staring at the Jason Otis, Maxwell Curtis connection on his computer screen. Jason Otis and Maxwell Curtis were half-brothers. Maxwell's father was a police officer. He was shot and killed in the line of duty when Maxwell was a little less than one year old. Mrs. Curtis remarried and took her new husband's last name of Otis. Jason Otis was a younger half sibling by a little less than four years. Keegan then punched Jason's name into the Columbia University database. He was not listed as an alumnus. Then he typed in college organizations. There it was on the screen in front of him, another totally unexpected connection between Jason, Maxwell and Kendra. Keegan wrote down the specifics and decided to save this information for the upcoming staff debriefing this case demanded.

Keegan took time to bring up the CNN page on his computer. The latest news from North Korea was that Kim Jong-Il had relapsed slightly. Keegan didn't understand this turn of events as he had seen firsthand the significant improvement on a day-by-day basis when the C1 Extraction medication was administered to Señor Quinonez. This caused him to rethink his analysis. Maybe he was in error and the medication Kim Jong-Il was receiving was not the C1 Extraction. No, some other unknown must have slipped into the equation, because he now had connections between Jason, Maxwell and Kendra. Keegan decided to call The Keeper and update her on the situation. After a twenty-minute conversation, he hit the end call button on his cell phone.

Keegan determined that there were no security matters demanding attention, so he decided to stay in Philadelphia until at least Sunday. He felt his stomach growl and realized he hadn't eaten any breakfast, and it was approaching noon. He decided to take another shower and spruce up a little before picking April up for their lunch date.

Chapter 74

Keegan chose a nearby Applebee's restaurant for lunch with April. As soon as they were seated, they again discussed the incidents leading up to April's kidnapping. April asked what the next step would be. Keegan informed her he was still conducting background research on Jason and Dr. Curtis. He didn't mention Kendra.

Then Keegan decided to change topics. As much as he hated to, he knew he had to bring up Jason and April's relationship. He noticed that April was not wearing the engagement ring Jason had given her. "April, I know you loved Jason and how betrayed you must feel. Would you like to talk about it?"

"I don't want to, but I suppose I have to sooner or later."

"You are a smart young lady, April. You know you need to talk about the mess he put you through as part of the healing process. If you would feel more comfortable talking with a professional, I can set up an appointment for you or maybe you already know a good counselor."

"No, that's not necessary. I'll talk with you. You're pretty straightforward and won't mince words. Let's see. Where do I start? I thought things were going along fine in our relationship. That Friday night he created a special meal for us and told me he had a surprise. I was blindsided. When I felt the handcuffs cinch around my wrists I thought he was playing a practical joke. Then fear set in. The next thing that came to my mind was he was going to rape me. From that point on, I had to cope with fear of the unknown. The situation seemed like a Dr. Jekyl and Mr. Hyde scene. For months Jason was easy going, always agreeable, loving and gracious. The night he abducted me, he turned into a person I had never seen before. He was arrogant, edgy, scary and unconcerned about my feelings. I have never felt so helpless in my life. Even after he pulled the pistol out and threatened me with it, the scenario didn't seem real. I had a melt down and fell under his control. As much as I wanted to struggle, my body wouldn't let me."

"That was your basic survival instinct kicking in. Your brain told you what you had to do to survive."

"Every time I looked at him I could sense the anger in his eyes. He had never given me a reason to distrust him. When I told him he didn't have to do this and asked him why he would treat me this way if he loved me, his response was he loved me but not enough to be with me forever. That was when I felt like my insides were being twisted in a vice. The real message was I was a sucker, and our relationship meant nothing to him." April's eyes filled with tears, and she started crying. Keegan knew this was what April needed. He took his white hanky out of his back pants pocket and handed it to her. She accepted it and wiped her tears away. She could see black streaks from her mascara.

"I am so sorry you had to go through this, April."

"I prayed to God that he would protect me. I felt peace and wasn't afraid until we pulled into the garage and Jason directed me to the chain link fence enclosure. All I could think of was some psycho who left girls to starve to death in a basement dungeon. You know. It's the stuff you hear on the news and see on the television shows. I thank God that through all of this, Jason and the others involved never assaulted me. You have no idea how helpless and alone I felt and how afraid I was, Keegan."

"I'm sorry, April. I couldn't sleep while you were gone. I replayed the abduction over and over again in my mind. I couldn't bear to think what you were going through. I kept blaming myself for not protecting you or seeing this coming. All I could envision was your death. I decided I couldn't continue as head of security with Thornburg Genetics. I questioned if I could go on living if something horrific happened to you. Can you ever forgive me for my failure, April?"

April looked at Keegan's face. She could see a tear trickle down his cheek. She hadn't expected this. It had never occurred to her that Keegan's emotions could run so deep. Then she realized that even though his job was in the field of security, he was just as human as she was.

"There is nothing to forgive. You did everything possible to keep my family and me safe. I'm sorry I never took the time to consider how you might feel. Now that I think about it you were under a load of pressure. Are you alright?"

Keegan reached across the table and took April's hands in his. He felt her warmth. "April, I have something to share with you. I don't want to share it, and I can only hope you will not hold it against me. I don't even know how to start, so I guess I'll just blurt it out." He paused and looked at April's face. He had fallen in love with April and knew his next sentence would hurt her. If only someone else could tell her, but he knew it was up to him. He took a deep breath. "Jason was involved with another woman while he was seeing you."

April stared at Keegan and said nothing. Keegan could see a blank stare and then the tears started again. He looked around the restaurant and was glad there were only a few people left from the lunch crowd. The man and woman in the adjacent booth turned their heads away and pretended not to notice when Keegan glanced their way.

In a quiet voice, April asked, "Who is she?"

"I can't tell you right now, April. She is part of our ongoing investigation."

"Is she pretty? What does she look like?"

"I guess you could say she is pretty. She is slim. Her facial features are nice, and she has long blond hair."

"Where was he seeing her?" April continued in her soft voice.

Keegan hesitated. Why did April have to ask questions like this? The whole conversation was painful. "Our surveillance personnel observed Jason with her at a hotel."

April was crying less now, but her face was still red. She didn't know why she was crying. She knew any relationship with Jason was over, and she never wanted to see him again.

"Is she a girlfriend, a prostitute or what?"

"Does it really matter? Why don't we move on to some other topic?"

"I want to know, Keegan."

"We believe she is a girlfriend, and it is quite possible he is with her now."

"So I have been played as a fool for months now. How long have you known? Why didn't you tell me, Keegan? I could have married this guy. Were you ever going to tell me?"

"I have only known for a short time. I wanted to tell you, but I couldn't."

"Your dumb security reasons, right?"

"Partially."

"What's the rest of the excuse?"

"I didn't want you to think I was meddling in your personal life. Think about it for a minute. How would it look for Keegan McGrath if he walked up to April James and said, 'I think you should know your fiancé has a girlfriend?' Would you thank me and consider me your best friend or would you hate me forever for being an intruder? I was caught in the middle of a no-win situation."

"So the other day you told me you loved me, but you didn't have the guts to tell me my fiancé had a girlfriend."

"I'm sorry, April. I would have told you soon. I never would have let you marry Jason without knowing about another woman. I had to wait for the appropriate time. I can't believe you think it was easy for me to know that Jason was having a fling behind your back. I called him a dirt bag more times than I can count. I wanted to punch him. I wanted to ride in on a white horse and save your honor like a knight in shining armor, and because of logistics, I couldn't."

"I guess whether you told me or not doesn't matter. He had no intentions of marrying me anyway. All he was doing for months was using me. My insides are all twisted, and I hurt, Keegan." April started to cry again.

"I don't know what else to say. I'm sorry this happened and I'm even sorrier I'm the one who had to tell you." Keegan continued to look at April. Her face was beet red from crying so much. His heart ached for her, and he squeezed her hands a little harder. "What can I do to help you?"

"Would you hug me, Keegan?"

Keegan didn't expect this response and was caught off guard. April broke a small smile when she saw the questioning look on his face. "Are you sure?"

April nodded, "I'm sure."

Keegan slid out of his booth seat and slid in next to April. He felt like he was on display when he put his arm around her shoulders and she nestled her head next to his neck. April had stopped crying. Keegan turned and kissed April on her forehead. She gave a smile of approval. After a few minutes he suggested they leave. April held Keegan's hand as he drove them back to her apartment.

Chapter 75

The next morning, Keegan woke up at 7:00 AM when his alarm clock buzzed. He was tired of living in a motel room. He checked his email and the news online. Kim Jong-Il's health had deteriorated further. On day number four of the cancer treatment, every television station reported the updated news release. Kim Jong-Il, Supreme Leader of the Democratic People's Republic of Korea had died. A formal statement had been read by Ri Yong Ho, Chief of General Staff. Other than proclaiming his death, the statement told of his many virtues and accomplishments as the Supreme Leader. The podium was then turned over to Dr. Maxwell Curtis. Keegan took note of every word he said as each sentence was translated into the Korean language. Keegan was sure there was a time delay on the speech or it was prerecorded in case Dr. Curtis made an unfavorable statement.

"Good morning, ladies and gentlemen. As you know, Kim Jong-Il recently suffered from a rare form of liver and kidney cancer. With my extensive medical background in cancer research and treatment, I was asked to assist in treating this cancer. The Supreme Commander was prescribed an experimental drug in an attempt to eliminate the cancer and bring about a full recovery. The initial dose showed favorable results. However, subsequent doses failed to produce the desired results. This drug has produced numerous positive results when administered to patients with similar cancer types in the past several months. However, I must reiterate the drug used is still classified as experimental. My sympathy goes out to the family of Kim Jong-Il and the people of the Democratic People's Republic of Korea. I thank you for allowing me to briefly share the facts with you in this time of grief."

As soon as Dr. Curtis finished speaking, the cameras showed him being escorted off the podium. No questions were taken from reporters, and there were no flashes of light from camera bulbs when they left the area. The next scene was from the United States' White House and an American correspondent. "You have seen the brief press release concerning the death of the North Korean leader, Kim Jong-Il. The president has called the Chief of General Staff, Ri Yong Ho and the leader's son Kim Jong-Un to express his condolences. A complete synopsis of ramifications concerning this situation will be discussed on this station in a special news broadcast within the hour. Stay tuned to this station. This is Robert Baker, Fox News, Washington."

Keegan started to rehash the facts of the C1 Extraction heist again. Maybe Dr. Curtis wasn't involved. Maybe the drugs dispensed to Kim Jong-Il were different drugs altogether. It had only been a few days since April's abduction. Something did not fit together. Keegan knew he had to find the missing pieces.

It was Saturday. Keegan and April were invited back to Dr. Hoffman's house for dinner at six. Keegan picked up April, and they started their drive to the Hoffman's. April insisted they stop at a super market on the way. They purchased a large bouquet of fresh flowers as a house-warming gift. When they arrived, Elizabeth was ecstatic about the bouquet. She said carnations were one of her favorite flowers, and she arranged the red, pink and white flowers in a vase, which she placed in the center of the dining room table.

As they dined on baked haddock, rice and fresh cooked green beans, the topic of conversation turned to the death of Kim Jong-Il. Keegan looked at Dr. Hoffman. "I should have called you sooner to see if you know Dr. Curtis."

"Yes. You are always in investigation mode, Mr. McGrath."

"I'm curious by nature, and my job demands it."

"Yes. I am aware of his work, but I did not know him in person. He lived in Europe I believe. Sweden I think. He has written several research papers dealing with experimental cancer drugs. He was also a renowned cancer surgeon."

"What do you mean was?"

"This may not be a good time to discuss this situation. Perhaps we should wait until after dinner."

Keegan looked at April and Elizabeth. "Do either of you mind if we discuss Dr. Curtis?" Both of them shook their heads no. "Now you have my interest peaked," said April. "Mine too," said Elizabeth.

"Very well; I will proceed then. I assume you did not hear about the recent demise of Dr. Curtis in an automobile accident."

"You're kidding me," said Keegan.

"So why all the hype?" asked April.

Keegan turned and looked at Elizabeth. He didn't know whether to continue the conversation. Dr. Hoffman picked up on his unease. "It is okay to talk with Elizabeth here. I know she has the Noah Gene, and anything we discuss will stay in the confines of our house. I have already briefed her on the C1 Extraction incident."

Keegan hesitated, but then spoke. "I'm almost positive the experimental drug administered to Kim Jong-Il was the C1 Extraction drug."

"That fast?" asked April. "This whole chain of events just started a week ago."

"And if you were someone in power, with money and no alternatives, how hard would it be to convince you an experimental drug was the only option, especially if it was recommended by a top cancer surgeon," said Keegan.

"Yes. It could not have been the C1 Extraction drug," said Dr. Hoffman. "That is a powerful drug. If you show signs of improvement the first day your health will improve on a day-by-day basis until you are healed after seven days. If the drug does not work, which is the case with only a few types of cancer, there is no improvement on the first day."

"There must be exceptions," said Keegan. "Maybe he had other physical ailments that weren't accounted for."

"Our research does not indicate additional problems if there is improvement of health on the first day."

"So what doesn't fit in this situation then? This Dr. Curtis prescribes an experimental drug to a high-profile patient. The patient shows significant signs of improvement the first day, but dies a few days later. Next, Dr. Curtis is killed in an automobile accident. It sounds more like an automobile assassination to me. My guess is this was a form of retaliation for prescribing an ineffective medication."

"It sure seems suspicious, doesn't it?" said Elizabeth.

"I hate to be boring and verging on rude, but do you mind if we watch the news for a few minutes after supper? I would like to see if we can get an update on the alleged car accident," said Keegan.

"That will be fine," said Elizabeth. "We can check out more information on the computer too. Why don't we have our dessert in the living room? The seven o'clock report should update the event."

"That's not necessary, Elizabeth. I didn't mean to get carried away and upset the fine meal you prepared for us."

"Don't be silly, Mr. McGrath. I was isolated for so long I enjoy keeping up with current events. Why don't you and Raymond go into the living room while April and I clear the table. We'll bring you a fresh cup of coffee and a piece of the best chocolate cream pie in town."

"That sounds delicious."

"Yes. Let's follow Elizabeth's instructions," said Dr. Hoffman as he pushed his chair back, stood up and walked toward the living room. "It was a fine meal, Elizabeth."

"It was a superb meal," said Keegan.

"Thank you both for the compliments. Now off to the living room with you. April and I will join you there in a few minutes."

Keegan followed Dr. Hoffman into the living room. Dr. Hoffman sat in his normal recliner while Keegan sat in a brown, overstuffed chair that must have been forty years old, but was unbelievably comfortable.

Dr. Hoffman picked up the remote control from the stand next to his recliner and turned the television on. Fox News flashed onto the screen. After ten minutes of uneventful news, Elizabeth and April showed up with large mugs of coffee and a piece of pie for each of them. It was seven o'clock and the world news broadcast started. The first story dealt with new banking and financial legislation in England. Then an update dealing with Somalian pirates hijacking a massive oil tanker and holding it for ransom was portrayed. News from North Korea was the third topic. The female news anchor again reported the death of Kim Jong-II and a brief mention of the experimental cancer drug was made. She then described the grief the Supreme Leader's family and the country of North Korea were going through. Then she talked about Dr. Curtis and his role in attempting to cure the cancer. The news station started to replay his speech after the death of Kim Jong-II. As his speech started, April jumped up off the couch, holding the plate with her half eaten piece of pie in her hand. She pointed at the television with her fork and hollered; "That's him! That's him!"

"That's who?" asked Keegan.

"That's him! The benefactor! That's his voice!"

"Are you sure April?"

"That's him. There's no doubt whatsoever. He made my life miserable. He made Elizabeth's life miserable, and who knows how many other lives he ruined. He was a jerk. If he's dead he got what he deserved. Wait a minute. If he's dead, Keegan, do you remember what I told you about Jason's plans?"

"Do you mean Dr. Curtis took Elizabeth hostage?" asked Dr. Hoffman. "I can't believe someone of his stature would be driven to such an action. I wonder if the robotic voice on the phone that threatened Elizabeth was his?"

"I've never heard his voice," said Elizabeth.

Chapter 76

"I'm sorry about your brother, Jason."

"I'm sure his death breaks your heart, Sheila."

"That's not nice to say. Max was a decent guy, honey."

"I thought they might put him in jail for life, but I never thought they would execute him."

"It was a car accident, honey."

"If he even died in a car, it was no accident. It was a message sent to the world that you don't make mistakes when you deal with the leaders of North Korea. Either way, the results are the same for us. You know they will make an effort to locate the pill manufacturer, and they will swarm every bank account possible to retrieve the money they spent on those pills."

"It's a good thing our bank accounts are secured. Can you think of any way they can trace pills or money back to us?"

"No way at all, babe. Our offshore Cayman bank account information is impossible for any outsider to retrieve, and even if they find out I'm Max's half-brother, they cannot tie me to the medication fraud. They can't hold me responsible because I'm a relative. Who knows where Max got the experimental cancer drug. He's been doing research for years and in numerous labs. They will find Max's car at the airport. It's a rental car and we never touched it, so our fingerprints won't be on it. There is no way to trace anything back to us. The North Korean leaders in charge of obtaining the cancer treatment have to be fuming."

"We could send them an anonymous letter and tell them the medication was derived from Thornburg Genetics."

"If we do that, babe, there is a chance of tracing it back to us. You sure do hold a grudge against Thornburg, don't you?"

"I could have been one of their star researchers, but they refused to let me work to my full potential. All they handed me were mundane science projects a first year college student could have completed."

"I know, honey, but now you have your own lab, and we have a potential hundred and fifty million dollars or so to survive on thanks to Thornburg Genetics. I believe we can handle that. Don't you?"

Chapter 77

April didn't say any more about the benefactor while they were at the Hoffmans' house. The up-to-date news about Dr. Maxwell Curtis was over, so Dr. Hoffman shut off the television. The four of them discussed more current events to help Elizabeth catch up from her two years of isolation. About nine o'clock, Keegan suggested to April that they leave.

As soon as they pulled out of the driveway, April began talking about the benefactor. "That was him, Keegan. There is no doubt. It was his voice. As soon as I heard him, I felt my hair stand on end, and I had goose bumps on my arms. Remember when I told you the money they would receive from selling the C1 Extraction pills was supposed to be split three ways, but Jason said it would soon be two?"

"I remember. That means Jason and Kendra must have set Dr. Curtis up for failure. The death of the first client to receive the C1 Extraction pills was preplanned. It wouldn't have mattered whether or not the first customer was the North Korean leader. The first customer they lined up was scheduled to die. If the first customer had not been high profile, Jason and Sheila must have had some other plan to kill Maxwell Curtis. Their plan was creative. Make millions of dollars off their first customer and still retain the original one hundred C1 Extraction pills. It appears that neither Jason nor Sheila have any morals when it comes to the sanctity of life. They must have given Maxwell placebos to administer to Kim Jong-Il. Their game is all about the money. With just two people in the picture they stand to gain well over one hundred million dollars between the two of them. Jason threw his half-brother to the wolves. I don't think a human being can sink much lower than that. However, he did not harm you or Elizabeth. I guess Jason is into selective cruelty."

"What do you mean, half-brother? This Dr. Curtis and Jason are half-brothers?"

"I just discovered the connection yesterday."

"So Jason framed his own half-brother for the sake of millions of dollars that they were supposed to split between them?"

"It sure appears that way."

There was silence as April thought through this new portrayal of Jason. She had fallen in love with him and considered him the perfect man. Now his actions made him look like a beast. She started to cry again. "So what happens now, Keegan?"

"I have to drop you off at your apartment and continue some serious security work and brainstorming."

"I don't want you to drop me off. I want to spend time with you. Maybe I can come over to your motel room and watch you work."

"Watching me work should be on the bottom of the heap for excitement and besides that, I've been at the motel for ten days now. My room is a mess."

"I could tidy it up for you and maybe you'll have important questions that need my input."

"Okay. You can come to paradise with me, but remember, you are entering at your own risk."

When they arrived at the motel, Keegan opened the door and let April enter first. "It's a little messy, but not too bad. I can have the place cleaned up in no time."

"I would appreciate it. It's a little embarrassing and I should help, but I have to hit the computer, April."

April went about restoring order to the bachelor pad. In fifteen minutes she had folded towels, discarded empty coffee cups and wiped down the tops of the television stand and table. Then she took the two plastic bags of trash she had collected and set them in the hallway. "What kind of room service do you have here? It doesn't look like your room attendant has cleaned once."

"I don't let anybody into my room unless I'm here and not busy, which is never. Every couple of days, I go to the front desk and swap my towels for a clean set. At this point the sheets are about due for a clean set too."

"You sure make it easy for housekeeping. Maybe I can get a part-time job here. You know I have so much free time." April watched Keegan flick through screen after screen on the computer. She could feel her eyes starting to droop. "I think I'll lie down and take a short nap. I feel a little tired."

"Why don't you use the bed by the door? Those sheets are fresh. I've been sleeping in the bed closest to the window."

April slipped her shoes off and crawled under the queen size bedspread. Keegan could hear her breathing pattern change and knew she was asleep. He turned away from the computer screen and looked at her. The bedspread was pulled up to her neck. He pushed himself out of the chair and walked to the side of his bed and sat down where he could see her face. She looked relaxed with a strand of long brown hair rolled over her cheek. Keegan knew her body and emotions had been taxed over the last few days. Most normal people don't look for trouble, but trouble happens just the same. Thank God she was alive. He knew he loved her, and he was sure she loved him. He was not about to let her get away. After Keegan admired her for several minutes, he shut the bed light off and went back to his computer. He took a second look at all of the press releases dealing with the deaths of Kim Jong-Il and Maxwell Curtis. Then he reviewed all the information he had obtained on Jason, Sheila, alias Kendra, and Maxwell. Finally he checked all of his notes on Dr. Hoffman, April, Elizabeth and the contacts made by the benefactor, now identified as Dr. Maxwell Curtis. When he had completed the review, he made notes and placed all of the information in chronological order. It was almost three o'clock in the morning. Keegan took his time under the hot shower, then slid into a pair of gym shorts and crawled into his bed. April hadn't moved since she fell asleep. Keegan thought of beautiful April as he drifted into sleep.

The next morning, Keegan woke to the smell of coffee. April was sitting on her bed, staring at him. He could see that her hair was damp and knew she had taken a shower.

"What time is it?"

"It's a little after nine. What time did you go to bed?"

"It was about three o'clock."

"Three o'clock! Do you want to sleep some more?"

"No. I'm ready to get up. The coffee smells good."

"There is no guarantee on taste. It's one of those gourmet hotel coffee packets." April poured two cups of coffee and dumped a packet of powdered creamer in hers. "So, did you decide what to do next?"

"We need to have a meeting and get all of our minds together. Today is Sunday. I'm going to call Lexis in a while and see if we can set up a meeting for Tuesday."

"What are you going to do the rest of today?"

"Spend time with you, my pretty lass."

"Why don't we go to a church service?"

"Sure. I'll go. It's a shame I don't spend much time in church. My job demands so much time, and I never know what city I'll be in from week to week. I can call Lexis this afternoon."

"We have to run back to my apartment first, so I can change into something more appropriate and clean."

After the morning church service, Keegan and April went out to lunch. Keegan called Lexis and set up a meeting for Tuesday at his hotel. He contacted everybody he wanted in attendance.

"I have a question, Keegan."

"What's your question?"

"If neither Jason nor Sheila, Kendra or whatever her name is, cared if Maxwell was killed, what would stop either of them from doing away with the other and not having to split the money from the C1 Extraction pills at all? A one-way split is twice as good as a two-way split."

"I never considered that. Who knows what kind of relationship Jason and Sheila really have. Maybe they truly love each other more than they love money. Maybe they have a business deal where they need each other, or maybe they will plot to write the other one out of the picture. Who knows? We're all set as long as we can keep them away from Thornburg Genetics."

Chapter 78

On Tuesday morning at 9:00 AM, Keegan started the meeting in the small motel conference room. Three undercover Thornburg Genetics security staff were watching the building from strategic locations and one floater was monitoring the conference room door. In attendance were April, Lexis, Dr. Hoffman, Tanya and Mark.

It took Keegan an hour to pour over the details of the security breach from start to finish. He included the role of each person involved and discussed the release of the C1 Extraction medication and how Dr. Hoffman had been compromised. Then he went into both Elizabeth's and April's kidnapping experience and eventual release. He concluded with the death of Kim Jong-Il and Dr. Maxwell Curtis.

"Now," said Keegan, "We must make some serious decisions. At this point in time, this entire situation has been kept in-house. There has been no law enforcement involvement and limited military involvement. I can assure you all of this information is top secret and will never be revealed to the general public. The question is: do we want to keep it this way? If we get law enforcement involved in the theft of the C1 Extraction pills, Elizabeth's kidnapping and April's abduction, Thornburg Genetics will be under investigation and scrutiny for years. We will be required to go through rigorous interviews with investigators. Due to the alleged Noah Gene, most of the interviews will not go well, and the investigators will conclude we are withholding information if we aren't completely candid during interviews. That's what they do for a living."

"I am sure we will be required to discuss multiple facts about our research departments that we don't want exposed. We can fall back on 'don't touch us' due to top-secret military research operations, but even certain military personnel can be squeezed for information if politics come into play. We can only thank God both April and Elizabeth returned safely and nobody on our side was harmed through this whole situation."

"Another problem is Jason will be exposed if we bring in law enforcement. I'm sure you are asking yourselves who cares, but I would guess his picture will end up in the newspapers and on television news worldwide. I doubt the North Koreans have any idea where the prescribed medication for Kim Jong-Il originated, but you can bet they will know if Jason's name comes up. Because of the death of their leader, they will follow every lead in their desire to retaliate. I have no idea what consequences this may have on Thornburg Genetics, either as a company or on an individual level."

"What do you mean on an individual level?" asked Lexis.

"To be blunt, I expect someone must pay for the death of the Supreme leader. An example must be made. Someone or numerous people will die."

"But you said Dr. Curtis was dead due to the medication foul up."

"His death was a start. I am sure the North Koreans paid a huge sum of money to obtain the miracle cancer-curing drug. My guess is the money was placed in an account that is not traceable. They will be looking for the money and anyone else involved. If Jason's photo is splattered throughout the world media, we will have placed a big target on his back and set him up for death. The North Korean military will find him and execute him, but only after they have extracted all the information he knows about the C1 Extraction medication. They may even get their hands on the remainder of the one hundred pills. Who knows what their chemists will unleash and be able to trace back to Thornburg Genetics. There are no positive aspects for this whole scenario."

"If we do nothing, our dear Mr. Jason and Sheila, who I will refer to as Kendra, make millions of dollars off the C1 Extraction pills in their possession. It makes me sick to think they can get away with the plot they created, and we have to keep our fingers crossed they don't discover the explosive capabilities of the medication they have. If they blow themselves up, the whole matter ends. If they discover the explosive capabilities and attempt to sell the information, we have a major breach-of-security issue that will have to be handled by the military. According to Dr. Hoffman, the chances of discovering the explosive capabilities of the C1 Extraction medication are a million to one. I'm going with the Doctor's statistics. While Kendra may love research, I believe she and Jason were disgruntled employees looking for money. Jason and Kendra will have millions of tax-free dollars as they sell the pills. As Dr. Hoffman pointed out, Kendra will be obsessed with duplicating the C1 Extraction formula. She will fail, because she does not have access to the correct rare plant compounds required for the medication. Am I correct Dr. Hoffman?"

"Yes. That is a correct assumption. We have found no way to duplicate the rare plant compound required to produce the C1 Extraction medication by genetic engineering."

"Thank you, Doctor. When Kendra fails, there is a chance someone in Thornburg Genetics may again be contacted. We don't know if any insider other than Jason has been planted in Thornburg Genetics. My calculations are no. I believe they set this operation up as a one-time hit because Dr. Hoffman refused to follow the perpetrators' demands for months. They released both April and Elizabeth unharmed. I consider this a good-faith gesture on their part to show closure to their involvement. Could they put pressure on April or Dr. Hoffman again?

Anything is possible, but we'll be ready. We will come up with a plan of action so we are ready to shut down these thugs if they ever contact us again. It will be easy to use the death of Kim Jong-Il against them. From this incident we can create our own espionage story and threaten to release it worldwide if Jason and Kendra attack us again. Time is on our side, because the North Koreans will not stop until they find them and their money. By the time North Korea finds them, the C1 Extraction pill inventory will most likely be depleted, and they will be on the run and looking over their shoulders for the rest of their lives. I can almost guarantee they won't want that misfortune. Jason and Kendra are smart individuals. I don't see them compromising millions of dollars by making a stupid move."

"In my eyes this situation is a catch twenty-two. If Thornburg Genetics attempts to capture or retaliate against Jason and Kendra, Thornburg Genetics research operations may be exposed much more than we want. If Jason and Kendra ever attempt to blackmail us, we threaten to release their personal information to the North Korean government and expose them as accessories to the murder of Kim Jong-Il." Keegan paused to let his conclusion sink in. "Did I miss anything? Does anyone have any additional thoughts?"

"What if those two or anyone else kidnaps another employee or family member of Thornburg Genetics?" asked April.

"First, we will locate Jason and Kendra and monitor their moves. I am sure they are in a foreign country. Can we swoop down and capture them? I doubt it. Most foreign countries don't like covert operations. Also, if we expose their operation, it exposes us. Your question deals with potential kidnappers. It took years for Jason and Kendra, and probably Max, to infiltrate our company as far as they did. It also took a unique set of circumstances, many of which we orchestrated. Remember April, we put you out there as a decoy. I just don't see kidnapping as a threat at this time. However, I will say each of you needs to be the eyes and ears in Thornburg Genetics. My security staff is top notch, but we are only as good as the information we are given. If anything looks suspicious, we need to know. We will determine the value of the information you give us. No bit of information is too small or unimportant. Is there anything else?"

"Yes," said Dr. Hoffman. "I don't like the fact that Jason and Kendra are making millions of dollars off our medication and research. There must be some way to track down the money they receive and cut them off."

"Their money will be in a Swiss bank account or some type of offshore account. Believe me when I tell you that attempting to track down an account like this is an effort in futility. As a side note, we did cash a $100,000 check given to April by the benefactor. I realize this does not make up for millions of dollars, but at least it's something."

"But these people held Elizabeth hostage for two years and now they are getting away with such a crime and making large sums of cash."

"Dr. Hoffman. You need to let this matter go. Be thankful Elizabeth is back with you and enjoy your life. I hate to remind you of this, but I have no choice. I had a plan formulated to stop the Thornburg Genetics security breach. I am confident my plan would have worked. The plan had to be abandoned because you took security matters into your own hands. In effect you gave the perpetrators the C1 Extraction medication. I admire you and your research, however, you need to concentrate on your research and continue to develop new and improved pharmaceuticals. That is your specialty. I am a security specialist. My job is to stop the loss of the research information, trade secrets and products you are creating as well as any potential loss of life. You have to let me do my job without interference. Again I say, let this matter go. Any attempt at revenge will be of no benefit to anyone. Concentrate on the positive and let go of the negative."

"Do we have any idea how these three have been able to communicate with inside sources if they do not have the alleged Noah Gene?" asked Lexis. "I know we have suspicions that chemo or radiation treatments may cause some type of gene mutation where the Noah Gene is, shall we say, led astray. Both Kendra and Jason worked for Thornburg Genetics, but neither appeared to be candidates to move up to a level six or seven security clearance."

"This was on my list of topics to discuss. As you know, medical records are held in strictest confidence. I have no way to access medical records without breaking the law. However, I do have information none of you were privy to that may prove beneficial to the Noah Gene theory. While medical records are confidential, organization attendance records are not. I scrutinized the backgrounds of Jason, Kendra and Maxwell even further. I was stunned by the results, and I'm sure all of you will be too. Jason Otis and Maxwell Curtis are half-brothers. The only place I was able to locate this information was in their hometown newspaper archives. An obituary showed that Maxwell's father died soon after Maxwell was born. His mother remarried about a year later and a birth announcement showed Jason Otis was born two years later. The real, almost scary, connection is Jason, Maxwell, and Kendra all attended Columbia University graduate school at the same time, although in different capacities. The campus had a small group of students that met together on a regular basis. The group was for cancer survivors. The chances are great that all three were cancer survivors. This brings up a lot of what ifs. What if they received radiation and chemotherapy? What if this mutated the alleged Noah Gene? What if this sequence of events allowed them to access vital secret Thornburg information and on and on? The written tests Jason and Kendra took certainly did not verify either of them as a potential Noah Gene carrier, but somehow they were able to obtain enough information to procure the C1 Extraction pills. April, did you feel any apprehension when Jason told you to give up the pills and formula when he was in your apartment?"

"Now that you mention it, I did not."

"I believe all three of them had compromised immune systems. I would even guess they used the first batch of fifty C1 Extraction pills to heal their own cancer-ridden bodies. Once they found out how effective the drug was, they hatched their plot to obtain more for resale."

There was silence in the group. Keegan could tell they were each mulling over the information he had just portrayed. After several minutes Dr. Hoffman spoke. "This almost verifies our theory about the Noah Gene. I will conduct more research on the chemo and radiation gene mutation theory. Perhaps this will allow a backdoor approach to verify the Noah Gene existence. I can't tell you how exciting this is. It is unfortunate it took such a severe event to bring it to the surface."

"I would rather see you concentrate on the Noah Gene theory than on retaliation, Doctor. What do you think?"

"I believe that is a good idea."

"Great. Are there any other questions or ideas?" There was silence as Keegan studied each face in the room. "Let me say this in closing. Thornburg Genetics is a huge organization. Even with the time and effort my security staff and I put into safeguarding the assets of Thornburg Genetics, we will never be perfect. The potential of a security breach always looms in the future. Our measure of success can only be determined by how much loss we can avoid; loss of pharmaceuticals, research, rare plants, and, most importantly, human life. The criminals scored this time. This event has been a learning experience for all of us, and we must do our best to avoid another incident. Please make sure all security level seven employees contact us with any incident that seems the least bit out of the ordinary. I still have more background work to do, but our meeting today has dictated the final results of this matter. This case will probably be closed out within a month. I thank each of you for your input and sacrifice. With that said, this meeting is closed."

"Thank you, Keegan," said Lexis as she stood up. "As Keegan said, please be aware of your surroundings and don't let your guard down. Keep an eye out for suspicious situations. The Noah Gene will kick in unless we come across another chance fluke. I ask you to try to put this incident behind you. It's over and according to Keegan it will be over for some time. It may be nothing more will ever come from it. Dr. Hoffman and April, I thank you for enduring all of the hardships you have been subjected to. Tanya and Mark, do you have anything to add?"

Tanya shook her head. "I have nothing to add. I'm still trying to analyze the whole incident."

"Mark?"

"No, Lexis. I have to say that security issues are not my strong point. I am shocked this happened. I never saw it coming."

"I know what you mean, Mark. Very well, let's adjourn our meeting. Tanya, Mark and I are going down to the Thornburg building. Why don't the three of you take the rest of the day off and get some well-deserved rest."

"Yes," said Dr. Hoffman. "I believe I will get back to my research work now that Mr. McGrath has confirmed some of our theories about the Noah Gene. I had all of last week off. That was sufficient."

"It sounds like April and Keegan are on their own," Lexis said with a smirk as she looked their way.

Lexis, Tanya, Mark and Dr. Hoffman all made their way out of the conference room.

"Would you care for some lunch, April?"

"I thought you would never ask."

"So, what's in store for April James now? Life will be pretty boring compared to the last few weeks."

"As a matter of fact, this incident has been somewhat life changing. My goal is to live life to the fullest. When Jason pointed a pistol at my head, I realized how short life could be. At that moment, I understood two things. First, I want to live my life with more gusto and help even more people. Second, I want a deeper relationship with God." April paused. "I have decided to resign from Thornburg Genetics."

April watched Keegan's mouth drop open as he stared at her. "You're what? You can't resign. What about your name recognition campaign? What about the Thornburg Vision of Hope Charity and all of the great work you can do to help people? What about, mmm, I don't know. You can't just quit. Where will you go? What will you do?"

"Aren't you going to say it?"

"Say what?"

"You know, you hard-headed Irish security goon, that you'll miss my smiling face, great looks and wonderful company."

"No, I won't say it. I'm not going to miss you, because I'm not going to let you go anywhere."

"Well, since you put it that way, I guess I have no choice but to stay. I mean, could you get any more romantic?"

"Oh. I see. You're playing me hard, Miss April James. You catch me way off guard then play your little innocent act. That's not fair."

"Of course it's fair. Remember when you told me to use my intuition?"

Keegan put his arms around April, drew her close to him and kissed her. They kissed gently for several minutes. Then Keegan looked April in the eyes and rubbed his thumb across her cheek. "Shall we go to lunch now?"

April rolled her eyes. "Sure, why not. Maybe if I get you fed you can concentrate on me. By the way, did I tell you I have a date with a nice college boy in Allentown this coming Saturday morning?"

"What do you mean?"

"My new friend Aaron is going to escort me to the nicest little waterfall in the state of Pennsylvania. He goes there to take photos early in the morning. If there is any amount of humidity, the reflection from the mist gives off a fluorescent rainbow. I thought I might take him out to lunch afterwards. I think he has some friends that want to meet the crazy lady he discovered in the woods."

"Just the two of you are going to the falls?"

"Just the two of us. I'll bring you back a photo."

"That's just hilarious."

Chapter 79

"Well Jason, it's been exactly one month now since your brother passed away. Nobody from Thornburg Genetics or North Korea has made any attempt to contact us. Our millions of dollars are free and clear," said Sheila.

"You are more optimistic than I am, babe. I doubt the North Koreans will give up on their search for the money they spent on the cancer medication. If it were my money, I wouldn't, and Thornburg is not going to stop looking for us either."

"Jason, honey, we are in the clear. Trust me. Our bank account is out of everyone's reach but ours, and the deed to this house is listed under a fictitious name. You have a new identity. We are untouchable."

"You have covered all the bases I can think of to disappear off the face of the earth, but I still have to stay cautious. It's my nature."

"Speaking of Thornburg, honey, I'm going to take a little excursion."

"What do you mean by excursion?"

"I have a message to deliver to Thornburg Genetics."

"Can't you just be happy performing your plant research and enjoying our millions of dollars?"

"Jason, you know what I think of Thornburg Genetics. They didn't appreciate my research capabilities, and they didn't offer to pay me nearly as much as I was worth. Now they have to pay for their crucial errors in judgment. As long as I'm on earth, I'm going to drive their security unit and upper level management crazy. They can spend the money they should have spent on me wondering where those exotic, almost extinct, plants appear from. I know they have more plants than what I have seen. It will cost them a fortune in security upgrades."

"I know you have a personal vendetta, but isn't this going a little overboard? I don't suppose it will do me any good to ask you to stop because I'm madly in love with you, and I don't want to see anything bad happen to you."

"Do you know why you are madly in love with me, honey? It's because I take risks and like to live on the edge. Besides, they will never catch me. I'm too smart."

"I hate to admit it, babe, but you are right on all counts."

"My plane leaves tomorrow. I'll be back in a few days. I have four select aloe vera gold plants I must deliver in person to America."

The next morning, Sheila went to the basement in her house. She slid on a Tyvek™ protective suit, rubber gloves and a respirator. Jason watched through the picture window as she opened the door to her greenhouse. He felt a slight movement of air from the negative air pressure that flowed from the greenhouse into the rest of the basement. Sheila spent several minutes walking through the four rows of thriving plants. Jason could tell she was admiring each of them. Then she walked up to the aloe vera gold plants. She talked to the plants as she placed four small plants into a stainless steel tray designed to hold four, four-inch pots. "You are my babies. We have to take a little trip. I don't know if I will ever see you again, but if I don't, I want you to know that I love you." Then she slid the tray into a plywood box and closed the airtight door. Sheila knew the lithium batteries would keep the grow lights, thermostat and air filtration system operating for days. The twelve-inch wide by twelve-inch long by sixteen-inch high box was a mini greenhouse impervious to outside forces. Sheila had designed it herself. Sheila exited the greenhouse and stripped off the respirator, rubber gloves and Tyvek™ suit.

"How are you going to get those on a plane?"

"I have connections now, honey. I'm a stewardess. Remember?"

Chapter 80

It was 10:00 on Saturday night. A medium built, bald man carrying a plywood box banged twice on the glass window of the Princeton University campus steel entry door. Behind the door and down a hundred foot corridor was the greenhouse that housed the university's rare plant collection. The entryway was well lit. A campus security officer looked with interest at monitor number four on his control panel. He watched the frumpy looking man tip his head up and wave at the security camera, then point at the box he was carrying. The officer decided it was some fraternity student playing a hoax. He reached down and pushed button number four on the control panel, then spoke into the microphone. "This is security. How can I help you?"

"I know it's late, but I have some plants I simply must place in the greenhouse tonight. I'm afraid they won't live until Monday."

The security officer wasn't sure what to think. The man's voice sounded very feminine. It must be a sorority house playing a hoax. Probably the box had a snake in it or worms or cow manure. He had seen enough pranks on campus to know he didn't want to be in the middle of one, but he was bored and thought maybe he would play along for a while just to see what the joke was this time.

"I'll be there in a minute."

He took his time walking to the door. There was no sense in rushing just for a prank. When he arrived at the door, he could see the man patiently waiting. He had set the box on the ground. The officer tapped on the door window. "My orders are not to let anyone into this building after hours."

"I understand sir, but this is an urgent matter. I probably should have called in advance, but I didn't know if I would be able to acquire these plants until the last minute."

Then the frumpy looking man picked up a cup of coffee and a Dunkin' Donuts bag that was sitting in a cardboard carrier on the wooden box. "I brought you a jumbo Dunkin' Donuts coffee to drink with two cream filled éclairs for your trouble."

This hoax has got to be the best one yet, thought the security officer. Maybe he has a tarantula in that box. I hate spiders.

"Let me see inside the box."

"Sure thing, sir." The man set the coffee and bag back in the carrier and set it on the ground. He lifted the box up to window level and slid a panel open, so the officer could see four plants lit up through a glass barrier.

"I need to see your campus ID card."

The man pulled an ID card from his pocket and pressed it against the entry door window. The officer pulled a flashlight from the carrier on his belt, turned it on and inspected the card. It looked legitimate. Professor Anthony Mendillo, Botany Professor. Another frumpy looking professor with sloppy clothes he thought. He must have picked them up at some yard sale. No wonder the college kids he saw were such slobs. Look at this lackluster role model.

"Let me see inside the bag."

The botany professor set the box holding the plants down, picked up the bag, opened it and held it in front of the window glass. The officer could see donuts in the bottom. He decided to open the door and let the professor in. He had keys to every other door off this foyer, and they were all locked and secured.

"Back up a step and I'll open the door. This had better be on the up and up. You are on our security cameras." The security officer opened the door. Professor Mendillo picked up the coffee carrier with two coffees in it, the Dunkin' Donuts bag, and then the plywood box's handle with his other hand. He walked inside and set the box down. The security officer made sure the building's self-locking door was closed tight behind him. The professor handed the officer the tray with two cups of coffee and the bag.

"I brought us both a cup of coffee and I brought you two éclairs. The jumbo coffee is for you. I hope it's still hot enough."

The officer noticed skintight rubber gloves on the professor's hands.

"What are the gloves for?"

"Oh, I always wear rubber gloves when I'm transporting rare plant specimens. You must have seen some of the other professors and graduate students wearing them. It is one of our standard operating procedures."

"No, I don't see many people on this shift professor."

"I didn't think about that. Sorry."

The professor felt the heat radiate from the jumbo cup of coffee as he lifted it out of the tray and opened the flap on the lid. He handed it to the officer, then took his own cup and opened the flap and sipped. "Mine is still hot. How about yours?"

The officer took a sip. "Just right. Thanks a lot Professor Mendillo."

The professor handed the officer the bag. He opened it with caution and looked inside. There were two éclairs inside just as promised.

"You act like the boogie man was going to jump out of that bag or something."

"The college kids are always trying to play some prank on us. We can never be too careful. I can tell you a hundred prank stories. Anyhow, thanks for the coffee and éclairs. These will hit the spot."

"You are more than welcome. Thanks for letting me in. I've been worried for two hours that I would have to make a dozen phone calls for approval to access the greenhouse with these rare plants. You saved the day for me. I assume that greenhouse door B is locked. I would like to drop these plants off and get home. It's been a long day."

"Sure thing professor. Go ahead, I'm right behind you." The officer took another sip of coffee. "This sure is good."

The professor walked down the hallway to the door of greenhouse B. The greenhouse was under negative pressure, and the professor could feel a hint of a breeze exit when the security officer unlocked and opened the door. The professor set his cup of coffee down on the floor and donned a facemask he had in his pocket.

"You must wait outside the door. This is a greenhouse designed with special filters to stop outside pollutants from entering. You can watch me through the door window. It will only take a minute to drop off these plants," said the professor.

"Yeah, my boss told me never to go into this greenhouse for any reason. Are you sure you are allowed in here?"

"Of course. That is why I have this special environmentally controlled box to carry these plants and I'm wearing rubber gloves and a mask. The air in the box is filtered to imitate the air in the greenhouse. We have to be so careful that I sometimes feel like we are preparing for surgery."

The officer glanced at the professor's plant box again. He was having second thoughts about letting anyone into the building without calling his supervisor first. If something went wrong, he knew his supervisor would kill him. How would he explain why he had allowed anybody access and disobeyed orders. "Think," he thought to himself. The professor's ID was acceptable, because it showed he was a botany professor. He had on rubber gloves and a breathing mask. Nobody would do that unless they were legitimate, and who else would want to get into a greenhouse after hours. The security guard stepped aside allowing access to greenhouse B.

The officer shut the door behind Professor Mendillo and peered through the door window. He watched the professor walk down the main aisle and turn left a few rows down. The officer gave a big yawn as he watched and took a large swallow of coffee. The professor stopped in plain view of the officer and opened his plant box. He took his time removing the aloe vera gold plants and adjusted them on the rack to his satisfaction. Professor Mendillo then pulled a cell phone out of his pocket and checked the time. He nodded his head in approval, picked up his plywood box and walked back to the greenhouse door. The officer was not looking through the glass. Professor Mendillo had to push the door hard to get out. The building security officer was lying in front of it, passed out.

"I guess he just can't handle his coffee. Maybe next time he should try decaf." The professor laughed at his own joke as he stepped over the officer's outstretched body.

It was forty minutes later when additional campus security staff found the officer sleeping in a pool of coffee in front of the greenhouse B door. He had not made his scheduled eleven o'clock security telephone call to headquarters. The officer's supervisor, Sgt. Mann, forced him to drink as much water as he could. The officer pointed to a spot on his head. Sgt. Mann felt a large bump where the officer had apparently hit the floor. Within a few minutes the officer was somewhat coherent.

"I have a splitting headache. I think the professor drugged me." The officer's voice was slurred, but Sgt. Mann got the gist of what he was telling him.

"What professor? What happened?"

"A botany professor stopped to drop off some plants in the greenhouse. The next thing I know, here I am." The officer knew he was in big trouble.

"What was the professor's name?"

"His ID card said Mendillo."

The sergeant retrieved his smart phone and called for the campus nurse on duty. He then looked up the college personnel list. There was no Professor Mendillo listed. Then he and another officer reviewed the surveillance tape in the building's security control room. The tape showed a person knocking at the front entrance door. They followed each camera in order and watched as the alleged professor entered greenhouse B. The sergeant had been trained on emergency procedures for this building. His first order of business was to call the botany department chairwoman, Dr. Zhang, and notify her of the security breach. Sgt. Mann disliked Dr. Zhang and tried to avoid her at all costs. He made the mistake of calling her a professor when she first arrived at the University. She explained the difference between a professor and a doctor to him in great detail, and then informed him her name was Dr. Zhang, not Professor Zhang. He felt sorry for any students who were stuck with her for a teacher. Sgt. Mann briefed Dr. Zhang about the situation. She informed him she would drive to the facility and should arrive in a few minutes. Sgt. Mann had been trained to follow specific protocol should he ever have to enter the rare plant greenhouse B. He slipped on a special Tyvek™ suit, placed a breathing mask over his nose and mouth, slid on a pair of latex gloves and entered the greenhouse. Sgt. Mann walked down the main aisle, retracing the intruder's path he had just observed on the surveillance tape. It wasn't hard to locate the four plants that had been dropped off. The sergeant picked up one of the plants. Printed on the pot in bold magic marker was a message. 'THORNBURG, I KNOW WHAT YOU HAVE.' The sergeant could see the same writing on the three other pots as well. He set the pot back on the rack and walked back to the main greenhouse door, where he sent another officer to his car to retrieve a roll of crime scene tape. Sgt. Mann then cordoned off the area surrounding the plants and the entire greenhouse with the bright yellow tape. When he exited the greenhouse, he placed a section of tape on that door as well.

The crowd had grown in the lobby outside greenhouse B. Sgt. Mann said hello to Dr. Zhang and the University Dean. The campus nurse was scrutinizing the building officer's lump on his head. There were also two other people he did not recognize. Dr. Zhang assumed the lead role.

"When we have emergency practice drills, we never expect an emergency will happen to us. We always think it will happen to someone else. I don't know exactly what we are dealing with in this situation, but Sgt. Mann briefed me and he appears to have followed security protocol to the letter. Thank you for an excellent job, Sgt. Mann. Do you have additional information you can share with us?"

"I have information I need to share with you in private, Dr. Zhang."

"In private? I believe we can all be advised of any pertinent information Sgt. Mann. What information do you have?"

"I insist that we speak in private."

"I don't know what information could be so secretive, but if you insist. Let's go down the hall to my office."

As soon as the office door was closed, Sgt. Mann told Dr. Zhang about the writing on the clay pots. He told her he had no idea who Thornburg was, but it sounded like a threat of some type and questioned if the local sheriff's office should be called.

"My guess is Thornburg is referring to the pharmaceutical company, Thornburg Genetics," said Dr. Zhang. "They are a top-ranked research company in the field of plant biochemistry and genetics. First, I will check the university directory to see if we have any staff or students by the name of Thornburg. Was Thornburg spelled with an 'e' or 'u'?"

"It was Thornburg with a 'u', Dr. Zhang."

Dr. Zhang pulled a smartphone from the front left pocket of her slacks. After touching the screen several times, she looked up at Sgt. Mann. "There is no record of anyone by the name of Thornburg associated with our university. Let me make a phone call to the Thornburg Genetics offices. I doubt we will be able to talk with anyone at this hour of the night, but we will try. I see they have an emergency number." Again she touched the smartphone screen several times and then raised the phone to her ear. "Hello. This is Dr. Zhang, Department Chairwoman of Botany at Princeton University. I am calling to discuss an unusual situation. We had a break-in at our rare plant greenhouse B at approximately 10:00 PM. Someone disguised as a professor deposited four potted plants inside the greenhouse. On each of the pots are the words, quote, 'Thornburg, I know what you have.' Who in your organization would know something about this?" There was a pause, then Dr. Zhang said thank you.

"They are referring me to their security department," Dr. Zhang whispered.

"Hello. This is Thornburg Genetics security. This is Officer Taber speaking. How may I help you?"

"Hello. This is Dr. Zhang. I am Chairwoman of Botany at Princeton University. I am calling to discuss an unusual situation. We had a break-in at our rare plant greenhouse B at approximately 10:00 PM. Someone with a Princeton ID card disguised as a professor deposited four potted plants inside our greenhouse. On each of the pots are the words, quote, 'Thornburg, I know what you have.' I checked our university directory. We have no one employed in this university by the name Thornburg nor do we have any students by that name. Does this mean anything to your company?"

"It may be a Thornburg Genetics security issue, Dr. Zhang. How many people know about this situation?"

"Two of us know about the writing on the pots. Seven or eight people are aware of the break-in."

"May I have the names of the other people involved please?"

"We don't just hand out names, Officer Taber. What do you need names for?"

"It's a standard security procedure ma'am in case we require further information from an individual in the future."

"My name is Dr. Zhang, not ma'am."

"Yes, Dr. Zhang. Sorry."

"Sgt. Mann of Princeton University security is the officer that discovered the writing on the pots."

"Thank you, Dr. Zhang. You said the two of you are the only ones that know about the writing?"

"That is what I said, Officer Taber!"

"Thank you, Dr. Zhang. I am going to call the head of Thornburg security and advise him of this situation. May I put you on hold for a minute?"

"You may put me on a short hold. I reiterate the word short."

"It should be less than one minute. Please hold."

In less than one minute, Keegan McGrath was on the line. "Hello, Dr. Zhang. This is Keegan McGrath. I am head of security for Thornburg Genetics."

"Do you have a title, Mr. McGrath?"

"My title is Head of Security. I have been briefed by my colleague about your discovery in the rare plants greenhouse. I was also told that only you and a Sgt. Mann are aware of the writing on the pots. Is that information correct?"

"This is the third time I have affirmed this, Head of Security Mc-Grath."

"Very well, Dr. Zhang. I will send a team of security specialists from Thornburg Genetics to evaluate the situation. They will arrive in approximately two hours. Please do not tell anyone else about this situation and do not let anyone into the greenhouse itself until we inspect and clear it. This has the potential of being a dangerous situation. How many people are in the immediate area right now?"

"We have four or five civilian staff and four or five campus security staff either in the building or in the area."

"Okay. Please do not let any more people into the area, and I will need the names, telephone numbers and titles of all people involved in any way up to this point in time. Can I count on your cooperation, Dr. Zhang?"

"Since this is considered an emergency situation, it is my call what procedures we will follow, Head of Security McGrath. At this point in time I believe we need to contact the local authorities and apprise them of the situation."

"Dr. Zhang. Please listen to me. This may be a volatile situation that requires our expertise. The local authorities will not know what potential dangers exist. We do know. I implore you not to contact outside agencies until we can get to the university and evaluate the situation."

"As I stated, Head of Security McGrath, this is an emergency situation and each decision is my call. The entire botany program is under my jurisdiction in an emergency situation. I feel that local police must be notified. That is my final decision."

"I am doing my best to work with you, Dr. Zhang. I need your cooperation in this matter."

"I will not be bullied into making a bad decision, Head of Security McGrath. Good evening." Dr. Zhang hit the off button on her smartphone.

"What was that all about, Dr. Zhang?"

"I talked with Thornburg Genetics Head of Security McGrath. He insisted this situation not be reported to the local police. He stated this might be a volatile situation that his security staff should handle. I disagree with his assessment."

"If he knows something we don't, what will it hurt to wait for his security team to travel here and check things out? You can always call the police after they arrive if they don't do a satisfactory job."

"Thornburg Genetics is not affiliated with Princeton University, and I will not have them dictating our security procedures, Sgt. Mann. It is time to notify our local police department about this situation."

There was a knock on Dr. Zhang's door as the University Dean walked in. "I just received a telephone call from a Keegan McGrath who is head of security for a company called Thornburg Genetics. Did you just talk to a Mr. McGrath, Dr. Zhang?"

"Yes. I talked to a Head of Security McGrath from Thornburg Genetics. He considered this matter a possible emergency and tried to set up protocol I did not agree with."

"He stated that you were calling the local police. Have you called the police about this situation?"

"I have not. My next telephone call is to 911 to report this emergency."

"Dr. Zhang. You will not call the police. You will follow every instruction given to you by Mr. McGrath and you will tell no one else about this matter. Is that clear?"

"I must object. I have authority over this area in an emergency situation. I feel it is necessary to contact the local police."

"Your objection is overruled. If you value your employment here, you will follow every order given by Mr. McGrath. If I hear of one move to the contrary, you will be fired; and I will personally make sure you are never hired at another major university in this country. Do I make myself clear?"

"Yes, very clear. I value my job, and I will follow your instructions."

"Good. Sgt. Mann is now in charge. You will wait here in your office until security staff arrives from Thornburg Genetics. Since you were one of the first people on the scene, I believe they will want to interview you. You are to cooperate with their investigation to the fullest extent. You are not to talk to or share information with anyone else about this incident. That includes using your phone. I will remain in this building as long as required. We will discuss your role in emergency situations further on Monday morning in my office at 9:00 AM."

"Sgt. Mann, security staff from Thornburg Genetics will arrive within two hours. You are to follow their instructions. Start a timed log listing the names of everyone here and anyone who comes or goes. This whole ordeal is to be kept quiet. No information leaks. Is that understood?"

"Yes, ma'am."

Chapter 81

In less than two hours a trained Thornburg Genetics plant inspector and two Thornburg Genetics security staff arrived at the Princeton University rare plant greenhouse B. Keegan McGrath was one of the security staff. The University Dean and Sgt. Mann welcomed them.

After introductions, Keegan and the other Thornburg security officer followed Sgt. Mann to the building security control room. The sergeant set up the incident tape for review and waited outside the door as requested by Keegan. As they reviewed the tape, Keegan whistled and said to his comrade, "Déjà vu?"

"We've seen this before, boss. It's that same little frumpy man from the University of Washington botany caper."

"It sure is. There he goes down the aisle with the plant box in hand. He pulls out four plants, one at a time. He places them on the rack, admires his handiwork, checks his cell phone, and then back up the aisle he walks. It looks like he has a little problem exiting back through the door, then away he goes."

Keegan opened the control room door. "Sgt. Mann, are there any copies of this surveillance tape other than the original?"

"No, sir. The original is actually in our security office. You are viewing it from that location."

"What other cameras are recording this area?"

"We have a front door camera, a camera over the door leading into the greenhouse, the camera view you just observed, and one at the opposite end of the greenhouse."

"Would you please let me have all of those originals to take with me and any other views from the security cameras dealing with this situation from 9:00 PM to present? We have to do an extensive amount of research on these tapes. No copies should be made, and the cameras in this area should be turned off at this moment."

"I'm not about to let these tapes out of my possession. I need them for reference to make sure the security officer that pulled this dumb stunt will be in the unemployment line."

"I understand how you feel about the security officer, and I understand how you feel about letting these tapes out of your possession. However, this is a high-profile, sensitive and top secret issue. Only a few people are aware of this situation. I assume all of your college staff signs a confidentiality statement. Please make sure it is enforced or this whole scenario could get ugly. I have to meet with the University Dean to let her know where we stand and that confidentiality is of the utmost importance. Maybe we can meet together and discuss the tapes.

What do you think, Sergeant?"

"My orders are to follow your orders. I will have the tapes delivered to this building right away."

"Thank you for your cooperation, Sergeant. I'm not trying to antagonize you; I'm trying to work with you. Situations like this only happen on occasion, and I like to have a good working relationship with all of the security staff I come in contact with. By the way, I think you will find the officer who allowed this breach of security may turn into an excellent officer unless you have some other reason to terminate his employment. From past experience, a mistake like this really jolts an officer to improve his or her work ethic. If you keep him on staff, he will be forever beholden to you. That's just something for you to think about. Is there anything else we should know?"

"We have one piece of evidence we believe is incident-related just down the walkway from the building. It hasn't been touched, and the area has been cordoned off with one of my staff guarding the area."

"Okay. Before we check that out, we need to go into greenhouse B." Keegan and the Thornburg plant inspector, Hector Rodriquez, took Tyvek™ jumpsuits out of a duffle bag they brought with them and opened the plastic bags they were sealed in. After donning the suits, they put on latex gloves and face masks. Sgt. Mann ushered them to greenhouse B. After removing the crime scene tape, Sgt. Mann unlocked and opened the door. Keegan led the way down the main aisle and turned left down a side aisle, following the path of the intruder as seen on the security tape. He could see the plants he was searching for as the clay pots had writing on them. "These are the plants Hector. Check them out."

Hector picked up one of the plants and read the writing on the pot. THORNBURG, I KNOW WHAT YOU HAVE. He lifted the plant high in the air and scrutinized the underside of the leaves. Then he repeated the process with the other three plants. "They are definitely the aloe vera gold, variety XR 51, boss. They're ours." Hector opened the special climate-controlled box he was carrying and gently placed the plants inside, closed the box door and turned on the battery pack to the miniature filtration system. He knew the plants were volatile, but not the degree of volatility.

Keegan noticed how hesitant Hector was about handling the plants. "What's the matter Hector? Is there a problem?"

"We are told in training that all of the plants we search for are volatile, but we never know what that means from specie to specie. We are just told to do our inspections, call in a sighting if we find a plant considered 'out of circulation' and leave the premises as soon as possible.

For all I know, this thing could blow up in my face."

Keegan laughed. "Sorry about the laugh Hector. This plant needs additional chemical catalysts to become volatile. It is perfectly safe to carry. I will make sure your future training courses cover the volatility aspects of our plants in more detail."

"Thanks, boss. That's a big relief."

Keegan and Hector walked down the main aisle and back out of greenhouse B. Keegan removed all of the crime scene tape as they retreated. After they removed their Tyvek™ suits, gloves, and masks, Keegan and the second Thornburg security officer followed Sgt. Mann outside the building door to the sight of the suspected piece of evidence. It looked like a rubber mask, but the way it was laying on top of a hosta plant in the dark made it hard to tell. Keegan took a small flashlight out of a pouch he wore on his belt and shone it at the object.

"Do you have an evidence bag, Sgt. Mann?"

"Right here, Mr. McGrath."

"Would you please hold this flashlight for me?"

Keegan took the bag and retrieved a sealed, sterile rubber glove from his pants pocket. He broke the seal, put the glove on and picked the object out of the hosta plant. He turned it from side to side as he walked thirty feet to a streetlight for a closer look.

"I don't believe it."

The object was a rubber full head coverage mask. Keegan recognized the face and balding head as the same man he had viewed on the security camera just minutes before. It was also a duplicate of the face and balding head mask retrieved two years before from the University of Washington. It was the same person who removed the aloe vera gold plants from that facility. Keegan slipped the mask in the evidence bag and went back to the location where he had retrieved the mask. It only took a minute before his flashlight picked up a reflection from a pair of outdated black eyeglasses under a hosta plant. He slipped those into a separate evidence bag. Keegan took his cell phone out of his shirt pocket and walked a short distance from the evidence scene. He dialed the emergency number.

"Lexis, you are not going to believe this!"

Bible Verses

Bible verses which inspired portions of this novel are as follows:

I Kings 4:33: Solomon described plant life, from the cedar of Lebanon to the hyssop that grows out of the walls. (NIV)

Luke 21:16: You will be betrayed even by parents and brothers, relatives and friends, and they will put some of you to death. (NKJV)

I Timothy 6:10: For the love of money is a root of all kinds of evil. Some people, eager for money, have wandered from the faith and pierced themselves with many griefs. (NIV)

Thank you for reading The Noah Document.

Visit us at: www.garygoodnough.com